KT-500-640

LC542

7/9

2 3 SEP 2018

1 0 DEC 2019

Twens
~~OAC~~
SHF 12/19

WITHDRAWN

Books should be returned or renewed by the
last date stamped above

_____

_____

_____

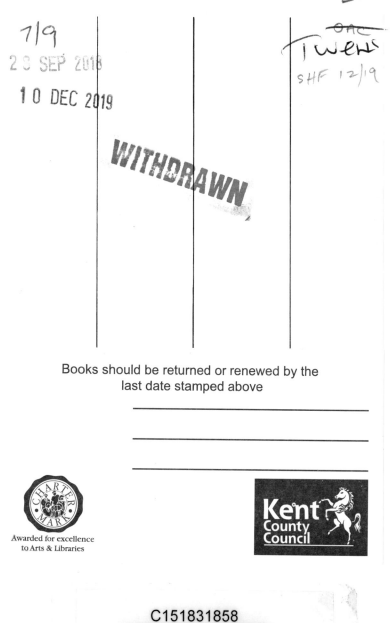

CHARTER MARK
Awarded for excellence
to Arts & Libraries

Kent
County
Council

C151831858

# The Apprentice

# The Apprentice

## Tess Gerritsen

**Wheeler Publishing • Chivers Press**
**Waterville, Maine USA • Bath, England**

KENT
ARTS & LIBRARIES

C1S1831858

This Large Print edition is published by Wheeler Publishing, USA and by Chivers Press, England.

Published in 2002 in the U.S. by arrangement with The Ballantine Publishing Group, a division of Random House, Inc.

Published in 2003 in the U.K. by arrangement with Transworld Publishers Ltd.

U.S. Hardcover 1-58724-322-9 (Wheeler Hardcover Series)
U.K. Hardcover 0-7540-1875-X (Windsor Large Print)
U.K. Softcover 0-7540-9244-5 (Paragon Large Print)

Copyright © 2002 by Tess Gerritsen

All rights reserved.

This is a work of fiction. Names, characters, places, and incidents either are a product of the author's imagination or are used fictitiously.

The text of this Large Print edition is unabridged.
Other aspects of the book may vary from the original edition.

Set in 16 pt. Plantin by Christina S. Huff.

Printed in Great Britain by
Antony Rowe Ltd, Chippenham, Wiltshire.

**British Library Cataloguing-in-Publication Data available**

**Library of Congress Cataloging-in-Publication Data**

Gerritsen, Tess.
 The apprentice / Tess Gerritsen.
  p. cm.
 ISBN 1-58724-322-9 (lg. print : hc : alk. paper)
 1. Police — Massachusetts — Boston — Fiction. 2. Boston
(Mass.) — Fiction. 3. Serial murders — Fiction.
 4. Policewomen — Fiction. 5. Large type books. I. Title.
PS3557.E687 A84 2002b
 813'.54—dc21         2002029632

To Terrina and Mike

# Acknowledgments

Throughout the writing of this book, I've had a wonderful team cheering me on, offering advice, and providing me with the emotional nourishment I needed to keep forging ahead. Many, many thanks to my agent, friend, and guiding light, Meg Ruley, and to Jane Berkey, Don Cleary, and the fabulous folks at the Jane Rotrosen Agency. I owe thanks as well to my superb editor, Linda Marrow, to Gina Centrello, for her unflagging enthusiasm, to Louis Mendez, for keeping me on top of things, and to Gilly Hailparn and Marie Coolman, for supporting me through the sad, dark days after September 11th, and guiding me safely home. Thanks also to Peter Mars for his information on the Boston P.D., and to Selina Walker, my cheerleader on the other side of the pond.

Finally, my deepest thanks to my husband, Jacob, who knows just how difficult it is to live with a writer — and sticks with me anyway.

# Prologue

*Today I watched a man die.*

*It was an unexpected event, and I still marvel at the fact that this drama unfolded at my very feet. So much of what passes for excitement in our lives cannot be anticipated, and we must learn to savor the spectacles as they come, and appreciate the rare thrills that punctuate the otherwise monotonous passage of time. And my days do pass slowly here, in this world behind walls, where men are merely numbers, distinguished not by our names, nor by our God-given talents, but by the nature of our trespasses. We dress alike, eat the same meals, read the same worn books from the same prison cart. Every day is like another. And then some startling incident reminds us that life can turn on a dime.*

*So it happened today, August second, which ripened gloriously hot and sunny, just the way I like it. While the other men sweat and shuffle about like lethargic cattle, I stand in the center of the exercise yard, my face turned to the sun like a lizard soaking up warmth. My eyes are closed, so I do not see the knife's thrust, nor do I see the man stumble backward and fall. But I hear the rumble of agitated voices, and I open my eyes.*

*In a corner of the yard, a man lies bleeding. Ev-*

eryone else backs away and assumes their usual see-nothing, know-nothing masks of indifference.

I alone walk toward the fallen man.

For a moment I stand looking down at him. His eyes are open and sentient; to him, I must be merely a black cutout against the glaring sky. He is young, with white-blond hair, his beard scarcely thicker than down. He opens his mouth and pink froth bubbles out. A red stain is spreading across his chest.

I kneel beside him and tear open his shirt, baring the wound, which is just to the left of the sternum. The blade has slid in neatly between ribs, and has certainly punctured the lung, and perhaps nicked the pericardium. It is a mortal wound, and he knows it. He tries to speak to me, his lips moving without sound, his eyes struggling to focus. He wants me to bend closer, perhaps to hear some deathbed confession, but I am not the least bit interested in anything he has to say.

I focus, instead, on his wound. On his blood.

I am well acquainted with blood. I know it down to its elements. I have handled countless tubes of it, admired its many different shades of red. I have spun it in centrifuges into bicolored columns of packed cells and straw-colored serum. I know its gloss, its silken texture. I have seen it flow in satiny streams out of freshly incised skin.

The blood pours from his chest like holy water from a sacred spring. I press my palm to the wound, bathing my skin in that liquid warmth, and blood coats my hand like a scarlet glove. He believes I am trying to help him, and a brief spark of gratitude lights his eyes. Most likely this man has not received much charity in his short life; how ironic that I should be mistaken as the face of mercy.

Behind me, boots shuffle and voices bark commands: "Back! Everyone get back!"

Someone grasps my shirt and hauls me to my feet. I am shoved backward, away from the dying man. Dust swirls and the air is thick with shouts and curses as we are herded into a corner. The instrument of death, the shiv, lies abandoned on the ground. The guards demand answers, but no one saw anything, no one knows anything.

No one ever does.

In the chaos of that yard, I stand slightly apart from the other prisoners, who have always shunned me. I raise my hand, still dripping with the dead man's blood, and inhale its smooth and metallic fragrance. Just by its scent, I know it is young blood, drawn from young flesh.

The other prisoners stare at me, and edge even farther away. They know I am different; they have always sensed it. As brutal as these men are, they are leery of me, because they understand who — and what — I am. I search their faces, seeking my blood brother among them. One of my kind. I do not see him, not here, even in this house of monstrous men.

But he does exist. I know I am not the only one of my kind who walks this earth.

Somewhere, there is another. And he waits for me.

# One

Already the flies were swarming. Four hours on the hot pavement of South Boston had baked the pulverized flesh, releasing the chemical equivalent of a dinner bell, and the air was alive with buzzing flies. Though what remained of the torso was now covered with a sheet, there was still much exposed tissue for scavengers to feast on. Bits of gray matter and other unidentifiable parts were dispersed in a radius of thirty feet along the street. A skull fragment had landed in a second-story flower box, and clumps of tissue adhered to parked cars.

Detective Jane Rizzoli had always possessed a strong stomach, but even she had to pause, eyes closed, fists clenched, angry at herself for this moment of weakness. *Don't lose it. Don't lose it.* She was the only female detective in the Boston P.D. homicide unit, and she knew that the pitiless spotlight was always trained on her. Every mistake, every triumph, would be noted by all. Her partner, Barry Frost, had already tossed up his breakfast in humiliatingly public view, and he was now sitting with his head on his knees in their air-conditioned vehicle, waiting for his stomach to settle. She could not afford to fall victim to nausea. She was the most visible law enforcement officer on the scene, and from the other side of the police tape the public stood watching, registering every move she made, every detail of her appearance. She knew she looked younger than her age of thirty-four, and she was self-conscious about maintaining an air of authority. What she lacked in height she compensated for with her direct gaze, her squared shoulders. She had learned the art of dominating a scene, if only through sheer intensity.

But this heat was sapping her resolve. She had started off dressed in her usual blazer and slacks and with her hair neatly combed. Now the blazer was off, her blouse was wrinkled, and the humidity had frizzed her dark hair into unruly coils. She felt assaulted on all fronts by the smells, the flies, and the piercing sunlight. There was too much to focus on all at once. And all those eyes were watching her.

Loud voices drew her attention. A man in a dress shirt and tie was trying to argue his way past a patrolman.

"Look, I gotta get to a sales conference, okay? I'm an hour late as it is. But you've got your goddamn police tape wrapped around my car, and now you're saying I can't drive it? It's my own friggin' car!"

"It's a crime scene, sir."

"It's an accident!"

"We haven't determined that yet."

"Does it take you guys all day to figure it out?

Why don't you listen to us? The whole neighborhood heard it happen!"

Rizzoli approached the man, whose face was glazed with sweat. It was eleven-thirty and the sun, near its zenith, shone down like a glaring eye.

"What, exactly did you hear, sir?" she asked.

He snorted. "Same thing everyone else did."

"A loud bang."

"Yeah. Around seven-thirty. I was just getting outta the shower. Looked out my window, and there he was, lying on the sidewalk. You can see it's a bad corner. Asshole drivers come flying around it like bats outta hell. Must've been a truck hit him."

"Did you see a truck?"

"Naw."

"Hear a truck?"

"Naw."

"And you didn't see a car, either?"

"Car, truck." He shrugged. "It's still a hit-and-run."

It was the same story, repeated half a dozen times by the man's neighbors. Sometime between seven-fifteen and seven-thirty A.M., there'd been a loud bang in the street. No one actually saw the event. They had simply heard the noise and found the man's body. Rizzoli had already considered, and rejected, the possibility that he was a jumper. This was a neighborhood of two-story buildings, nothing tall enough to explain such catastrophic damage to a jumper's body. Nor did she see any evidence of an explosion as the cause of this much anatomical disintegration.

"Hey, can I get my car out now?" the man said. "It's that green Ford."

"That one with the brains splattered on the trunk?"

"Yeah."

"What do you think?" she snapped, and walked away to join the medical examiner, who was crouched in the middle of the road, studying the asphalt. "People on this street are jerks," said Rizzoli. "No one gives a damn about the victim. No one knows who he is, either."

Dr. Ashford Tierney didn't look up at her but just kept staring at the road. Beneath sparse strands of silver hair, his scalp glistened with sweat. Dr. Tierney seemed older and more weary than she had ever seen him. Now, as he tried to rise, he reached out in a silent request for assistance. She took his hand and she could feel, transmitted through that hand, the creak of tired bones and arthritic joints. He was an old southern gentleman, a native of Georgia, and he'd never warmed to Rizzoli's Boston bluntness, just as she had never warmed to his formality. The only thing they had in common was the human remains that passed across Dr. Tierney's autopsy table. But as she helped him to his feet, she was saddened by his frailty and reminded of her own grandfather, whose favorite grandchild she had been,

13

perhaps because he'd recognized himself in her pride, her tenaciousness. She remembered helping him out of his easy chair, how his stroke-numbed hand had rested like a claw on her arm. Even men as fierce as Aldo Rizzoli are ground down by time to brittle bones and joints. She could see its effect in Dr. Tierney, who wobbled in the heat as he took out his handkerchief and dabbed the sweat from his forehead.

"This is one doozy of a case to close out my career," he said. "So tell me, are you coming to my retirement party, Detective?"

"Uh . . . what party?" said Rizzoli.

"The one you all are planning to surprise me with."

She sighed. Admitted, "Yeah, I'm coming."

"Ha. I always could get a straight answer from you. Is it next week?"

"Two weeks. And I didn't tell you, okay?"

"I'm glad you did." He looked down at the asphalt. "I don't much like surprises."

"So what do we have here, Doc? Hit-and-run?"

"This seems to be the point of impact."

Rizzoli looked down at the large splash of blood. Then she looked at the sheet-draped corpse, which was lying a good twelve feet away, on the sidewalk.

"You're saying he first hit the ground here, and then bounced way over there?" said Rizzoli.

"It would appear so."

"That's got to be a pretty big truck to cause this much splatter."

"Not a truck," was Tierney's enigmatic answer. He started walking along the road, eyes focused downward.

Rizzoli followed him, batting at swarms of flies. Tierney came to a stop about thirty feet away and pointed to a grayish clump on the curb.

"More brain matter," he noted.

"A truck didn't do this?" said Rizzoli.

"No. Or a car, either."

"What about the tire marks on the vic's shirt?"

Tierney straightened, his eyes scanning the street, the sidewalks, the buildings. "Do you notice something quite interesting about this scene, Detective?"

"Apart from the fact there's a dead guy over there who's missing his brain?"

"Look at the point of impact." Tierney gestured toward the spot in the road where he'd been crouching earlier. "See the dispersal pattern of body parts?"

"Yeah. He splattered in all directions. Point of impact is at the center."

"Correct."

"It's a busy street," said Rizzoli. "Vehicles do come around that corner too fast. Plus, the vic has tire marks on his shirt."

"Let's go look at those marks again."

As they walked back to the corpse, they were

joined by Barry Frost, who had finally emerged from the car, looking wan and a little embarrassed.

"Man, oh man," he groaned.

"Are you okay?" she asked.

"You think maybe I picked up the stomach flu or something?"

"Or something." She'd always liked Frost, had always appreciated his sunny and uncomplaining nature, and she hated to see his pride laid so low. She gave him a pat on the shoulder, a motherly smile. Frost seemed to invite mothering, even from the decidedly unmaternal Rizzoli. "I'll just pack you a barf bag next time," she offered.

"You know," he said, trailing after her, "I really do think it's just the flu. . . ."

They reached the torso. Tierney grunted as he squatted down, his joints protesting the latest insult, and lifted the disposable sheet. Frost blanched and retreated a step. Rizzoli fought the impulse to do the same.

The torso had broken into two parts, separated at the level of the umbilicus. The top half, wearing a beige cotton shirt, stretched east to west. The bottom half, wearing blue jeans, lay north to south. The halves were connected by only a few strands of skin and muscle. The internal organs had spilled out and lay in a pulpified mass. The back half of the skull had shattered open, and the brain had been ejected.

"Young male, well nourished, appears to be of

Hispanic or Mediterranean origin, in his twenties to thirties," said Tierney. "I see obvious fractures of the thoracic spine, ribs, clavicles, and skull."

"Couldn't a truck do this?" Rizzoli asked.

"It's certainly possible a truck could have caused massive injuries like these." He looked at Rizzoli, his pale-blue eyes challenging hers. "But no one heard or saw such a vehicle. Did they?"

"Unfortunately, no," she admitted.

Frost finally managed a comment. "You know, I don't think those are tire tracks on his shirt."

Rizzoli focused on the black streaks across the front of the victim's shirt. With a gloved hand, she touched one of the smears, and looked at her finger. A smudge of black had transferred to her latex glove. She stared at it for a moment, processing this new information.

"You're right," she said. "It's not a tire track. It's grease."

She straightened and looked at the road. She saw no bloody tire marks, no auto debris. No pieces of glass or plastic that would have shattered on impact with a human body.

For a moment, no one spoke. They just looked at one another, as the only possible explanation suddenly clicked into place. As if to confirm the theory, a jet roared overhead. Rizzoli squinted upward, to see a 747 glide past, on its landing approach to Logan International

Airport, five miles to the northeast.

"Oh, Jesus," said Frost, shading his eyes against the sun. "What a way to go. Please tell me he was already dead when he fell."

"There's a good chance of it," said Tierney. "I would guess his body slipped out as the wheels came down, on landing approach. That's assuming it was an inbound flight."

"Well, yeah," said Rizzoli. "How many stowaways are trying to get *out* of the country?" She looked at the dead man's olive complexion. "So he's coming in on a plane, say, from South America —"

"It would've been flying at an altitude of at least thirty thousand feet," said Tierney. "Wheel wells aren't pressurized. A stowaway would be dealing with rapid decompression. Frostbite. Even in high summer, the temperatures at those altitudes are freezing. A few hours under those conditions, he'd be hypothermic and unconscious from lack of oxygen. Or already crushed when the landing gear retracted on takeoff. A prolonged ride in the wheel well would probably finish him off."

Rizzoli's pager cut into the lecture. And a lecture it would surely turn into; Dr. Tierney was just beginning to hit his professorial stride. She glanced at the number on her beeper but did not recognize it. A Newton prefix. She reached for her cell phone and dialed.

"Detective Korsak," a man answered.

"This is Rizzoli. Did you page me?"

"You on a cell phone, Detective?"

"Yes."

"Can you get to a landline?"

"Not at the moment, no." She did not know who Detective Korsak was, and she was anxious to cut this call short. "Why don't you tell me what this is about?"

A pause. She heard voices in the background and the crackle of a cop's walkie-talkie. "I'm at a scene out here in Newton," he said. "I think you should come out and see this."

"Are you requesting Boston P.D. assistance? Because I can refer you to someone else in our unit."

"I tried reaching Detective Moore, but they said he's on leave. That's why I'm calling you." Again he paused. And added, with quiet significance: "It's about that case you and Moore headed up last summer. You know the one."

She fell silent. She knew exactly what he was referring to. The memories of that investigation still haunted her, still surfaced in her nightmares.

"Go on," she said softly.

"You want the address?" he asked.

She took out her notepad.

A moment later, she hung up and turned her attention back to Dr. Tierney.

"I've seen similar injuries in sky divers whose parachutes fail to open," he said. "From that height, a falling body would reach terminal velocity. That's nearly two hundred feet per second. It's enough to cause the disintegration we see here."

"It's a hell of a price to pay to get to this country," said Frost.

Another jet roared overhead, its shadow swooping past like an eagle's.

Rizzoli gazed up at the sky. Imagined a body falling, tumbling a thousand feet. Thought of the cold air whistling past. And then warmer air, as the ground spins ever closer.

She looked at the sheet-draped remains of a man who had dared to dream of a new world, a brighter future.

*Welcome to America.*

The Newton patrolman posted in front of the house was just a rookie, and he did not recognize Rizzoli. He stopped her at the perimeter of the police tape and addressed her with a brusque tone that matched his newly minted uniform. His name tag said: RIDGE.

"This is a crime scene, ma'am."

"I'm Detective Rizzoli, Boston P.D. Here to see Detective Korsak."

"I.D., please."

She hadn't expected such a request, and she had to dig in her purse for her badge. In the city of Boston, just about every patrolman knew exactly who she was. One short drive out of her territory, into this well-heeled suburb, and suddenly she was reduced to fumbling for her badge. She held it right up to his nose.

He took one look and flushed. "I'm really sorry, ma'am. See, there was this asshole reporter who talked her way past me just a few minutes ago. I wasn't gonna let that happen again."

"Is Korsak inside?"

"Yes, ma'am."

She eyed the jumble of vehicles parked on the street, among them a white van with COMMONWEALTH OF MASSACHUSETTS, OFFICE OF THE MEDICAL EXAMINER stenciled on the side.

"How many victims?" she asked.

"One. They're getting ready to move him out now."

The patrolman lifted the tape to let her pass into the front yard. Birds chirped and the air smelled like sweet grass. *You're not in South Boston anymore,* she thought. The landscaping was immaculate, with clipped boxwood hedges and a lawn that was bright AstroTurf green. She paused on the brick walkway and stared up at the roofline with its Tudor accents. *Lord of the fake English manor* was what came to mind. This was not a house, nor a neighborhood, that an honest cop could ever afford.

"Some digs, huh?" Patrolman Ridge called out to her.

"What did this guy do for a living?"

"I hear he was some kind of surgeon."

*Surgeon.* For her, the word had special meaning, and the sound of it pierced her like an icy needle, chilling her even on this warm day. She

21

looked at the front door and saw that the knob was sooty with fingerprint powder. She took a deep breath, pulled on latex gloves, and slipped paper booties over her shoes.

Inside, she saw polished oak floors and a stairwell that rose to cathedral heights. A stained-glass window let in glowing lozenges of color.

She heard the *whish-whish* of paper shoe covers, and a bear of a man lumbered into the hallway. Though he was dressed in businesslike attire, with a neatly knotted tie, the effect was ruined by the twin continents of sweat staining his underarms. His shirtsleeves were rolled up, revealing beefy arms bristling with dark hair. "Rizzoli?" he asked.

"One and the same."

He came toward her, arm outstretched, then remembered he was wearing gloves and let his hand fall again. "Vince Korsak. Sorry I couldn't say more over the phone, but everyone's got a scanner these days. Already had one reporter worm her way in here. What a bitch."

"So I heard."

"Look, I know you're probably wondering what the hell you're doing way out here. But I followed your work last year. You know, the Surgeon killings. I thought you'd want to see this."

Her mouth had gone dry. "What've you got?"

"Vic's in the family room. Dr. Richard Yeager, age thirty-six. Orthopedic surgeon. This is his residence."

She glanced up at the stained-glass window.

"You Newton boys get the upscale homicides."

"Hey, Boston P.D. can have 'em all. This isn't supposed to happen out here. Especially weird shit like this."

Korsak led the way down the hall, into the family room. Rizzoli's first view was of brilliant sunlight flooding through a two-story wall of ground-to-ceiling windows. Despite the number of crime scene techs at work here, the room felt spacious and stark, all white walls and gleaming wood floor.

And blood. No matter how many crime scenes she walked into, that first sight of blood always shocked her. A comet's tail of arterial splatter had shot across the wall and trickled down in streamers. The source of that blood, Dr. Richard Yeager, sat with his back propped up against the wall, his wrists bound behind him. He was wearing only boxer shorts, and his legs were stretched out in front of him, the ankles bound with duct tape. His head lolled forward, obscuring her view of the wound that had released the fatal hemorrhage, but she did not need to see the slash to know that it had gone deep, to the carotid and the windpipe. She was already too familiar with the aftermath of such a wound, and she could read his final moments in the pattern of blood: the artery spurting, the lungs filling up, the victim aspirating through his severed windpipe. Drowning in his own blood. Exhaled tracheal spray had dried on his bare chest. Judging by his broad shoulders and his musculature, he had been physically fit — surely capable of fighting back against an attacker. Yet he had died with head bowed, in a posture of obeisance.

The two morgue attendants had already brought in their stretcher and were standing by the body, considering how best to move a corpse that was frozen in rigor mortis.

"When the M.E. saw him at ten A.M.," said Korsak, "livor mortis was fixed, and he was in full rigor. She estimated the time of death somewhere between midnight and three A.M."

"Who found him?"

"His office nurse. When he didn't show up at the clinic this morning and he didn't answer his phone, she drove over to check on him. Found him around nine A.M. There's no sign of his wife."

Rizzoli looked at Korsak. "Wife?"

"Gail Yeager, age thirty-one. She's missing."

The chill Rizzoli had felt standing by the Yeagers' front door was back again. "An abduction?"

"I'm just saying she's missing."

Rizzoli stared at Richard Yeager, whose muscle-bound body had proved no match for Death. "Tell me about these people. Their marriage."

"Happy couple. That's what everyone says."

"That's what they always say."

"In this case, it does seem to be true. Only been married two years. Bought this house a year ago. She's an O.R. nurse at his hospital, so they had the same circle of friends, same work schedule."

"That's a lot of togetherness."

"Yeah, I know. It'd drive me bonkers if I had to hang around with my wife all day. But they seemed to get along fine. Last month, he took two whole weeks off, just to stay home with her after her mother died. How much you figure an orthopedic surgeon makes in two weeks, huh? Fifteen, twenty thousand bucks? That's some expensive comfort he was giving her."

"She must have needed it."

Korsak shrugged. "Still."

"So you found no reason why she'd walk out on him."

"Much less whack him."

Rizzoli glanced at the family room windows. Trees and shrubbery blocked any view of neighboring houses. "You said the time of death was between midnight and three."

"Yeah."

"Did the neighbors hear anything?"

"Folks to the left are in Paris. Ooh la la. Neighbors to the right slept soundly all night."

"Forced entry?"

"Kitchen window. Screen pried off, used a glass cutter. Size eleven shoeprints in the flower bed. Same prints tracked blood in this room." He took out a handkerchief and wiped his moist forehead. Korsak was one of those unlucky individuals for whom no antiperspirant was powerful enough. Just in the few minutes they'd been conversing, the sweat stains in his shirt had spread.

"Okay, let's slide him away from the wall," one of the morgue attendants said. "Tip him onto the sheet."

"Watch the head! It's slipping!"

"Aw, Jesus."

Rizzoli and Korsak fell silent as Dr. Yeager was laid sideways on a disposable sheet. Rigor mortis had stiffened the corpse into a ninety-degree angle, and the attendants debated how to arrange him on the stretcher, given his grotesque posture.

Rizzoli suddenly focused on a chip of white lying on the floor, where the body had been sitting. She crouched down to retrieve what appeared to be a tiny shard of china.

"Broken teacup," said Korsak.

"What?"

"There was a teacup and saucer next to the victim. Looked like it fell off his lap or something. We've already packed it up for prints." He saw her puzzled look and he shrugged. "Don't ask me."

"Symbolic artifact?"

"Yeah. Ritual tea party for the dead guy."

She stared at the small chip of china lying in her gloved palm and considered what it meant. A knot had formed in her stomach. A terrible sense of familiarity. *A slashed throat. Duct tape bindings. Nocturnal entry through a window. The victim or victims surprised while asleep.*

*And a missing woman.*

"Where's the bedroom?" she asked. Not wanting to see it. Afraid to see it.

"Okay. This is what I wanted you to look at."

The hallway that led to the bedroom was hung with framed black-and-white photographs. Not the smiling-family poses that most houses displayed, but stark images of female nudes, the faces obscured or turned from the camera, the torsos anonymous. A woman embracing a tree, smooth skin pressed against rough bark. A seated woman bent forward, her long hair cascading down between her bare thighs. A woman reaching for the sky, torso glistening with the sweat of vigorous exercise. Rizzoli paused to study a photo that had been knocked askew.

"These are all the same woman," she said.

"It's her."

"Mrs. Yeager?"

"Looks like they had a kinky thing going, huh?"

She stared at Gail Yeager's finely toned body. "I don't think it's kinky at all. These are beautiful pictures."

"Yeah, whatever. Bedroom's in here." He pointed through the doorway.

She stopped at the threshold. Inside was a king-size bed, its covers thrown back, as though its occupants had been abruptly roused from sleep. On the shell-pink carpet, the nylon pile had been flattened in two separate swaths leading from the bed to the doorway.

Rizzoli said, softly, "They were both dragged from the bed."

Korsak nodded. "Our perp surprises them in bed. Somehow subdues them. Binds their wrists and ankles. Drags them across the carpet and into the hallway, where the wood floor begins."

She was baffled by the killer's actions. She imagined him standing where she was now, looking in at the sleeping couple. A window high over the bed, uncurtained, would have spilled enough light to see which was the man and which the woman. He would go to Dr. Yeager first. It was the logical thing to do, to control the man. Leave the woman for later. This much Rizzoli could envision. The approach, the initial attack. What she did not understand was what came next.

"Why move them?" she said. "Why not kill Dr. Yeager right here? What was the point of bringing them out of the bedroom?"

"I don't know." He pointed through the doorway. "It's all been photographed. You can go in."

Reluctantly she entered the room, avoiding the drag marks on the carpet, and crossed to the bed. She saw no blood on the sheets or the covers. On one pillow was a long blond strand — Mrs. Yeager's side of the bed, she thought. She turned to the dresser, where a framed photograph of the couple confirmed that Gail

Yeager was indeed a blonde. A pretty one, too, with light-blue eyes and a dusting of freckles on deeply tanned skin. Dr. Yeager had his arm draped around her shoulder and projected the brawny confidence of a man who knows he is physically imposing. Not a man who would one day end up dead in his underwear, his hands and feet bound.

"It's on the chair," said Korsak.

"What?"

"Look at the chair."

She turned to face the corner of the room and saw an antique ladder-back chair. Lying on the seat was a folded nightgown. Moving closer, she saw bright spatters of red staining the cream satin.

The hairs on the back of her neck were suddenly bristling, and for a few seconds she forgot to breathe.

She reached down and lifted one corner of the garment. The underside of the fold was spattered as well.

"We don't know whose blood it is," said Korsak. "It could be Dr. Yeager's; it could be the wife's."

"It was already stained before he folded it."

"But there's no other blood in this room. Which means it got splattered in the other room. Then he brought it into this bedroom. Folded it nice and neat. Placed it on that chair, like a little parting gift." Korsak paused. "Does that remind you of someone?"

She swallowed. "You know it does."

"This killer is copying your boy's old signature."

"No, this is different. This is all different. The Surgeon never attacked couples."

"The folded nightclothes. The duct tape. The victims surprised in bed."

"Warren Hoyt chose single women. Victims he could quickly subdue."

"But look at the similarities! I'm telling you, we've got a copycat. Some wacko who's been reading about the Surgeon."

Rizzoli was still staring at the nightgown, remembering other bedrooms, other scenes of death. It had happened during a summer of unbearable heat, like this one, when women slept with their windows open and a man named Warren Hoyt crept into their homes. He brought with him his dark fantasies and his scalpels, the instruments with which he performed his bloody rituals on victims who were awake and aware of every slice of his blade. She gazed at that nightgown, and a vision of Hoyt's utterly ordinary face sprang clearly to mind, a face that still surfaced in her nightmares.

*But this is not his work. Warren Hoyt is safely locked away in a place he can't escape. I know, because I put the bastard there myself.*

"The *Boston Globe* printed every juicy detail," said Korsak. "Your boy even made it into the *New York Times*. Now this perp is reenacting it."

"No, your killer is doing things Hoyt never did. He drags this couple out of the bedroom, into another room. He props up the man in a sitting position, then slashes his neck. It's more like an execution. Or part of a ritual. Then there's the woman. He kills the husband, but what does he do with the wife?" She stopped, suddenly remembering the shard of china on the floor. The broken teacup. Its significance blew through her like an icy wind.

Without a word, she walked out of the bedroom and returned to the family room. She looked at the wall where the corpse of Dr. Yeager had been sitting. She looked down at the floor and began to pace a wider and wider circle, studying the spatters of blood on the wood.

"Rizzoli?" said Korsak.

She turned to the windows and squinted against the sunlight. "It's too bright in here. And there's so much glass. We can't cover it all. We'll have to come back tonight."

"You thinking of using a Luma-lite?"

"We'll need ultraviolet to see it."

"What are you looking for?"

She turned back to the wall. "Dr. Yeager was sitting there when he died. Our unknown subject dragged him from the bedroom. Propped him up against that wall, and made him face the center of the room."

"Okay."

"Why was he placed there? Why go to all that

31

trouble while the victim's still alive? There had to be a reason."

"What reason?"

"He was put there to watch something. To be a witness to what happened in this room."

At last Korsak's face registered appalled comprehension. He stared at the wall, where Dr. Yeager had sat, an audience of one in a theater of horror.

"Oh, Jesus," he said. "Mrs. Yeager."

# Two

Rizzoli brought home a pizza from the deli around the corner and excavated an ancient head of lettuce from the bottom of her refrigerator vegetable bin. She peeled off brown leaves until she reached the barely edible core. It was a pale and unappetizing salad, which she ate out of duty and not for pleasure. She had no time for pleasure; she ate only to refuel for the night ahead, a night that she did not look forward to.

After a few bites, she pushed her food away and stared at the vivid smears of tomato sauce on the plate. The nightmares catch up with you, she thought. You think you're immune, that you're strong enough, detached enough, to live with them. And you know how to play the part, how to fake them all out. But those faces stay with you. The eyes of the dead.

Was Gail Yeager among them?

She looked down at her hands, at the twin scars knotting both palms, like healed crucifixion wounds. Whenever the weather turned cold and damp, her hands ached, a punishing reminder of what Warren Hoyt had done to her a year ago, the day he had pierced her flesh with his blades. The day she had thought would be her last on earth. The old wounds were aching now, but she could not blame this on the weather. No, it was because of what she had seen today in Newton. The folded nightgown. The fantail of blood on the wall. She had walked into a room where the air itself was still charged with terror, and she had felt Warren Hoyt's lingering presence.

Impossible, of course. Hoyt was in prison, exactly where he should be. Yet here she sat, chilled by the memory of that house in Newton, because the horror had felt so familiar.

She was tempted to call Thomas Moore, with whom she had worked the Hoyt case. He knew the details as intimately as she did, and he understood how tenacious was the fear that Warren Hoyt had spun like a web around all of them. But since Moore's marriage, his life had diverged from Rizzoli's. His newfound happiness was the very thing that now made them strangers. Happy people are self-contained; they breathe different air and are subject to different laws of gravity. Though Moore might not be aware of the change between them, Rizzoli had felt it, and she mourned the loss, even as she felt ashamed for envying his happiness. Ashamed, too, of her jealousy of the woman who had captured Moore's heart. A few days ago, she had received his postcard from London, where he and Catherine were vacationing. It was a brief hello scrawled on the back of a souvenir card from the Scotland Yard Museum, just a few words to let Rizzoli know their stay was pleasant and all was right in their world. Thinking of that note now, with its cheery optimism, Rizzoli knew she could not trouble him about this case; she could not bring the shadow of Warren Hoyt back into their lives.

She sat listening to the sounds of traffic on the street below, which only seemed to emphasize the utter stillness inside her apartment. She looked around, at the starkly furnished living room, at the blank walls where she had yet to hang a single picture. The only decoration, if it could be called that, was a city map, tacked to the wall above her dining table. A year ago, the map had been studded with colored pushpins marking the Surgeon's kills. She'd been so hungry for recognition, for her colleagues to acknowledge that, yes, she was their equal, that she had lived and breathed the hunt. Even at home, she had eaten her meals in grim view of murder's footprints.

Now the Surgeon pushpins were gone, but the map remained, waiting for a fresh set of pins to mark another killer's movements. She wondered what it said about her, what pitiful interpretation one could draw, that even after two years in this apartment, the only adornment hanging on her walls was this map of Boston. My beat, she thought.

My universe.

The lights were off inside the Yeager residence when Rizzoli pulled into the driveway at nine-ten P.M. She was the first to arrive, and since she did not have access to the house, she sat in her car with the windows open to let in fresh air as she waited for the others to arrive. The house stood on a quiet cul-de-sac, and both neighbors' homes were dark. This would work to their advantage tonight, as there would be less ambient light to obscure their search. But at that moment, sitting alone and contemplating that house of horrors, she craved bright lights and human company. The windows of the Yeager home stared at her like the glassy eyes of a corpse. The shadows around her took on myriad forms, none of them benign. She took out her weapon, unlatched the safety, and set it on her lap. Only then did she feel calmer.

Headlights beamed in her rearview mirror. Turning, she was relieved to see the crime scene unit van pull up behind her. She slipped her weapon back in her purse.

A young man with massive shoulders stepped out of the van and walked toward her car. As he bent down to peer in her window, she saw the glint of his gold earring.

"Hey, Rizzoli," he said.

"Hey, Mick. Thanks for coming out."

"Nice neighborhood."

"Wait till you see the house."

A new set of headlights flickered into the cul-de-sac. Korsak had arrived.

"Gang's all here," she said. "Let's get to work."

Korsak and Mick did not know each other. As

Rizzoli introduced them by the glow of the van's dome light, she saw that Korsak was staring at the CST's earring and noticed his hesitation before he shook Mick's hand. She could almost see the wheels turning in Korsak's head. *Earring. Weight lifter. Gotta be gay.*

Mick began unloading his equipment. "I brought the new Mini Crimescope 400," he said. "Four-hundred-watt arc lamp. Three times brighter than the old GE three-fifty watt. Most intense light source we ever worked with. This thing's even brighter than five-hundred-watt Xenon." He glanced at Korsak. "You mind carrying in the camera stuff?"

Before Korsak could respond, Mick thrust an aluminum case into the detective's arms, then turned back to the van for more equipment. Korsak just stood there for a moment holding the camera case, wearing a look of disbelief. Then he stalked off toward the house.

By the time Rizzoli and Mick got to the front door with their various cases containing the Crimescope, power cords, and protective goggles, Korsak had turned on the lights inside the house and the door was ajar. They pulled on shoe covers and walked in.

As Rizzoli had done earlier that day, Mick paused in the entryway, staring up in awe at the soaring stairwell.

"There's stained glass at the top," said Rizzoli. "You should see it with the sun shining through."

An irritated Korsak called out from the family

room, "We getting down to business here, or what?"

Mick flashed Rizzoli a *what an asshole* look, and she shrugged. They headed down the hall.

"This is the room," said Korsak. He was wearing a different shirt from the one he'd worn earlier that afternoon, but this shirt, too, was already blotted with sweat. He stood with his jaw jutting out, his feet planted wide apart, like an ill-tempered Captain Bligh on the deck of his ship. "We focus here, this area of the floor."

The blood had lost none of its emotional impact. While Mick set up his equipment, plugging in the power cord, readying the camera and tripod, Rizzoli found her gaze drawn to the wall. No amount of scrubbing would completely erase that silent testimony to violence. The biochemical traces would always remain in a ghostly imprint.

But it was not blood they sought tonight. They were searching for something far more difficult to see, and for that, they required an alternate light source that was intense enough to reveal what was now invisible to the unaided eye.

Rizzoli knew that light was simply electromagnetic energy that moved in waves. Visible light, which the human eye can detect, had wavelengths between 400 and 700 nanometers. Shorter wavelengths, in the ultraviolet range, were not visible. But when UV light shines on a number of different natural and man-made substances, it sometimes excites electrons within those substances, releasing visible light in a process called fluorescence. UV light could reveal body fluids, bone fragments, hairs, and fibers. That's why she had requested the Mini Crimescope. Under its UV lamp, a whole new array of evidence might become visible.

"We're about ready here," said Mick. "Now we need to get this room as dark as possible." He looked at Korsak. "Can you start by turning off those hall lights, Detective Korsak?"

"Wait. What about goggles?" said Korsak. "That UV light's gonna blast my eyes, right?"

"At the wavelengths I'm using, it won't be all that harmful."

"I'd like a pair, anyway."

"They're in that case. There's goggles for everyone."

Rizzoli said, "I'll get the hall lights." She walked out of the room and flipped the switches. When she returned, Korsak and Mick were still standing as far apart as possible, as though afraid of exchanging some communicable disease.

"So which areas are we focusing on?" said Mick.

"Let's start at that end, where the victim was found," said Rizzoli. "Move outward from there. The whole room."

Mick glanced around. "You've got a beige area rug over there. It's probably going to fluoresce. And that white couch is gonna light up under UV, too. I just want to warn you, it'll be tough to spot anything against that background." He glanced at Korsak, who was already wearing his goggles and now looked like some pathetic middle-aged loser trying to appear cool in wraparound sunglasses.

"Hit those room lights," said Mick. "Let's see how dark we can get it in here."

Korsak flipped the switch, and the room dropped into darkness. Starlight shone in faintly through the large uncurtained windows, but there was no moon and the backyard's thick trees blocked out the lights of neighboring houses.

"Not bad," said Mick. "I can work with this. Better than some crime scenes, where I've had to crawl around under a blanket. You know, they're developing imaging systems that can be used in daylight. One of these days, we won't have to stumble around like blind men in the dark."

"Can we cut to the chase and get started?" Korsak snapped.

"I just thought you'd be interested in some of this technology."

"Some other time, okay?"

"Whatever," said Mick, unruffled.

Rizzoli slipped on her goggles as the Crimescope's blue light came on. The eerie glow of fluorescing shapes appeared like ghosts in the dark room, the rug and the couch bouncing back light as Mick had predicted. The blue light moved toward the opposite wall, where Dr.

40

Yeager's corpse had been sitting, and bright slivers glowed on the wall.

"Kind of pretty, isn't it?" said Mick.

"What is that?" asked Korsak.

"Strands of hair, adhering to the blood."

"Oh, yeah. That's *real* pretty."

"Shine it on the floor," said Rizzoli. "That's where it'll be."

Mick aimed the UV lens downward, and a new universe of revealed fibers and hairs glowed at their feet. Trace evidence that the initial vacuuming by the CSU had left behind.

"The more intense the light source, the more intense the fluorescence," said Mick as he scanned the floor. "That's why this unit is so great. At four hundred watts, it's bright enough to pick up everything. The FBI bought seventy-one of these babies. It's so compact, you can bring it on a plane as a carry-on."

"What are you, some techno freak?" said Korsak.

"I like cool gadgets. I was an engineering major."

"You were?"

"Why do you sound so surprised?"

"I didn't think guys like you were into that stuff."

"Guys like me?"

"I mean, the earring and all. You know."

Rizzoli sighed. "Open mouth, insert foot."

"What?" said Korsak. "I'm not putting them down or anything. I just happen to notice that not many of them go into engineering. More like theater and the arts and stuff. I mean, that's *good*. We *need* artists."

"I went to U. Mass," said Mick, refusing to take offense. He continued to scan the floor. "Electrical engineering."

"Hey, electricians make good money."

"Um, that's not quite the same career."

They were moving in an ever-widening circle, the UV light continuing to pick up the occasional fleck of hair, fibers, and other unidentifiable particles. Suddenly they moved into a startlingly bright field.

"The rug," said Mick. "Whatever these fibers are, they're fluorescing like crazy. Won't be able to see much against this background."

"Scan it anyway," said Rizzoli.

"Coffee table's in the way. Could you move it?"

Rizzoli reached down toward what appeared to her as only a geometric shadow against a fluorescing background of white. "Korsak, get the other end," she said.

With the coffee table moved aside, the area rug was a bright oval pool that glowed bluish-white.

"How we gonna spot anything on that background?" said Korsak. "It's like trying to see glass floating in water."

"Glass doesn't float," said Mick.

"Oh, right. You're the engineer. So what's *Mick* short for, anyway? *Mickey?*"

"Let's do the couch," Rizzoli cut in.

Mick redirected the lens. The couch fabric also glowed under UV, but it was a softer fluorescence, like snow under moonlight. Slowly he scanned the padded frame, then the cushions, but spotted no suspicious smears, only a few long stray hairs and dust particles.

"These were tidy people," said Mick. "No stains, not even much dust. I'll bet this couch is brand-new."

Korsak grunted. "Must be nice. Last new couch I bought was when I got married."

"Okay, there's some more floor space back there. Let's move that way."

Rizzoli felt Korsak bump into her, and she smelled his doughy odor of sweat. His breathing was noisy, as though he had sinus problems, and the darkness seemed to amplify his snuffling. Annoyed, she stepped away from him and slammed her shin against the coffee table.

*"Shit."*

"Hey, watch where you're going," said Korsak.

She bit back a retort; things were already tense enough in this room. She bent down to rub her leg. The darkness and the abrupt change in position made her dizzy and disoriented. She had to squat down so she wouldn't lose her balance. For a few seconds she crouched in the blackness, hoping Korsak wouldn't trip over her, since he was heavy enough to squash her flat. She could hear the two men moving about a few feet away.

"The cord's tangled," said Mick. The Crime-scope light suddenly shifted in Rizzoli's direction as he turned to free up the power cord.

The beam washed across the rug where Rizzoli was crouched. She stared. Framed by the background fluorescence of the rug fibers was a dark irregular spot, smaller than a dime.

"Mick," she said.

"Can you lift that end of the coffee table? I think the cord's wrapped around the leg."

*"Mick."*

"What?"

"Bring the scope over here. Focus on the rug. Right where I am."

Mick came toward her. Korsak did, too; she could hear his adenoidal breathing moving closer.

"Aim at my hand," she said. "I've got my finger near the spot."

Bluish light suddenly bathed the rug, and her hand was a black silhouette against the fluorescing background.

"There," she said. "What is it?"

Mick crouched beside her. "A stain of some kind. I should get a photo of that."

"But it's a dark spot," said Korsak. "I thought we were looking for something that fluoresces."

"When the background's highly fluorescent, like these carpet fibers, body fluids may actually look dark, because they don't fluoresce as brightly. This stain could be anything. The lab will have to confirm it."

"So what, are we gonna cut a piece out of this nice rug, just because we've found an old coffee stain or something?"

Mick paused. "There's one more trick we can try."

"What?"

"I'm going to change the wavelength on this scope. Bring it down to UV shortwave."

"What does that do?"

"It's real cool if it happens."

Mick adjusted the settings, then focused the light on the area of rug containing the dark blot. "Watch," he said, and flipped off the power to the Crimescope.

The room went pitch-black. All except for one bright spot glowing at their feet.

"What the hell is *that?*" said Korsak.

Rizzoli felt as though she were hallucinating. She stared at the ghostly image, which seemed to burn with green fire. Even as she watched, the spectral glow began to fade. Seconds later, they were in complete blackness.

"Phosphorescence," said Mick. "It's delayed fluorescence. It happens when UV light excites electrons in certain substances. The electrons take a little extra time to return to their baseline energy state. As they do, they release photons of light. That's what we were seeing. We've got a stain here that phosphoresces bright green after exposure to short-wavelength UV light. That's very suggestive." He rose and switched on the room lights.

In the sudden brightness, the rug they had been staring at with such fascination appeared utterly ordinary. But she could not look at it now without feeling a sense of revulsion, because she knew what had taken place there; the evidence of Gail Yeager's ordeal still clung to those beige fibers.

"It's semen," she said.

"It very well could be," said Mick as he set up the camera tripod and attached the Kodak Wratten filter for UV photography. "After I get a shot of this, we'll cut out this section of the rug. The lab will have to confirm with acid phosphatase and microscopic."

But Rizzoli needed no confirmation. She turned toward the blood-spattered wall. She remembered the position of Dr. Yeager's body, and she remembered the teacup that had fallen from his lap and shattered on the wood floor. The spot of phosphorescing green on the rug confirmed what she had feared. She understood what had happened, as surely as if the scene were playing out before her eyes.

*You dragged them from their beds to this room, with its wood floor. Bound the doctor's wrists and ankles and taped over his mouth so he could not cry out, could not distract you. You sat him there, against that wall, making him your mute audience of one. Richard Yeager is still alive, and fully aware of what you are about to do. But he cannot fight back. He cannot protect his wife. And to alert you to his movements, his struggles, you place a teacup and saucer on his lap, as an early-warning system. It will clatter on this hard floor should he manage to rise to his feet. In the throes of your own pleasure, you cannot keep an eye on what Dr. Yeager is doing, and you do not want to be taken by surprise.*

*But you want him to watch.*

She stared down at the spot that had glowed bright green. Had they not moved the coffee table, had they not been searching specifically for those trace leavings, they might have missed it.

*You claimed her, here on this rug. Took her in full view of her husband, who could do nothing to save her, who could not even save himself. And when it was done, when you had taken your spoils, one small drop of semen was left on these fibers, drying to an invisible film.*

Was killing the husband part of the pleasure? Did the unsub pause, his hand gripping the knife, to savor the moment? Or was it merely a practical conclusion to the events that preceded it? Did he feel anything at all as he grasped Richard Yeager by the hair and pressed the blade to his throat?

The room lights went off. Mick's camera shutter clacked again and again, capturing the dark smear, surrounded by the fluorescent glow of the rug.

*And when the task is done, and Dr. Yeager sits with head bowed, his blood dripping on the wall behind him, you perform a ritual borrowed from another killer's bag of tricks. You fold Mrs. Yeager's spattered nightgown and place it on display in the bedroom, just as Warren Hoyt used to do.*

*But you are not finished yet. This was just the first act. More pleasures, terrible pleasures, lie ahead.*

*For that, you take the woman.*

The room lights came back on, and the glare was like a stab to her eyes. She was stunned and shaking, rocked by terrors that she had not felt in months. And humiliated that these two men must surely see it in her white face, her unsteady hands. Suddenly she could not breathe.

She walked out of the room, out of the house. Stood in the front yard, drawing in desperate breaths of air. Footsteps followed her out, but she did not turn to see who it was. Only when he spoke did she know it was Korsak.

"You okay, Rizzoli?"

"I'm fine."

"You didn't look fine."

"I was just feeling a little dizzy."

"It's a flashback to the Hoyt case, isn't it? Seeing this, it's gotta shake you up."

"How would you know?"

A pause. Then, with a snort: "Yeah, you're right. How the hell would I know?" He started back to the house.

She turned and called out: "Korsak?"

"What?"

They stared at each other for a moment. The night air was not unpleasant, and the grass smelled cool and sweet. But dread was thick as nausea in her stomach.

"I know what she's feeling," she said softly. "I know what she's going through."

"Mrs. Yeager?"

"You have to find her. You have to pull out all the stops."

"Her face is all over the news. We're following up every phone tip, every sighting." Korsak shook his head and sighed. "But you know, at this point, I gotta wonder if he's kept her alive."

"He has. I know he has."

"How can you be so sure?"

She hugged herself to quell the trembling and looked at the house. "It's what Warren Hoyt would have done."

# Three

Of all her duties as a detective in Boston's homicide unit, it was the visits to the unobtrusive brick building on Albany Street that Rizzoli disliked most. Though she suspected she was no more squeamish than her male colleagues, she in particular could not afford to reveal any vulnerability. Men were too good at spotting weaknesses, and they would inevitably aim for those tender places with their barbs and their practical jokes. She had learned to maintain a stoic front, to gaze without flinching upon the worst the autopsy table had to offer. No one suspected how much sheer nerve it took for her to walk so matter-of-factly into that building. She knew the men thought of her as the fearless Jane Rizzoli, the bitch with the brass balls. But sitting in her car in the parking lot behind the M.E.'s office, she felt neither fearless nor brassy.

Last night, she had not slept well. For the first time in weeks, Warren Hoyt had crept back into her dreams, and she had awakened drenched in sweat, her hands aching from the old wounds.

She looked down at her scarred palms and suddenly wanted to start the car and drive away, anything to avoid the ordeal that awaited her inside the building. She did not have to be here; this was, after all, a Newton homicide — not her responsibility. But Jane Rizzoli had never been a coward, and she was too proud to back down now.

She stepped out of the car, slammed the door shut with a fierce bang, and walked into the building.

She was the last to arrive in the autopsy lab, and the other three people in the room gave her quick nods of greeting. Korsak was draped in an extra-large O.R. gown and wearing a bouffant paper cap. He looked like an overweight house-wife in a hairnet.

"What have I missed?" she asked as she, too, pulled on a gown to protect her clothes from unexpected splatter.

"Not much. We're just talking about the duct tape."

Dr. Maura Isles was performing the autopsy. The Queen of the Dead was what the homicide unit had dubbed her a year ago, when she'd first joined the Commonwealth of Massachusetts medical examiner's office. Dr. Tierney himself had lured her to Boston from her plum faculty position at the U.C. San Francisco Medical School. It did not take long for the local press to start calling her by her Queen of the Dead nick-name as well. At her first Boston court appear-ance, testifying for the M.E.'s office, she had arrived dressed in Goth black. The TV cameras had followed her regal figure as she strode up the courthouse steps, a strikingly pale woman with a slash of red lipstick, shoulder-length raven hair with blunt bangs, and an attitude of cool imperviousness. On the stand, nothing had rattled her. As the defense attorney flirted, cajoled, and finally resorted in desperation to outright bullying, Dr. Isles had answered his questions with unfailing logic, all the while maintaining her Mona Lisa smile. The press loved her. Defense attorneys dreaded her. And homicide cops were both spooked and fascinated by this woman who'd chosen to spend her days in communion with the dead.

Dr. Isles presided over the autopsy with her usual dispassion. Her assistant, Yoshima, was equally matter-of-fact as he quietly set up instruments and angled lights. They both regarded the body of Richard Yeager with the cool gaze of scientists.

Rigor mortis had faded since Rizzoli had seen the body yesterday, and Dr. Yeager now lay flaccid. The duct tape had been cut away, the boxer shorts removed, and most of the blood rinsed from his skin. He lay with arms limp at his sides, both hands swollen and purplish, like bruise-colored gloves, from the combination of tight bindings and livor mortis. But it was the slash wound across his neck that everyone now focused on.

"Coup de grâce," said Isles. With a ruler she measured the dimensions of the wound. "Fourteen centimeters."

"Weird, how it doesn't seem all that deep," said Korsak.

"That's because the cut was made along Langer's Lines. Skin tension pulls the edges back together so it hardly gapes. It's deeper than it looks."

"Tongue depressor?" said Yoshima.

"Thanks." Isles took it from him and gently slipped the rounded wooden edge into the wound, murmuring under her breath: "Say *ah*. . . ."

"What the hell?" said Korsak.

"I'm measuring wound depth. Nearly five centimeters."

Now Isles pulled a magnifier over the wound and peered into the meat-red slash. "The left carotid artery and the left jugular have both been transected. The trachea has also been in-cised. The level of tracheal penetration, just below the thyroid cartilage, suggests to me that the neck was extended first, before the slash was made." She glanced up at the two detec-tives. "Your unknown subject pulled the vic-tim's head back, and then made a very deliberate incision."

"An execution," said Korsak.

Rizzoli remembered how the Crimescope had picked up the glow of hairs adhering to the blood-spattered wall. Dr. Yeager's hairs, torn from his scalp as the blade cut into his skin.

"What kind of blade?" she asked.

Isles did not immediately respond to the

question. Instead, she turned to Yoshima and said, "Sticky tape."

"I've already got the strips laid out here."

"I'll approximate the margins. You apply the tape."

Korsak gave a startled laugh as he realized what they were doing. "You're taping him back together?"

Isles shot him a glance of dry amusement. "You prefer Super Glue?"

"That supposed to hold his head on, or what?"

"Come on, Detective. Sticky tape wouldn't hold even your head on." She looked down through the magnifier and nodded. "That's fine, Yoshima. I can see it now."

"See what?" said Korsak.

"The wonders of Scotch tape. Detective Rizzoli, you asked me what kind of blade he used."

"Please tell me it's not a scalpel."

"No, it's not a scalpel. Take a look."

Rizzoli stepped toward the magnifier and peered at the wound. The incised edges had been pulled together by the transparent tape, and what she now saw was a clearer approximation of the weapon's cross-sectional shape. There were parallel striations along one edge of the incision.

"A serrated blade," she said.

"At first glance, it does appear that way."

Rizzoli looked up and met Isles's quietly challenging gaze. "But it's not?"

"The cutting edge itself is not serrated, because the other edge of the incision is absolutely smooth. And notice how these parallel scratches appear along only one-third of the incision? Not the entire length. Those scratch marks were made as the blade was being withdrawn. The killer started his incision under the left jaw, and sliced toward the front of the throat, ending the incision just on the far side of the tracheal ring. The scratch marks appear as he's ending his cut, and slightly twisting the blade as he withdraws."

"So what made those scratches?"

"It's not from the cutting edge. This weapon has serrations on the back edge, and they made the parallel scratches as the weapon was pulled out." Isles looked at Rizzoli. "This is typical of a Rambo or survival-type knife. Something a hunter might use."

*A hunter.* Rizzoli looked at the thickly muscled shoulders of Richard Yeager and thought: This was not a man who'd meekly assume the role of prey.

"Okay, so let me get this straight," said Korsak. "This vic, Dr. Weight Lifter here, watches our perp pull out a big friggin' Rambo knife. And he just sits there and lets him cut his throat?"

"His wrists and ankles were bound," said Isles.

"I don't care if he's trussed up like Tutankhamen. Any red-blooded man's gonna squirm like hell."

Rizzoli said, "He's right. Even with your

wrists and ankles bound, you can still kick. You can even head-butt. But he was just sitting there, against the wall."

Dr. Isles straightened. For a moment, she didn't say anything, just stood as regally as though her surgical gown were a priestess's robe. She looked at Yoshima. "Hand me a wet towel. Direct that light over here. Let's really wipe him down and go over his skin. Inch by inch."

"What're we looking for?" asked Korsak.

"I'll tell you when I see it."

Moments later, when Isles lifted the right arm, she spotted the marks on the side of the chest. Beneath the magnifying lens, two faint red bumps stood out. Isles ran her gloved finger over the skin. "Wheals," she said. "It's a Lewis Triple Response."

"Lewis what?" asked Rizzoli.

"Lewis Triple Response. It's a signature effect on the skin. First you see erythema — red spots — and then a flare caused by cutaneous arteriolar dilatation. And finally, in the third stage, wheals pop up due to increased vascular permeability."

"It looks to me like a Taser mark," said Rizzoli.

Isles nodded. "Exactly. This is the classic skin response to an electrical shock from a Taser-like device. It would certainly incapacitate him. Zap, and he loses all neuromuscular control. Certainly long enough for someone to bind his wrists and ankles."

"How long do these wheals usually last?"

"On a living subject, they normally fade after two hours."

"And on a dead subject?"

"Death arrests the skin process. That's why we can still see it. Although it's very faint."

"So he died within two hours of receiving this shock?"

"Correct."

"But a Taser only brings you down for a few minutes," said Korsak. "Five, ten at the most. To keep him down, he'd have to be shocked again."

"And that's why we're going to keep looking for more," said Isles. She shifted the light farther down the torso.

The beam mercilessly spotlighted Richard Yeager's genitals. Up till that moment, Rizzoli had avoided looking at that region of his anatomy. To stare at a corpse's sexual organs always struck her as a cruel invasion, yet one more outrage, one more humiliation visited upon the victim's body. Now the light was focused on the limp penis and scrotum, and the violation of Richard Yeager seemed complete.

"There are more wheals," said Isles, wiping away a smear of blood to reveal the skin. "Here, on the lower abdomen."

"And on his thigh," Rizzoli said softly.

Isles glanced up. "Where?"

Rizzoli pointed to the telltale marks, just to the left of the victim's scrotum. So these are

Richard Yeager's last terrible moments, she thought. Fully awake and alert, but he cannot move. He cannot defend himself. The bulging muscles, the hours at the gym, mean nothing in the end, because his body will not obey him. His limbs lie useless, short-circuited by the electrical storm that has sizzled through his nervous system. He is dragged from his bedroom, helpless as a stunned cow on the way to slaughter. Propped up against the wall, to witness what comes next.

But the Taser's effect is brief. Soon his muscles twitch; his fingers clench into fists. He watches his wife's ordeal, and rage floods his body with adrenaline. This time, when he moves, his muscles obey. He tries to rise, but the clatter of the teacup falling from his lap betrays him.

It takes only another burst of the Taser and he collapses, despairing, like Sisyphus tumbling back down the hill.

She looked at Richard Yeager's face, at the eyelids slitted open, and thought of the last images his brain must have registered. His own legs, stretched useless in front of him. His wife, lying conquered on the beige rug. And a knife, gripped in the hunter's hand, closing in for the kill.

*It is noisy in the dayroom, where men pace like the caged beasts they are. The TV blares, and the metal stairs leading to the upper tier of cells clang with every footfall. We are never out of our watchers' sights. Surveillance cameras are everywhere, in the shower room, even in the toilet area. From the windows of the guard station, our keepers look down on us as we mingle here in the well. They can see every move we make. Souza-Baranowski Correctional Center is a level-six facility, the newest in the Massachusetts Correctional Institute system, and it is a technical marvel. The locks are keyless, operated by computer terminals in the guard tower. Commands are issued to us by bodiless voices over intercoms. The doors to every cell in this pod can be opened or closed by remote access, without a human being ever appearing. There are days when I wonder if any of our guards are flesh and blood or if the silhouettes we see, standing behind glass, are merely animatronic robots, torsos swiveling, heads nodding. Whether by man or by machine, I am being watched, yet it does not bother me, as they cannot see into my mind; they cannot enter the dark landscape of my fantasies. That place belongs only to me.*

*As I sit in the dayroom, watching the six o'clock news on the TV, I am wandering that very landscape. It is the woman newscaster, smiling from the screen, who makes the journey with me. I imagine her dark hair as a splash of black upon the pillow. I see sweat glistening on her skin. And in my world, she is not smiling; oh no, her eyes are wide, the dilated pupils like bottomless pools, the lips drawn back in a rictus of terror. All this I imagine as I gaze at the pretty newscaster in her jade-green suit. I see* her smile, hear her well-modulated voice, and I wonder what her screams would sound like.

Then a new image comes on the TV, and all thoughts of the newscaster vanish. A male reporter stands in front of the Newton home of Dr. Richard Yeager. In a somber voice, he reveals that, two days after the doctor's murder and the abduction of his wife, no arrests have been made. I am already acquainted with the case of Dr. Yeager and his wife. Now I lean forward, staring intently at the screen, waiting for a glimpse.

I finally see her.

The camera has swung toward the house, and it catches her in close-up as she walks out the front door. A heavyset man emerges right behind her. They stand talking in the front yard, unaware that at that moment the TV cameraman has zoomed in on them. The man looks coarse and piggish with his sagging jowls and sparse strands of hair combed over a bare scalp. Beside him, she looks small and insubstantial. It has been a long time since I last saw her, and much about her seems changed. Oh, her hair is still an unruly mane of black curls, and she wears yet another one of her navy-blue pantsuits, the jacket hanging too loose on her shoulders, the cut unflattering to her petite frame. But her face is different. Once it was square-jawed and confident, not particularly beautiful, but arresting nonetheless, because of the fierce intelligence of her eyes. Now she looks worn and troubled. She has lost weight. I see new shadows in her face, in the hollows of her cheeks.

*Suddenly she spots the TV camera and she stares, looking straight at me, her eyes seeming to see me, even as I see her, as though she stands before me in the flesh. We have a history together, she and I, a shared experience so intimate we are as forever bonded as lovers.*

*I rise from the couch and walk to the TV. Press my hand to the screen. I am not listening to the reporter's voice-over; I am focused only on her face. My little Janie. Do your hands still trouble you? Do you still rub your palms, the way you did in the courtroom, as though worrying at a splinter trapped in your flesh? Do you think of the scars the way I do, as love tokens? Little reminders of my high regard for you?*

*"Get the fuck away from the TV! We can't see!" someone yells.*

*I do not move. I stand in front of the screen, touching her face, remembering how her coal-dark eyes once stared up at me in submission. Remembering the slickness of her skin. Perfect skin, unadorned by even the lightest stroke of the makeup brush.*

*"Asshole, move!"*

*Suddenly she is gone, vanished from the screen. The female newscaster in the jade-green jacket is back. Only a moment ago, I had been content to settle for this well-groomed mannequin in my fantasies. Now she strikes me as vapid, just another pretty face, another slender throat. It took only one glimpse of Jane Rizzoli to remind me of what is truly worthy prey.*

*I return to the couch and sit through a commer-cial for Lexus automobiles. But I am no longer watching the TV. Instead, I am remembering what it was like to walk in freedom. To wander city streets, inhaling the scents of women who pass by me. Not the chemist's busy florals that come from bottles, but the real perfume of a woman's sweat, or a woman's hair warmed by the sun. On summer days, I would join the other pedestrians waiting for the crosswalk light to turn green. In the press of a crowded street corner, who would notice that the man behind you has leaned close to sniff your hair? Who would no-tice that the man beside you is staring at your neck, marking your pulse points, where he knows your skin smells sweetest?*

*But they don't notice. The crosswalk light turns green. The crowd begins to move. And the woman walks on, never knowing, never suspecting, that the hunter has caught her scent.*

"The folding of the nightgown does not in it-self mean you're dealing with a copycat," said Dr. Lawrence Zucker. "This is merely a demon-stration of control. The killer displaying his mastery over the victims. Over the crime scene."

"The way Warren Hoyt used to do," said Rizzoli.

"Other killers have done this as well. It's not unique to the Surgeon."

Dr. Zucker was watching her with a strange, almost feral glint in his eye. He was a criminal psychologist at Northeastern University and he frequently consulted for the Boston Police Department. He had worked with the homicide unit during the Surgeon investigation a year ago, and the criminal profile he'd compiled of the unknown subject at that time had turned out to be eerily accurate. Sometimes, Rizzoli wondered how normal Zucker himself could be. Only a man intimately familiar with the territory of evil could have insinuated himself so deeply into the mind of a man like Warren Hoyt. She had never been comfortable with this man, whose sly, whispery voice and intense stares made her feel invaded and vulnerable. But he was one of the few who had truly understood Hoyt; perhaps he would understand a copycat as well.

Rizzoli said, "It's not just the folded nightclothes. There are other similarities. Duct tape was used to bind this victim."

"Again, not unique. Did you ever watch the TV show *MacGyver*? He showed us a thousand and one uses for duct tape."

"Nocturnal entry through a window. The victims surprised in bed —"

"When they're most vulnerable. It's a logical time to attack."

"And the single slash, across the neck."

Zucker shrugged. "A quiet and efficient way to kill."

"But add it all together. The folded nightgown. The duct tape. The method of entry. The coup de grâce —"

63

"And what you get is an unknown subject who is choosing rather common strategies. Even the teacup on the victim's lap — it's a variation on what's been done before, by serial rapists. They set a plate or other dishes on the husband. If he moves, the falling chinaware alerts the perp. These are common strategies because they work."

In frustration, Rizzoli pulled out the Newton crime scene photos and laid them across his desk. "We're trying to find a missing woman, Dr. Zucker. So far we have no leads. I don't even want to think about what she's going through right now — if she's still alive. So you take a good long look at these. Tell me about this unsub. Tell me how we can find him. How we can find *her*."

Dr. Zucker slipped on his glasses and picked up the first photo. He said nothing, just stared for a moment, then reached for the next in the series of images. The only sounds were the creak of his leather chair and his occasional murmur of interest. Through his office window Rizzoli could see the campus of Northeastern University, nearly deserted on this summer's day. Only a few students were lolling on the grass outside, backpacks and books spread around them. She envied those students, envied their carefree days and their innocence. Their blind faith in the future. And their nights, uninterrupted by dark dreams.

"You said you found semen," said Dr. Zucker.

Reluctantly she turned from the view of sunning students and looked at him. "Yes. On that oval rug in the photo. The lab confirms it's a different blood type from the husband's. The DNA's been entered into the CODIS database."

"Somehow, I doubt this unsub is careless enough to be identified by a national database match. No, I'm betting his DNA isn't in CODIS." Zucker looked up from the photo. "And I'll bet he left no fingerprints."

"Nothing that popped up on AFIS. Unfortunately, the Yeagers had at least fifty visitors at the house following the funeral for Mrs. Yeager's mother. Which means we're looking at a lot of unidentified prints."

Zucker gazed down at the photo of Dr. Yeager, slumped against the blood-splattered wall. "This homicide was in Newton."

"Yes."

"Not an investigation you'd normally take part in. Why are you involved?" He looked up again, his gaze holding hers with discomforting intensity.

"I was asked by Detective Korsak —"

"Who is nominally in charge. Right?"

"Right. But —"

"Aren't there enough homicides in Boston to keep you busy, Detective? Why do you feel the need to take this on?"

She stared back, feeling as though he had somehow crawled inside her brain, that he was poking around, searching for just the tender spot to torment. "I told you," she said. "The woman may still be alive."

"And you want to save her."

"Don't you?" she shot back.

"I'm curious, Detective," said Zucker, unruffled by her anger. "Have you talked to anyone about the Hoyt case? I mean, about its impact on you, personally?"

"I'm not sure I know what you mean."

"Have you received any counseling?"

"Are you asking if I've seen a shrink?"

"It must have been a pretty awful experience, what happened to you in that basement. Warren Hoyt did things to you that would haunt any cop. He left scars, both emotional and physical. Most people would have lingering trauma. Flashbacks, nightmares. Depression."

"The memories aren't any fun. But I can deal with them."

"That's always been your way, hasn't it? To tough it out. Never complain."

"I bitch about things like everyone else."

"But never about anything that would make you look weak. Or vulnerable."

"I can't stand whiners. I refuse to be one myself."

"I'm not talking about whining. I'm talking about being honest enough to acknowledge you're having problems."

"What problems?"

"You tell me, Detective."

"No, you tell me. Since you seem to think I'm all fucked up."

"I didn't say that."

"But you think that."

"You're the one who used the term *fucked up*. Is that how you feel?"

"Look, I came about *that*." She pointed to the Yeager crime scene photos. "Why are we talking about me?"

"Because when you look at these photos, all you see is Warren Hoyt. I'm just wondering why."

"That case is closed. I've moved on."

"Have you? Really?"

The question, asked so softly, made her fall silent. She resented his probing. Resented, most of all, that he'd recognized a truth she could not admit. Warren Hoyt *had* left scars. All she had to do was look down at her hands to be reminded of the damage he'd inflicted. But the worst damage was not physical. What she had lost, in that dark basement last summer, was her sense of invincibility. Her sense of confidence. Warren Hoyt had taught her how vulnerable she really was.

"I'm not here to talk about Warren Hoyt," she said.

"Yet he's the reason you're here."

"No. I'm here because I see parallels between these two killers. I'm not the only one who does. Detective Korsak sees it, too. So let's stick to the subject, okay?"

He regarded her with a bland smile. "Okay."

"So what about this unsub?" She tapped on the photos. "What can you tell me about him?"

Once again, Zucker focused on the image of Dr. Yeager. "Your unknown subject is obviously organized. But you already know that. He came to the scene fully prepared. The glass cutter, the stun gun, the duct tape. He managed to subdue this couple so quickly, it makes you wonder . . ." He glanced at her. "No chance there's a second perp? A partner?"

"Only one set of footprints."

"Then your boy is very efficient. And meticulous."

"But he left his semen on the rug. He's handed us the key to his identity. That's one hell of a mistake."

"Yes, it is. And he certainly knows it."

"So why assault her right there, in the house? Why not do it later, in a safe place? If he's organized enough to pull off a home invasion and control the husband —"

"Maybe that's the real payoff."

"What?"

"Think about it. Dr. Yeager sits there, bound and helpless. Forced to watch while another man takes possession of his property."

"Property," she repeated.

"In this unsub's mind, that's what the woman is. Another man's property. Most sexual predators wouldn't risk attacking a couple. They'd choose the lone woman, the easy target. Having a man in the picture makes it dangerous. Yet this unsub had to know there was a husband in the picture. And he came prepared to deal with him. Could it be that was part of the pleasure, part of the excitement? That he had an audience?"

*An audience of one.* She looked down at the photo of Richard Yeager, slumped against the wall. Yes, that had been her immediate impression when she'd walked into the family room.

Zucker's gaze shifted to the window. A moment passed. When he spoke again, his voice was soft and sleepy, as though the words were drifting up in a dream state.

"It's all about power. And control. About dominance over another human being. Not just the woman, but over the man as well. Maybe it's really the man who excites him, who's a vital part of this fantasy. Our unsub knows the risks, yet he's compelled to carry out his impulses. His fantasies control him, and he, in turn, controls his victims. He's all-powerful. The dominator. His enemy sits immobilized and helpless, and our unsub does what victorious armies have always done. He's captured his prize. He rapes the woman. His pleasure is heightened by Dr. Yeager's utter defeat. This attack is more than sexual aggression; it's a display of masculine power. One man's victory over another. The conqueror claiming his spoils."

Outside, the students on the lawn were gathering up their backpacks, brushing grass from

their clothes. The afternoon sun washed everything in hazy gold. And what would the day
hold next for those students? Rizzoli wondered.
Perhaps an evening of leisure and conversation,
pizza and beer. And a sound sleep, without
nightmares. The sleep of the innocent.

*Something I'll never again know.*

Her cell phone chirped. "Excuse me," she
said, and flipped open the phone.

The call was from Erin Volchko, in the hair,
fiber, and trace evidence lab. "I've examined
those strips of duct tape taken off Dr. Yeager's
body," said Erin. "I've already faxed the report
to Detective Korsak. But I knew you'd want to
know as well."

"What have we got?"

"A number of short brown hairs caught in the
adhesive. Limb hairs, pulled from the victim
when the tape was peeled off."

"Fibers?"

"Those as well. But here's the really interesting thing. On the strip pulled from the victim's ankles, there was a single dark-brown hair
strand, twenty-one centimeters long."

"His wife is a blonde."

"I know. That's what makes this particular
strand interesting."

The unsub, thought Rizzoli. It's from our
killer. She asked, "Are there epithelial cells?"

"Yes."

"So we might be able to get DNA off that hair
strand. If it matches the semen —"

"It won't match the semen."

"How do you know that?"

"Because there's no way this strand came from the killer." Erin paused. "Unless he's a zombie."

# Four

For detectives in Boston P.D.'s homicide unit, a visit to the crime lab required only a short walk down a pleasantly sun-washed hallway to the south wing of Schroeder Plaza. Rizzoli had strode down this hall countless times, her gaze often straying to the windows that overlooked the troubled neighborhood of Roxbury, where shops were barricaded at night behind bars and pad-locks and every parked car came equipped with the Club. But today, she was in single-minded pursuit of answers, and she did not even glance sideways but headed in a beeline to Room S269, the hair, fiber, and trace evidence lab.

In this windowless room, crammed tight with microscopes and a gammatech prism gas chromatograph, criminalist Erin Volchko reigned supreme. Cut off from sunlight and outdoor views, she focused her gaze, instead, on the world beneath her microscope lens, and she had the pinched eyes, the perpetual squint, of someone who has been staring too long into an eyepiece. As Rizzoli came into the room, Erin swiveled around to face her.

"I've just put it under the microscope for you. Take a look."

Rizzoli sat down and peered into the teaching eyepiece. She saw a hair shaft stretched horizontally across the field.

"This is that long brown strand I recovered from the strip of duct tape binding Dr. Yeager's ankles," said Erin. "It's the only such strand trapped in the adhesive. The others were short hairs from the victim's limbs, plus one of the vic's head hairs, on the strip taken from his mouth. But this long one is an orphan strand. And it's quite a puzzling one. It doesn't match either the victim's head hair or the hairs we got from the wife's hairbrush."

Rizzoli moved the field, scanning the hair shaft. "It's definitely human?"

"Yes, it's human."

"So why can't it be our perp's?"

"Look at it. Tell me what you see."

Rizzoli paused, calling back to mind all that she had learned about forensic hair examination. She knew Erin must have a reason for taking her so systematically through the process; she could hear quiet excitement in her voice. "This strand is curved, degree of curl about point one or point two. And you said the shaft length was twenty-one centimeters."

"In the range of a woman's hairstyle," said Erin. "But rather long for a man."

"Is it the length that concerns you?"

"No. Length doesn't tell us gender."

"Then what am I supposed to focus on, anyway?"

"The proximal end. The root. Do you notice anything strange?"

"The root end looks a little ragged. Kind of like a brush."

"That's exactly the word I would use. We call that a brushlike root end. It's a collection of cortical fibrils. By examining the root, we can tell what stage of hair growth this strand was in. Care to venture a guess?"

Rizzoli focused on the bulbous root end, with its gossamer-like sheath. "There's something transparent clinging to the root."

"An epithelial cell," said Erin.

"That means it was in active growth."

"Yes. The root itself is slightly enlarged, so this hair was in late anagen. It was just ending its active growth phase. And that epithelial cell might give us DNA."

Rizzoli raised her head and looked at Erin. "I don't see what this has to do with zombies."

Erin gave a soft laugh. "I didn't mean that literally."

"What did you mean?"

"Look at the hair shaft again. Follow it as it leads away from the root."

Once again, Rizzoli gazed into the microscope and focused on a darker segment of the hair shaft. "The color's not uniform," she said.

"Go on."

"There's a black band on the shaft, a short way from the root. What is that?"

"It's called distal root banding," said Erin.

"That's where the sebaceous gland duct enters the follicle. Sebaceous gland secretions include enzymes that actually break down cells, in a sort of digestive process. It causes this swelling and dark band formation near the root end of the hair. That's what I wanted you to see. The distal banding. It rules out any possibility this hair is your unsub's. It may have been shed from his clothes. But not his head."

"Why not?"

"Distal banding and brushlike root ends are both postmortem changes."

Rizzoli's head snapped up. She stared at Erin. "Postmortem?"

"That's right. It came from a decomposing scalp. The changes in that strand are classic, and they're pretty specific for the decomposition process. Unless your killer has risen from the grave, this hair could not have come from his head."

It took a moment for Rizzoli to find her voice again. "How long would the person have to be dead? For the hair to show these changes?"

"Unfortunately, banding changes aren't helpful in determining the postmortem interval. It could have been pulled from the deceased's scalp anywhere from eight hours to several weeks after death. Hair from corpses embalmed years ago could also look like this."

"What if you pull someone's hair out while they're still alive? Leave those hairs lying around for a while? Would the changes show up then?"

"No. These decompositional changes only appear while the hair remains in the dead victim's scalp. They have to be plucked out later, after death." Erin met Rizzoli's stunned gaze. "Your unknown subject has had contact with a corpse. He picked up that hair on his clothes, then shed it onto the tape, while he was binding Dr. Yeager's ankles."

Rizzoli said, softly: "He has another victim."

"That's one possibility. I'd like to propose another." Erin crossed to another countertop and returned with a small tray bearing a section of duct tape lying adhesive-side up. "This piece was peeled off Dr. Yeager's wrists. I want to show it to you under UV. Hit that wall switch, will you?"

Rizzoli flipped the switch. In the sudden darkness, Erin's small UV lamp glowed an eerie blue-green. It was a far less powerful light source than the Crimescope that Mick had used in the Yeager residence, but as its beam washed across the strip of tape, startling details were nonetheless revealed. Adhesive tape left behind at crime scenes can be a detective's treasure trove. Fibers, hairs, fingerprints, even a criminal's DNA left behind in skin cells, may adhere to tape. Under UV, Rizzoli could now see bits of dust and a few short hairs. And, along one edge of the tape, what looked like a very fine fringe of fibers.

"Do you see how these fibers at the extreme edge are continuous?" said Erin. "They run the whole length of the tape taken from his wrists, as well as from his ankles. They almost look like a manufacturer's artifact."

"But they're not?"

"No, they're not. If you lay a roll of tape on its side, the edges pick up traces of whatever the roll is lying on. These are fibers from that surface. Everywhere we go, we pick up traces of our environment. And we later leave behind those traces in other locations. So has your unsub." Erin switched on the room lights and Rizzoli blinked in the sudden glare.

"What sort of fibers are these?"

"I'll show you." Erin removed the slide containing the strand of hair and replaced it with another slide. "Take a look through the teaching head. I'll explain what we're seeing."

Rizzoli peered into the eyepiece and saw a dark fiber, curled into a **C**.

"This is from the edge of the duct tape," said Erin. "I used forced hot air to peel apart all the various layers of the tape. These dark-blue fibers ran along the entire length. Now let me show you the cross section." Erin reached for a file folder, from which she removed a photograph. "This is how it looks under the scanning electron microscope. See how the fiber has a delta shape? Like a little triangle. It's manufactured this way to reduce dirt trapping. This delta shape is characteristic of carpet fibers."

"So this is man-made material?"

"Right."

"What about birefringence?" Rizzoli knew that when light passed through a synthetic fiber, it often came out polarized in two different planes, as though shining through a crystal. The double refraction was called birefringence. Each type of fiber had a characteristic index, which could be measured with a polarizing microscope.

"This particular blue fiber," said Erin, "has a birefringence index of point zero six three."

"Is that characteristic for something in particular?"

"Nylon six, six. Commonly used in carpets, because it's resistant to stains, it's resilient, and it's tough. In particular, this fiber's cross-sectional shape and infrared spectrograph match a Dupont product called Antron, used in carpet manufacture."

"And it's dark blue?" said Rizzoli. "That's not a color most people would choose for a home. It sounds like auto carpet."

Erin nodded. "In fact, this particular color, number eight-oh-two blue, has long been offered as a standard option in luxury-priced American cars. Cadillacs and Lincolns, for instance."

Rizzoli immediately understood where this was going. She said, "Cadillac makes hearses."

Erin smiled. "So does Lincoln."

They were both thinking the same thing: *The killer is someone who works with corpses.*

Rizzoli considered all the people who might

come into contact with the dead. The cop and the medical examiner who are called to the scene of an unattended death. The pathologist and his assistant. The embalmer and the funeral director. The restorer, who washes the hair and applies makeup, so the loved one is presentable for final viewing. The dead pass through a succession of living guardians, and traces of this passage might cling to any and all who have laid hands on the deceased.

She looked at Erin. "The missing woman. Gail Yeager . . ."

"What about her?"

"Her mother died last month."

Joey Valentine was making the dead come alive.

Rizzoli and Korsak stood in the brightly lit prep room of the Whitney Funeral Home and Chapel and watched as Joey dug through his Graftobian makeup kit. Inside were tiny jars of cream highlighters and rouges and lipstick powders. It looked like any theatrical makeup kit, but these creams and rouges were meant to breathe life into the ashen skin of corpses. Elvis Presley's velvet voice sang "Love Me Tender" on a boom box while Joey pressed modeling wax onto the corpse's hands, plugging the various holes and incisions left by multiple I.V. catheters and arterial cut-downs.

"This was Mrs. Ober's favorite music," he said as he worked, glancing occasionally at the three snapshots clipped to the easel, which he'd set up beside the prep table. Rizzoli assumed they were images of Mrs. Ober, although the living woman who appeared in those photos bore little resemblance to the gray and wasted corpse on which Joey was now laboring.

"Son says she's an Elvis freak," said Joey. "Went to Graceland three times. He brought over that cassette, so I could play it while I do her makeup. I always try to play their favorite song or tune, you know. Helps me get a feeling for them. You learn a lot about someone just by what music they listen to."

"What's an Elvis fan supposed to look like?" asked Korsak.

"You know. Brighter lipstick. Bigger hair. Nothing like someone who listens to, say, Shostakovich."

"So what music did Mrs. Hallowell listen to?"

"I don't really remember."

"You worked on her only a month ago."

"Yes, but I don't always remember the details." Joey had finished his wax job on the hands. Now he moved to the head of the table, where he stood nodding to the beat of "You Ain't Nothing but a Hound Dog." Dressed in black jeans and Doc Martens, he looked like a hip young artist contemplating a blank canvas. But his canvas was cold flesh, and his medium was the makeup brush and the rouge pot. "Touch of Bronze Blush Light, I think," he said, and reached for the appropriate jar of rouge.

With a mixing spatula, he began blending colors on a stainless-steel palette. "Yeah, this looks about right for an old Elvis girl." He began smoothing it onto the corpse's cheeks, blending it all the way up to the hairline, where silver roots peeked beneath the black dye job.

"Maybe you remember talking to Mrs. Hallowell's daughter," said Rizzoli. She pulled out a photo of Gail Yeager and showed it to Joey.

"You should ask Mr. Whitney. He handles most of the arrangements here. I'm just his assistant —"

"But you and Mrs. Yeager must have discussed her mother's makeup for the funeral. Since you prepared the remains."

Joey's gaze lingered on Gail Yeager's photograph. "I remember she was a really nice lady," he said softly.

Rizzoli gave him a questioning look. "Was?"

"Look, I've been following the news. You don't really think Mrs. Yeager's still alive, do you?" Joey turned and frowned at Korsak, who was wandering around the prep room, peeking into cabinets. "Uh . . . Detective? Are you looking for something in particular?"

"Naw. Just wondered what kind of stuff you keep in a mortuary." He reached into one of the cabinets. "Hey, is this thing a curling iron?"

"Yes. We do shampoos and waves. Manicures. Everything to make our clients look their best."

"I hear you're pretty good at it."

"They've all been satisfied with my work."

Korsak laughed. "They can tell you that themselves, huh?"

"I mean, their families. Their families are satisfied."

Korsak put down the curling iron. "You've been working for Mr. Whitney, what, seven years now?"

"About that."

"Must've been right out of high school."

"I started off washing his hearses. Cleaning the prep room. Answering the night calls for pickup. Then Mr. Whitney had me help him with the embalming. Now that he's getting on in years, I do almost everything here."

"So I guess you got an embalmer's license, huh?"

A pause. "Uh, no. I never got around to applying. I just help Mr. Whitney."

"Why don't you apply? Seems like it'd be a step up."

"I'm happy with my job the way it is." Joey turned his attention back to Mrs. Ober, whose face had now taken on a rosy glow. He reached for an eyebrow comb and began to stroke brown coloring onto her gray eyebrows, his hands working with almost loving delicacy. At an age when most young men are eager to tackle life, Joey Valentine had chosen instead to spend his days with the dead. He had shepherded corpses from hospitals and nursing homes to this clean, bright room. He had washed and dried them, shampooed their hair, brushed on creams and powders to grant them the illusion of life. As he stroked color on Mrs. Ober's cheeks, he murmured: "Nice. Oh yes, that's really nice. You're going to look fabulous. . . ."

"So, Joey," said Korsak. "You been working here seven years, right?"

"Didn't I just tell you that?"

"And you never bothered to apply for any, like, professional credentials?"

"Why do you keep asking me that?"

"Is that because you knew you wouldn't get a license?"

Joey froze, his hand about to stroke on lipstick. He said nothing.

"Does old Mr. Whitney know about your criminal record?" asked Korsak.

At last Joey looked up. "You didn't tell him, did you?"

"Maybe I should. Seeing as how you scared the shit out of that poor girl."

"I was only eighteen. It was a mistake —"

"A mistake? What, you peeped in the wrong window? Spied on the wrong girl?"

"We went to high school together! It wasn't like I didn't know her!"

"So you only peep in windows of girls you know? What else you done, you never got caught for?"

"I told you, it was a mistake!"

"You ever sneak into someone's house? Go into their bedroom? Maybe filch a little something like a bra, or a nice pair of panties?"

"Oh, Jesus." Joey stared down at the lipstick he'd just dropped on the floor. He looked as though he was about to be sick.

"You know, Peeping Toms have a way of going on to other things," said Korsak, unrelenting. "Bad things."

Joey went to the boom box and shut it off. In the silence that followed, he stood with his back turned to them, staring out the window at the cemetery across the road. "You're trying to fuck up my life," he said.

"No, Joey. We're just trying to have a frank conversation here."

"Mr. Whitney doesn't know."

"And he doesn't have to."

"Unless?"

"Where were you on Sunday night?"

"At home."

"By yourself?"

Joey sighed. "Look, I know what this is all about. I know what you're trying to do. But I told you, I hardly knew Mrs. Yeager. All I did was take care of her mother. I did a good job, you know. Everyone told me so, afterward. How alive she looked."

"You mind if we take a peek in your car?"

"Why?"

"Just to check it out."

"Yes, I mind. But you're going to do it anyway, aren't you?"

"Only with your permission." Korsak paused.

"You know, cooperation is a two-way street."

Joey just kept staring out the window. "There's a burial out there today," he said softly. "See all the limousines? Ever since I was a kid, I've loved watching funeral processions. They're so beautiful. So dignified. It's the one thing people still do right. The one thing they haven't ruined. Not like weddings, where they do stupid things like jumping out of planes. Or saying their vows on national television. At funerals, we still show respect for what's proper. . . ."

"Your car, Joey."

At last, Joey turned and crossed to one of the cabinet drawers. Reaching inside, he pulled out a set of keys, which he handed to Korsak. "It's the brown Honda."

Rizzoli and Korsak stood in the parking lot, staring down at the taupe carpet that lined the trunk of Joey Valentine's car.

"Shit." Korsak slammed down the trunk hood. "I'm not through with this guy."

"You haven't got a thing on him."

"You see his shoes? Looked to me like size eleven. And the hearse has navy-blue carpet."

"So do thousands of other cars. It doesn't make him your man."

"Well, it sure ain't old Whitney." Joey's boss, Leon Whitney, was sixty-six years old.

"Look, we already got the unsub's DNA," said Korsak. "All we need is Joey's."

"You think he'll just spit in a cup for you?"

"If he wants to keep his job. I think he'll sit up and beg like a dog for me."

She looked across the road, shimmering with heat, and gazed at the cemetery, where the funeral procession was now winding its dignified way toward the exit. Once the dead are buried, life moves on, she thought. Whatever the tragedy, life must always move on. *And so should I.*

"I can't afford to spend any more time on this," she said.

"What?"

"I've got my own caseload. And I don't think the Yeager case has anything to do with Warren Hoyt."

"That's not what you thought three days ago."

"Well, I was wrong." She crossed the parking lot to her car, opened the door, and rolled down the windows. Waves of heat rushed out at her from the baking interior.

"Did I tick you off or something?" he asked.

"No."

"So why are you bailing out?"

She slid behind the wheel. The seat felt searing, even through her slacks. "I've spent the last year trying to get over the Surgeon," she said. "I've got to let go of him. I've got to stop seeing his hand in everything I run across."

"You know, sometimes your gut feeling's the best thing you can go with."

"Sometimes, that's all it is. A feeling, not a fact. There's nothing sacred about a cop's instinct. What the hell is instinct, anyway? How many times does a hunch turn out dead wrong?" She turned on the engine. "Too damn often."

"So I didn't tick you off?"

She slammed her door shut. "No."

"You sure?"

She glanced through the open window at him. He stood squinting in the sunlight, eyes narrowed to slits under a bushy fringe of eyebrow. On his arms, dark hairs bristled, heavy as a pelt, and his stance, hips thrust forward, shoulders sagging, made her think of a slouching gorilla. No, he had not ticked her off. But she could not look at him without registering a twinge of distaste.

"I just can't spend any more time on this," she said. "You know how it is."

Back at her desk, Rizzoli focused her attention on all the paperwork that had accumulated. On top was the file for Airplane Man, whose identity remained unknown and whose ruined body still lay unclaimed in the M.E.'s office. She had neglected this victim too long. But even as she opened the folder and reviewed the autopsy photos, she was still thinking of the Yeagers and of a man who had corpse hair on his clothes. She reviewed the schedule of Logan Airport's jet landings and takeoffs, but it was Gail Yeager's face that stayed on her mind, smiling from the photo on the dresser. She remembered the gallery of women's photos that had been taped to the wall of the conference room a year ago, during the Surgeon investigation. Those women had been smiling, too, their faces captured at a moment when they were still warm flesh, when life still glowed in their eyes. She could not think of Gail Yeager without remembering the dead who had gone before her.

She wondered if Gail was already among them.

Her pager vibrated, the buzz like an electric shock from her belt. An advance warning of a discovery that would rock her day. She picked up the phone.

A moment later, she was hurrying out of the building.

# Five

The dog was a yellow Lab, excited to near hysteria by the police officers standing nearby. He capered and barked at the end of his leash, which was tied to a tree. The dog's owner, a wiry middle-aged man in running shorts, sat nearby on a large rock, head drooping into his hands, ignoring his dog's pleading yips for attention.

"Owner's name is Paul Vandersloot. Lives on River Street, just a mile from here," said Patrolman Gregory Doud, who had secured the scene and had already strung a semicircle of police tape on the trees.

They were standing on the edge of the municipal golf course, staring into the woods of Stony Brook Reservation, which directly abutted the golf course. Located at the southern tip of Boston's city limits, this reservation was surrounded by a sea of suburbs. But within Stony Brook's 475 acres was a rugged landscape of wooded hills and valleys, rocky outcroppings, and marshes fringed with cattails. In winter, cross-country skiers explored the park's ten miles of trails; in summer, joggers found refuge in its quiet forests.

And so had Mr. Vandersloot, until his dog led him to what lay among the trees.

"He says he comes here every afternoon to take his dog for a run," said Officer Doud. "Usually goes up the East Boundary Road trail first, through the woods, then loops back along this inside edge of the golf course. It's about a four-mile run. Says he keeps the dog on a leash the whole time. But today, the dog got away from him. They were going up the trail when the dog took off west, into the woods, and wouldn't come back. Vandersloot went chasing after him. Practically tripped right over the body." Doud glanced at the jogger, who was still huddled on the rock. "Called nine-one-one."

"He use a cell phone?"

"No, ma'am. Went to a phone booth down at the Thompson Center. I got here around two-twenty. I was careful not to touch anything. Just walked into the woods far enough to confirm it was a body. About fifty yards in, I could already smell it. Then, after another fifty yards, I saw it. Backed right out and secured the scene. Closed off both ends of the Boundary Road trail."

"And when did everyone else get here?"

"Detectives Sleeper and Crowe got here around three. The M.E. arrived around three-thirty." He paused. "I didn't realize you were coming in, too."

"Dr. Isles called me. I guess we're all parking on the golf course for now?"

"Detective Sleeper ordered it. Doesn't want

any vehicles visible from Enneking Parkway. Keeps us out of the public's eye."

"Any media turned up yet?"

"No, ma'am. I was careful not to radio it in. Used the call box down the road instead."

"Good. Maybe we'll get lucky and they won't turn up at all."

"Uh-oh," said Doud. "Could this be our first jackal arriving?"

A dark-blue Marquis rolled across the golf course grass and pulled up beside the M.E.'s van. A familiar overweight figure hauled himself out and smoothed his sparse hair over his scalp.

"He's not a reporter," said Rizzoli. "This guy I'm expecting."

Korsak lumbered toward them. "You really think it's her?" he asked.

"Dr. Isles says it's a strong possibility. If so, your homicide just moved into Boston city limits." She looked at Doud. "Which way do we approach it, so we don't contaminate things?"

"You're okay going from the east. Sleeper and Crowe have already videoed the site. The footprints and drag marks all come from the other direction, starting at Enneking Parkway. Just follow your nose."

She and Korsak slipped under the police tape and headed into the woods. This section of second-growth trees was as dense as any deep forest. They ducked beneath spiky branches that scratched their faces, and snagged their trouser legs on brambles. They emerged on the

East Boundary jogging trail and spotted a strand of police tape, fluttering from a tree.

"The jogger was running along this path when his dog got away from him," she said. "Looks like Sleeper left us a trail of tape."

They crossed the jogging path and plunged once again into the woods.

"Oh man. I think I can smell it already," said Korsak.

Even before they saw the body, they heard the ominous hum of flies. Dry twigs snapped beneath their shoes, the sound as startling as gunfire. Through the trees ahead, they saw Sleeper and Crowe, faces contorted in disgust as they waved away insects. Dr. Isles was crouched near the ground, a few diamonds of sunlight dappling her black hair. Drawing closer, they saw what Isles was doing.

Korsak uttered an appalled groan. "Ah, shit. That I didn't need to see."

"Vitreous potassium," said Isles, and the words sounded almost seductive in her smoky voice. "It'll give us another estimate for the postmortem interval."

The time of death would be difficult to determine, Rizzoli thought, gazing down at the nude corpse. Isles had rolled it onto a sheet, and it lay faceup, eyes bulging from the heat-expanded tissues inside the cranium. A necklace of disk-shaped bruises ringed the throat. The long blond hair was a stiff mat of straw. The abdomen was bloated, and the belly was tinted a liverish green. Blood vessels had been stained by the bacterial breakdown of blood, and the veins were startlingly visible, like black rivers flowing beneath the skin. But all these horrors paled in view of the procedure Isles was now performing. The membranes around the human eye are the most sensitive surface of the body; a single eyelash or the tiniest grain of sand caught beneath an eyelid can cause immense discomfort. So it made both Rizzoli and Korsak wince to watch Isles pierce the corpse's eye with a twenty-gauge needle. Slowly she sucked the vitreous fluid into a 10 cc syringe.

"Looks nice and clear," said Isles, sounding pleased. She placed the syringe in an ice-filled cooler, then rose to her feet and surveyed the site with a regal gaze. "Liver temp is only two degrees cooler than ambient temp," she said. "And there's no insect or animal damage. She hasn't been lying here very long."

"It's just a dump?" asked Sleeper.

"Lividity indicates she died while lying faceup. See how it's darker on the back, where the blood's pooled? But she was found lying here facedown."

"She was moved here."

"Less than twenty-four hours ago."

"Looks like she's been dead a lot longer than that," said Crowe.

"Yes. She's flaccid, and there's significant bloating. Skin's already slipping off."

"Is that a nosebleed?" asked Korsak.

"Decomposed blood. She's starting to purge. Fluids are being forced out by the internal buildup of gases."

"Time of death?" asked Rizzoli.

Isles paused, her gaze fixed for a moment on the grotesquely swollen remains of a woman they all believed was Gail Yeager. Flies buzzed, filling the silence with their greedy hum. Except for the long blond hair, there was little about the corpse that resembled the woman in the photographs, a woman who once had surely turned men's heads with just a smile. It was a disturbing reminder that both the beautiful and the homely are reduced by bacteria and insects to the grim equality of moldering flesh.

"I can't answer that," said Isles. "Not yet."

"More than a day?" pressed Rizzoli.

"Yes."

"The abduction was Sunday night. Could she have been dead since then?"

"Four days? It depends on the ambient temperature. The absence of insect damage makes me think the body was kept indoors until just recently. Protected from the environment. An air-conditioned room would slow down decomposition."

Rizzoli and Korsak exchanged glances, both of them wondering the same thing. Why would the unsub wait so long to dispose of a decomposing body?

Detective Sleeper's walkie-talkie crackled, and they heard Doud's voice: "Detective Frost just arrived. And the CSU van's here. You ready for 'em?"

"Stand by," said Sleeper. Already he looked exhausted, drained from the heat. He was the oldest detective in the unit, no more than five years from retirement, and he had no need to prove himself. He looked at Rizzoli. "We're coming in on the tail end of this case. You been working with Newton P.D. on it?"

She nodded. "Since Monday."

"So you gonna be lead?"

"Right," said Rizzoli.

"Hey," protested Crowe. "We were first on the scene."

"Abduction was in Newton," said Korsak.

"But the body's now in Boston," retorted Crowe.

"Jesus," said Sleeper. "Why the hell are we fighting over this?"

"It's mine," said Rizzoli. "I'm lead." She stared at Crowe, daring him to challenge her. Expecting their usual rivalry to flare up, as it always did. She saw one side of his mouth turn up in the beginning of an ugly sneer.

Then Sleeper said, into his walkie-talkie, "Detective Rizzoli is now lead investigator." He looked at her again. "You ready for CSU to come in?"

She glanced up at the sky. It was already five P.M., and the sun had dipped below the trees. "Let's get them in here while they can still see what they're doing."

An outdoor death scene, in fading daylight, was not a scenario she welcomed. In wooded areas, wild animals were always poised to descend, scattering remains and dragging off evidence. Rainstorms wash away blood and semen, and the winds scatter fibers. There were no doors to lock out trespassers, and perimeters were easily breached by the curious. So she felt a sense of urgency as the crime scene unit began its grid search. They brought with them metal detectors and sharp eyes and evidence sacks waiting to be filled with grotesque treasures.

By the time Rizzoli tramped back out of the woods and onto the golf course, she was sweating and filthy and tired of swatting at mosquitoes. She paused to brush twigs from hair and pluck burrs from her slacks. Straightening, she suddenly focused on a sandy-haired man in a suit and tie, who stood beside the M.E.'s van, a cell phone pressed to his ear.

She went to Patrolman Doud, who was still manning the perimeter. "Who's the suit over there?" she asked.

Doud glanced in the man's direction. "Him? Says he's FBI."

"What?"

"Flashed his badge and tried to talk his way past me. I told him he'd have to clear it with you first. Didn't seem too happy about that."

"What's a fibbie doing here?"

"You got me."

She stood watching the man for a moment,

disturbed by the arrival of a federal agent. As lead investigator, she wanted no blurring of the lines of authority, and this man, with his military bearing and businessman's suit, already looked as though he owned the scene. She walked toward him, but he did not acknowledge her presence until she was standing right beside him.

"Excuse me," she said. "I understand you're FBI?"

He snapped his cell phone shut and turned to face her. She saw strong, clean-cut features and a coolly impervious gaze.

"I'm Detective Jane Rizzoli, the lead on this case," she said. "May I see your I.D.?"

He reached into his jacket and pulled out the badge. As she studied it, she could feel him watching her, sizing her up. She resented his silent appraisal, resented the way he put her on guard, as though he was the one in control.

"Agent Gabriel Dean," she said, handing back the badge.

"Yes, ma'am."

"May I ask what the FBI's doing here?"

"I wasn't aware we were on opposing teams."

"Did I say we were?"

"You're giving me the distinct feeling I shouldn't be here."

"The FBI doesn't usually turn up at our crime scenes. I'm just curious what brings you to this one."

"We received an advisory from Newton P.D. about the Yeager homicide." It was an incomplete answer; he was leaving out too much, forcing her to fish. Withholding information was a form of power, and she understood the game he was playing.

"I imagine you guys get a lot of routine advisories," she said.

"Yes, we do."

"Every homicide, isn't that right?"

"We're notified."

"Is there something about this one that's special?"

He simply gazed at her with that impenetrable expression. "I think the victims would say so."

Her anger was working its way like a splinter to the surface. "This body was found only a few hours ago," she said. "Are these advisories now instantaneous?"

There was a faint twitch of a smile on his lips. "We're not entirely out of the loop, Detective. We'd appreciate it if you kept us apprised of your progress. Autopsy reports. Trace evidence. Copies of all witness statements —"

"That's a lot of paperwork."

"I realize that."

"And you want it all?"

"Yes."

"Any particular reason?"

"A murder and abduction shouldn't interest us? We'd like to follow this case."

As imposing as he was, she didn't hesitate to challenge him by stepping closer. "When do you plan to start calling the shots?"

"It remains your case. I'm only here to assist."

"Even if I don't see the need for it?"

His gaze shifted to the two attendants who'd emerged from the woods and were now loading the stretcher with the remains into the M.E.'s van. "Does it really matter who works the case?" he asked quietly. "As long as this unsub is caught?"

They watched the van drive away, carrying the already desecrated corpse to further indignities beneath the bright lights of the autopsy suite. Gabriel Dean's response had reminded her, with punishing clarity, just how unimportant were matters of jurisdiction. Gail Yeager did not care who took credit for the capture of her killer. All she demanded was justice, whoever might deliver it. Justice was what Rizzoli owed her.

But she'd known the frustration of watching her own hard work claimed by her colleagues. More than once, she had seen men step forward and arrogantly assume command of cases she herself had painstakingly built from scratch. She would not allow it to happen here.

She said, "I appreciate the Bureau's offer of help. But at the moment, I think we've got all bases covered. I'll let you know if we need you." With that, she turned and walked away.

"I'm not sure you understand the situation," he said. "We're part of the same team now."

"I don't recall asking for FBI assistance."

"It's been cleared through your unit commander: Lieutenant Marquette. Would you like to confirm it with him?" He held out his cell phone.

"I have my own cell phone, thank you."

"Then I urge you to call him. So we don't waste time on turf battles."

She was stunned by how easily he had stepped aboard. And by how accurately she had sized him up. This was a man who'd not stand quietly on the sidelines.

She took out her own phone and began punching in numbers. But before Marquette answered, she heard Patrolman Doud call out her name.

"Detective Sleeper's on comm for you," said Doud, and handed her his walkie-talkie.

She pressed the transmit button. "Rizzoli."

Through a burst of static, she heard Sleeper say: "You might want to get back here."

"What have you got?"

"Uh . . . you'd better see for yourself. We're about fifty yards north of where the other one was found."

*The other one?*

She thrust the walkie-talkie back at Doud and charged into the woods. She was in such a hurry she did not immediately notice that Gabriel Dean was following her. Only when she heard the snap of a twig did she turn and see that he was right behind her, his face grim and implacable. She didn't have the patience to argue with him, so she ignored him and plunged on.

She spotted the men standing in a grim circle

beneath the trees, like silent mourners with heads bowed. Sleeper turned and met her gaze.

"They'd just finished their first sweep with the metal detector," he said. "Crime scene tech was heading back to the golf course when the alarm went off."

She moved into the circle of men and crouched down to inspect what they had found.

The skull had been separated from the body and lay isolated from the rest of the nearly skeletonized remains. A gold crown glinted like a pirate's tooth from the row of dirt-stained teeth. She saw no clothing, no remnants of fabric, only exposed bones with leathery bits of decomposing flesh still adhering. Clumps of long brown hair were matted to leaves, suggesting that these remains were a woman's.

She straightened, her gaze scanning the forest floor. Mosquitoes lit on her face and fed off her blood, but she was oblivious to their sting. She focused only on the layers of dead leaves and twigs, the dense underbrush. A deeply sylvan retreat that she now regarded with horror.

*How many women are lying in these woods?*

"It's his dump site."

She turned and looked at Gabriel Dean, who had just spoken. He was crouched a few feet away, sifting through the leaves with gloved hands. She had not even seen him pull on gloves. Now he stood up, his gaze meeting hers.

"Your unsub has used this place before," said Dean. "And he'll probably use it again."

"If we don't scare him off."

"And that's the challenge. Keeping it quiet. If you don't alarm him, there's a chance he'll come back. Not just to dump another body, but to visit. To recapture the thrill."

"You're from the behavioral unit. Aren't you?"

He didn't answer her question but turned to survey the array of personnel standing around in the woods. "If we can keep this out of the press, we might have a chance. But we've got to clamp down on it now."

*We.* With that one word, he had stepped into a partnership with her that she had never sought, had never consented to. Yet here he was, issuing edicts. What made it especially galling was the fact that everyone else was listening to their conversation and understood that her authority was now being challenged.

Only Korsak, with his customary bluntness, dared step into the dialogue. "Excuse me, *Detective* Rizzoli," he said. "Who is this gentleman?"

"FBI," she said, her gaze still fixed on Dean.

"So could someone explain to me when this turned into a federal case?"

"It hasn't," she said. "And Agent Dean is about to leave the site. Could somebody show him the way?"

She and Dean gazed at each other for a moment. Then he tipped his head to her, a silent acknowledgment that he was conceding this round. "I can find my own way out," he said. He turned and walked back toward the golf course.

"What is it with these fibbies?" said Korsak. "Always think they're king of the hill. What's the Bureau doing here?"

Rizzoli stared at the woods into which Gabriel Dean had just vanished, a gray figure blending into the dusk. "I wish I knew."

Lieutenant Marquette arrived on the scene a half hour later.

The presence of brass was usually the last thing Rizzoli welcomed. She disliked having a superior officer look over her shoulder as she worked. But Marquette did not interfere and simply stood among the trees, silently appraising the situation.

"Lieutenant," she said.

He responded with a curt nod. "Rizzoli."

"What's with the Bureau? They had an agent here, expecting full access."

He nodded. "Request came through OPC."

So it had been approved at the top — the Office of the Police Commissioner.

She watched as the CSU crew packed up their kits and headed back toward the van. Though they were standing within Boston city limits, this dark corner of Stony Brook Reservation felt as isolated as the deep woods. The wind tossed leaves into the air and stirred the smell of decay. Through the trees she saw Barry Frost's flashlight bobbing in the darkness as he untied the crime scene tape, removing all traces of police activity. Tonight, the stakeout would begin, for an unsub whose craving for a whiff of decay might draw him back to this lonely park, to this silent grove of trees.

"So I don't have any choice?" she said. "I have to cooperate with Agent Dean."

"I assured OPC we would."

"What's the Bureau's interest in this case?"

"Did you ask Dean?"

"It's like talking to that tree over there. You get nothing back. I'm not thrilled about this. We have to give him everything, but he doesn't have to tell us squat."

"Maybe you didn't approach him the right way."

Anger shot like a poison dart into her bloodstream. She understood the unspoken meaning of his statement: *You've got an attitude, Rizzoli. You always tick off men.*

"You ever meet Agent Dean?" she asked.

"No."

She gave a laugh laced with sarcasm. "Lucky you."

"Look, I'll find out what I can. Just try to work with him, okay?"

"Does someone say I haven't?"

"Phone call says. I hear you chased him off the site. That's not exactly a cooperative relationship."

"He challenged my authority. I need to establish something right off the bat here. Am I in charge? Or am I not?"

A pause. "You're in charge."

"I trust Agent Dean will get that message, too."

"I'll see he does." Marquette turned and stared at the woods. "So now we've got two sets of remains. Both female?"

"Judging by the skeletal size, and the clumps of hair, the second one looks like another female. There's almost no soft tissue left. Postmortem scavenger damage, but no obvious cause of death."

"Are we sure there aren't more of them out here?"

"Cadaver dogs didn't find any."

Marquette gave a sigh. "Thank God."

Her pager vibrated. She glanced down at her belt and recognized the phone number on the digital readout. The M.E.'s office.

"It's just like last summer," murmured Marquette, still staring at the trees. "The Surgeon started killing around this time, too."

"It's the heat," said Rizzoli as she reached for her cell phone. "It brings the monsters out."

# Six

*I hold freedom in the palm of my hand.*

*It comes in the shape of a tiny white pentagon with* MSD 97 *stamped on one side. Decadron, four milligrams. Such a pretty shape for a pill, not just another boring disk or torpedo-shaped caplet like so many other medicines. This design took a leap of imagination, a spark of whimsy. I picture the marketing folks at Merck Pharmaceuticals, sitting around a conference table, asking each other: "How can we make this tablet instantly recognizable?" And the result is this five-sided pill, which rests like a tiny jewel in my hand. I have been saving it, hiding it away in a small tear in my mattress, waiting for just the right time to use its magic.*

*Waiting for a sign.*

*I sit curled up on the cot in my cell, a book propped up on my knees. The surveillance camera sees only a studious prisoner reading* The Complete Works of William Shakespeare. *It cannot see through the cover of the book. It cannot see what I hold in my hand.*

*Downstairs, in the well of the dayroom, a commercial blares on the TV and a Ping-Pong ball clacks back and forth on the table. Yet another ex-*

citing evening in Cell Block C. In an hour, the intercom will announce lights-out, and the men will climb the stairs to their cells, shoes clanging on metal steps. They will each walk into their cages, obedient rats minding their master in the squawk box. In the guard booth, the command will be typed into the computer, and all cell doors will simultaneously close, locking the rats in for the night.

I curl forward, bending my head to the page, as though the print is too small. I stare with fierce concentration at "Twelfth Night, Act 3, Scene Three: A street. Antonio and Sebastian approach . . ."

Nothing to watch here, my friends. Just a man on his cot, reading. A man who suddenly coughs and reflexively puts his hand to his mouth. The camera is blind to the small tablet in my palm. It does not see the flick of my tongue, or the pill clinging to it like a bitter wafer as it's drawn into my mouth. I swallow the tablet dry, needing no water. It is small enough to go down easily.

Even before it dissolves in my stomach, I imagine I can feel its power swirling through my bloodstream. Decadron is the brand name for dexamethasone, an adrenocortical steroid with profound effects on every organ in the human body. Glucocorticoids such as Decadron affect everything from blood sugar, to fluid retention, to DNA synthesis. Without them, the body collapses. They help us maintain our blood pressure and stave off the shock of injury and infection. They affect our bone growth and fertility, muscle development and immunity.

*They alter the composition of our blood.*

*When at last the cage doors slide shut and the lights go out, I lie on my cot, feeling my blood pulse through me. Imagining the cells as they tumble through my veins and arteries.*

*I have seen blood cells numerous times through the microscope. I know the shape and function of each one, and with just a glance through the lens I can tell you if a blood smear is normal. I can scan a field and immediately estimate the percentages of different leukocytes — the white blood cells that defend us from infection. The test is called a white blood cell differential, and I have performed it countless times as a medical technician.*

*I think of my own leukocytes circulating in my veins. At this very moment, my differential white count is changing. The tablet of Decadron, which I swallowed two hours ago, has by now dissolved in my stomach and the hormone is swirling through my system, performing its magic. A blood sample, drawn from my vein, will reveal a startling abnormality: an overwhelming host of white blood cells with multilobed nuclei and granular stippling. These are neutrophils, which automatically swarm into action when faced with the threat of overwhelming infection.*

*When one hears hoofbeats, medical students are taught, one must think of horses, not zebras. But the doctor who sees my blood count will surely think of horses. He will arrive at a perfectly logical conclusion. It will not occur to him that, this time, it is truly a zebra galloping by.*

★ ★ ★

Rizzoli suited up in the autopsy suite's changing room, donning gown and shoe covers, gloves, and a paper cap. She'd had no time to shower since tramping around Stony Brook Reservation, and in this overcooled room sweat chilled like rime on her skin. Nor had she eaten dinner, and she was light-headed with hunger. For the first time in her career, she considered using a dab of Vicks under her nose to block out the smells of the autopsy, but she resisted the temptation. Never before had she resorted to its use, because she'd thought it a sign of weakness. A homicide cop should be able to deal with every aspect of the job, however unpleasant, and while her colleagues might retreat behind a menthol shield, she had stubbornly endured the undisguised odors of the autopsy suite.

She took a deep breath, inhaling a last gulp of unfouled air, and pushed through the door into the next room.

She had expected to find Dr. Isles and Korsak waiting for her; what she had not expected was to find Gabriel Dean in the room as well. He stood across the table from her, a surgical gown covering his shirt and tie. While exhaustion showed plainly on Korsak's face and in the weary slump of his shoulders, Agent Dean looked neither tired nor bowed by the day's events. Only the five o'clock shadow darkening his jaw marred his crisp good looks. He regarded her with the unabashed gaze of one who knows he has every right to be there.

Under the bright exam lights, the body looked in far worse shape than when she had seen it, just hours ago. Purge fluid had continued to leak from the nose and mouth, trailing bloody streaks on the face. The abdomen was so bloated, it appeared to be in the advanced stages of pregnancy. Fluid-filled blisters ballooned beneath the skin, lifting it from the dermis in papery sheets. Skin was peeling away entirely from areas of the torso and had bunched like wrinkled parchment under the breasts.

Rizzoli noted that the fingerpads had been inked. "You've already taken prints."

"Just before you got here," said Dr. Isles, her attention focused on the tray of instruments that Yoshima had just wheeled to the table. The dead interested Isles more than the living did, and she was oblivious, as usual, to the emotional tensions vibrating in the room.

"What about the hands? Before you inked them?"

Agent Dean said, "We've completed the external exam. The skin's been sticky-taped for fibers, and the nail clippings have been collected."

"And when did *you* get here, Agent Dean?"

"He was here before me, too," said Korsak. "I guess some of us rate higher on the food chain."

If Korsak's comment was meant to feed her irritation, it worked. A victim's fingernails may harbor bits of skin clawed from the attacker. Hair or fibers may be clutched in a closed fist.

110

The examination of the victim's hands was a crucial step in the autopsy and she had missed it.

But Dean had not.

"We already have a positive I.D.," said Isles. "Gail Yeager's dental X rays are up on the light box."

Rizzoli crossed to the light box and studied the series of small films clipped there. Teeth glowed like a row of ghostly headstones on the film's black background.

"Mrs. Yeager's dentist did some crown work on her last year. You can see it there. The gold crown is number twenty on the periapical series. Also, she had silver amalgam fillings in numbers three, fourteen, and twenty-nine."

"It's a match?"

Dr. Isles nodded. "I have no doubt these are the remains of Gail Yeager."

Rizzoli turned back to the body on the table, her gaze falling on the ring of bruises around the throat. "Did you X-ray the neck?"

"Yes. There are bilateral thyroid horn fractures. Consistent with manual strangulation." Isles turned to Yoshima, whose silent and ghostly efficiency sometimes made one forget he was even in the room. "Let's get her into position for the vaginal swabs."

What followed next struck Rizzoli as the worst indignity that could befall a woman's mortal remains. It was worse than the gutting open of the belly, worse than the resection of heart and lungs. Yoshima maneuvered the flaccid legs into a froglike position, spreading the thighs wide for the pelvic exam.

"Excuse me, Detective?" Yoshima said to Korsak, who was standing closest to Gail Yeager's left thigh. "Could you hold that leg in position?"

Korsak stared at him in horror. "Me?"

"Just keep the knee flexed like that, so we can collect the swabs."

Reluctantly Korsak reached for the corpse's thigh, then jerked back as a layer of skin peeled off in his gloved hand. "Christ. Aw, Christ."

"The skin's going to slip, no matter what you do. If you could just hold the leg open, okay?"

Korsak let out a sharp breath. Through the stench of the room, Rizzoli caught a whiff of Vicks menthol. Korsak, at least, had not been too proud to dab it on his upper lip. Grimacing, he grabbed the thigh and rotated it sideways, exposing Gail Yeager's genitalia. "Like this is gonna make sex real appealing from now on," he muttered.

Dr. Isles directed the exam light onto the perineum. Gently she spread apart the swollen labia to reveal the introitus. Rizzoli, stoic as she was, could not bear to watch this grotesque invasion, and she turned away.

Her gaze met Gabriel Dean's.

Up till that moment, he had been observing the proceedings with quiet detachment. But at that instant, she saw anger in his eyes. It was the same rage she now felt toward the man who had brought Gail Yeager to this ultimate degradation. Staring at each other in shared outrage, their rivalry was temporarily forgotten.

Dr. Isles inserted a cotton swab into the vagina, smeared it across a microscope slide, and set the slide on a tray. Next she took a rectal swab, which would also be analyzed for the presence of sperm. When she'd completed the collection and Gail Yeager's legs were once again lying straight on the table, Rizzoli felt as though the worst was over. Even as Isles started the Y incision, cutting diagonally from the right shoulder down to the lower end of the sternum, Rizzoli thought that nothing could surpass the indignity of what had already been done to this victim.

Isles was just about to cut a matching incision from the left shoulder when Dean said, "What about the vaginal smear?"

"The slides will go to the crime lab," said Dr. Isles.

"Aren't you going to do a wet prep?"

"The lab can identify sperm perfectly well on a dry slide."

"This is your only chance to examine the fresh specimen."

Dr. Isles paused, scalpel tip poised over the skin, and gave Dean a puzzled look. Then she said to Yoshima, "Put a few drops of saline on that slide and slip it under the microscope. I'll take a look in just a second."

The abdominal incision came next, Dr. Isles's

scalpel slicing into the bloated belly. The stench of decomposing organs was suddenly more than Rizzoli could bear. She lurched away and stood gagging over the sink, regretting that she had so foolishly tried to prove her own fortitude. She wondered if Agent Dean was watching her now and feeling any sense of superiority. She had not seen Vicks glistening on *his* upper lip. She kept her back turned to the table and listened, rather than watched, as the autopsy proceeded behind her. She heard the air blowing steadily through the ventilation system and water gurgling and the clang of metal instruments.

Then she heard Yoshima call out, in a startled voice, "Dr. Isles?"

"Yes?"

"I've got the slide under the scope, and . . ."

"Is there sperm?"

"You really need to see this for yourself."

Her nausea fading, Rizzoli turned to watch as Isles peeled off her gloves and sat down at the microscope. Yoshima hovered over her as she gazed into the eyepiece.

"Do you see them?" he asked.

"Yes," she murmured. She sat back, looking stunned. She turned to Rizzoli. "The body was found around two P.M.?"

"About then."

"And it's now nine P.M. —"

"Well, is there sperm or not?" cut in Korsak.

"Yes, there's sperm," said Isles. "And it's motile."

Korsak frowned. "Meaning what? Like it's *moving?*"

"Yes. It's moving."

A silence dropped over the room. The significance of this finding had startled them all.

"How long does sperm stay motile?" asked Rizzoli.

"It depends on the environment."

"How long?"

"After ejaculation, they can remain motile for one or two days. At least half of the sperm under that microscope are moving. This is fresh ejaculate. Probably no more than a day old."

"And how long has the victim been dead?" asked Dean.

"Based on her vitreous potassium levels, which I drew about five hours ago, she's been dead at least sixty hours."

Another silence passed. Rizzoli saw the same conclusion register on everyone's faces. She looked at Gail Yeager, who now lay with torso split open, organs bared. Hand clapped to her mouth, Rizzoli spun toward the sink. For the first time in her career as a cop, Jane Rizzoli was sick.

"He knew," said Korsak. "That son of a bitch *knew.*"

They stood together in the parking lot behind the M.E.'s building, the tip of Korsak's cigarette glowing orange. After the chill air of the autopsy room, it almost felt good to be bathed in the steam of a summer night, to escape the harsh procedure lights and retreat into this cloak of darkness. She had been humiliated by her display of weakness, humiliated most of all that Agent Dean was there to see it. At least he'd been considerate enough to make no comment and had regarded her with neither sympathy nor ridicule, merely indifference.

"Dean's the one who asked for that test on the sperm," said Korsak. "Whatever he called it —"

"The wet prep."

"Yeah, the wet prep thing. Isles wasn't even gonna look at it fresh. She was gonna let it dry out first. So here's this fibbie guy telling the doc what to do. Like he knows exactly what he's looking for, exactly what we'll find. How did he know? And what the hell's the FBI doing on this case, anyway?"

"You did the background on the Yeagers. What's there to attract the FBI?"

"Not a thing."

"Were they into something they shouldn't have been?"

"You make it sound like the Yeagers got *themselves* killed."

"He was a doctor. Are we talking about drug deals here? A federal witness?"

"He was clean. His wife was clean."

"That coup de grâce — like an execution. Maybe that's the symbolism. A slice across the throat, to silence him."

"Jesus, Rizzoli. You've made a hundred-eighty-degree turn here. First we're thinking sex perp who kills for the thrill of it. Now you're into conspiracies."

"I'm trying to understand why Dean's involved. The FBI never gives a shit about what we're doing. They stay out of our way, we stay out of theirs, and that's how everybody likes it. We didn't ask for their help with the Surgeon. We handled it all in-house, used our own profiler. Their behavioral unit's too busy kissing up to Hollywood to give us the time of day. So what's different about this case? What makes the Yeagers special?"

"We didn't find a thing on them," said Korsak. "No debts, no financial red flags. No pending court cases. No one who'd say boo about either one of them."

"Then why the FBI interest?"

Korsak thought it over. "Maybe the Yeagers had friends in high places. Someone who's now screaming for justice."

"Wouldn't Dean just come out and tell us that?"

"Fibbies never like to tell you anything," said Korsak.

She looked back at the building. It was nearly midnight, and they had not yet seen Maura Isles leave. When Rizzoli had walked out of the autopsy suite, Isles had been dictating her report and had scarcely even waved good night. The Queen of the Dead paid scant attention to the living.

*Am I any different? When I lie in bed at night, it's the faces of the murdered I see.*

"This case is bigger than just the Yeagers," said Korsak. "Now we've got that second set of remains."

"I think this may let Joey Valentine off the hook," said Rizzoli. "It explains how our unsub picked up that corpse hair — from an earlier victim."

"I'm not done with Joey yet. One more twist of the screw."

"You got anything on him?"

"I'm looking; I'm looking."

"You'll need more than an old charge of voyeurism."

"But that Joey, he's weird. You gotta be weird to enjoy putting lipstick on dead ladies."

"Weirdness isn't enough." She stared at the building, thinking of Maura Isles. "In some ways, we're all weird."

"Yeah, but we're *normal* weird. Joey's got, like, no *normal* in his weirdness."

She laughed. This conversation had meandered into the absurd, and she was too tired to make sense of it any longer.

"What the hell'd I say?" Korsak asked.

She turned to her car. "I'm getting punchy. I need to go home and get some sleep."

"You gonna be here for the bone doctor?"

"I'll be here."

Tomorrow afternoon, a forensic anthropologist would be joining Isles to examine the skeletal remains of the second woman. Though she was not looking forward to another visit to this house of horrors, it was a duty Rizzoli could not avoid. She crossed to her car and unlocked the door.

"Hey, Rizzoli?" Korsak called out.

"Yeah?"

"Did you get dinner? Wanna go out for a burger or something?"

It was the sort of invitation any cop might extend to another. A hamburger, a beer, a few hours to unwind after a stressful day. Nothing unusual or untoward about it, yet it made her uncomfortable because she sensed the loneliness, the desperation, behind it. And she did not want to be entangled in this man's sticky web of need.

"Maybe another time," she said.

"Yeah. Okay," he said. "Another time." And with a quick wave, he turned and walked to his own car.

When she got home, she found a message from her brother Frankie on the answering machine. While she flipped through her mail, she listened to his voice boom out and could picture his swaggering stance, his bullying face.

"Hey, Janie? You there?" A long pause. "Aw, shit. Look, I forgot all 'bout Mom's birthday tomorrow. How 'bout us going in together on a present? Put my name on it, too. I'll mail you a check. Just tell me how much I owe ya, okay?

Bye. Oh, and hey, how ya doing?"

She threw her mail down on the table and muttered, "Yeah, Frankie. Like you paid me for the last gift." It was too late, anyway. The gift had already been delivered — a box of peach bath towels, monogrammed with Angela's initials. *This year, Janie gets full credit. For all the difference it makes.* Frankie was the man of a thousand excuses, all of them solid gold as far as Mom was concerned. He was a drill sergeant at Camp Pendleton, and Angela worried about him, obsessed over his safety, as though he faced enemy fire every day in that dangerous California scrub brush. She'd even wondered aloud if Frankie was getting enough to eat. Yeah, sure, Ma. The U.S. Marine Corps is gonna let your 220-pound baby starve to death. It was Jane who had not, in fact, eaten anything since noon. That embarrassing upchuck into the autopsy lab sink had emptied whatever was left in her stomach, and now she was ravenous.

She raided her cupboard and found the lazy woman's treasure: Starkist Tuna, which she ate straight out of the can, along with a handful of saltine crackers. Still hungry, she returned to the cupboard for sliced peaches and polished those off as well, licking the syrup from her fork as she stared at the map of Boston tacked to her wall.

Stony Brook Reservation was a broad swath of green surrounded by suburbia — West Roxbury and Clarendon Hills to the north,

Dedham and Readville to the south. On any summer day, the reservation would draw large numbers of families and joggers and picnickers. Who would notice a lone man in a car, driving along Enneking Parkway? Who would bother to watch as he pulled into one of the service parking areas and stared into the woods? A suburban park is irresistible to those weary of concrete and asphalt, jackhammers and blaring horns. Along with those seeking refuge in the coolness of woods and grass was one who came with an entirely different purpose in mind. A predator seeking a place to discard his prey. She saw it through his eyes: the dense trees, the carpet of dead leaves. A world where insects and forest animals would happily collaborate in the act of disposal.

She set down her fork, and its clatter against the table was startlingly loud.

From the bookshelf she picked up the packet of color-coded pushpins. She pressed a red one on the street where Gail Yeager had lived in Newton and pressed another red one in Stony Brook Reservation where Gail's body was found. She added a second pin in Stony Brook — this one blue — to represent the remains of the unknown woman. Then she sat down and considered the geography of the unsub's world.

During the Surgeon killings, she had learned to study a city map the way a predator studies his hunting grounds. She was, after all, a hunter as well, and to catch her prey she had to under-

121

stand the universe in which he lived, the streets he walked, the neighborhoods he roamed. She knew that human predators most often hunted in areas that were familiar to them. Like everyone else, they had their comfort zones, their daily routines. So when she looked at the pins on the map, she knew that she was seeing more than just the location of crime scenes and body dumps; she was seeing his sphere of activity.

The town of Newton was upscale and expensive, a suburb of professionals. Stony Brook Reservation was three miles southeast, in a neighborhood not nearly as tony as Newton. Was the unsub a resident of one of these neighborhoods, stalking prey that crossed his path as he moved between home and work? He would have to be someone who fit in, someone who did not rouse suspicion as an outsider. If he lived in Newton, he'd have to be a white-collar man with white-collar tastes.

And white-collar victims.

The grid of Boston streets blurred before her tired eyes, yet she did not give up and go to bed; she sat in a daze beyond exhaustion, a hundred details swimming in her head. She thought of fresh sperm in a decomposing corpse. She thought of skeletal remains with no name. Navy-blue carpet fibers. A killer who sheds the hair of his past victims. A stun gun, a hunter's knife, and folded nightclothes.

And Gabriel Dean. What was the FBI's role in all this?

She dropped her head in her hands, feeling as though it would explode with so much information. She had wanted to be lead detective, had even demanded it, and now the weight of this investigation was crushing her. She was too tired to think and too wound up to sleep. She wondered if this was what a breakdown felt like and ruthlessly suppressed the thought. Jane Rizzoli would never allow herself to be so spineless as to suffer a nervous breakdown. In the course of her career she had chased a perp across a rooftop, had kicked down doors, had confronted her own death in a dark cellar.

She had killed a man.

But until this moment, she had never felt so close to crumbling.

*The prison nurse is not gentle as she ties the tourniquet around my right arm, snapping the latex like a rubber band. It pinches my skin and tears at my hairs, but she does not care; to her, I am just another malingerer who has roused her from her cot and interrupted her normally uneventful shift in the prison clinic. She is middle-aged, or at least she looks it, with puffy eyes and overplucked brows, and her breath smells like sleep and cigarettes. But she is a woman, and I stare at her neck, loose and wattled, as she bends over my arm to locate a good vein. I think of what lies beneath her crepey white skin. The carotid artery, pulsing with bright blood, and beside it, the jugular vein, swollen with its darker river of venous blood. I am intimately familiar with the*

*anatomy of a woman's neck, and I study hers, un-
attractive as it is.*

*My antecubital vein has plumped up, and she
grunts in satisfaction. She opens an alcohol swab
and wipes it across my skin. It is a careless and slov-
enly gesture, not what one expects from a medical
professional, done out of habit and nothing more.*

*"You'll feel a poke," she announces.*

*I register the prick of the needle without flinching.
She has hit the vein cleanly, and blood streams into
the red-topped Vacutainer tube. I have worked with
the blood of countless others, but never my own, so I
stare at it with interest, noting that it is rich and
dark, the color of black cherries.*

*The tube is nearly full. She pulls it from the
Vacutainer needle and pops a second tube onto the
needle. This tube is a purple-top, for a complete
blood count. When this one, too, is filled, she pulls the
needle from my vein, snaps the tourniquet loose, and
jams a wad of cotton against the puncture site.*

*"Hold it," she commands.*

*Helplessly I rattle the handcuff on my left wrist,
which is fastened to the frame of the clinic cot. "I
can't," I say in a deflated voice.*

*"Oh, for God's sake," she sighs. No sympathy, just
irritation. There are some who despise the weak, and
she is one of them. Given absolute power, and a vulnerable subject, she could easily transform into the
same sort of monsters who tortured Jews in concentration camps. Cruelty is there beneath the surface,
disguised by the white uniform and the name tag
with R.N.*

She glances at the guard. "Hold it," she says.

He hesitates, then clamps his fingers against the cotton, pressing it to my skin. His reluctance to touch me is not because he's afraid of any violence on my part; I have always been well behaved and polite, a model prisoner, and none of the guards fear me. No, it is my blood that makes him nervous. He sees red oozing into the cotton and imagines all sorts of microbial horrors swarming toward his fingers. He looks relieved when the nurse tears open a bandage and tapes the cotton wad in place. At once he goes to the sink and washes his hands with soap and water. I want to laugh at his terror of something as elemental as blood. Instead I lie motionless on the cot, my knees drawn up, my eyes closed, as I release an occasional whimper of distress.

The nurse leaves the room with the tubes of my blood, and the guard, his hands thoroughly washed, sits down in a chair to wait.

And wait.

What feels like hours goes by in that cold and sterile room. We hear nothing from the nurse; it's as if she has abandoned us, forgotten us. The guard shifts in his chair, wondering what could be taking her so long.

I already know.

By now, the machine has completed its analysis of my blood, and she holds the results in her hand. The numbers alarm her. All concerns about a prisoner's malingering have fled; she sees the evidence, there in the printout, that a dangerous infection rages in my body. That my complaint of abdominal pain is

125

*surely genuine. Although she has examined my belly, felt my muscles flinch, and heard me groan at her touch, she did not quite believe my symptoms. She has been a prison nurse too long, and experience has made her skeptical of inmates' physical complaints. In her eyes we are all manipulators and con men, and our every symptom is just another pitch for drugs.*

*But a lab test is objective. The blood goes into the machine and a number comes out. She cannot ignore an alarming white blood cell count. And so she is surely on the telephone, consulting with the medical officer: "I have a prisoner here with severe abdominal pain. He does have bowel sounds, but his belly's tender in the right lower quadrant. What really worries me is his white count . . ."*

*The door opens, and I hear the squeak of the nurse's shoes on the linoleum. When she addresses me, there is none of that sneering tone she'd used earlier. Now she is civil, even respectful. She knows she is dealing with a seriously ill man and if anything should happen to me she will be held responsible. Suddenly I am not an object of contempt but a time bomb that could destroy her career. And she has already delayed too long.*

*"We're going to transfer you to the hospital," she says, and looks at the guard. "He needs to be moved immediately."*

*"Shattuck?" he asks, referring to the Lemuel Shattuck Hospital Correctional Unit in Boston.*

*"No, that's too far away. He can't wait that long. I've arranged a transfer to Fitchburg Hospital."*

*There is urgency in her voice, and the guard now glances at me with concern.*

*"So what's wrong with him?" he asks.*

*"It could be a ruptured appendix. I've got the paperwork all ready, and I've called the Fitchburg E.R. He'll have to go by ambulance."*

*"Aw, shit. Then I gotta ride with him. How long's this gonna take?"*

*"He'll probably be admitted. I think he needs surgery."*

*The guard glances at his watch. He is thinking about the end of his shift and whether someone will show up in time to relieve him at the hospital. He is not thinking about me but about the details of his own schedule, his own life. I am merely a complication.*

*The nurse folds a bundle of papers and slips them into an envelope. She hands this to the guard. "This is for the Fitchburg E.R. Be sure the doctor gets it."*

*"It's gotta be by ambulance?"*

*"Yes."*

*"Makes security a problem."*

*She glances at me. My wrist is still handcuffed to the cot. I lie perfectly still, with my knees bent — the classic position of a patient suffering from excruciating peritonitis. "I wouldn't worry too much about security. This one's way too sick to put up a fight."*

# Seven

"Necrophilia," said Dr. Lawrence Zucker, "or 'love of the dead,' has always been one of mankind's dark secrets. The word comes from the Greek, but as far back as the days of the pharaohs there was evidence of its practice. A beautiful or high-ranking woman who died at that time was always kept from the embalmers until at least three days after her death. This was to ensure that her body wasn't sexually abused by the men charged with preparing her for burial. Sexual abuse of the dead has been recorded throughout history. Even King Herod was said to have had sex with his wife for seven years after her death."

Rizzoli looked around the conference room and was struck by the eerie familiarity of this scene: a gathering of tired detectives, files and crime scene photos scattered on the table. The whispery voice of psychologist Lawrence Zucker, luring them into the nightmarish mind of a predator. And the chill — most of all, she remembered the chill of this room, and how it had seeped into her bones and numbed her hands. Many of the faces were the same as well: Detectives Jerry Sleeper and Darren Crowe and her partner, Barry Frost. The cops with whom she had worked on the Surgeon investigation a year ago.

Another summer, another monster.

But this time, one face was absent from the team. Detective Thomas Moore was not among them, and she missed his presence, missed his quiet assurance, his steadfastness. Though they'd had a falling-out during the Surgeon investigation, they had since mended their friendship, and now his absence was like a gaping hole in their team.

In Moore's place, sitting in the very chair Moore usually occupied, was a man she did not trust: Gabriel Dean. Anyone walking into this meeting would notice immediately that Dean was the outsider in this gathering of cops. From his well-tailored suit to his military posture, he stood out from the others, and they were all aware of the divide. No one spoke to Dean; he was the silent observer, the Bureau man whose role remained a mystery to them all.

Dr. Zucker continued. "Sex with a corpse is an activity most of us don't care to think about. But it's mentioned repeatedly in literature, in history, and in a number of criminal cases. Nine percent of serial killer victims are sexually violated postmortem. Jeffrey Dahmer, Henry Lee Lucas, and Ted Bundy all admitted to it." His gaze dropped to the autopsy photo of Gail Yeager. "So the presence of fresh ejaculate in this victim is not all that surprising."

Darren Crowe said, "They used to say this was something only the wackos did. That's what an FBI profiler once told me. That these are the nuts who wander around jabbering to themselves."

"Yes, it was once thought of as a sign of a severely disordered killer," said Zucker. "Someone who shuffles around in a psychotic daze. It's true, a number of these perps are psychotics who fall into the category of disorganized killers — neither sane nor intelligent. They have so little control over their own impulses that they'll leave all sorts of evidence behind. Hairs, semen, fingerprints. They're the easy ones to catch, because they don't know, or they don't care, about forensics."

"So what about this guy?"

"This unsub is not psychotic. He's an entirely different creature." Zucker opened the folder of photos from the Yeager house and arranged them on the table. Then he looked at Rizzoli. "Detective, you walked through the crime scene."

She nodded. "This unsub was methodical. He came with a murder kit. He was neat and efficient. He left almost no trace evidence behind."

"There was semen," Crowe pointed out.

"But not in a place we'd be likely to search for it. We might easily have missed it. In fact, we almost did."

"And your overall impression?" asked Zucker.

"He's organized. Intelligent." She paused.

And added, "Exactly like the Surgeon."

Zucker's gaze locked on hers. Zucker had always made her uneasy, and she felt invaded by his speculative look. But Warren Hoyt had to be on all their minds. She could not be the only one who felt this was a replay of an old nightmare.

"I agree with you," said Zucker. "This is an organized killer. He follows what some profilers would call a cognitive-object theme. His behavior isn't just to achieve immediate gratification. His actions have a specific goal, and that goal is to be in complete control of a woman's body — in this case, the victim, Gail Yeager. This unsub wants to possess her, use her even after her death. By assaulting her in front of the husband, he establishes this right of possession. He becomes the dominator, over both of them."

He reached for the autopsy photo. "I find it interesting that she was neither mutilated nor dismembered. Except for the natural changes of early decomposition, the corpse seems to be in rather good condition." He looked at Rizzoli for confirmation.

"There were no open wounds," she said. "The cause of death was strangulation."

"Which is the most intimate way to kill someone."

"Intimate?"

"Think of what it means to manually strangle someone. How personal it is. The close contact. Skin to skin. Your hands against her flesh.

Pressing her throat as you feel her life drain away."

Rizzoli stared at him in disgust. "Jesus."

"This is how *he* thinks. What *he* feels. This is the universe he inhabits, and we have to learn what that universe is like." Zucker pointed to Gail Yeager's photo. "He's driven to possess her body, to own it, dead or alive. This is a man who develops a personal attachment to a corpse, and he'll continue to fondle it. Sexually abuse it."

"Then why dispose of it?" asked Sleeper. "Why not keep it around for seven years? Like that King Herod did with his wife."

"Practical reasons?" Zucker offered. "He may live in an apartment building, where the smell of a decomposing body would attract notice. Three days is about as long as one would want to keep a corpse."

Crowe laughed. "Try three seconds."

"Then you're saying he has almost a lover's attachment to this body," said Rizzoli.

Zucker nodded.

"It must have been hard for him to just dump her there. In Stony Brook."

"Yes, it would have been difficult. Like having your lover leave you."

She thought of that place in the woods. The trees, the dappled shade. So far from the heat and noise of the city. "It's not just a dump site," she said. "Maybe it's consecrated ground."

They all looked at her.

"Say again?" said Crowe.

"Detective Rizzoli has hit on exactly the point I was getting at," said Zucker. "That spot, in the reserve, is not just a place to throw away used corpses. You have to ask yourself, Why didn't he bury them? Why does he leave them exposed to possible discovery?"

Rizzoli said, softly, "Because he visits them."

Zucker nodded. "These are his lovers. His harem. He returns again and again, to look at them, touch them. Maybe even embrace them. That's why he sheds corpse hairs. When he handles the bodies, he picks up their hairs on his clothes." Zucker looked at Rizzoli. "That postmortem strand matches the second set of remains?"

She nodded. "Detective Korsak and I started with the assumption this unsub picked up the strand from his workplace. Now that we know where that hair came from, does it make any sense to keep pursuing the funeral home angle?"

"Yes," said Zucker. "And I'll tell you why. Necrophiles are attracted to corpses. They get a sexual charge out of handling the bodies. Embalming them, dressing them. Applying their makeup. They may try to gain access to this thrill by choosing jobs in the death industry. An embalmer's assistant, for example, or a mortuary beautician. Keep in mind, that unidentified set of remains may not be a murder victim at all. One of the most well known necrophiles was a psychotic named Ed Gein, who started off by raiding cemeteries. Digging up women's bodies to bring home. It was only later that he turned to homicide as a means of obtaining corpses."

"Oh man," Frost muttered. "This just keeps getting better."

"It's one aspect of the wide spectrum of human behavior. Necrophiliacs strike us as sick and perverted. But they've always been with us, this subsegment of people driven by strange obsessions. Bizarre hungers. Yes, some of them are psychotic. But some of them are perfectly normal in every way."

*Warren Hoyt was perfectly normal, too.*

It was Gabriel Dean who spoke next. Up till then, he had not said a word during the entire meeting, and Rizzoli was startled to hear his deep baritone.

"You said that this unsub might return to the woods to visit his harem."

"Yes," said Zucker. "That's why the stakeout of Stony Brook should continue indefinitely."

"And what happens when he discovers his harem has vanished?"

Zucker paused. "He will not take it well."

The words sent a chill up Rizzoli's spine. *They are his lovers. How would any man react when his lover was stolen from him?*

"He'll be frantic," said Zucker. "Enraged that someone would take his possessions. And anxious to replace what he's lost. It will send him hunting again." Zucker looked at Rizzoli. "You have to keep this out of the media's eye, as long as possible. The stakeout may be your best chance to catch him. Because he *will* return to those woods, but only if he thinks it's safe. Only if he believes the harem is still there, waiting for him."

The conference room door opened. They all turned to see Lieutenant Marquette poke his head into the room. "Detective Rizzoli?" he said. "I need to speak to you."

"Right now?"

"If you don't mind. Let's go into my office."

Judging by the expressions of everyone else in the room, the same thought had occurred to them all: Rizzoli's being called to the woodshed. And she had no idea why. Flushing, she rose from her chair and walked out of the room.

Marquette was silent as they headed down the hall to the homicide unit. They stepped into his office and he shut the door. Through the glass partition, she saw detectives staring at her from their workstations. Marquette went to the window and snapped the blinds shut. "Why don't you sit down, Rizzoli?"

"I'm fine. I just want to know what's going on."

"Please." His voice quieter now, even gentle. "Sit down."

His new solicitousness made her uneasy. She and Marquette had never really warmed to each other. The homicide unit was still a boy's club, and she knew she was the bitch invader. She sank into a chair, her pulse starting to hammer.

135

For a moment he sat silent, as though trying to come up with the right words. "I wanted to tell you this before the others hear about it. Because I think this will be hardest on you. I'm sure it's just a temporary situation and it'll be resolved within days, if not hours."

"What situation?"

"This morning, around five A.M., Warren Hoyt escaped custody."

Now she understood why he'd insisted she sit down; he had expected her to crumble.

But she did not. She sat perfectly still, her emotions shut down, every nerve gone numb. When she spoke, her voice was so eerily calm, she scarcely recognized it as her own.

"How did it happen?" she asked.

"It was during a medical transfer. He was admitted last night to Fitchburg Hospital for an emergency appendectomy. We don't really know how it happened. But in the operating room . . ." Marquette paused. "There are no witnesses left alive."

"How many dead?" she asked. Her voice still flat. Still a stranger's.

"Three. A nurse and a female anesthetist, prepping him for surgery. Plus the guard who accompanied him to the hospital."

"Souza-Baranowski is a level-six facility."

"Yes."

"And they allowed him to go to a civilian hospital?"

"If it had been a routine admission, he would

have been transported to the Shattuck prison unit. But in a medical emergency, it's MCI policy to take prisoners to the nearest contracted facility. And the nearest one was in Fitchburg."

"Who decided it was an emergency?"

"The prison nurse. She examined Hoyt, and consulted with the MCI physician. They both concurred he needed immediate attention."

"Based on what findings?" Her voice was starting to sharpen now, the first note of emotion creeping in.

"There were symptoms. Abdominal pain —"

"He has medical training. He knew exactly what to tell them."

"They also had abnormal lab tests."

"What tests?"

"Something about a high white blood cell count."

"Did they understand who they were dealing with? Did they have *any* idea?"

"You can't fake a blood test."

"He could. He worked in a hospital. He knows how to manipulate lab tests."

"Detective —"

"For Christ's sake, he was a fucking *blood* technician!" The shrillness of her own voice startled her. She stared at him, shocked by her outburst. And overwhelmed by the emotions that were finally blasting through her. Rage. Helplessness.

And fear. All these months, she had suppressed it, because she knew it was irrational to be afraid of Warren Hoyt. He had been locked in a place where he could not reach her, could not hurt her. The nightmares had merely been aftershocks, lingering echoes of an old terror that she hoped would eventually fade. But now fear made perfect sense, and it had her in its jaws.

Abruptly she shot to her feet and turned to leave.

"Detective Rizzoli!"

She stopped in the doorway.

"Where are you going?"

"I think you know where I have to go."

"Fitchburg P.D. and the State Police have this under control."

"Do they? To them, he's just another con on the run. They'll expect him to make the same mistakes all the others do. But he won't. He'll slip right through their net."

"You don't give them enough credit."

"They don't give Hoyt enough credit. They don't understand what they're dealing with," she said.

*But I do. I understand perfectly.*

Outside, the parking lot shimmered white-hot under the glaring sun and the wind that blew from the street was thick and sulfurous. By the time she climbed into her car, her shirt was already soaked with sweat. Hoyt would like this heat, she thought. He thrived on it, the way a lizard thrives on the baking desert sand. And like any reptile, he knew how to quickly slither out of harm's way.

*They won't find him.*

As she drove toward Fitchburg, she thought of the Surgeon, loose in the world again. Imagined him walking city streets, the predator back among the prey. She wondered if she still had the fortitude to face him. If, having defeated him once, she had used up her lifetime quota of courage. She did not think of herself as a coward; she had never backed away from a challenge and had always plunged headlong into any fray. But the thought of confronting Warren Hoyt left her shaking.

*I fought him once, and it almost killed me. I don't know if I can do it again. If I can wrestle the monster back into his cage.*

The perimeter was unmanned. Rizzoli paused in the hospital corridor, glancing around for a uniformed officer, but saw only a few nurses standing nearby, two of them embracing each other for comfort, the others huddled together and spoke in low tones, faces gray with shock.

She ducked under the drooping yellow tape and walked unchallenged through the double doors, which automatically hissed open to admit her into the O.R. reception area. She saw the smears and busy tango steps of bloody footprints on the floor. A CST was already packing up his kit. This was a cold scene, picked over and trampled on, just waiting to be released for cleanup.

But cold as it was, contaminated though it was, she could still read what had happened in this room, for it was written on the walls in blood. She saw the dried arcs of arterial spray released from a victim's pulsing artery. It traced a sine wave across the wall and splattered the large erasable board where the day's surgery schedule had been written, listing the O.R. room numbers, patients' names, surgeons' names, and operative procedures. A full day's schedule had been booked. She wondered what had happened to the patients whose operations were abruptly canceled because the O.R. was now a crime scene. She wondered what the consequences were of a postponed cholecystectomy — whatever that was. That full schedule explained why the crime scene had been processed so quickly. The needs of the living must be served. One could not indefinitely shut down the town of Fitchburg's busiest O.R.

The arcs of spurted blood continued across the schedule board, around a corner, and onto the next wall. Here the peaks were smaller as the systolic pressure fell, and the pulsations began to trail downward, sliding toward the floor. They ended in a smeared lake next to the reception desk.

*The phone. Whoever died here was trying to reach the phone.*

Beyond the reception area, a wide corridor lined by sinks led past the individual operating rooms. Men's voices, and the crackle of a portable radio, drew her toward an open doorway. She walked along the row of scrub sinks, past a CST who scarcely gave her a glance. No one challenged her, even as she stepped into O.R. #4 and halted, appalled by the evidence of carnage. Though no victims remained in the room, their blood was everywhere, spattering walls, cabinets, and countertops and tracked across the floor by all those who had come in murder's wake.

"Ma'am? Ma'am?"

Two men in plainclothes stood by the instrument cabinet, frowning at her. The taller one crossed toward her, his paper shoe covers sucking against the sticky floor. He was in his mid-thirties, and he carried himself with that cocky air of superiority that all heavily muscled men exhibited. Masculine compensation, she thought, for his rapidly receding hairline.

Before he could ask the obvious question, she held out her badge. "Jane Rizzoli, Homicide. Boston P.D."

"What's Boston doing here?"

"I'm sorry. I don't know your name," she answered.

"Sergeant Canady. Fugitive Apprehension Section."

A Massachusetts State Police officer. She started to shake his hand, then saw he was wearing latex gloves. He didn't seem inclined to offer her the courtesy, in any event.

"Can we help you?" Canady asked.

"Maybe I can help *you*."

141

Canady did not seem particularly thrilled by the offer. "How?"

She looked at the multiple streamers of blood flung across the wall. "The man who did this — Warren Hoyt —"

"What about him?"

"I know him very well."

Now the shorter man joined them. He had a pale face and ears like Dumbo's, and although he, too, was obviously a cop, he did not seem to share Canady's sense of territoriality. "Hey, I know you. Rizzoli. You're the one put him away."

"I worked with the team."

"Naw, you're the one cornered him out in Lithia." Unlike Canady, he was not wearing gloves and he gave her a handshake. "Detective Arlen. Fitchburg P.D. You drive all the way out here just for this?"

"As soon as I heard." Her gaze drifted back to the walls. "You realize who you're up against, don't you?"

Canady cut in: "We have things under control."

"Do you know his history?"

"We know what he did here."

"But do you know *him?*"

"We have his files from Souza-Baranowski."

"And the guards there had no idea who they were dealing with. Or this wouldn't have happened."

"I've never failed to bring one back," said

Canady. "They all make the same mistakes."

"Not this one."

"He's only had six hours."

"Six hours?" She shook her head. "You've already lost him."

Canady bristled. "We're canvassing the neighborhood. Set up roadblocks and vehicle checks. Media's been alerted, and his photo's been broadcast on every local TV station. As I said, it's under control."

She didn't respond but turned her attention back to the ribbons of blood. "Who died in here?" she asked softly.

It was Arlen who answered. "The anesthetist and the O.R. nurse. Anesthetist was lying there, at that end of the table. The nurse was found over here, by the door."

"They didn't scream? They didn't alert the guard?"

"They would have had a hard time making any noise at all. Both women were slashed right through the larynx."

She moved to the head of the table and looked at the metal pole where a bag of I.V. solution hung, the plastic tube and catheter trailing toward a pool of water on the floor. A glass syringe lay shattered beneath the table.

"They had his I.V. going," she said.

"It was started in the E.R.," said Arlen. "He was moved directly here, after the surgeon examined him downstairs. They diagnosed a ruptured appendix."

"Why didn't the surgeon come up with him? Where was he?"

"He was seeing another patient in the E.R. Came up probably ten, fifteen minutes after all this happened. Walked through the double doors, saw the dead MCI guard lying out in the reception area, and ran straight for the phone. Practically the entire E.R. staff rushed up, but there was nothing they could do for any of the victims."

She looked at the floor and saw the swipes and smears of too many shoes, too much chaos to ever be interpreted.

"Why wasn't the guard in here, watching the prisoner?" she asked.

"The O.R.'s supposed to be a sterile zone. No street clothes allowed. He was probably told to wait outside the room."

"But isn't it MCI policy for their prisoners to be shackled at all times when they're out of the facility?"

"Yes."

"Even in the O.R., even under anesthesia, Hoyt should have had his leg or arm handcuffed to the table."

"He should have."

"Did you find the handcuffs?"

Arlen and Canady glanced at each other.

Canady said, "The cuffs were lying on the floor, under the table."

"So he *was* shackled."

"At one point, yes —"

"Why would they release him?"

"A medical reason, maybe?" suggested Arlen. "To start another I.V.? Reposition him?"

She shook her head. "They'd need the guard in here to unlock the cuffs. The guard wouldn't walk out, leaving his prisoner in here unshackled."

"Then he must have gotten careless," said Canady. "Everyone in the E.R. was under the impression Hoyt was a very sick man, in too much pain to put up a fight. Obviously, they didn't expect. . . ."

"Jesus," she murmured. "He hasn't lost his touch." She looked at the anesthesia cart and saw that one drawer was open. Inside, vials of thiopental sparkled under the bright O.R. lights. An anesthetic. They were about to put him to sleep, she thought. He is lying on this table, with that I.V. in his arm. Moaning, pain contorting his face. They have no idea what is about to happen; they are busy doing their jobs. The nurse is thinking about which instruments to set up, what the doctor will need. The anesthetist is calculating the doses of drugs, while she watches the patient's heart rate on the monitor. Maybe she sees his heart accelerate and assumes it's due to pain. She doesn't realize he is tensing for the lunge. For the kill.

And then . . . what happened then?

She looked at the instrument tray near the table. It was empty. "Did he use a scalpel?" she asked.

"We haven't found the weapon."

"It's his favorite instrument. He always used a scalpel . . ." A thought suddenly raised the hairs on the back of her neck. She looked at Arlen. "Could he still be in this building?"

Canady cut in, "He's not in the building."

"He's impersonated doctors before. He knows how to blend in with medical personnel. Have you searched this hospital?"

"We don't need to."

"Then how do you know he's not here?"

"Because we have proof he left the building. It's on video."

Her pulse quickened. "You caught him on security cameras?"

Canady nodded. "I suppose you'll want to see it for yourself."

# Eight

"It's weird, what he does," said Arlen. "We've watched this tape several times, and we still don't get it."

They had moved downstairs, into the hospital conference room. In the corner was a rolling cabinet with a TV and VCR. Arlen let Canady turn on all the power switches and work the remote. Controlling the remote was an alpha male's role, and Canady needed to be that male. Arlen was secure enough not to care.

Canady shoved in the tape and said, "Okay. Let's see if Boston P.D. can figure it out." It was the verbal equivalent of tossing down the gauntlet. He pressed PLAY.

A view of a closed door at the end of a corridor appeared onscreen.

"This is a ceiling-mounted camera in a first-floor hallway," said Arlen. "That door you see leads directly outside, to the staff parking lot, east of the building. It's one of four exits. The recording time's at the bottom."

"Five-ten," she read.

"According to the E.R. log, the prisoner was moved upstairs to the O.R. at around four forty-five, so this is twenty-five minutes later. Now

147

watch. It happens around five-eleven."

On-screen, the seconds counted forward. Then, at 5:11:13, a figure suddenly walked into view, moving at a calm, unhurried pace toward the exit. His back was turned to the camera, and they saw trim brown hair above the collar of the white lab coat. He was wearing surgeon's scrub pants and paper shoe covers. He made it all the way to the door and was pressing on the exit bar when he suddenly stopped.

"Watch this," said Arlen.

Slowly the man turned. His gaze lifted to the camera.

Rizzoli leaned forward, her throat dry, her eyes riveted on the face of Warren Hoyt. Even as she stared at him, he seemed to be staring directly at her. He walked toward the camera, and she saw he had something tucked under his left arm. A bundle of some kind. He kept walking until he was standing directly beneath the lens.

"Here's the weird part," said Arlen.

Still staring into the camera, Hoyt raised his right hand, palm facing forward, as though he were about to swear in court to tell the truth. With his left hand, he pointed to his open palm. And he smiled.

"What the hell's that all about?" said Canady.

Rizzoli didn't answer. In silence she watched as Hoyt turned, walked to the exit, and vanished out the door.

"Play it again," she said softly.

"You have any idea what that hand thing was all about?"

"Play it again."

Canady scowled and hit REWIND, then PLAY.

Once again, Hoyt walked to the door. Turned. Walked back to the camera, his gaze focused on those who were now watching.

She sat with every muscle tensed, her heart racing, as she waited for his next gesture. The one she already understood.

He raised his palm.

"Pause it," she said. "Right here!"

Canady hit PAUSE.

On the screen, Hoyt stood frozen with a smile on his face, his left index finger pointing to the open palm of his right hand. The image left her stunned.

It was Arlen who finally broke the silence. "What does it mean? Do you know?"

She swallowed. "Yes."

"Well, *what?*" snapped Canady.

She opened her hands, which had been closed into fists on her lap. On both her palms were the scars left from Hoyt's attack a year ago, thick knots that had healed over the two holes torn by his scalpels.

Arlen and Canady stared at her scars.

"Hoyt did that to you?" said Arlen.

She nodded. "That's what it means. That's why he raised his hand." She looked at the TV, where Hoyt was still smiling, his palm open to the camera. "It's a little joke, just between us.

His way of saying hello. The Surgeon is talking to me."

"You must have pissed him off big-time," said Canady. He waved the remote at the screen. "Look at that. It's like he's saying, 'Up yours.'"

"Or 'I'll be seeing you,'" Arlen said quietly.

His words chilled her. *Yes, I know I'll be seeing you. I just don't know when or where.*

Canady pressed PLAY, and the tape continued. They watched Hoyt lower his hand, and he turned once again toward the exit. As he walked away, Rizzoli focused on the bundle wedged under his arm.

"Stop it again," she said.

Canady hit PAUSE.

She leaned forward and touched the screen. "What is this thing he's carrying? It looks like a rolled-up towel."

"It is," said Canady.

"Why would he walk out with that?"

"It's not the towel. It's what he has inside it."

She frowned, thinking about what she had just seen upstairs in the O.R. Remembered the empty tray next to the table.

She looked at Arlen. "Instruments," she said. "He took surgical instruments."

Arlen nodded. "There's a laparotomy set missing from the room."

"Laparotomy? What's that?"

"It's medical-speak for cutting open the abdomen," said Canady.

On-screen, Hoyt had walked out the exit and they saw only an empty hallway, a closed door. Canady shut off the TV and turned to her. "Looks like your boy's anxious to go back to work."

The chirp of her cell phone made her flinch. She could feel her heart hammering as she reached for her phone. The two men were watching her, so she stood and turned to the window before answering the call.

It was Gabriel Dean. "You're aware the forensic anthropologist is meeting us at three o'clock?" he said.

She looked at her watch. "I'll be there on time." Barely.

"Where are you?"

"Look, I'll be there, okay?" She hung up. Staring out the window, she drew in a deep breath. I can't keep up, she thought. The monsters are stretching me too thin. . . .

"Detective Rizzoli?" said Canady.

She turned to him. "I'm sorry. I have to get back to the city. You'll call me the instant you hear anything about Hoyt?"

He nodded. Smiled. "We don't think it'll take long."

The last person she felt like speaking to was Dean, but as she drove into the M.E.'s parking lot she saw him stepping out of his car. She quickly pulled into a space and turned off her engine, thinking that if she just waited a few minutes, he would walk into the building first, and she could avoid any unnecessary conversation with him. Unfortunately, he had already spotted her, and he stood waiting in the parking lot, an unavoidable obstacle. She had no choice but to deal with him.

She stepped out into the wilting heat and walked toward him, at the pace of one with no time to waste.

"You never came back to the meeting this morning," he said.

"Marquette called me into his office."

"He told me about it."

She stopped and looked at him. "Told you what?"

"That one of your old perps is out."

"That's right."

"And that's shaken you up."

"Marquette told you that, too?"

"No. But since you didn't come back to the meeting, I assumed you were upset."

"Other matters required my attention." She started to walk toward the building.

"You are the lead on this case, Detective Rizzoli," he called after her.

She stopped, turned to look at him. "Why do you feel the need to remind me?"

Slowly he walked toward her, until he was close enough to be intimidating. Perhaps that was his intention. They now stood face-to-face, and although she would never give ground, she couldn't help flushing under his gaze. It was not just his physical superiority that made her feel threatened; it was her sudden realization that he was a desirable man — an utterly perverse reaction, in light of her anger. She tried to suppress the attraction, but it had already planted its claws and she could not shake it off.

"This case is going to require your full attention," he said. "Look, I do understand you're upset about Warren Hoyt's escape. It's enough to rattle any cop. Enough to knock you off balance —"

"You hardly know me. Don't try to be my shrink."

"I just wonder if you're feeling focused enough to head up this investigation. Or if you have other issues that will interfere."

She managed to hold her temper. To ask, quite calmly: "Do you know how many people Hoyt killed this morning? Three, Agent Dean. A man and two women. He slashed their throats, and he walked away, just like that. The way he always manages to do." She raised her hands, and he stared at her scars. "These are the souvenirs he gave me last year, just before he was about to cut my throat." She dropped her hands and laughed. "So yeah, you're absolutely right. I do have issues with him."

"You also have a job to do. Right here."

"I'm doing it."

"You're distracted by Hoyt. You're letting him get in the way."

"The only issue that keeps getting in my way is

*you*. I don't even know what you're doing here."

"Interagency cooperation. Isn't that the party line?"

"I'm the only one cooperating. What are you giving me in return?"

"What is it you expect?"

"You could start by telling me why the Bureau's involved. It's never stepped in on any of my cases before. What makes the Yeagers different? What do you know about them that I don't?"

"I know as much about them as you do," he said.

Was it the truth? She didn't know. She couldn't read this man. Now sexual attraction had added to her confusion, scrambling any and all messages between them.

He looked at his watch. "It's after three. They're waiting for us."

He started toward the building, but she didn't immediately follow him. For a moment she stood alone in the parking lot, shaken by her reaction to Dean. At last she took a breath and walked into the morgue, bracing herself for another visit with the dead.

This one, at least, did not turn her stomach. The overpowering stench of putrefaction that had sickened her during the autopsy of Gail Yeager was largely absent from the second set of remains. Nevertheless, Korsak had taken his usual precautions and once again had smeared

Vicks under his nose. Only a few bits of leathery connective tissue still adhered to the bones, and while the smell was certainly unpleasant, at least it did not send Rizzoli reeling for the sink. She was determined to avoid a repeat of last night's embarrassing performance, especially with Gabriel Dean now standing directly across from her, able to watch every twitch on her face. She maintained a stoic front as Dr. Isles and the forensic anthropologist, Dr. Carlos Pepe, unsealed the box and carefully removed the skeletal remains, laying them on the sheet-draped morgue table.

Sixty years old and bent like a gnome, Dr. Pepe was as excitable as a child as he lifted out the box's contents, eyeing each item as though it were gold. While Rizzoli saw only a random collection of dirt-stained bones, as featureless as twigs from a tree, Dr. Pepe saw radii and ulnas and clavicles, which he efficiently identified and placed in anatomical position. Disarticulated ribs and breastbone clattered against the covered stainless steel. Vertebrae, two of them surgically fused together, formed a knobby chain down the center of the table to the hollow ring of the pelvis, shaped like a macabre crown for a king. Arm bones formed spindly limbs that ended in clusters of what looked like dirty pebbles but were in reality the tiny bones that give human hands such miraculous versatility. Immediately obvious was evidence of an old injury: steel surgical pins in the left thigh bone. At the head of the table Dr. Pepe placed the skull and disarticulated jawbone. Gold teeth gleamed through crusted dirt. All the bones now lay displayed.

But the box was not yet empty.

He turned it over, pouring the last of the contents onto a cloth-draped tray. A shower of dirt and leaves and clumps of matted brown hair spilled out. He directed the exam light onto the tray and, with a pair of tweezers, began picking through the dirt. Within seconds, he found what he was looking for: a tiny black nugget, shaped like a fat grain of rice.

"Puparium," he said. "Often mistaken as rat droppings."

"That's what I would've said," said Korsak. "Rat poop."

"There are lots of them in here. You just have to know what you're looking for." Dr. Pepe plucked out a few more black grains and set them aside in a small pile. "*Calliphoridae* species."

"What?" said Korsak.

Gabriel Dean said, "Blowflies."

Dr. Pepe nodded. "These are the casings the blowfly larvae develop in. They're like cocoons. It's the exoskeleton for the third-stage larvae. They emerge from these as adult flies." He moved the magnifier over the puparia. "These are all eclosed."

"What does that mean? Eclosed?" asked Rizzoli.

"It means they're empty. The flies have hatched."

Dean asked, "What's the developmental time for *Calliphoridae* in this region?"

"At this time of year, it's about thirty-five days. But notice how these two puparia differ in color and weathering? They're all from the same species, but this casing's had longer exposure to the elements."

"Two different generations," said Isles.

"That would be my guess. I'll be interested to hear what the entomologist has to say."

"If each generation takes thirty-five days to mature," said Rizzoli, "does that mean we're talking seventy days of exposure? Is that how long this victim has been lying there?"

Dr. Pepe glanced at the bones on the table. "What I see here is not inconsistent with a post-mortem interval of two summer months."

"You can't get more specific than that?"

"Not with skeletonized remains. This individual may have been lying in those woods for two months. Or six months."

Rizzoli saw Korsak roll his eyes, so far unimpressed by their bone expert.

But Dr. Pepe was just getting started. He shifted his focus to the remains on the table. "A single individual, female," he said, surveying the array of bones. "On the small side — not much taller than five-foot-one. Healed fractures are obvious. We have an old comminuted femoral fracture, treated with a surgical screw."

"Looks like a Steinman pin," said Isles. She pointed to the lumbar spine. "And she's had a surgical fusion of L-2 and L-3."

"Multiple injuries?" asked Rizzoli.

"This victim has had a major traumatic event."

Dr. Pepe continued his inventory. "Two left ribs are missing, as well as . . ." He shuffled through the collection of tiny hand bones. ". . . three carpals and most of the phalanges from the left hand. Some scavenger made off with a snack, I'd say."

"A hand sandwich," said Korsak. No one laughed.

"Long bones are all present. So are all the vertebrae. . . . He paused, frowning at the neck bones. "The hyoid's missing."

"We couldn't find it," said Isles.

"You sifted?"

"Yes. I went back to the site myself to look for it."

"It may have been scavenged," said Dr. Pepe. He picked up a scapula — one of the wing bones that flare out behind the shoulder. "See the **V**-shaped punctures here? They were made by canine and carnissial teeth." He looked up. "Was the head found separated from the body?"

Rizzoli answered, "It was lying a few feet from the torso."

Pepe nodded. "Typical of dogs. For them, a head is like a big ball. A plaything. They'll roll it around, but they can't really sink their teeth into a head, the way they can a limb or a throat."

"Wait," said Korsak. "Are we talking Fifi and Rover here?"

"All canids, wild and domestic, behave in similar ways. Even coyotes and wolves like to play with balls, just like Fifi and Rover. Since these remains were in a suburban park, surrounded by residences, domestic dogs would almost certainly have frequented those woods. Like all canids, their instinct is to scavenge. They'll gnaw on any areas they can get their jaws around. The margins of the sacrum, the spinous processes. The ribs and iliac crests. And of course, they'll tear away any soft tissue that still remains."

Korsak looked appalled. "My wife has a little Highland terrier. That's the last friggin' time I let him lick *me* on the face."

Pepe reached for the cranium and shot Isles a mischievous look. "So let's play pimp time, Dr. Isles. What's your call on this?"

*"Pimp time?"* asked Korsak.

"It's a term from medical school," said Isles. "*Pimping someone* means to test their knowledge. To put them on the spot."

"Something I'm sure you used to do to your pathology students at U.C.," said Pepe.

"Ruthlessly," Isles admitted. "They'd cringe whenever I looked their way. They knew a tough question was coming."

"Now I get to pimp you," he said, with a touch of glee. "Tell us about this individual."

She focused on the remains. "The incisors,

palate shape, and skull length are consistent with the Caucasoid race. The skull is on the small side, with minimal supraorbital ridges. Then there's the pelvis. The shape of the inlet, the suprapubic angle. It's a Caucasian female."

"And the age?"

"There's incomplete epiphyseal fusion of the iliac crest. No arthritic changes on the spine. A young adult."

"I concur." Dr. Pepe picked up the mandible. "Three gold crowns," he noted. "And there's been extensive amalgam restoration. Have you done X rays?"

"Yoshima did them this morning. They're on the light box," said Isles.

Pepe crossed to look at them. "She's had two root canals." He pointed to the film of the mandible. "Looks like gutta percha canal fillings. And look at this. See how the roots of seven through ten and twenty-two through twenty-seven are short and blunt? There's been orthodontic movement."

"I didn't notice that," said Isles.

Pepe smiled. "I'm glad there's something left to teach you, Dr. Isles. You're beginning to make me feel quite superfluous."

Agent Dean said, "So we're talking about someone with the means to pay for dental work."

"Quite expensive dental work," added Pepe.

Rizzoli thought of Gail Yeager and her perfectly straight teeth. Long after the heart ceased to beat, long after the flesh decayed, it was the condition of the teeth that distinguished the rich from the poor. Those who struggled to pay the rent would neglect the aching molar, the unsightly overbite. The characteristics of this victim were beginning to sound hauntingly familiar.

*Young female. White. Well-to-do.*

Pepe set down the mandible and shifted his attention to the torso. For a moment he studied the collapsed cage of ribs and sternum. He picked up a disarticulated rib, arched it toward the breastbone, and studied the angle made by the two bones.

"Pectus excavatum," he said.

For the first time, Isles looked dismayed. "I didn't notice that."

"What about the tibias?"

Immediately she moved to the foot of the table and reached for one of the long bones. She stared at it, her frown deepening. Then she picked up the matching bone from the other limb and placed them side by side.

"Bilateral genu varum," she said, by now sounding quite disturbed. "Maybe fifteen degrees. I don't know how I missed it."

"You were focused on the fracture. That surgical pin's staring you in the face. And this isn't a condition one sees much anymore. It takes an old guy like me to recognize it."

"That's no excuse. I should have noticed it immediately." Isles was silent a moment, her vexed gaze flitting from the leg bones to the chest. "This does not make sense. It's not consistent with the dental work. It's as if we're dealing with two different individuals here."

Korsak cut in, "You mind telling us what you're talking about? What doesn't make sense?"

"This individual has a condition known as genu varum," said Dr. Pepe. "Commonly known as bowed legs. Her shinbones were curved about fifteen degrees from straight. That's twice the normal degree of curvature for a tibia."

"So why're you getting all excited? Lotta folks have bow legs."

"It's not just the bow legs," said Isles. "It's also the chest. Look at the angle the ribs make with the sternum. She has pectus excavatum, or funnel chest. Abnormal bone and cartilage formation caused the sternum — the breast bone — to be sunken in. If it's severe, it can cause shortness of breath, cardiac problems. In this case, it was mild, and probably gave her no symptoms. The condition would have been primarily cosmetic."

"And this is due to abnormal bone formation?" said Rizzoli.

"Yes. A defect in bone metabolism."

"What kind of illness are we talking about?"

Isles hesitated and looked at Dr. Pepe. "Her stature *is* short."

"What's the Trotter-Gleiser estimate?"

Isles took out a measuring tape, whisked it over the femur and tibia. "I'd guess about sixty-one inches. Plus or minus three."

"So we've got pectus excavatum. Bilateral genu varus. Short stature." He nodded. "It's strongly suggestive."

Isles looked at Rizzoli. "She had rickets as a child."

It was almost a quaint word, *rickets.* For Rizzoli, it conjured up visions of barefoot children in tumbledown shacks, crying babies, and the grime of poverty. A different era, colored in sepia. *Rickets* was not a word that matched a woman with three gold crowns and orthodontically straightened teeth.

Gabriel Dean had also taken note of this contradiction. "I thought rickets is caused by malnutrition," he said.

"Yes," Isles answered. "A lack of vitamin D. Most children get an adequate supply of D from either milk or sunlight. But if the child is malnourished, and kept indoors, she'll be deficient in the vitamin. And that affects calcium metabolism and bone development." She paused. "I've actually never seen a case before."

"Come out on a dig with me someday," said Dr. Pepe. "I'll show you plenty of cases from the last century. Scandinavia, northern Russia —"

"But today? In the U.S.?" asked Dean.

Pepe shook his head. "Quite unusual. Judging by the bony deformities, as well as her small stature, I would guess this individual lived in impoverished circumstances. At least through her adolescence."

163

"That isn't consistent with the dental work."

"No. That's why Dr. Isles said we seem to be dealing with two different individuals here."

The child and the adult, thought Rizzoli. She remembered her own childhood in Revere, their family crammed into a hot little rental house, a place so small that for her to enjoy any privacy she had to crawl into her secret space beneath the front porch. She remembered the brief period after her father was laid off, the frightened whispers in her parents' bedroom, the suppers of canned corn and Potato Buds. The bad times had not lasted; within a year, her father was back at work and meat was once again on the table. But a brush with poverty leaves its mark, on the mind if not the body, and the three Rizzoli siblings had all chosen careers with steady, if not spectacular, incomes — Jane in law enforcement, Frankie in the Marines, and Mikey in the U.S. Postal Service, all of them striving to escape the insecurity of childhood.

She looked at the skeleton on the table and said, "Rags to riches. It does happen."

"Like something out of Dickens," said Dean.

"Oh yeah," said Korsak. "That Tiny Tim kid."

Dr. Isles nodded. "Tiny Tim suffered from rickets."

"And then he lived happily ever after, 'cause old Scrooge probably left him a ton of money," said Korsak.

*But you didn't live happily ever after,* thought

Rizzoli, gazing at the remains. No longer were these just a sad collection of bones, but a woman whose life was now beginning to take shape in Rizzoli's mind. She saw a child with crooked legs and a hollow chest, growing stunted in the mean soil of poverty. Saw that child passing into adolescence, wearing blouses with mismatched buttons, the fabric worn to frayed transparency. Even then, was there something different, something special about this girl? A look of determination in her eyes, an upward tilt to the jaw that announced she was destined for a better life than the one into which she'd been born?

Because the woman she grew into lived in a different world, where money bought straight teeth and gold crowns. Good luck or hard work or perhaps the attention of the right man had lifted her to far more comfortable circumstances. But the poverty of her childhood was still carved in her bones, in the bowing of her legs, and in the trough in her chest.

There was evidence of pain as well, a catastrophic event that had shattered her left leg and spine, leaving her with two fused vertebrae and a steel rod permanently embedded in her thighbone.

"Judging by her extensive dental work, and by her probable socioeconomic status, this is a woman whose absence would be noted," said Dr. Isles. "She's been dead at least two months. Chances are, she's in the NCIC database."

"Yeah, her and about a hundred thousand others," said Korsak.

The FBI's National Crime Information Center maintained a missing persons file, which could be cross-checked against unidentified remains to produce a list of possible matches.

"We have nothing local?" asked Pepe. "No open missing persons cases that might be a match?"

Rizzoli shook her head. "Not in the state of Massachusetts."

Exhausted as she was that night, she could not sleep. She got out of bed once to recheck the locks on her door and the latch on the window leading to the fire escape. Then, an hour later, she heard a noise and imagined Warren Hoyt walking up the hallway toward her bedroom, a scalpel in his hand. She grabbed her weapon from the nightstand and dropped to a crouch in the darkness. Drenched in sweat, she waited, gun poised, for the shadow to materialize in her doorway.

She saw nothing, heard nothing, except the drumming of her own heart and the throb of music from a car passing on the street below.

At last she eased into the hallway and switched on the lights.

No intruder.

She moved into the living room, flipped on another light. In one quick glance she saw the door chain was in place, the fire escape window latched tight. She stood gazing at a room that was exactly as she'd left it and thought: I'm losing my mind.

She sank onto the couch, put down her gun, and dropped her head in her hands, wishing she could squeeze all thoughts of Warren Hoyt from her brain. But he was always there, like a tumor that could not be excised, metastasizing into every waking moment of her life. In bed, she had not been thinking of Gail Yeager or the unnamed woman whose bones she had just examined. Nor had she been thinking of Airplane Man, whose file remained on her desk at work, staring at her in silent reproach for her neglect. So many names and reports demanded her attention, but when she lay down at night and stared into the darkness, only Warren Hoyt's face came to mind.

The phone rang. She snapped straight, her heart battering against her chest. It took her a few breaths to calm down enough to pick up the receiver.

"Rizzoli?" said Thomas Moore. It was not a voice she'd expected to hear, and she was caught off guard by a sudden sense of longing. Only a year ago, she and Moore had worked together as partners during the Surgeon investigation. Though their relationship had never gone beyond that of two colleagues, they had trusted each other with their lives, and in some ways that was a level of intimacy as deep as any marriage could be. Hearing his voice now reminded her how much she missed him. And how much his marriage to Catherine still stung her.

"Hey, Moore," she said, her casual reply revealing none of these emotions. "What time is it over there?"

"It's nearly five. I'm sorry for calling you at this hour. I didn't want Catherine to hear this."

"It's okay. I'm still awake."

A pause. "You're having trouble sleeping, too." Not a question but a statement. He knew the same ghost was haunting them both.

"Marquette called you?" she said.

"Yes. I was hoping that by now —"

"There's nothing. It's been nearly twenty-four hours, and there hasn't been a single goddamn sighting."

"So the trail's gone cold."

"The trail was never there to begin with. He kills three people in the O.R., turns into the invisible man, and walks out of the hospital. Fitchburg and State Police canvassed the whole neighborhood, set up roadblocks. His face is all over the evening news. Nothing."

"There's one place he'll be drawn to. One person . . ."

"Your building's already staked out. Hoyt goes anywhere near it, we've got him."

There was a long silence. Then Moore said, quietly: "I can't bring her home. I'm keeping her right here, where I know she's safe."

Rizzoli heard fear in his voice, not for himself but for his wife, and she wondered, with a twinge of envy: What would it be like to be loved so deeply?

"Does Catherine know he's out?" she asked.

"Yes. I had to tell her."

"How's she taking it?"

"Better than I am. If anything, she's trying to calm *me* down."

"She's already faced the worst, Moore. She's beaten him twice. Proven she's stronger than he is."

"She *thinks* she's stronger. That's when things get dangerous."

"Well, she has you now." *And I have only myself.* The way it had always been and probably always would be.

He must have heard the note of weariness in her voice, for he said: "This has got to be hell on you, too."

"I'm okay."

"Then you're handling it better than I am."

She laughed, a sharp and startling sound that was all bluster. "Like I've got time to worry about Hoyt. I'm riding herd on a new task force. We found a body dump over at Stony Brook Reservation."

"How many victims?"

"Two women, plus a man he killed during the abduction. It's another bad one, Moore. You know it's bad when Zucker gives him a nickname. We're calling this unsub the Dominator."

"Why the Dominator?"

"It's what he seems to get off on. The power

trip. The absolute control over the husband. Monsters and their sick rituals."

"It sounds like a replay of last summer."

*Only this time you're not here to watch my back. You've got other priorities.*

"Any progress?" he asked.

"Slow. We've got multiple jurisdictions involved, multiple players. Newton P.D.'s on it, and — get this — the friggin' Bureau's stepped in."

"What?"

"Yeah. Some fibbie named Gabriel Dean. Says he's an *adviser,* but his hands are all over this case. You ever had that happen before?"

"Never." A pause. "Something's not right, Rizzoli."

"I know."

"What does Marquette say?"

"He's rolled over and playing dead, 'cause OPC's ordered us to cooperate."

"What's Dean's story?"

"We're talking tight-lipped here. You know, the if-I-tell-you-then-I'll-have-to-kill-you kind of guy." She paused, remembering Dean's gaze, his eyes as piercing as shards of blue glass. Yes, she could imagine him pulling a trigger without even flinching. "Anyway," she said, "Warren Hoyt's not my number one concern right now."

"But he's mine," said Moore.

"If there's any news, you'll be the first one I call."

She hung up, and in the silence the bravado

she'd felt, talking to Moore, instantly collapsed. Once again she was alone with her fears, sitting in an apartment with the door barred and the windows latched and only a gun to keep her company.

Maybe you're the best friend I have, she thought. And she picked up the weapon and carried it back to her bedroom.

# Nine

"Agent Dean came to see me this morning," said Lieutenant Marquette. "He has doubts about you."

"The feelings are mutual," Rizzoli said.

"He's not questioning your skills. He thinks you're a fine cop."

"But?"

"He wonders if you're the right detective to be lead on this one."

She said nothing for a moment, just sat calmly facing Marquette's desk. When he'd called her into his office this morning, she had already guessed what the meeting was about. She had walked in determined to maintain ironclad control over her emotions, to offer him no glimpse of what he was waiting for: a sign that she was already over the edge, in need of being replaced.

When she spoke, it was in a quiet and reasonable voice. "What are his concerns?"

"That you're distracted. That you have unresolved issues having to do with Warren Hoyt. That you're not fully recovered from the Surgeon investigation."

"What did he mean by *not recovered?*" she asked.

Already knowing exactly what he'd meant.

Marquette hesitated. "Jesus, Rizzoli. This isn't easy to say. You know it isn't."

"I'd just like you to come out and say it."

"He thinks you're unstable, okay?"

"What do you think, Lieutenant?"

"I think you've got a lot on your plate. I think Hoyt's escape knocked the wind out of you."

"Do you think I'm unstable?"

"Dr. Zucker has also expressed some concerns. You never went for counseling last fall."

"I was never ordered to."

"Is that the only way it works with you? You have to be ordered?"

"I didn't feel I needed it."

"Zucker thinks you haven't let go of the Surgeon yet. That you see Warren Hoyt under every rock. How can you lead this investigation if you're still reliving the last one?"

"I guess I'd like to hear it from you, Lieutenant. Do *you* think I'm unstable?"

Marquette sighed. "I don't know. But when Agent Dean comes in here and lays out his concerns, I've got to take notice."

"I don't believe Agent Dean is an entirely reliable source."

Marquette paused. Leaned forward with a frown. "That's a serious charge."

"No more serious than the charge he's leveling at me."

"You have anything to back it up?"

"I called the FBI's Boston office this morning."

"Yes?"

"They know nothing about Agent Gabriel Dean."

Marquette sat back in his chair and regarded her for a moment, saying nothing.

"He came here straight from Washington," she said. "The Boston office had nothing to do with it. That's not the way it's supposed to work. If we ask them for a criminal profile, it always goes through their area field division coordinator. This didn't go through their field division. It came straight from Washington. Why is the FBI mucking around in my investigation in the first place? And what does Washington have to do with it?"

Still, Marquette said nothing.

She pressed on, her frustration building, her control starting to crack. "You told me the order to cooperate came through the police commissioner."

"Yes, it did."

"Who in the FBI approached OPC? Which part of the Bureau are we dealing with?"

Marquette shook his head. "It wasn't the Bureau."

"What?"

"The request didn't come from the FBI. I spoke to OPC last week, the day Dean showed up. I asked them that same question."

"And?"

"I promised them I'd keep this confidential. I

expect the same from you." Only after she'd given a nod of assent did he continue. "The request came from Senator Conway's office."

She stared at him in bewilderment. "What does our senator have to do with all this?"

"I don't know."

"OPC wouldn't tell you?"

"They may not know, either. But it's not a request they'd brush off, not when it comes direct from Conway. And he's not asking for the moon. Just interagency cooperation. We do it all the time."

She leaned forward and said, quietly: "Something's wrong, Lieutenant. You know it. Dean hasn't been straight with us."

"I didn't call you in here to talk about Dean. We're talking about you."

"But it's his word you're relying on. Does the FBI now dictate orders to Boston P.D.?"

This seemed to take Marquette aback. Abruptly straightening, he eyed her across the desk. She had hit just the right nerve. *The Bureau versus Us. Are you really in charge?*

"Okay," he said. "We talked. You listened. That's good enough for me."

"For me, too." She stood up.

"But I'll be watching, Rizzoli."

She gave him a nod. "Aren't you always?"

"I've found some interesting fibers," Erin Volchko said. "They were lifted with sticky tape from the skin of Gail Yeager."

175

"More navy-blue carpet?" asked Rizzoli.

"No. To be honest, I'm not sure what these are."

Erin did not often admit that she was baffled. That alone piqued Rizzoli's interest in the slide now under the microscope. Through the lens, she saw a single dark strand.

"We're looking at a synthetic fiber, whose color I'd characterize as drab green. Based on its refractive indices, this is our old friend Dupont nylon, type six, six."

"Just like the navy-blue carpet fibers."

"Yes. Nylon six, six is a very popular fiber due to its strength and resilience. You'll find it in a large variety of fabrics."

"You said this was lifted off Gail Yeager's skin?"

"These fibers were found clinging to her hips, her breasts, and a shoulder."

Rizzoli frowned. "A sheet? Something he used to wrap her body?"

"Yes, but not a sheet. Nylon wouldn't be appropriate for that use, due to its low moisture absorbency. Also, these particular threads are made up of extremely fine thirty-denier filaments, ten filaments to a thread. And the thread's finer than a human hair. This kind of fiber would produce a finished product that's very tight. Maybe weatherproof."

"A tent? A tarp?"

"Possible. That's the kind of fabric one might use to wrap a body."

Rizzoli had a bizarre vision of packaged tarps

hanging in Wal-Mart, the manufacturer's sug-gested uses printed on the label: PERFECT FOR CAMPING, WEATHERPROOFING, AND WRAP-PING DEAD BODIES.

"If it's just a tarp, we're dealing with a pretty generic piece of fabric," said Rizzoli.

"C'mon, Detective. Would I drag you over here to look at a perfectly generic fiber?"

"It's not?"

"It's actually quite interesting."

"What's interesting about a nylon tarp?"

Erin reached for a folder on the lab counter-top and pulled out a computer-generated graph, on which a line traced a silhouette of jagged peaks. "I ran an ATR analysis on these fibers. This is what popped out."

"ATR?"

"Attenuated Total Reflection. It uses infrared microspectroscopy to examine single fibers. In-frared radiation is beamed at the fiber, and we read the spectra of light that bounces back. This graph shows the IR characteristics of the fiber itself. It simply confirms that it's nylon six, six, as I told you earlier."

"No surprise."

"Not yet," said Erin, a sly smile playing at her lips. She took a second graph from the folder, laid it beside the first. "Here we see the IR tracing of exactly the same fiber. Notice anything?"

Rizzoli gazed back and forth. "They're dif-ferent."

"Yes, they are."

"But if these are from the same fiber, the graphs should be identical."

"For this second graph, I altered the image plane. This ATR is the reflection from the *surface* of the fiber. Not the core."

"So the surface and the core are different."

"Right."

"Two different fibers twisted together?"

"No. It's a single fiber. But the fabric has had a surface treatment. That's what the second ATR is picking up — the surface chemicals. I ran it through the chromatograph, and it seems to be silicone-based. After the fibers were woven and dyed, a silicone rub was applied to the finished fabric."

"Why?"

"I'm not sure. Waterproofing? Tear resistance? It must be an expensive process. I think this fabric has some very specific purpose. I just don't know what it is."

Rizzoli leaned back on the lab stool. "Find this fabric," she said, "and we'll find our perp."

"Yes. Unlike generic blue carpet, this fabric is unique."

The monogrammed towels were draped over the coffee table for all the party guests to see, the letters AR, for Angela Rizzoli, entwined in baroque curlicues. Jane had chosen them in peach, her mother's favorite color, and had paid extra for the deluxe birthday gift wrapping with apricot ribbons and a cluster of silk flowers.

They'd been delivered specifically by Federal Express, because her mother associated those red, white, and blue trucks with surprise packages and happy events.

And Angela Rizzoli's fifty-ninth birthday party should have qualified as a happy event. Birthdays were a very big deal in the Rizzoli family. Every December, when Angela bought a fresh calendar for the new year, the first thing she did was flip through the months, marking the family's various birthdays. To forget a loved one's special day was a serious transgression. To forget your *mother's* birthday was an unforgivable sin, and Jane knew better than to ever let the day slip by uncelebrated. She'd been the one to buy ice cream and string up the decorations, the one who'd sent out invitations to the dozen neighbors who were now gathered in the Rizzoli living room. She was the one now slicing the cake and passing the paper plates to guests. She'd done her duty as always, but this year the party had fallen flat. And all because of Frankie.

"Something's wrong," Angela said. She sat flanked on the couch by her husband and younger son, Michael, and she stared without joy at the gifts displayed on her coffee table — enough bath oil beads and talcum powder to keep her smelling sweet into the next decade. "Maybe he's sick. Maybe there's been an accident and nobody's called me yet."

"Ma, Frankie's fine," said Jane.

"Yeah," Michael chimed in. "Maybe they sent him out on — what do you call it? When they play war games?"

"Maneuvers," said Jane.

"Yeah, some kinda maneuvers. Or even out of the country. Some place he's not supposed to tell anyone about, where he can't get to a phone."

"He's a drill sergeant, Mike. Not Rambo."

"Even Rambo sends his mother a birthday card," snapped Frank Senior.

In the sudden hush, all the guests ducked for cover and took simultaneous bites of cake. They spent the next few seconds chewing with fierce concentration.

It was Gracie Kaminsky, the Rizzolis' next-door neighbor, who bravely broke the silence. "This cake is *so* good, Angela! Who baked it?"

"Baked it myself," said Angela. "Imagine that, having to bake my own birthday cake. But that's how it goes in this family."

Jane flushed as though slapped. This was all Frankie's fault. He was the one Angela was really furious with, but as always, Jane caught the ugly spillover. She said quietly reasonably: "I offered to bring the cake, Ma."

Angela shrugged. "From a bakery."

"I didn't have the time to bake one."

It was the truth, but oh, it was the wrong thing to say. She knew it as soon as the words left her lips. She saw her brother Mike cringe into the couch. Saw her dad flush, bracing himself.

"Didn't have the time," said Angela.

Jane gave a desperate laugh. "My cakes are always a mess, anyway."

"Didn't have the time," Angela repeated.

"Ma, do you want some ice cream? How about —"

"Since you're so *busy,* I guess I should get down on my knees and *thank you* for even making it to your only mother's *birthday.*"

Her daughter said nothing, just stood there with her face stung red, fighting to keep her tears under control. Guests went back to frantically devouring cake, no one daring to look at anyone else.

The phone rang. Everyone froze.

At last, Frank Senior answered it. Said, "Your mother's right here," and handed the portable phone to Angela.

*Jesus, Frankie, what took you so long?* With a sigh of relief, Jane began gathering up used paper plates and plastic forks.

"What gift?" her mother said. "I haven't gotten it."

Jane winced. *Oh no, Frankie. Don't try to pin the blame on me.*

In the next breath, all the anger magically melted from her mother's voice.

"Oh, Frankie, I understand, honey. Yes, I do. The marines, they work you so hard, don't they?"

Shaking her head, Jane was walking toward the kitchen when her mother called out:

"He wants to talk to you."

"Who, me?"

"That's what he says."

Jane took the phone. "Hey, Frankie," she said.

Her brother shot back: "What the fuck, Janie?"

"Excuse me?"

"You know what I'm talking about."

At once she walked out of the room, carrying the phone into the kitchen, and let the door swing shut behind her.

"I asked you for *one* fucking favor," he said.

"Are you talking about the gift?"

"I call to say happy birthday, and she lights into me."

"You could've expected that."

"I bet you're thinking this is *so* cool, aren't you? Getting me on her shit list."

"You got yourself on it. And it sounds like you weaseled right off it again, too."

"And that's what pisses you off, isn't it?"

"I don't really care, Frankie. It's between you and Ma."

"Yeah, but you're always in there, sneaking around behind my back. Anything to make me look bad. Couldn't even add my fucking name to your fucking gift."

"*My* gift was already delivered."

"And I guess it was too much *trouble* just to pick up a little something for me?"

"Yes, it was. I'm not here to wipe your ass. I'm working eighteen-hour days."

"Oh yeah. I hear that all the time from you.

'Poor little me, working so hard I only get fifteen minutes of sleep at night.' "

"Besides, you didn't pay me for the last gift."

"Sure I did."

"No, you didn't." *And it still pisses me off that Ma refers to it as "that nice lamp Frankie gave me."*

"So it's all about the money, is that it?" he said.

Her beeper went off, rattling against her belt. She looked at the number. "I don't give a shit about the money. It's the way you keep getting away with things. You don't even try, but somehow you always get full credit."

"Is this the *'poor shitty me'* act again?"

"I'm hanging up, Frankie."

"Give me back to Ma."

"First I got to answer my page. You call back in a minute."

"What the hell? I'm not racking up another long-distance —"

She disconnected. Paused for a moment to let her temper cool down, then punched in the number from her beeper readout.

Darren Crowe answered.

She was in no mood to deal with yet another disagreeable man, and she snapped back: "Rizzoli. You paged me."

"Jeez, try a little Midol, why don't you?"

"You want to tell me what's going on?"

"Yeah, we got a ten fifty-four. Beacon Hill. Sleeper and I got here 'bout half an hour ago."

She heard laughter in her mother's living

room and glanced toward the closed door. Thought of the scene that was sure to come if she made an exit during Angela's birthday party.

"You'll want to see this one," said Crowe.

"Why?"

"It'll be obvious when you get here."

# Ten

Standing on the front stoop, Rizzoli caught the scent of death through the open doorway and paused, reluctant to take that first step into the house. To view what she already knew waited inside. She would have preferred to delay an extra moment or two, to prepare herself for the ordeal, but Darren Crowe, who'd opened the door to admit her, now stood watching her, and she had no choice but to pull on gloves and shoe covers and get on with what needed to be done.

"Is Frost here yet?" she asked as she snapped on gloves.

"Got here about twenty minutes ago. He's inside."

"I would've been here sooner, but I had to drive in from Revere."

"What's in Revere?"

"Mom's birthday party."

He laughed. "Sounded like you were having a *real* good time there."

"Don't ask." She pulled on the last shoe cover and straightened, her face all business now. Men like Crowe respected only strength, and strength was all she allowed him to see. As they stepped inside, she knew his gaze was on her, that he would be watching for her reaction to whatever she was about to confront. Testing, always testing, waiting for the moment when she would come up short. Knowing that, sooner or later, it would happen.

He closed the front door and suddenly she felt claustrophobic, cut off from fresh air. The stench of death was stronger, her lungs filling with its poison. She let none of these emotions show as she took in the foyer, noting the twelve-foot ceilings, the antique grandfather clock — not ticking. She'd always considered the Beacon Hill section of Boston as her dream neighborhood, the place she'd move to if she ever won the lottery or, even more far-fetched, ever married Mr. Right. And this would have qualified as her dream home. Already she was unnerved by the similarity to the Yeager crime scene. A fine home in a fine neighborhood. The scent of slaughter in the air.

"Security system was off," said Crowe.

"Disabled?"

"No. The vics just didn't turn it on. Maybe they didn't know how to work it, since it's not their house."

"Whose house is it?"

Crowe flipped open his notebook and read, "Owner is Christopher Harm, age sixty-two. Retired stock trader. Serves on the board of the Boston Symphony Orchestra. Spending the summer in France. He offered the use of his home to the Ghents while they're on tour in Boston."

"What do you mean, on tour?"

"They're both musicians. Flew in a week ago from Chicago. Karenna Ghent is a pianist. Her husband Alexander was a cellist. Tonight was supposed to be their final performance at Symphony Hall."

It did not escape her notice that Crowe had referred to the man in the past tense but not the woman.

Their paper shoe covers whished across the wood floor as they walked up the hall, drawn toward the sound of voices. Stepping into the living room, Rizzoli did not see the body at first, because it was blocked from her view by Sleeper and Frost, who stood with their backs turned to her. What she did see was the by-now familiar horror story written on the walls: multiple arcs of arterial splatter. She must have drawn in a sharp breath, because both Frost and Sleeper simultaneously turned to look at her. They stepped aside, to reveal Dr. Isles, crouched beside the victim.

Alexander Ghent sat propped up against the wall like a sad marionette, his head tilted backward, revealing the gaping wound that had been his throat. *So young,* was her first shocked reaction as she stared at the disconcertingly unworried face, the open blue eye. *He is so very young.*

"An official from the Symphony Hall — name's Evelyn Petrakas — came to pick them

up around six o'clock for their evening performance," said Crowe. "They didn't answer the
door. She found it was unlocked, so she walked
in to check on them."

"He's wearing a pajama bottom," said Rizzoli.

"He's in rigor mortis," said Dr. Isles as she
rose to her feet. "And there's been significant
cooling. I'll be more specific when I get the vitreous potassium results. But right now, I'd estimate time of death between sixteen and twenty
hours ago. Which would make it . . ." She
glanced at her watch. "Sometime between one
and five A.M."

"The bed's unmade," said Sleeper. "The last
time anyone saw the couple was yesterday night.
They left Symphony Hall around eleven, and
Ms. Petrakas dropped them off here."

The victims were asleep, thought Rizzoli,
staring at Alexander Ghent's pajama bottom.
Asleep and unaware that someone was in their
house. Walking toward their bedroom.

"There's an open kitchen window that leads
to a little courtyard in back," said Sleeper. "We
found several footprints in the flower bed, but
they're not all the same size. Some of them may
belong to a gardener. Or even the victims."

Rizzoli stared down at the duct tape binding
Alex Ghent's ankles. "And Mrs. Ghent?" she
asked. Already knowing the answer.

"Missing," said Sleeper.

Her gaze moved in an ever larger circle
around the corpse, but she saw no broken tea-

cup, no fragments of chinaware. Something is wrong, she thought.

"Detective Rizzoli?"

She turned and saw a crime scene tech standing in the hallway.

"Patrolman says there's some guy outside, claims to know you. He's raising a holy stink, demanding access. You want to check him out?"

"I know who it is," she said. "I'll go walk him in."

Korsak was smoking a cigarette as he paced the sidewalk, so furious about the indignity of being reduced to the status of civilian bystander that smoke seemed to be rising from his ears as well. He saw her and immediately threw down the butt and squashed it as though it were a disgusting bug.

"You shutting me out or what?" he said.

"Look, I'm sorry. The patrolman didn't get the word."

"Goddamn rookie. Didn't show any respect."

"He didn't know, okay? It was my fault." She lifted the crime scene tape and he ducked under it. "I want you to see this."

At the front door, she waited while he pulled on shoe covers and latex gloves. He stumbled as he tried to balance on one foot. Catching him, she was shocked to smell alcohol on his breath. She had called him from her car, had reached him at home on a night when he was off duty. Now she regretted having alerted him at all. He was already angry and belligerent, but she could not refuse him entry without precipitating a noisy and very public scene. She only hoped he was sober enough not to embarrass them both.

"Okay," he huffed. "Show me what we got."

In the living room he stared without comment at the corpse of Alexander Ghent, slumped in a pool of blood. Korsak's shirt had come untucked, and he breathed with his usual adenoidal snuffle. She saw Crowe and Sleeper glance their way, saw Crowe roll his eyes, and suddenly she was furious at Korsak for showing up in this condition. She had called him because he'd been the first detective to walk the Yeager death scene, and she'd wanted his impression on this one as well. What she got instead was a drunk cop whose very presence was starting to humiliate her.

"It could be our boy," said Korsak.

Crowe snorted. "No shit, Sherlock."

Korsak turned his bloodshot gaze on Crowe. "You're one of those boy geniuses, huh? Know it all."

"Not like it takes a genius to see what we've got."

"What do you think we've got?"

"A replay. Nocturnal home invasion. Couple surprised in bed. Wife abducted, husband gets the coup de grâce. It's all here."

"So where's the teacup?" Impaired though he was, Korsak had managed to zero in on precisely the detail that had bothered Rizzoli.

190

"There isn't one," said Crowe.

Korsak stared at the victim's empty lap. "He's got the vic posed. Got him sitting up against the wall to watch the show, like the last time. But he left out the warning system. The teacup. If he assaults the wife, how does he keep track of the husband?"

"Ghent's a skinny guy. Not much of a threat. Besides, he's all trussed up. How's he gonna get up and defend his wife?"

"It's a change; that's all I'm saying."

Crowe shrugged and turned away. "So he rewrote the script."

"Pretty boy just knows it all, doesn't he?"

The room fell silent. Even Dr. Isles, who was often ready with an ironic comment, said nothing, but just watched with a vaguely amused expression.

Crowe turned, his gaze like laser beams on Korsak. But his words were addressed to Rizzoli: "Detective, is there a reason this man is trespassing on our crime scene?"

Rizzoli grasped Korsak's arm. It was doughy and moist, and she could smell his sour sweat. "We haven't seen the bedroom yet. Come on."

"Yeah," Crowe laughed. "Don't wanna miss the bedroom."

Korsak yanked away from her and took an unsteady step toward Crowe. "I been working this perp way before you, asshole."

"Come on, Korsak," said Rizzoli.

". . . chasing down every fucking lead there is.

I'm the one shoulda been called here first, 'cause I know him now. I can smell him."

"Oh. Is that what I'm smelling?" said Crowe.

"Come *on*," said Rizzoli, about to lose it. Afraid of all the rage that might come roaring out if she did. Rage against both Korsak and Crowe for their stupid head butting.

It was Barry Frost who gracefully stepped in to defuse the tension. Rizzoli's instinct was usually to leap into any argument with both feet first, but Frost's was to play peacemaker. It's the curse of growing up the middle child, he'd once told her, the kid who knows his face will otherwise catch the fists of all parties involved. He did not even try to calm down Korsak but instead said to Rizzoli, "You've got to see what we found in the bedroom. It ties these two cases together." He walked across the living room and headed into another hallway, his matter-of-fact stride announcing: *If you want to go where the action is, follow me.*

After a moment, Korsak did.

In the bedroom, Frost, Korsak, and Rizzoli gazed at the rumpled sheets, the thrown-back covers. And at the twin swaths carved in the carpet.

"Dragged from their beds," Frost said. "Like the Yeagers."

But Alexander Ghent had been smaller and far less muscular than Dr. Yeager, and the unsub would have had an easier time moving him into the hallway and posing him against the wall. An easier time grasping his hair and baring his throat.

"It's on the dresser," said Frost.

It was a powder-blue teddy, size 4, neatly folded and speckled with blood. Something a young woman would wear to attract a lover, excite a husband. Surely Karenna Ghent had never imagined the violent theater in which this garment would serve as both costume and prop. Beside it were a pair of Delta Airline ticket envelopes. Rizzoli glanced inside them and saw the itinerary, which had been arranged through the Ghents' talent agency.

"They were due to fly out tomorrow," she said. "Next stop was Memphis."

"Too bad," said Korsak. "They never got to see Graceland."

Outside, she and Korsak sat in his car with the windows open while he smoked a cigarette. He drew in deeply, then released a sigh of satisfaction as the smoke worked its poisonous magic in his lungs. He seemed calmer, more focused than when he'd arrived three hours ago. The blast of nicotine had sharpened his mind. Or perhaps the alcohol had finally worn off.

"You have any doubt this is our boy?" he asked her.

"No."

"Crimescope didn't pick up any semen."

"Maybe he was neater this time."

"Or he didn't rape her," said Korsak. "And

that's why he didn't need the teacup."

Annoyed by his smoke, she turned her face to the open window and waved her hand to clear the air. "Murder doesn't follow a set script," she said. "Every victim reacts differently. It's a two-character play, Korsak. The killer *and* the victim. Either one can affect the outcome. Dr. Yeager was a much bigger man than Alex Ghent. Maybe our unsub felt less confident about controlling Yeager, so he used the china-ware as a warning signal. Something he didn't feel he needed to do with Ghent."

"I don't know." Korsak flicked an ash out the window. "It's such a weird-ass thing to do, that teacup. Part of his signature. Something he wouldn't leave out."

"Everything else was identical," she pointed out. "Well-to-do couple. The man bound and posed. The woman missing."

They fell silent as the same grim thought surely occurred to them both: *The woman. What has he done to Karenna Ghent?*

Rizzoli already knew the answer. Though Karenna's image would soon appear on TV screens across the city and a plea would go out for the public's help, though Boston P.D. would scramble to follow up every phone tip, every sighting of a dark-haired woman, Rizzoli knew what the outcome would be. She could feel it, like a cold stone in her stomach. Karenna Ghent was dead.

"Gail Yeager's body was dumped about two

days after her abduction," said Korsak. "It's now been — what? Around twenty hours since this couple was attacked."

"Stony Brook Reservation," said Rizzoli. "That's where he'll bring her. I'll reinforce the surveillance team." She glanced at Korsak. "You see any way Joey Valentine fits into this one?"

"I'm working on it. He finally gave me a sample of his blood. DNA's pending."

"That doesn't sound like a guilty man. You still watching him?"

"I was. Till he filed a complaint that I was harassing him."

"Were you?"

Korsak laughed, snorting out a lungful of smoke. "Any grown man who gets off powder-puffing dead ladies is gonna squeal like a girl, no matter what I do."

"How, exactly, do girls squeal?" she countered in irritation. "Kind of like boys do?"

"Aw, jeez. Don't give me that bra-burning shit. My daughter's always doing that. Then she runs out of money and comes whining to chauvinist-pig daddy for help." Suddenly Korsak straightened. "Hey. Look who just showed up."

A black Lincoln had pulled into a parking space across the street. Rizzoli saw Gabriel Dean emerge from the car, his trim, athletic figure pulled straight from the pages of *GQ*. He stood gazing up at the redbrick facade of the residence. Then he approached the patrolman manning the perimeter and showed his badge.

The patrolman let him through the tape.

"Get a load of that," said Korsak. "Now *that* pisses me off. That same cop made me stand outside till you came out to get me. Like I'm just another bum off the street. But Dean, all he has to do is wave the magic badge and say 'federal fucking agent' and he's golden. Why the hell does he get a pass?"

"Maybe because he bothered to tuck in his shirt."

"Oh yeah, like a nice suit would do it for me. It's all in the attitude. Look at him. Like he owns the goddamn world."

She watched as Dean gracefully balanced on one leg to pull on a shoe cover. He thrust his long hands into gloves, like a surgeon preparing to operate. Yes, it was all in the attitude. Korsak was an angry pugilist who expected the world to kick him around. Naturally it did.

"Who called him here?" said Korsak.

"I didn't."

"Yet he just happens to show up."

"He always does. Someone's keeping him in the loop. It's no one on my team. It goes higher."

She stared at the front door again. Dean had stepped inside, and she imagined him standing in the living room, surveying the bloodstains. Reading them the way one reads a field report, the bright splatter detached from the humanity of its source.

"You know, I been thinking about it," said

Korsak. "Dean didn't show up on the scene until nearly three days after the Yeagers were attacked. First time we see him is over at Stony Brook Reservation, when Mrs. Yeager's body was found. Right?"

"Right."

"So what took him so long? The other day, we were playing around with the idea it was an execution. Some trouble the Yeagers had gotten into. If they were already on the feds' radar screen — under investigation, say, or being watched — you'd think the fibbies would be on the case the instant Dr. Yeager was whacked. But they waited three days to step in. What finally pulled them in? What got them interested?"

She looked at him. "Did you file a VICAP report?"

"Yeah. Took me a whole friggin' hour to finish it. A hundred eighty-nine questions. Weird shit like, 'Was any body part bitten off? What objects got shoved into which orifices?' Now I gotta file a supplementary report on Mrs. Yeager."

"Did you request a profile evaluation when you transmitted the form?"

"No. I didn't see the point of having some FBI profiler tell me what I already know. I just did my civic duty and sent in the VICAP form."

VICAP, or the Violent Criminals Apprehension Program, was the FBI's database of violent crimes. Compiling that database required the cooperation of often-harried law enforcement

197

officers who, when confronted with the long VICAP questionnaire, many times did not even bother.

"When did you file the report?" she asked.

"Right after the postmortem on Dr. Yeager."

"And that's when Dean showed up. A day later."

"You think that's it?" asked Korsak. "That's what pulled him in?"

"Maybe your report tripped an alarm."

"What would get their attention?"

"I don't know." She looked at the front door, through which Dean had vanished. "And it's pretty clear he's not going to tell us."

# Eleven

Jane Rizzoli was not a symphony kind of gal. The extent of her exposure to music was her collection of easy-listening CDs and the two years she'd played trumpet in the middle school band, one of only two girls who'd chosen that instrument. She'd been drawn to it because it produced the loudest, brassiest sound of all, not like those tooty clarinets or the chirpy flutes the other girls played. No, Rizzoli wanted to be heard, and so she sat shoulder to shoulder with the boys in the trumpet section. She loved it when the notes came blasting out.

Unfortunately, they were too often the wrong notes.

After her father banished her to the backyard for her practice sessions and then the neighborhood dogs began to howl in protest, she finally put the trumpet away for good. Even she could recognize that raw enthusiasm and strong lungs were not enough to make up for a discouraging lack of talent.

Since then, music had meant little more to her than white noise aboard elevators and thudding bass notes in passing cars. She had been inside the Symphony Hall on the corner of

Huntington and Mass Ave. only twice in her life, both times as a high school student attending field trips to hear BSO rehearsals. In 1990, the Cohen Wing had been added, a part of Symphony Hall that Rizzoli had never before visited. When she and Frost entered the new wing, she was surprised by how modern it looked — not the dark and creaky building that she remembered.

They showed their badges to the elderly security guard, who snapped his kyphotic spine a little straighter when he saw the two visitors were from Homicide.

"Is this about the Ghents?" he asked.

"Yes, sir," said Rizzoli.

"Terrible. Just terrible. I saw them last week, right after they got into town. They dropped by to check out the hall." He shook his head. "Seemed like such a nice young couple."

"Were you on duty the night they performed?"

"No, ma'am. I just work here during the day. Have to leave at five to pick up my wife from day care. She needs twenty-four-hour supervision, you know. Forgets to turn off the stove . . ." He stopped, suddenly reddening. "But I guess you folks aren't here to pass the time. You come to see Evelyn?"

"Yes. Which way to her office?"

"She's not there. I saw her go into the concert hall a few minutes ago."

"Is there a rehearsal going on or something?"

"No, ma'am. It's our quiet season. Orchestra stays out in Tanglewood during the summer. This time of year, we just get a few visiting performers."

"So we can walk right into the hall?"

"Ma'am, you got the badge. Far as I'm concerned, you can go anywhere."

They did not immediately spot Evelyn Petrakas. As Rizzoli stepped into the dim auditorium, all she saw at first was a vast sea of empty seats, sweeping down toward a spotlighted stage. Drawn toward the light, they started down the aisle, wood floor creaking like the timbers of an old ship. They had already reached the stage when a voice called out, faintly:

"Can I help you?"

Squinting against the glare, Rizzoli turned to face the darkened rear of the auditorium. "Ms. Petrakas?"

"Yes?"

"I'm Detective Rizzoli. This is Detective Frost. Can we speak to you?"

"I'm here. In the back row."

They walked up the aisle to join her. Evelyn did not rise from her seat but remained huddled where she was, as though hiding from the light. She gave the detectives a dull nod as they took the two seats beside her.

"I've already spoken to a policeman. Last night," Evelyn said.

"Detective Sleeper?"

"Yes. I think that was his name. An older man, quite nice. I know I was supposed to wait and talk to some other detectives, but I had to leave. I just couldn't stay at that house any longer . . ." She looked toward the stage, as though mesmerized by a performance only she could see. Even in the gloom, Rizzoli could see it was a handsome face, perhaps forty, with premature streaks of silver in her dark hair. "I had responsibilities here," Evelyn said. "All the ticket refunds. And then the press started showing up. I had to come back and deal with it." She gave a tired laugh. "Always putting out fires. That's my job."

"What is your job here exactly, Ms. Petrakas?" asked Frost.

"My official title?" She gave a shrug. " 'Program coordinator for visiting artists.' What it means is, I try to keep them happy and healthy while they're in Boston. It's amazing how helpless some of them can be. They spend their lives in rehearsal halls and studios. The real world's a puzzle to them. So I recommend places for them to stay. Arrange for their pickup at the airport. Fruit basket in the room. Whatever extra comforts they need. I hold their hands."

"When did you first meet the Ghents?" asked Rizzoli.

"The day after they arrived in town. I went to pick them up at the house. They couldn't take a taxi because Alex's cello case made it a tight squeeze. But I have an SUV with a backseat that folds down."

"You drove them around town while they were here?"

"Only back and forth between the house and Symphony Hall."

Rizzoli glanced in her notebook. "I understand the house on Beacon Hill belongs to a symphony board member. A Christopher Harm. Does he often invite musicians to stay there?"

"During the summer, when he's in Europe. It's so much nicer than a hotel room. Mr. Harm trusts classical musicians. He knows they'll take good care of his home."

"Have any guests at Mr. Harm's house ever complained of problems there?"

"Problems?"

"Trespassers. Burglaries. Anything that's made them uneasy."

Evelyn shook her head. "It's Beacon Hill, Detective. You couldn't ask for a nicer neighborhood. I know Alex and Karenna loved it there."

"When did you last see them?"

Evelyn swallowed. Said, softly: "Last night. When I found Alex . . ."

"I meant while he was still alive, Ms. Petrakas."

"Oh." Evelyn gave an embarrassed laugh. "Of course, that's what you meant. I'm sorry; I'm not thinking. It's just so hard to concentrate." She shook her head. "I don't know why I even bothered to come in to work today. It just seemed like something I needed to do."

"The last time you saw them?" Rizzoli prompted her.

This time Evelyn answered in a steadier voice. "It was the night before last. After their performance, I drove them back to Beacon Hill. It was around eleven or so."

"Did you just drop them off? Or did you go inside with them?"

"I let them off right in front of their house."

"Did you see them actually walk in?"

"Yes."

"So they didn't ask you inside."

"I think they were pretty tired. And they were feeling a little depressed."

"Why?"

"After all the anticipation about performing in Boston, it wasn't as big an audience as they'd expected. And we're supposed to be the city of music. If this was the best we could draw here, what could they hope for in Detroit or Memphis?" Evelyn stared unhappily toward the stage. "We're dinosaurs, Detective. Karenna said that, in the car. Who appreciates classical music anymore? Most young people would rather watch music videos. People jiggling around with metal studs in their faces. It's all about sex and glitter and stupid costumes. And why does that singer, what's his name, have to stick his tongue out? What's that got to do with music?"

"Absolutely nothing," Frost agreed, warming at once to the topic. "You know, Ms. Petrakas, my wife and I had this very same conversation the other day. Alice, she loves classical music. Really loves it. Every year, we buy season tickets to the symphony."

Evelyn gave him a sad smile. "Then I'm afraid you're a dinosaur, too."

As they rose to leave, Rizzoli spotted a glossy program lying on the seat in front of her. She reached across to pick it up. "Are the Ghents in here?" she asked.

"Turn to page five," said Evelyn. "There. That's their publicity photo."

It was a picture of two people in love.

Karenna, slim and elegant in an off-the-shoulder black gown, gazed up into her husband's smiling eyes. Her face was luminous, her hair as dark as a Spaniard's. Alexander looked down at her with a boyish smile, an unruly forelock of pale hair dipping over his eye.

Evelyn said softly: "They were beautiful, weren't they? It's strange, you know. I never got the chance to sit down and really talk with them. But I did know their music. I've listened to their recordings. I've watched them perform, up on that stage. You can tell a lot about someone just by listening to their music. And the one thing I remember was how tenderly they played. I think that's the word I'd use to describe them. They were such tender people."

Rizzoli looked at the stage and imagined Alexander and Karenna on the night of their final performance. Her black hair lustrous under the stage lights, his cello gleaming. And their music, like the voices of two lovers singing to each other.

"The night they performed," said Frost. "You said it was a disappointing turnout."

"Yes."

"How big was the audience?"

"I believe we sold around four hundred fifty tickets."

Four hundred fifty pairs of eyes, thought Rizzoli, all of them focused on the stage, where a couple in love were wreathed in light. What emotions did the Ghents inspire in their audience? The pleasure of music, well played? The joy of watching two young people in love? Or had other, darker emotions stirred in the heart of someone seated in this very hall? Hunger. Envy. The bitterness of wanting what another man possesses.

She looked down again, at the photo of the Ghents.

*Was it her beauty that caught your eye? Or was it the fact they were in love?*

She drank black coffee and stared at the dead piling up on her desk. Richard and Gail Yeager. Rickets Lady. Alexander Ghent. And Airplane Man, who, although no longer considered a homicide victim, still weighed on her mind. The dead always did. A never-ending supply of corpses, each one demanding her attention, each one with his or her own tale of horror to

206

tell, if Rizzoli would just dig deep enough to lay bare the bones of their stories. She'd been digging so long that all the dead she'd ever known were beginning to blend together like skeletons tangled in a mass grave.

When the DNA lab paged her at noon, she was relieved to escape, at least for the moment, that accusing stack of files. She left her desk and headed down the hall to the south wing.

The DNA lab was in S253, and the criminalist who'd paged her was Walter De Groot, a blond Dutchman with a pale man-in-the-moon face. Usually he winced when he saw her, since her visits were almost always for the purpose of prodding or cajoling him, anything to hurry along a DNA profile. Today, though, he gave her a broad grin.

"I've developed the autorad," he said. "It's hanging there now."

An autorad, or autoradiogram, was an X-ray film that captured the pattern of DNA fragments. De Groot took down the film from the drying line and clipped it onto a light box. Parallel rows of dark blots tracked from top to bottom.

"What you see here is the VNTR profile," he said. "That's short for 'variable numbers of tandem repeats.' I've extracted the DNA from the different sources you've provided, and isolated the fragments with the particular loci we're comparing. These aren't really genes, but sections of the DNA strand that repeat with no clear purpose. They make good identification markers."

"So what are these various tracks? What do they correspond to?"

"The first two lanes, starting at the left, are the controls. Number one is a standard DNA ladder, to help us estimate the relative positions for the various samples. Lane two is a standard cell line, again used as a control. Lanes three, four, and five are evidentiary lines, taken from known origins."

"Which origins?"

"Lane three is suspect Joey Valentine's. Lane four is Dr. Yeager's. Lane five is Mrs. Yeager's."

Rizzoli's gaze lingered on lane five. She tried to wrap her mind around the concept that this was part of the blueprint that had created Gail Yeager. That a unique human being, from the precise shade of her blond hair to the sound of her laughter, could be distilled down to this chain of dark blots. She saw no humanity in this autorad, nothing of the woman who had loved a husband and mourned a mother. *Is this all we are? A necklace of chemicals? Where, in the double helix, does the soul lie?*

Her gaze shifted to the final two lanes. "And what are these last ones?" she asked.

"These are the unidentifieds. Lane six is from that semen stain on the Yeagers' rug. Lane seven is the fresh semen collected from Gail Yeager's vaginal vault."

"These last two look like a match."

"That's correct. Both unidentified DNA samples are from the same man. And, you'll notice, it's not Dr. Yeager or Mr. Valentine. This effectively eliminates Mr. Valentine as the semen source."

She stared at the two unidentified lanes. The genetic fingerprint of a monster.

"There's your unsub," said De Groot.

"Have you called CODIS? Any chance we could talk them into moving a little faster on a data search?"

CODIS was a national DNA data bank. It stored the genetic profiles of thousands of convicted offenders, as well as unidentified profiles from crime scenes across the country.

"Actually, that's the reason I paged you. I sent them the rug stain DNA last week."

She sighed. "Meaning we'll hear back from them in a year."

"No, Agent Dean just called me. Your unsub's DNA isn't in CODIS."

She looked at him in surprise. "Agent Dean gave you the news?"

"He must have cracked the whip at them or something. In all my time here, I've never seen a CODIS request expedited this fast."

"Did you confirm that directly with CODIS?"

De Groot frowned. "Well, no. I assumed that Agent Dean would know —"

"Please call them. I want it confirmed."

"Is there some, uh, question about Dean's reliability?"

"Let's just play it safe, okay?" She looked, once again, at the light box. "If it's true our boy's not in CODIS . . ."

"Then you've got yourself a new player, Detective. Or someone who's managed to stay invisible to the system."

She stared in frustration at the chain of blots. We have his DNA, she thought. We have his genetic profile. But we still don't know his name.

Rizzoli slipped a disk into her CD player and sank onto the couch as she toweled off her wet hair. The rich strains of a solo cello poured from the speaker like melted chocolate. Though she was not a fan of classical music, she had bought a CD of Alex Ghent's early recordings in the Symphony Hall gift shop. If she was to familiarize herself with every aspect of his death, so, too, should she know about his life. And much of his life was music.

Ghent's bow glided over the cello strings, the melody of Bach's Suite no. 1 in G Major rising and falling like the swells of an ocean. It had been recorded when he was only eighteen. When he'd sat in a studio, his fingers warm flesh as they'd pressed the strings, steadied the bow. Those same fingers now lay white and chilled in the morgue refrigerator, their music silenced. She had watched his autopsy that morning and had noted the fine, long fingers, had imagined them flying up and down the cello's neck. That human hands could unite with mere wood and strings to produce such rich sounds seemed a miracle.

She picked up the CD cover and studied his photograph, taken when he was still only a boy. His eyes gazed downward, and his left arm was draped around the instrument, embracing its curves, as he would one day embrace his wife, Karenna. Though Rizzoli had searched for a CD featuring both of them, all their joint recordings were sold out in the gift shop. Only Alexander's was in stock. The lonely cello, calling to its mate. And where was that mate now? Alive and in torment, facing the ultimate terror of death? Or was she beyond pain and already in the early stages of decomposition?

The phone rang. She turned down the CD player and picked up the receiver.

"You're there," said Korsak.

"I came home to take a shower."

"I called just a few minutes ago. You didn't answer."

"Then I guess I didn't hear it. What's up?"

"That's what I want to know."

"If anything turns up, you'll be the first one I call."

"Yeah. Like you called me even *once* today? I had to hear about Joey Valentine's DNA from the lab guy."

"I didn't get the chance to tell you. I've been running around like crazy."

"Remember, I'm the one who first brought you in on this."

"I haven't forgotten."

"You know," said Korsak, "it's going on fifty hours since he took her."

And Karenna Ghent has probably been dead for two days, she thought. But death wouldn't deter her killer. It would whet his appetite. He'd look at her corpse and see only an object of desire. Someone he can control. She doesn't resist him. She is cool, passive flesh, yielding to any and all indignities. She is the perfect lover.

The CD was still playing softly, Alexander's cello weaving its mournful spell. She knew where this was going, knew what Korsak wanted. And she didn't know how to turn him down. She rose from the couch and turned off the CD. Even in the silence, the strains of the cello seemed to linger.

"If it's like the last time, he'll dump her tonight," said Korsak.

"We'll be ready for him."

"So am I part of the team or what?"

"We've already got our stakeout crew."

"You don't have me. You could use another warm body."

"We've already assigned the positions. Look, I'll call you as soon as anything —"

"Fuck this 'calling me' shit, okay? I'm not gonna sit by the phone like some goddamn wallflower. I've known this perp longer than you, longer than anyone. How would you feel, someone cuts in on your dance? Leaves you outta the take-down? You think about that."

She did. And she understood the anger that

was now raging through him. Understood it better than anyone, because it had once happened to her. The shunting aside, the bitter view from the sidelines while others moved in to claim her victory.

She looked at her watch. "I'm leaving right now. If you want to join me, you'll have to meet me there."

"What's your stakeout position?"

"The parking area across the road from Smith Playground. We can meet at the golf course."

"I'll be there."

# Twelve

At two A.M. in Stony Brook Reservation, the air was muggy and thick as soup. Rizzoli and Korsak sat in her parked car, closely abutting dense shrubbery. From their position, they could observe all cars entering Stony Brook from the east. Additional surveillance vehicles were stationed along Enneking Parkway, the main thoroughfare winding through the reservation. Any vehicle that pulled off onto one of the dirt parking areas could swiftly be hemmed in on all sides by converging vehicles. It was a purse-string trap, from which no car could escape.

Rizzoli was sweating in her vest. She rolled down the window and breathed in the scent of decaying leaves and damp earth. Forest smells.

"Hey, you're letting in mosquitoes," complained Korsak.

"I need the fresh air. It smells like cigarettes in here."

"I only lit up one. I don't smell it."

"Smokers never do."

He looked at her. "Jeez, you been snapping at me all night. You got a problem with me, maybe we should talk about it."

She stared out the window, toward the road,

214

which remained dark and untraveled. "It's not about you," she said.

"Who, then?"

When she didn't answer, he gave a grunt of comprehension. "Oh. Dean again. So what'd he do now?"

"Few days ago, he complained about me to Marquette."

"What'd he tell him?"

"That I'm not the right man for the job. That maybe I need counseling for *unresolved issues.*"

"He talking about the Surgeon?"

"What do you think?"

"What an asshole."

"And today, I find out we got instant feedback from CODIS. It's never happened before. All Dean has to do is snap his fingers, and everyone jumps. I just wish I knew what he was doing here."

"Well, that's the thing about fibbies. They say information is power, right? So they keep it from us, 'cause it's a macho game to them. You and me, we're just pawns to Mr. James Fucking Bond."

"You're getting confused with the CIA."

"CIA, FBI." He shrugged. "All those alphabet agencies, they're all about secrets."

The radio crackled. "Watcher Three. We got a vehicle, late-model sedan, moving south on Enneking Parkway."

Rizzoli tensed, waiting for the next team to report in.

Now Frost's voice, in the next vehicle. "Watcher Two. We see him. Still moving south. Doesn't look like he's slowing down."

Seconds later, a third unit reported: "Watcher Five. He's just passed the intersection of Bald Knob Road. Heading out of the park."

*Not our boy.* Even at this early-morning hour, Enneking Parkway was well traveled. They had lost count of how many vehicles they'd tracked through the reservation. Too many false alarms punctuating long intervals of boredom had burned up all her adrenaline, and she was fast sliding into sleep-deprived torpor.

She leaned back with a disappointed sigh. Beyond the windshield she saw the blackness of woods, lit only by the occasional spark of a firefly. "Come on, you son of a bitch," she murmured. "Come to Mama. . . ."

"You want some coffee?" asked Korsak.

"Thanks."

He poured a cup from his thermos and handed it to her. The coffee was black and bitter and utterly disgusting, but she drank it anyway.

"Made it extra strong tonight," he said. "Two scoops of Folgers instead of one. Puts hair on your chest."

"Maybe that's what I need."

"I figure, I drink enough of this stuff, some of that hair might migrate back up to my head."

She looked off toward the woods, where darkness hid rotting leaves and foraging animals. Animals with teeth. She remembered the

216

gnawed remains of Rickets Lady and thought of raccoons chewing on ribs and dogs rolling skulls around like balls, and what she imagined, staring into the trees, was not Bambi.

"I can't even talk about Hoyt anymore," she said. "Can't mention him without people giving me that pitying *look*. Yesterday, I tried to point out the parallels between the Surgeon and our new boy, and I could see Dean thinking: *She's still got the Surgeon on the brain.* He thinks I'm obsessed." She sighed. "Maybe I am. Maybe that's how it'll always be. I'll walk onto any crime scene and I'll see his handiwork. Every perp will have his face."

They both glanced at the radio as Dispatch said, "We have a request for a premises check, Fairview Cemetery. Any units in the area?"

No one responded.

Dispatch repeated the request: "We have a call for a premises check, Fairview Cemetery. Possible unauthorized entry. Unit Twelve, are you still in the area?"

"Unit Twelve. We're on the ten-forty, River Street. It's a code one. We're unable to re-spond."

"Roger that. Unit Fifteen? What's your ten-ten?"

"Unit Fifteen. West Roxbury. Still on that Missile six. These folks are not calming down. Estimate at least a half hour, hour till we can get to Fairview."

"Any units?" said Dispatch, trolling the radio

waves for an available patrol car. On a warm Saturday night, a routine premises check of a cemetery was not a high-priority call. The dead are beyond caring about frolicking couples or teenage vandals. It is the living who must command a cop's first attention.

Radio silence was broken by a member of Rizzoli's stakeout team. "Uh, this is Watcher Five. We're situated on Enneking Parkway. Fairview Cemetery's in our immediate vicinity —"

Rizzoli grabbed the mike and hit the transmit button. "Watcher Five, this is Watcher One," she cut in. "Do not abandon your position. You copy?"

"We have five vehicles on stakeout —"

"The cemetery is *not* our priority."

"Watcher One," said Dispatch. "All units are on calls right now. Any chance you could release one?"

"Negative. I want my team to hold position. Copy, Watcher Five?"

"Ten-four. We are holding. Dispatch, we can't respond to that premises-check call."

Rizzoli huffed out a sigh. There might be complaints about this come morning, but she was not going to release a single vehicle from her surveillance team, not for a trivial call.

"It's not like we're swamped with action," said Korsak.

"When it happens, it'll be fast. I'm not going to let anything foul this up."

"You know that thing we were talking about

218

earlier? About you being obsessed?"

"Don't start in now."

"No, I'm not gonna go there. You'll bite off my head." He shoved open his door.

"Where you going?"

"Take a leak. I need permission?"

"Just asking."

"That coffee's going right through me."

"No wonder. Your coffee'd burn a hole through cast iron."

He stepped out of the car and walked into the woods, his hands already fumbling at his fly. He didn't bother to step behind any tree but just stood there, urinating into the bushes. This she didn't need to see, and she averted her gaze. Every class has its gross-out kid, and Korsak was it, the boy who openly picked his nose and belched with gusto and wore his lunch on the front of his shirt. The kid whose moist and pudgy hands you avoided touching at all costs, because you were sure to catch his cooties. She felt both repelled by him and sorry for him. She looked down at the coffee he'd poured for her, and she tossed what was left out the window.

Fresh chatter erupted over the radio, startling her.

"We got a vehicle moving east on Dedham Parkway. Looks like a Yellow Cab."

Rizzoli responded, "A taxicab at three A.M.?"

"That's what we got."

"Where's he going?"

"Just turned north onto Enneking."

"Watcher Two?" said Rizzoli, calling the next unit on the route.

"Watcher Two," said Frost. "Yeah, we see him. Just went past us. . . ." A silence. Then, with sudden tension: "He's slowing down . . ."

"Doing what?"

"Braking. Looks like he's about to pull over —"

"Location?" snapped Rizzoli.

"The dirt parking area. He's just pulled into the parking area!"

*It's him.*

"Korsak, we're hot!" she hissed out the window. As she slipped on her personal comm unit and adjusted the earpiece, every nerve was singing with excitement.

Korsak zipped up his fly and scrambled back into the car. "What? What?"

"Vehicle just pulled off Enneking — Watcher Two, what's he doing?"

"Just sitting there. Lights are off."

She hunched forward, pressing the headset to her ear in concentration. The seconds ticked by, transmissions silent, everyone waiting for the suspect's next move.

*He's checking out the area. Confirming that it's safe to proceed.*

"It's your call, Rizzoli," said Frost. "We move on him?"

She hesitated, weighing their options. Afraid to spring the trap too soon.

"Wait," said Frost. "He just turned his headlights back on. Ah, shit, he's backing out. He's changed his mind."

"Did he spot you? Frost, did he spot you?"

"I don't know! He's pulled back onto Enneking. Proceeding north —"

"We've spooked him!" In that split second, the only possible decision was crystal clear to her. She barked into her comm unit: "All units, go, go, *go!* Box him in *now!*"

She started the car, jammed the gear into drive. Her tires spun, digging a trough through soft dirt and fallen leaves, branches whipping at the windshield. She heard her team's rapid-fire transmissions and the far-off blare of multiple sirens.

"Watcher Three. We now have Enneking north blocked off —"

"Watcher Two. In pursuit —"

"Vehicle is approaching! He's braking —"

"Box him in! Box him in!"

"Do not confront without backup!" Rizzoli ordered. "Wait for backup!"

"Roger that. Vehicle has halted. We are holding position."

By the time Rizzoli screeched to a halt, Enneking Parkway was a knot of cruisers and throbbing blue lights. Rizzoli felt temporarily blinded as she stepped out of her car. The surge of adrenaline had excited them all to fever pitch and she could hear it in their voices, the crackling tension of men on the edge of violence.

Frost yanked open the suspect's door, and

half a dozen weapons were pointed at the driver's head. The cabbie sat blinking and disoriented, blue lights pulsing on his face.

"Step out of the vehicle," Frost ordered.

"What — what'd I do?"

*"Step out of the vehicle."* On this adrenaline-drenched night, even Barry Frost had transformed into someone frightening.

The cabbie slowly emerged, hands held high. The instant both his feet touched the ground, he was spun around and shoved facedown against the hood of the cab.

"What'd I *do?*" he cried as Frost patted him down.

"State your name!" said Rizzoli.

"I don't know what this is all about —"

"Your *name!*"

"Wilensky." He gave a sob. "Vernon Wilensky —"

"Check," said Frost, reading the cabbie's I.D. "Vernon Wilensky, white male, born 1955."

"Matches the carriage permit," said Korsak, who'd leaned into the cab to check the I.D. clipped to the visor.

Rizzoli glanced up, eyes narrowing against the glare of oncoming headlights. Even at three A.M., there was traffic moving along the parkway, and with the road now blocked by police vehicles, they'd soon have cars backing up in both directions.

She focused again on the cabbie. Grabbing his shirt, she turned him around to face her and aimed her flashlight in his eyes. She saw a middle-aged man, blond hair gone thin and scraggly, skin sallow in the harsh beam of light. This was not the face she'd envisioned as their unsub. She had looked into the eyes of evil more times than she cared to count and carried, in her memory all the faces belonging to the monsters she had encountered in her career. This scared man did not belong in that gallery.

"What are you doing here, Mr. Wilensky?" she said.

"I was just — just picking up a fare."

"What fare?"

"A guy called for a cab. Said he ran outta gas on Enneking Parkway —"

"Where is he?"

"I don't know! I stopped where he said he'd be waiting, and he wasn't there. Please, it's all a mistake. Call my dispatcher! She'll back me up!"

Rizzoli said to Frost: "Pop open the trunk."

Even as she walked to the rear of the cab, a sick feeling was building in her stomach. She lifted the trunk hood and aimed her Maglite. For a solid five seconds she stared into that empty trunk, the sick feeling now worsening to full-blown nausea. She pulled on gloves. Felt her face flushing hot and bright, her chest going hollow with despair, as she peeled back the gray carpet lining the trunk. She saw a spare tire, a jack, and a few tools. She began yanking on the carpet, peeling it back farther, all her rage focused on ripping away every square inch of it, exposing every dark nook it might conceal. She was like a madwoman, clawing desperately for the scraps of her own redemption. When she could tear away no more and the trunk was exposed down to bare metal, she just stared at the empty space, refusing to accept what was plain to see. The irrefutable evidence that she had screwed up.

*A setup. This was just a setup, meant to distract us. But from what?*

The answer came to her with dizzying speed. A call erupted from their radios.

"Ten fifty-four, ten fifty-four, Fairview Cemetery. All units, ten fifty-four, Fairview Cemetery."

Frost's gaze met hers, both of them struck in that instant by the same terrible realization. Ten fifty-four. Homicide.

"Stay with the cab!" she ordered Frost, and she sprinted to her car. In the tangle of vehicles, hers was the easiest to extract, the quickest to turn around. Even as she scrambled in behind the wheel and twisted the key, she was cursing her own stupidity.

"Hey! *Hey!*" shouted Korsak. He was running beside the car, pounding on the door.

She braked just long enough to let him scramble in and yank his door shut. Then she floored the accelerator, flinging him back against his seat.

"What the fuck, you gonna leave me back there?" he yelled.

"Buckle up."

"I'm not just some ride-along."

"*Buckle up!*"

He dragged his seat belt over his shoulder and snapped it shut. Even over the voices chattering on the radio, she could hear his labored breathing, wet with mucousy wheezes.

"Watcher One, responding to the ten fifty-four," she said to Dispatch.

"Your ten-ten?"

"Enneking Parkway, just passed the intersection with Turtle Pond. ETA less than a minute."

"You'll be first on the scene."

"Situation?"

"No further information. Assume ten fifty-eight."

*Armed and believed dangerous.*

Rizzoli's foot was lead on the pedal. The road to Fairview Cemetery came up so fast she almost missed it. They took the turn with tires screaming, Rizzoli wrestling the wheel for control.

"Whoa!" gasped Korsak as they nearly slammed into a row of roadside boulders. The wrought-iron gate hung open and she drove through. The cemetery was unlit, and beyond her headlights were rolling lawns, gravestones jutting up like white teeth.

A vehicle from a private security patrol was parked a hundred yards from the cemetery gate. The driver's door was open and the dome light was glowing. Rizzoli braked and was already reaching for her weapon as she stepped out, the reflex so automatic she did not even register the action. Too many other details were assaulting her: The smell of freshly mown grass and damp earth. The punch of her heartbeat against her breastbone.

And the fear. As her gaze swept the darkness, she felt the icy lick of fear because she knew that if the cab was a setup, then this could be, too. A bloody game that she had not even been aware she was part of.

She froze, her eyes focusing on a puddle of shadow near the base of a memorial obelisk. Aiming her Maglite, she saw the security guard's crumpled body.

As she stepped toward him, she smelled the blood. There was no other scent like it, and it rang primitive alarms in her brain. She knelt down on grass that was wet with it, still warm with it. Korsak was right beside her, shining his flashlight as well, and she could hear his snuffling breaths, the piggy noises he always made when he'd exerted himself.

The guard was lying facedown. She rolled him onto his back.

"Jesus!" yelped Korsak, jerking away with such violence his flashlight beam shot wildly toward the sky.

Rizzoli's beam was trembling as well as she stared at the nearly severed neck, nubs of cartilage gleaming whitely from the butchered flesh. Man down, all right. Down, out, and barely attached to his own head.

Flashing blue lights cut through the night, a surreal kaleidoscope weaving toward them. She rose to her feet, and her slacks were sticky with blood, the fabric adhering to her knees. Eyes narrowed against the glare of approaching cruisers, she turned away, facing the black expanse of the cemetery. In that instant, as the advancing headlights cut an arc through the darkness, an image froze on her retinas: a figure, moving among the headstones. It was just a split second's glimpse, and in the next pulse of light the figure was lost in the sea of jutting marble and granite.

"Korsak," she said. "Someone moving — two o'clock."

"Can't see a damn thing."

She stared. Saw it again, moving down the slope, toward the cover of trees. In an instant she was sprinting, weaving through the obstacle course of headstones, feet pounding across the sleeping dead. She heard Korsak close behind, wheezing like an accordion, but he couldn't keep up. Within seconds she was on her own, legs pumping on the rocket fuel of adrenaline. She was almost to the trees, closing in on where she had last spotted the figure, but she saw no moving silhouettes, no flitting of darkness across darkness. She slowed, stopped, her gaze sweeping back and forth, seeking the slightest movement in the shadows.

Though she was now at a standstill, her pulse accelerated, driven by fear. By the skin-crawling certainty that *he* was nearby. *He* was watching her. Yet she was reluctant to turn on her flashlight, to send out a beacon announcing her location.

The snap of a twig made her whirl to her right. The trees loomed in front of her, an impenetrable black curtain. Through the roar of her own blood, the rush of air through her lungs, she heard leaves rustle and more twigs crack.

*He is walking toward me.*

She dropped to a crouch, weapon aimed, nerves honed to a hair trigger.

The footsteps suddenly stopped.

She snapped on the Maglite and shone it dead ahead. Saw him, then, dressed in black, standing among the trees. Caught in the beam of light, he twisted away arm rising to shield his eyes.

*"Freeze!"* she yelled. "Police!"

The man went perfectly still, his face turned, his hand reaching toward his face. He said, quietly, "I'm going to take off my goggles."

"No, asshole! You're going to freeze right where you are."

"And then what, Detective Rizzoli? Shall we exchange badges? Pat each other down?"

She stared, suddenly recognizing the voice. Slowly, deliberately, Gabriel Dean removed his goggles and turned to face her. With the light in his eyes, he could not see her, but she could see him just fine, and his expression was cool and composed. With the flashlight she made a vertical sweep of his body, saw black clothes, a weapon holstered at his hip. And in his hand, the night-vision goggles which he'd just removed. Korsak's words shot straight to mind: *Mr. James Fucking Bond.*

Dean took a step toward her.

Instantly her weapon snapped up. "Stay right where you are."

"Easy Rizzoli. No reason to shoot my head off."

"Isn't there?"

"I'm just walking closer. So we can talk."

"We can talk fine from this distance."

He looked toward the flashing lights of the cruisers. "Who do you suppose radioed in the homicide call?"

She held steady didn't let her aim waver.

"Use your head, Detective. I assume you've got a good one." He took another step.

"Just fucking *freeze* right there."

"Okay." He held up his hands. Said again, lightly, "Okay."

"What are you doing here?"

"Same thing you are. This is where the action is."

"How did you know? If you're the one who called in that ten fifty-four, how did you know the action was here?"

"I didn't."

"You just *happened* to come along and find him?"

"I heard Dispatch call for a property check of

Fairview Cemetery. A possible trespasser."

"So?"

"So I wondered if it was our unsub."

"You *wondered?*"

"Yes."

"You must have had a good reason."

"Instinct."

"Don't bullshit me, Dean. You turn up fully dressed for night ops, and I'm supposed to believe you just moseyed on over to check out a trespasser?"

"My instincts are good."

"You'd have to have ESP to be that good."

"We're wasting time here, Detective. Either arrest me or work with me."

"I'm leaning toward the first choice."

He regarded her with an unruffled expression. There was too much he wasn't telling her, too many secrets she'd never get out of him. Not here, not tonight. At last she lowered her weapon but did not holster it. Gabriel Dean didn't inspire that level of trust.

"Since you were first on the scene, what did you see?"

"I found the security guard already down. I used his car radio to call Dispatch. The blood was still warm. I thought there was a chance our boy'd be close by. So I went looking."

She gave a dubious snort. "In the trees?"

"I saw no other vehicles in the cemetery. Do you know what neighborhood surrounds us, Detective?"

She hesitated. "Dedham's to the east. Hyde Park north and south."

"Exactly. Residential neighborhoods on all sides, with lots of places to park a car. From there it's just a short stroll to this cemetery."

"Why would the unsub come here?"

"What do we know about him? Our boy is obsessed with the dead. He craves the smell of them, the touch of them. He holds on to corpses until the stench becomes impossible to disguise, to hide. Only then does he surrender the remains. This is a man who probably gets turned on just by walking through a cemetery. So here he was, in the dark, indulging in a little erotic adventure."

"This is sick."

"Look into *his* mind, *his* universe. We may think it's sick, but for him, this place is a little slice of paradise. A place where the dead are laid to rest. Just the place the Dominator would come. He walks around here and probably imagines a whole harem of sleeping women right beneath his feet.

"But then he's disturbed, surprised by the arrival of a security patrol. A guard who's probably expecting to deal with nothing more dangerous than a few teenagers looking for a little nighttime adventure."

"And the guard lets a lone man stroll right up and cut his throat?"

Dean was silent. For this he had no explanation. Neither did Rizzoli.

By the time they walked back up the slope, the night was pulsing with blue lights, and her team was already stringing crime scene tape between stakes. Rizzoli stared at the grim carnival of activity and suddenly she felt too weary to deal with any of it. Seldom had she questioned her own judgment, doubted her own instincts. But tonight, faced with the evidence of her failure, she wondered if Gabriel Dean wasn't right — that she had no business leading this investigation. That the trauma inflicted on her by Warren Hoyt had so damaged her that she could no longer function as a cop. Tonight she had made the wrong choice, had refused to release anyone from her team to answer the call for a premises check. *We were only a mile away. Sitting in our cars, waiting for nothing, while this man was dying.*

The string of defeats had piled up so heavily on her shoulders that she felt her back sag as though under the weight of real stones. She returned to her car and flipped open her cell phone; Frost answered.

"Yellow Cab dispatcher confirms the cabbie's story," he told her. "They got the call at two-sixteen. Male claiming his car was out of gas on Enneking Parkway. She dispatched Mr. Wilensky. We're trying to track down the number the call came from."

"Our boy's not stupid. The call's going to lead nowhere. A pay phone. Or a stolen cell phone. *Shit.*" She slapped the dashboard.

"So what about the cabbie? He comes up clean."

"Release him."

"You sure?"

"It was all a game, Frost. The unsub knew we'd be waiting for him. He's playing with us. Demonstrating he's in control. That he's smarter than us." *And he just proved it.*

She hung up and sat for a moment, collecting the energy to step out of the car and face what came next. Another death investigation. All the questions that would surely follow about her decisions tonight. She thought of how fiercely she had pinned her hopes on the belief that the unsub would adhere to his pattern. Instead he had used that very pattern to taunt her. To produce the fiasco she was now staring at.

Several of the cops standing by the crime scene tape turned and looked her way — a signal that, tired as she was, she could not hide in her car much longer. She remembered Korsak's thermos of coffee; awful as it was, she could use the shot of caffeine. She reached around to retrieve the thermos behind her seat and suddenly stopped.

She looked up at the law enforcement personnel standing among the cruisers. She saw Gabriel Dean, lean and sleek as a black cat as he walked the crime scene perimeter. She saw cops scanning the ground, flashlights sweeping back and forth. But she did not see Korsak.

She stepped out of the car and approached

Officer Doud, who'd been part of the stakeout team. "Have you seen Detective Korsak?" she asked.

"No, ma'am."

"He wasn't here when you arrived? He wasn't waiting by the body?"

"I haven't seen him here at all."

She stared toward the trees, where she had encountered Gabriel Dean. *Korsak was running right behind me. But he never caught up. And he didn't come back here. . . .*

She began walking toward the trees, retracing the route she had run across the cemetery. During that sprint, she'd been so focused on pursuit that she'd paid little attention to Korsak, who'd trailed behind her. She remembered her own fear, the pounding heart, the night wind rushing past her face. She remembered his heavy breathing as he'd struggled to keep up. Then he'd fallen behind, and she'd lost track of him.

She moved faster now, her flashlight sweeping left and right. Was this the route she'd taken? No, no, she'd gone down a different row of headstones. She recognized an obelisk looming to the left.

Correcting course, she headed for the obelisk and almost tripped over Korsak's legs.

He lay crumpled beside a headstone, the shadow of his bulky torso merging with the granite. At once she was on her knees, screaming for assistance as she rolled him onto his back. One glance at his swollen, dusky face told her he was in cardiac arrest.

She felt his neck, wanting so desperately to detect a carotid pulse that she almost mistook the bounding pulse of her own fingers for his. But he had none.

She slammed her fist down on his chest. Even that violent punch did not jolt his heart awake.

She tilted his head back and tugged his sagging jaw forward to open the airway. So many things about Korsak had once repelled her. The smell of his sweat and cigarettes, his noisy sniffling, his doughy handshake. None of that registered now as she sealed her mouth against his and blew air into his lungs. She felt his chest expand, heard a noisy wheeze as his lungs expelled the air again. She planted her hands on his chest and began CPR, doing the work his heart refused to do. She kept pumping as other cops arrived to assist, as her arms began to tremble and sweat soaked into her vest. Even as she pumped, she was mentally flogging herself. How had she overlooked him, lying here? Why hadn't she noticed his absence? Her muscles burned and her knees ached, but she did not stop. She owed that much to him and would not abandon him a second time.

An ambulance siren screamed closer.

She was still pumping as the paramedics arrived. Only when someone took her arm and firmly tugged her away did she relinquish her role. She stood back, legs trembling, as the paramedics took over, inserting an I.V. line, hanging a bag of saline. They tilted Korsak's head back and thrust a laryngoscope blade down his throat.

"I can't see the vocal cords!"

"Jesus, he's got a big neck."

"Help me reposition."

"Okay. Try it again!"

Again the paramedic inserted the laryngoscope, straining to hold up the weight of Korsak's jaw. With his massive neck and swollen tongue, Korsak looked like a freshly slaughtered bull.

"Tube's in!"

They tore away the rest of Korsak's shirt, baring a thick mat of hair, and slapped on defibrillator paddles. On the EKG monitor, a jagged line appeared.

"He's in V-tach!"

The paddles discharged, a jolt of electrical current slicing through Korsak's chest. The seizure jerked his heavy torso right off the grass and dropped him back in a flaccid mound. The cops' multiple flashlight beams revealed every cruel detail, from the pale beer belly to the almost feminine breasts that are the embarrassment of so many overweight men.

"Okay! He's got a rhythm. Sinus tach —"

"BP?"

The cuff whiffed tight around his meaty arm. "Ninety systolic. Let's move him!"

Even after they'd transferred Korsak into the

ambulance and the taillights had winked away into the night, Rizzoli did not move. Numb with exhaustion, she stared after it, imagining what would follow for him. The harsh lights of the E.R. More needles, more tubes. It occurred to her that she should call his wife, but she did not know her name. In fact, she knew almost nothing about his personal life, and it struck her as unbearably sad that she knew far more about the dead Yeagers than about the living, breathing man who'd worked beside her. The partner she'd failed.

She looked down at the grass where he'd been lying. It still bore the imprint of his weight. She imagined him running after her but too short of breath to keep up. He would have pushed himself anyway, driven by male vanity, by pride. Did he clutch his chest before he went down? Did he try to call for help?

*I would not have heard him anyway. I was too busy trying to run down shadows. Trying to salvage my own pride.*

"Detective Rizzoli?" said Officer Doud. He'd approached so quietly, she had not even realized he was standing beside her.

"Yes?"

"I'm afraid we've found another one."

"What?"

"Another body."

Stunned, she could say nothing as she followed Doud across the damp grass, his flashlight lighting the way through the blackness. A flicker of more lights far ahead marked their destination. By the time she finally detected the first whiff of decay, they were several hundred yards from where the security guard had fallen.

"Who found it?" she asked.

"Agent Dean."

"Why was he searching all the way out here?"

"I guess he was doing a general sweep."

Dean turned to face her as she approached. "I think we've found Karenna Ghent," he said.

The woman lay atop a grave site, her black hair splayed around her, clusters of leaves arranged among the dark strands in mock decoration of mortified flesh. She had been dead long enough for her belly to bloat, for purge fluid to trickle from her nostrils. But the impact of all these details faded in the greater horror of what had been done to the lower abdomen. Rizzoli stared at the gaping wound. A single transverse slice.

The ground seemed to give way beneath her feet and she stumbled backward, blindly reaching for support and finding only air.

It was Dean who caught her, grasping her firmly by the elbow. "It's not a coincidence," he said.

She was silent, her gaze still fixed on that terrible wound. She remembered similar wounds on other women. Remembered a summer even hotter than this one.

"He's been following the news," said Dean. "He knows you're the lead investigator. He knows how to turn the tables, how to make a game of cat and mouse go both ways. That's what it is to him, now. A game."

Although she registered his words, she didn't understand what he was trying to tell her. "What game?"

"Didn't you see the name?" He aimed his flashlight at the words carved into the granite headstone:

*Beloved husband and father*
*Anthony Rizzoli*
*1901–1962*

"It's a taunt," said Dean. "And it's aimed straight at you."

# Thirteen

The woman sitting at Korsak's bedside had lank brown hair that looked as if it had been neither washed nor combed in days. She did not touch him but simply gazed at the bed with vacant eyes, her hands resting in her lap, lifeless as a mannequin's. Rizzoli stood outside the ICU cubicle, debating whether to intrude. Finally the woman looked up and met her gaze through the window, and Rizzoli could not simply walk away.

She stepped into the cubicle. "Mrs. Korsak?" she asked.

"Yes?"

"I'm Detective Rizzoli. Jane. Please call me Jane."

The woman's expression remained blank; clearly she did not recognize the name.

"I'm afraid I don't know your first name," said Rizzoli.

"Diane." The woman was silent for a moment; then she frowned. "I'm sorry. Who are you again?"

"Jane Rizzoli. I'm with Boston P.D. I've been working with your husband on a case. He may have mentioned it."

Diane gave a vague shrug and looked back at her husband. Her face revealed neither grief nor fear. Only the numb passivity of exhaustion.

For a moment Rizzoli simply stood in silent vigil over the bed. So many tubes, she thought. So many machines. And at their center was Korsak, reduced to senseless flesh. The doctors had confirmed a heart attack, and although his cardiac rhythm was now stable, he remained stuporous. His mouth hung agape, an endotracheal tube protruding like a plastic snake. A reservoir hanging at the side of the bed collected a slow trickle of urine. Though the bedsheet concealed his genitals, his chest and abdomen were bare, and one hairy leg protruded from beneath the sheet, revealing a foot with yellow unclipped toenails. Even as she took in these details, she felt ashamed of invading his privacy, of seeing him at his most vulnerable. Yet she could not look away. She felt compelled to stare, eyes drawn to all the intimate details, the very things that, were he awake, he would not want her to see.

"He needs a shave," said Diane.

Such a trivial concern, yet it was the one spontaneous remark Diane had made. She had not moved a muscle but sat perfectly motionless, hands still limp, her placid expression carved in stone.

Rizzoli searched for something to say, something she thought she *should* say to comfort her, and settled on a cliché. "He's a fighter. He won't give up easily."

Her words dropped like stones into a bottomless pond. No ripples, no effect. A long silence passed before Diane's flat blue eyes at last focused on her.

"I'm afraid I've forgotten your name again."

"Jane Rizzoli. Your husband and I were working a stakeout together."

"Oh. You're the one."

Rizzoli paused, suddenly stricken by guilt. *Yes, I'm the one. The one who abandoned him. Who left him lying alone in the darkness because I was so frantic to salvage my fucked-up night.*

"Thank you," said Diane.

Rizzoli frowned. "For what?"

"For whatever you did. To help him."

Rizzoli looked into the woman's vague blue eyes, and for the first time she noticed the tightly constricted pupils. The eyes of the anesthetized, she thought. Diane Korsak was in a narcotic daze.

Rizzoli looked at Korsak. Remembered the night she had called him to the Ghent death scene and he'd arrived intoxicated. She remembered, too, the night they had stood together in the M.E.'s parking lot and Korsak had seemed reluctant to go home. Is this what he faced every evening? This woman with her blank stare and her robot voice?

*You never told me. And I never bothered to ask.*

She moved to the bed and squeezed his hand. Recalled how his moist handshake had once repelled her. Not today; today, she would have rejoiced had he squeezed back. But the hand in hers remained limp.

It was eleven A.M. when she finally walked into her apartment. She turned the two dead bolts, pressed the button lock, and fastened the chain. Once, she would have thought all these locks were a sign of paranoia; once, she'd been satisfied with a simple knob lock and a weapon in her nightstand drawer. But a year ago Warren Hoyt had changed her life, and her door had since acquired these gleaming brass accessories. She stared at her array of locks, suddenly struck by how much she had become like every other victim of violent crime, desperate to barricade her home and shut out the world.

The Surgeon had done this to her.

And now this new unsub, the Dominator, had added his voice to the chorus of monsters braying outside her door. Gabriel Dean had understood at once that the choice of the grave on which Karenna Ghent's corpse had been deposited was no accident. Although the tenant of that grave, Anthony Rizzoli, was not her relation, their shared name was clearly a message intended for her.

*The Dominator knows my name.*

She did not remove her holster until she had made the complete walk-through of her apartment. It was not a large space, and it took less than a minute to glance in the kitchen and the living room, then move down the short hallway to her bedroom, where she opened the closet, peeked under the bed. Only then did she un-buckle her holster and slip the weapon into her nightstand drawer. She peeled off her clothes and went into the bathroom. She locked the door — yet another automatic reflex, and com-pletely unnecessary, but it was the only way she could step into the shower and summon the nerve to pull the curtain shut. Moments later, her hair still slick with conditioner, she was seized by the feeling that she was not alone. She yanked open the curtain and stared at the empty bathroom, her heart hammering, the water streaming down her shoulders and onto the floor.

She turned off the faucet. Leaned back against the tiled wall, breathing deeply, waiting for her heartbeat to slow. Through the *whoosh* of her own pulse she heard the hum of the ventila-tion fan. The rumble of pipes in her building. Everyday sounds that she had never bothered to register until now, when their very ordinariness served as a blessed focus.

By the time her heartbeat finally slowed to normal, the water had chilled on her skin. She stepped out, toweled off, then knelt down to mop up the wet floor as well. For all her swag-gering at work, her tough-cop act, she was now reduced to little more than shivering flesh. She saw, in the mirror, how fear had changed her. Staring back was a woman who had lost weight, whose already slim frame was slowly melting into gauntness. Whose face, once square and sturdy, now seemed thin as a wraith's, the eyes large and dark in their deepening hollows.

She fled the mirror and went into the bedroom. Hair still damp, she sank onto her bed and lay with eyes open, knowing she should try to catch at least a few hours' sleep. But daylight winked brightly through the cracks in the window blinds, and she could hear traffic in the street below. It was noon, and she had been awake for nearly thirty hours and had not eaten in nearly twelve. Yet she could summon up neither an appetite nor the will to fall asleep. The events of that early morning still buzzed like a current through her nervous system, the memories crackling in a recurrent loop. She saw the security guard's throat gaping open, his head turned at an impossible angle from his torso. She saw Karenna Ghent, leaves scattered in her hair.

And she saw Korsak, his body bristling with tubes and wires.

The three images cycled in her head like a strobe light, and she could not shut them off. She could not silence the buzzing. Was this what insanity felt like?

Weeks ago, Dr. Zucker had urged her to seek counseling and she had angrily brushed him off. Now she wondered if he had detected something in her words, her gaze, that even she had not been aware of. The first cracks in her sanity, shearing deeper and wider, since the Surgeon had rocked her life.

★ ★ ★

The ringing phone awakened her. It seemed that she'd only just closed her eyes, and the first emotion that bubbled up as she groped for the phone was rage, that she could not be granted even a moment's rest. She answered with a curt: "Rizzoli."

"Uh . . . Detective Rizzoli, this is Yoshima at the M.E.'s office. Dr. Isles was expecting you to come in for the Ghent postmortem."

"I am coming in."

"Well, she's already started, and —"

"What time is it?"

"Nearly four. We tried to page you, but you didn't answer."

She sat up so abruptly the room spun. She gave her head a shake and stared at the clock by her bed: 3:52. She had slept right through her alarm, as well as the sound of her pager. "I'm sorry," she said. "I'll be there as soon as I can."

"Hold on a minute. Dr. Isles wants to speak to you."

She heard the clang of instruments on a metal tray; then Dr. Isles's voice came on the phone. "Detective Rizzoli, you are coming in, right?"

"It'll take me half an hour to get there."

"Then we'll wait for you."

"I don't mean to hold you up."

"Dr. Tierney is coming in as well. You both need to see this."

This was highly unusual. With all the pathologists on staff to choose from, why would Dr. Isles

246

call Dr. Tierney back from his recent retirement?

"Is there some sort of problem?" asked Rizzoli.

"That wound on the victim's abdomen," said Dr. Isles. "It's not just a simple slash. It's a surgical incision."

Dr. Tierney was already garbed and standing in the autopsy room when Rizzoli arrived. Like Dr. Isles, he normally shunned the use of a respirator, and tonight his only facial protection was a plastic shield, through which Rizzoli could read his grim expression. Everyone in the room looked equally somber, and they regarded Rizzoli with unnerving silence as she entered the room. By now, the presence of Agent Dean no longer surprised her, and she acknowledged his gaze with only a faint nod, wondering if he had managed to catch a few hours' sleep as well. For the first time she saw fatigue in his eyes. Even Gabriel Dean was slowly being ground down by the weight of this investigation.

"What have I missed?" she asked. Not yet ready to confront the remains, she kept her gaze on Isles.

"We've completed the external examination. The criminalists have already taped for fibers, collected nail clippings, and combed hairs."

"What about the vaginal swabs?"

Isles nodded. "There was motile sperm."

Rizzoli took a breath and finally focused on the body of Karenna Ghent. The foul odor nearly overwhelmed the Vicks menthol that, for the first time, she had dabbed under her nostrils. She no longer trusted her own stomach. So much had gone wrong these last few weeks, and she'd lost confidence in the very strengths that had sustained her through other investigations. When she'd stepped in this room, what she'd dreaded wasn't the autopsy itself; rather, it was her own response to it. She could not predict, nor control, how she would react, and this, more than anything else, was what frightened her.

She'd eaten a handful of crackers at home so that she would not face this ordeal on an empty stomach, and she was relieved not to feel even a twinge of nausea despite the odors, despite the grotesque condition of the remains. She was able to maintain her composure as she regarded the liverish-green abdomen. The Y-incision had not yet been made. The single gaping wound was the one thing she could not bring herself to look at. Instead, she focused on the neck, on the discoid bruises, visible even against the underlying postmortem discoloration, under both angles of the jaw. The marks left by the killer's fingers, pressing into flesh.

"Manual strangulation," said Isles. "Like Gail Yeager."

*The most intimate way to kill someone,* Dr. Zucker had called it. *Skin to skin. Your hands against her flesh. Pressing her throat as you feel her life drain away.*

"And the X rays?"

"A fracture of the left thyroid horn."

Dr. Tierney cut in, "It's not the neck that concerns us. It's the wound. I suggest you put on a pair of gloves, Detective. You'll need to examine this yourself."

She crossed to the cabinet where the gloves were stored. Took her time pulling on a pair of Smalls, using the delay to steel herself. At last she turned back to the table.

Dr. Isles already had the overhead light focused on the lower abdomen. The edges of the wound gaped like blackened lips.

"The skin layer was opened with a single clean slice," said Dr. Isles. "Made with a nonserrated blade. Once through the skin, deeper incisions followed. First the superficial fascia, then the muscle, and finally the pelvic peritoneum."

Rizzoli stared into the maw of the wound, thinking of the hand that had held the blade, a hand so steady that it had traced the incision with a single confident slice.

She asked, softly: "Was the victim alive when this was done?"

"No. He used no suture, and there was no bleeding. This was a postmortem excision, performed after the patient's heart stopped, after circulation ceased. The manner in which this procedure was done — the methodical sequence of incisions — indicates he has had surgical experience. He's done this before."

Dr. Tierney said, "Go ahead, Detective. Examine the wound."

She hesitated, her hands chilled to ice in the latex gloves. Slowly she slipped her hand into the incision, burrowing deep into the pelvis of Karenna Ghent. She knew exactly what she would find, yet she was still shaken by the discovery. She looked at Dr. Tierney and saw confirmation in his eyes.

"The uterus was removed," he said.

She pulled her hand from the pelvis. "It's him," she said softly. "Warren Hoyt did this."

"Yet everything else is consistent with the Dominator," said Gabriel Dean. "The abduction, the strangulation. Postmortem intercourse —"

"But not this," she said, staring at the wound. "This is Hoyt's fantasy. This is what turns him on. The cutting, the taking of the very organ that defines them as women and gives them a power he'll never have." She looked straight at Dean. "I know his work. I've seen it before."

"We both have," Dr. Tierney said to Dean. "I performed the autopsies last year, on Hoyt's victims. This is his technique."

Dean shook his head in disbelief. "Two different killers? Combining techniques?"

"The Dominator and the Surgeon," said Rizzoli. "They've found each other."

# Fourteen

She sat in her car, warm air blasting from the AC vent, sweat beading on her face. Even the night's heat could not dispel the chill she still felt from the autopsy room. I must be coming down with a virus, she thought, massaging her temples. And no wonder; she had been going full throttle for days, and now it was catching up with her. Her head ached and all she wanted to do was crawl into bed and sleep for a week.

She drove straight home. Walked into her apartment and once again performed the ritual that had become such an important part of maintaining her sanity. The turning of the dead bolts, the sliding of the chain into its groove, were performed with deliberate care, and only after she completed her security checklist and had locked every lock, peered into every closet, did she finally kick off her shoes, peel off her slacks and blouse. Stripped down to her underwear, she sank onto the bed and sat massaging her temples, wondering if she still had any aspirin in the medicine cabinet yet feeling too drained to get up and look.

Her apartment intercom buzzed. She snapped straight, pulse galloping, alarms lighting up every nerve. She was not expecting visitors, nor did she want any.

The buzzer rang again, the sound like steel wool against raw nerve endings.

She rose and went into the living room to press the intercom button. "Yes?"

"It's Gabriel Dean. May I come up?"

Of all people, his was the last voice she'd expected to hear. She was so startled that for a moment she didn't respond.

"Detective Rizzoli?" he said.

"What is this about, Agent Dean?"

"The autopsy. There are issues we need to talk about."

She pressed the lock release and almost immediately wished she hadn't. She didn't trust Dean, yet she was about to let him into the safe haven of her apartment. With the careless press of a button, the decision had been made, and now she could not change her mind.

She'd barely had time to pull on a cotton bathrobe when he knocked. Through the fish-eye lens of the door's peephole his sharp features appeared distorted. Ominous. By the time she'd unfastened all the various locks, that grotesquely distorted image had solidified in her mind. Reality was far less threatening. The man who stood in her doorway had tired eyes and a face that registered the strain of having witnessed too many horrors on too little sleep.

Yet his first question was about her: "Are you holding up all right?"

She understood the implication of that question: That she was *not* all right. That she was in need of checking up on, an unstable cop about to fracture into brittle shards.

"I'm perfectly fine," she said.

"You left soon after the autopsy. Before we had the chance to talk."

"About what?"

"Warren Hoyt."

"What do you want to know about him?"

"Everything."

"I'm afraid that would take all night. And I'm tired." She tugged her bathrobe tighter, suddenly self-conscious. It had always been important to her to appear professional, and she usually slipped on a blazer before heading to a crime scene. Now she stood before Dean in nothing more than her robe and underwear, and she did not like this feeling of vulnerability.

She reached for the door, a gesture with an unmistakable message: *This conversation is over.*

He didn't budge from her doorway. "Look, I admit I made a mistake. I should have listened to you from the start. You were the one who saw it first. I didn't recognize the parallels with Hoyt."

"That's because you never knew him."

"So tell me about him. We need to work together, Jane."

Her laughter was sharp as glass. "Now you're interested in teamwork? This is new and different."

Resigned to the fact that he was not leaving, she turned and walked into the living room. He followed her, shutting the door behind him.

"Talk to me about Hoyt."

"You can read his file."

"I already have."

"Then you've got everything you need."

"Not everything."

She turned to face him. "What else is there?"

"I want to know what you know." He stepped closer, and she felt a thrill of alarm because she was at such a disadvantage, standing before him in her bare feet, too exhausted to fend off his assault. *It felt* like an assault, all these demands he was making and the way his gaze seemed to penetrate what little clothing she wore.

"There's some sort of emotional bond between you two," he said. "An attachment."

"Don't call it a fucking *attachment*."

"What would you call it?"

"He was the perp. I'm the one who cornered him. It's as simple as that."

"Not so simple, from what I've heard. Whether or not you want to admit it, there *is* an attachment between you two. He's purposefully stepped back into your life. That grave site where they left Karenna Ghent's body was not chosen at random."

She said nothing. On that point she could not disagree.

"He's a hunter, just like you are," said Dean.

"You both hunt humans. That's one bond between you. Common ground."

"There is no common ground."

"But you understand each other. No matter what your feelings are, you're linked to him. You saw his influence on the Dominator before anyone else did. You were way ahead of us."

"And you thought I needed a shrink."

"Yes. At the time, I did."

"So now I'm not crazy. I'm brilliant."

"You've got the inside track into his mind. You can help us figure out what he'll do next. What does he want?"

"How should I know?"

"You got a more intimate look at him than any other cop has."

"Intimate? Is that what you call it? That son of a bitch almost *killed* me."

"And there's nothing more intimate than murder. Is there?"

She hated him at that moment, because he had stated a truth she wanted to cringe from. He had pointed out the very thing she could not bear to acknowledge: That she and Warren Hoyt were forever bound to each other. That fear and loathing are more powerful emotions than love could ever be.

She sank onto the couch. Once, she would have fought back. Once, she'd been fierce enough to match any man word for word. But tonight, she was tired, so tired, and she did not have the strength to fend off Dean's questions.

He would continue to push and prod until he had answers, and she might as well surrender to the inevitable. Get it over with so that he would leave her alone.

She straightened and found herself staring at her hands, at the matching scars on her palms. These were only the most obvious souvenirs left by Hoyt; the other scars were not so visible: the healed fractures of her ribs and facial bones, which could still be seen on X ray. Least visible of all were the fracture lines that still split her life, like cracks left by an earthquake. In the last few weeks, she had felt those cracks begin to widen, as though the ground itself threatened to give way beneath her feet.

"I didn't realize he was still there," she whispered. "Standing right behind me in that cellar. In that house . . ."

He sat down in the chair across from her. "You're the one who found him. The only cop who knew where to look."

"Yes."

"Why?"

She gave a shrug, a laugh. "Dumb luck."

"No, it's got to be more than that."

"Don't give me credit I don't deserve."

"I don't think I've given you enough credit, Jane."

She looked up and found him staring at her with a directness that made her want to hide. But there was no place to retreat to, no defense she could mount against a gaze so piercing.

How much does he see? she wondered. Does he know how exposed he makes me feel?

"Tell me what happened in the cellar," he said.

"You know what happened. It's in my statement."

"People leave things out of statements."

"There's nothing more to tell."

"You're not even going to try?"

Anger ripped through her like shrapnel. "I don't *want* to think about it."

"Yet you can't help returning to it. Can you?"

She stared at him, wondering what game he was playing and how she'd been so easily sucked into it. She had known other men who were charismatic, men who could draw a woman's gaze so fast she'd get whiplash. Rizzoli had enough good sense to keep her distance from such men, to regard them for what they were: the genetically blessed among mere mortals. She had little use for such men, and they had little for her. But tonight, she had something Gabriel Dean needed, and he was focusing the full force of his attraction on her. And it was working. Never before had a man made her feel so confused and aroused all at once.

"He had you trapped in the cellar," said Dean.

"I walked right into it. I didn't know."

"Why didn't you?"

It was a startling question and it made her pause. She thought back to that afternoon, standing at the open cellar door, dreading the descent down those dark stairs. She remembered the suffocating heat of the house and how the sweat had soaked into her bra, her shirt. She remembered how fear had lit up every nerve in her body. Yes, she *had* known something was not right. She'd known what waited for her at the bottom of the steps.

"What went wrong, Detective?"

"The victim," she whispered.

"Catherine Cordell?"

"She was in the cellar. Tied to a cot in the cellar . . ."

"The bait."

She closed her eyes and could almost smell the scent of Cordell's blood, of damp earth. Of her own sweat, sour with fear. "I took it. I took the bait."

"He knew you would."

"I should have realized —"

"But you were focused on the victim. On Cordell."

"I wanted to save her."

"And that was your mistake."

She opened her eyes and looked at him in anger. "Mistake?"

"You didn't secure the area first. You left yourself open to attack. You committed the most basic of errors. Surprising, for someone so capable."

"You weren't there. You don't know the situation I faced."

"I read your statement."

"Cordell was lying there. Bleeding —"

"So you responded the way any normal human being would. You tried to help her."

"Yes."

"And it got you into trouble. You forgot to think like a cop."

Her look of outrage did not seem to disturb him in the least. He merely gazed back at her, his expression immobile, his face so composed, so assured, that it only served to magnify her own turmoil.

"I *never* forget to think like a cop," she said.

"In that cellar, you did. You let the victim distract you."

"My primary concern is always the victim."

"When it endangers you both? Is that logical?"

*Logical.* Yes, that was Gabriel Dean. She had never met anyone like this man, who could regard both the living and the dead with an equal absence of emotion.

"I couldn't let her die," she said. "That was my first — my only — thought."

"You knew her? Cordell?"

"Yes."

"You were friends?"

"No." Her answer was so immediate, Dean's eyebrow slanted up in a silent query. Rizzoli took a breath and said, "She was part of the Surgeon investigation. That's all."

"You didn't like her?"

Rizzoli paused, taken aback by Dean's penetrating insight. She said, "I didn't warm to her. Let's put it that way." *I was jealous of her. Of her beauty. And her effect on Thomas Moore.*

"Yet Cordell was a victim," said Dean.

"I wasn't sure *what* she was. Not at first. But toward the end, it became clear she was the Surgeon's target."

"You must have felt guilty. About doubting her."

Rizzoli said nothing.

"Is that why you needed so badly to save her?"

She stiffened, insulted by his question. "She was in danger. I didn't need any other reason."

"You took risks that weren't prudent."

"I don't think *risk* and *prudent* are words that go together in the same sentence."

"The Surgeon set the trap. You took the bait."

"Yeah, okay. It was a mistake —"

"One he knew you'd make."

"How could he possibly know that?"

"He knows a lot about you. It's that bond, again. That connection between you two."

She shot to her feet. "This is bullshit," she said, and walked out of the living room.

He followed her into the kitchen, relentlessly pursuing her with his theories, theories she didn't want to hear. The thought of any emotional link between herself and Hoyt was too repellent to consider, and she couldn't stand listening any longer. But here he was, crowding into her already claustrophobic kitchen, forcing her to hear what he had to say.

"Just as you have a direct channel into Warren Hoyt's psyche," Dean said, "he has one into yours."

"He didn't know me at the time."

"Can you be sure of that? He would have been following the investigation. Would have known you were on the team."

"And that's all he would have known about me."

"I think he understands more than you give him credit for. He feeds off women's fears. It's all written there, in his psychological profile. He's attracted to damaged women. To the emotionally battered. The whiff of a woman's pain turns him on, and he's exquisitely sensitive to its presence. He can detect it using the most subtle of clues. A woman's tone of voice. The way she holds her head or refuses eye contact. All the tiny physical signs that the rest of us might miss. But he picks up on them. He knows which women are wounded, and those are the ones he wants."

"I'm no victim."

"You are now. He made you one." He moved closer, so close they were almost touching. She felt the sudden wild urge to lean into his arms and press herself against him. To see how he would react. But pride and common sense kept her perfectly rigid.

She forced out a laugh. "Who's the victim here, Agent Dean? Not me. Don't forget, *I'm* the one who put him away."

"Yes," he answered quietly. "You put the Surgeon away. But not without a great deal of damage to yourself."

She stared back, silent. *Damaged.* That was exactly the word for what had been done to her. A woman with scars on her hands and a fortress of locks on her door. A woman who would never again feel August's hot breath without remembering the heat of that summer day and the smell of her own blood.

Without a word, she turned and walked out of the kitchen, back into the living room. There she sank on the couch and sat in dazed silence. He did not immediately follow her, and for a moment she was left blessedly alone. She wished he would simply vanish, walk out of her apartment and grant her the seclusion that every suffering animal craves. She was not so lucky. She heard him emerge from the kitchen, and she looked up to see him holding two glasses. He held one out to her.

"What's this?" she said.

"Tequila. I found it in your cupboard."

She took the glass and frowned at it. "I forgot I had it. It's ancient."

"Well, it hadn't been opened."

That's because she did not care for the taste of tequila. The bottle was just another one of those useless boozy gifts her brother Frankie brought home from his travels, like the Kahlúa liqueur from Hawaii and the sake from Japan. Frankie's way of showing off what a man of the

262

world he was, thanks to the U.S. Marine Corps. This was as good a time as any to sample his souvenir from sunny Mexico. She took a sip and blinked away the sting of tears. As the tequila warmed its way into her stomach, she suddenly thought of a detail from Warren Hoyt's past. His early victims had first been incapacitated by the drug Rohypnol, slipped into their drinks. How easy it is to catch us unguarded, she thought. When a woman is distracted or has no reason to distrust the man who hands her a drink, she is just another lamb in the chute. Even she had accepted a glass of tequila without question. Even she had allowed a man she did not know well into her apartment.

She looked at Dean again. He was sitting across from her, and their gazes were now level. The drink, tossed into her empty stomach, was already asserting itself, and her limbs felt nerveless. The anesthesia of alcohol. She was detached and calm, dangerously so.

He leaned toward her, and she did not pull away with her usual defensiveness. Dean was invading her personal space, the way few men had ever tried to do, and she let him. She surrendered to him.

"We're no longer dealing with a single killer," he said. "We're dealing with a partnership. And one of those two partners is a man you know better than anyone else does. Whether you want to admit it or not, you have a special link to

Warren Hoyt. Which makes you a link to the Dominator as well."

She released a deep breath and said, softly: "It's the way Warren works best. It's what he craves. A partner. A mentor."

"He had one in Savannah."

"Yes. A doctor named Andrew Capra. After Capra was killed, Warren was left on his own. That's when he came to Boston. But he never stopped looking for a new partner. Someone who'd share his cravings. His fantasies."

"I'm afraid he's found him."

They gazed at each other, both understanding the grim consequences of this new development.

"They're twice as effective now," he said. "Wolves work better in a pack than they do alone."

"Cooperative hunting."

He nodded. "It makes everything easier. The stalking. The cornering. Maintaining control of the victims . . ."

She sat up straight. "The teacup," she said.

"What about it?"

"There wasn't one at the Ghent death scene. Now we know why."

"Because Warren Hoyt was there to help him."

She nodded. "The Dominator had no need for a warning system. He had a partner who could alert him if the husband moved. A partner who stood by and watched the whole thing. And Warren would get off on it. He'd enjoy it. It's part of his fantasy. To watch as the woman is assaulted."

"And the Dominator craves an audience."

She nodded. "That's why he's chosen couples. So there'd be someone to watch. To see him enjoy ultimate power over a woman's body."

The ordeal she described was so intimate a violation that she found it painful to look Dean in the eyes. But she held her gaze. The sexual assault of women was a crime that awakened the prurient curiosity of too many men. As the lone woman in the room at morning investigative conferences, she had watched her male colleagues discuss the details of such assaults and had heard the electric hum of interest in their voices, even as they strove to maintain the appearance of sober professionalism. They lingered over the pathologist's reports of sexual injuries, stared too long at the crime scene photos of women with legs splayed apart. Their reactions made Rizzoli feel personally violated as well, and over the years she had developed a hair-trigger sensitivity to even a flicker of unseemly interest in a cop's eyes whenever the subject was rape. Now, looking into Dean's eyes, she searched for that disturbing flicker but saw none. Nor had she seen anything but grim determination in his eyes when he had stared down at the violated corpses of Gail Yeager and Karenna Ghent. Dean was not turned on by these atrocities; he was deeply appalled.

"You said that Hoyt craves a mentor," he said.

"Yes. Someone to lead the way. To teach him."

"Teach him what? He already knows how to kill."

She paused to take another sip of tequila. When she looked at him again, she found he had leaned even closer, as though afraid to miss her softest utterance.

"Variations on a theme," she said. "Women and pain. How many ways can you defile a body? How many ways can you inflict torture? Warren had a pattern he stuck to for several years. Maybe he's ready to expand his horizons."

"Or this unsub is ready to expand his."

She paused. "The Dominator?"

"We may have turned it around. Maybe it's our unknown subject who seeks a mentor. And he's chosen Warren Hoyt as his teacher."

She stared at him, chilled by the thought. The word *teacher* implied mastery. Authority. Was this the role into which Hoyt had transformed during his months behind prison walls? Had confinement nurtured his fantasies, honed his urges to razor-sharp purpose? He had been formidable enough before his arrest; she did not even want to think about a more powerful incarnation of Warren Hoyt.

Dean sank back in the chair, blue eyes regarding his glass of tequila. He had sipped only sparingly, and now he set the glass down on the coffee table. He'd always struck her as a man who never let his discipline weaken, who had learned to keep all impulses in check. But fatigue was taking its toll, and his shoulders were slumping, his eyes shot through with red. He rubbed his hand across his face. "How do two monsters manage to connect in a city the size of Boston?" he said. "How do they find each other?"

"And so fast?" she added. "The Ghents were attacked only two days after Warren escaped."

Dean lifted his head and looked at her. "They already knew each other."

"Or they knew *of* each other."

Certainly the Dominator would have known about Warren Hoyt. It was impossible to read a Boston newspaper last fall and be ignorant of the atrocities he had committed. Even if they had not met, Hoyt would know about the unsub as well, if only through news reports. He would have heard about the Yeagers' deaths, would have known that there existed a monster very much like him. He would wonder who this other predator might be, this brother in blood. Communication through murder, the message relayed via TV news shows and the *Boston Globe*.

*He's seen me on TV as well. Hoyt knew I was at the Yeager death scene. And now he is trying to make my reacquaintance.*

Dean's touch made her flinch. He was frowning at her, leaning even closer than before, and it seemed to her that no man had ever focused on her so intently.

*No man except the Surgeon.*

"It's not the Dominator who's playing games with me," she said. "It's Hoyt. The stakeout fiasco — it was meant to bring me down. It's the only way he can approach a woman, by bringing her down first. Demoralizing her, tearing away bits and pieces of her life. It's why he chose rape victims to kill. Women who'd already been symbolically destroyed. Before he attacks, he needs to have us weak. Afraid."

"You're the last woman I'd ever characterize as weak."

She flushed at the praise, because she knew it was not deserved. "I'm just trying to explain to you the way he works," she said. "How he stalks his prey. Incapacitates them before he moves in. He did it with Catherine Cordell. Before his final attack, he played mind games to terrify her. Sent her messages to let her know he could walk in and out of her life without her knowing he was there. Like a ghost, walking through walls. She didn't know when he'd appear next, or what direction the attack would come from. But she knew it was coming. That's how he wears you down. By letting you know that someday, when you least expect it, he'll come for you."

Despite the chilling nature of her words, she had maintained a calm voice. Unnaturally calm. Through it all, Dean watched her with quiet intensity, as though searching for a glimpse of real emotion, real weakness. She let him see none.

"Now he has a partner," she said. "Someone

he can learn from. Someone he can teach in return. A hunting team."

"You think they'll stay together."

"Warren would want to. He'd want a partner.
They've already killed together once. That's a
powerful bond, sealed in blood." She took a
final sip of her drink, draining the glass. Would
it numb her brain of nightmares tonight? Or was
she beyond the comforts of anesthesia?

"Have you requested protection?"

His question startled her. "Protection?"

"A cruiser, at the very least. To watch your
apartment."

"I'm a cop."

He tilted his head, as though waiting for the
rest of the answer.

"If I were a man," she said, "would you have
asked that question?"

"You're not a man."

"That means I automatically need protection?"

"Why do you sound so offended?"

"Why does my being a woman make me inca-
pable of defending my own home?"

He sighed. "Do you always have to outdo the
men, Detective?"

"I've worked hard to be treated like everyone
else," she said. "I'm not going to ask for special
favors because I'm a woman."

"It's *because* you're a woman that you're in
this position. The Surgeon's sexual fantasies are
about women. And the Dominator's attacks

aren't about the husbands, but about the wives. He rapes the wives. You can't tell me that your being female is irrelevant to this situation."

She flinched at the mention of rape. Up till now, the discussion of sexual assault had been about other women. That she was a potential victim brought the focus to a far more intimate level, a level she was not comfortable discussing with any man. Even more than the subject of rape, it was Dean himself who made her uneasy. The way he studied her, as though she held some secret he was eager to mine.

"It's not about you being a cop, or whether you're capable of defending yourself," he said. "It's about you being a woman. A woman Warren Hoyt has probably fantasized about all these months."

"Not me. Cordell's the one he wants."

"Cordell is out of his reach. He can't touch her. But you're right here. You're within his grasp, the very woman he almost defeated. The woman he pinned to the floor in that cellar. He had his blade at your throat. He could already smell your blood."

"Stop it, Dean."

"In a way, he's already claimed you. You're already his. And you're out in the open every day, working the very crimes he leaves behind. Every dead body's a message meant for your eyes. A preview of what he has planned for you."

"I said, *stop it*."

"And you think you don't need protection?

270

You think a gun and an attitude is all it takes to stay alive? Then you're ignoring your own gut feelings. You know what he'll do next. You know what he craves, what turns him on. And what turns him on is you. What he plans to do to *you*."

"Shut the fuck up!" Her outburst startled them both. She stared at him, dismayed by her loss of control and by the tears that sprang from nowhere. Goddamn it, goddamn it, she would not cry. She had never let a man see her crumble, and she wouldn't allow Dean to be the first.

She took a deep breath and said, quietly, "I want you to leave now."

"I'm only asking you to listen to your own instincts. To accept the same protection you'd offer any other woman."

She stood and went to the door. "Good night, Agent Dean."

For a moment he did not move, and she wondered what it would take to eject this man from her home. At last he rose to leave, but when he reached the door he stopped and looked down at her. "You're not invincible, Jane," he said. "And no one expects you to be."

Long after he'd walked out, she stood with her back pressed to the locked door, her eyes closed, trying to calm the turmoil left in the wake of his visit. She knew she was not invincible. She had learned that a year ago, when she'd looked up into the Surgeon's face and waited for the bite of his scalpel. She did not need to be reminded of that, and she resented the brutal manner in which Dean had brought home that lesson.

She crossed back to the couch and picked up the phone from the end table. It would not be dawn yet in London, but she could not delay making this call.

Moore answered on the second ring, his voice gruff but alert despite the hour.

"It's me," said Rizzoli. "Sorry to wake you."

"Let me go into the other room."

She waited. Over the phone she heard the creak of box springs as he got out of bed, then the sound of a door closing behind him.

"What's going on?" he said.

"The Surgeon's hunting again."

"There's been a victim?"

"I saw the autopsy a few hours ago. It's his work."

"He didn't waste any time."

"It gets worse, Moore."

"How could it get any worse?"

"He has a new partner."

A long pause. Then, softly: "Who is it?"

"We think it's the same unsub who killed that couple in Newton. Somehow, he and Hoyt found each other. They're hunting together."

"So quickly? How could they link up just like that?"

"They knew each other. They had to know each other."

"Where did they meet? When?"

"That's what we have to find out. It could be

key to the Dominator's identity." Suddenly she thought of the operating room from which Hoyt had escaped. *The handcuffs.* It had not been the guard who'd unlocked them. Someone else had walked into that O.R. to free Hoyt, someone disguised perhaps in an orderly's scrub suit or a doctor's borrowed lab coat.

"I should be there," said Moore. "I should be working this with you —"

"No, you shouldn't. You should be right where you are, with Catherine. I don't think Hoyt can find her. But he'll be trying. He never gives up; you know that. And now there are two of them, and we have no idea what this partner looks like. If he turns up in London, you won't know his face. You need to be ready."

As if anyone could be ready for the Surgeon's attack, she thought as she hung up. A year ago, Catherine Cordell had thought she was ready. She'd turned her home into a fortress and lived her life as though under siege. Yet Hoyt had slipped through her defenses; he had struck when she least expected it, in a place she thought was safe.

*Just as I think my home is safe.*

She rose and crossed to the window. Looking down at the street, she wondered if, at that moment, anyone was looking at *her,* watching her as she stood framed in the window's light. She would not be difficult to find. All the Surgeon had to do was look in the phone book under "RIZZOLI J."

On the street below, a vehicle slowed down and pulled over to the curb. A police cruiser. She watched it for a moment, but it did not move, and the engine lights shut off, indicating it had settled in for a stay. She had not requested protective surveillance, but she knew who had.

Gabriel Dean.

*History echoes with the screams of women.*

*The pages of textbooks pay scant attention to the lurid details that we hunger to know. Instead we are told dry accounts of military strategies and flank attacks, of the cunning of generals and the massing of armies. We see illustrations of men in armor, swords locked, muscled bodies twisting in the throes of combat. We see paintings of leaders astride noble mounts, gazing at fields where soldiers stand like rows of wheat awaiting the scythe. We see maps with arrows tracing the march of conquering armies, and read the lyrics of war ballads, sung in the name of king and country. The triumphs of men are always writ large, in the blood of soldiers.*

*No one speaks of the women.*

*But we all know they were there, soft flesh and smooth skin, their perfume wafting through history's pages. We all know, though we may not speak of it, that war's savagery is not confined to the battlefield. That when the last enemy soldier has fallen, and one army stands victorious, it is toward the conquered women that the army next turns its attentions.*

*So it has always been, though the brutal reality is*

*seldom mentioned in the history books. Instead, I read of wars that are as shiny as brass, with glory for all. Of Greeks battling under the watchful eyes of the Gods, and of the fall of Troy, which the poet Virgil tells us was a war fought by heroes: Achilles and Hector, Ajax and Odysseus, names now enshrined for eternity. He writes of clanging swords and flying arrows and blood-soaked earth.*

*He leaves out the best parts.*

*It is the playwright Euripides who tells us of the aftermath for the Trojan women, but even he is circumspect. He does not dwell on the titillating details. He tells us that a terrified Cassandra was dragged from Athena's temple by a Greek chieftain, but we are left to fantasize about what comes next. The tearing open of her robes, the baring of her skin. His thrusts between her virgin thighs. Her shrieks of pain and despair.*

*Across the fallen city of Troy, such shrieks would have echoed from other women's throats, as the victorious Greeks took what was due them, marking their victory in the flesh of conquered women. Were any men of Troy left alive to watch? The ancients do not mention it. But what better way to crow victory than to abuse the body of your enemy's beloved? What more powerful proof is there that you have defeated him, humiliated him, than to force him to watch as you take your pleasure, again and again?*

*This much I understand: triumph requires an audience.*

*I am thinking of the Trojan women as our car glides along Commonwealth Avenue, steady with the flow of traffic. It is a busy road, and even at nine P.M., cars move slowly, giving me time to leisurely study the building.*

*The windows are dark; neither Catherine Cordell nor her new husband are at home.*

*That's all I allow myself, that one look, and then the building slides out of view. I know the block is being watched, yet I could not resist that glimpse of her fortress, as impregnable as the walls of any castle. An empty castle, now, no longer of any interest to those who would storm it.*

*I look at my driver, whose face is hidden in shadow. I see only a silhouette and the gleam of eyes, like two hungry sparks in the night.*

*On the Discovery Channel, I have watched videos of lions at night, the green fire of their eyes burning in the darkness. I am reminded of those lions, of how they stared with hungry purpose, waiting for the moment to spring. I now see that hunger in the eyes of my companion.*

*The same hunger he surely sees in mine.*

*I roll down my window and inhale deeply as the warm scent of the city wafts in. The lion, sniffing the air over the savanna. Searching for the scent of prey.*

# Fifteen

They drove together in Dean's car, heading west toward the town of Shirley, forty-five miles from Boston. Dean said little during the drive, but the silence between them only seemed to magnify her awareness of his scent, his calm assurance. She scarcely gave him a glance for fear he'd see, in her eyes, the turmoil he'd inspired.

Instead, she glanced down and saw dark-blue carpet at her feet. She wondered if it was nylon six, six, #802 blue, wondered how many cars had similar carpeting. Such a popular color; it seemed that everywhere she looked now, she saw blue carpets, and imagined countless shoe soles trailing #802 nylon fibers all over the streets of Boston.

The air conditioner was too cold; she shut the vent by her knees and stared out at fields of tall grass, longing to feel the heat outside this over-cooled bubble. Outside, morning haze hung like gauze over green fields and trees stood motionless, their leaves unstirred by even the faintest breeze. Rizzoli seldom ventured into rural Massachusetts. She was a city girl, born and bred, and she felt no affinity for the countryside with its empty spaces and biting bugs. Nor did she feel its lure today.

Last night, she had not slept well. She had startled awake several times, had lain with heart pounding as she listened for footsteps, for the whisper of an intruder's breath. At five A.M. she rose from bed feeling drugged and unrested. Only after two cups of coffee had she felt alert enough to call the hospital and ask about Korsak's condition.

He was still in the ICU. Still on a ventilator.

She lowered the window a crack and warm air blew in, smelling of grass and earth. She considered the sad possibility that Korsak might never again enjoy such smells or feel the wind in his face. She tried to remember if the last words they'd exchanged were good ones, friendly ones, but she could not remember.

At Exit 36, Dean followed the signs to MCI-Shirley. Souza-Baranowski, the level-six security facility where Warren Hoyt had been housed, loomed off to their right. He parked in the visitors' lot and turned to look at her.

"You feel the need to walk out any time," he said, "just do it."

"Why are you expecting me to bail?"

"Because I know what he did to you. Anyone in your position would have problems working this case."

She saw genuine concern in his eyes, and she did not want it; it only reinforced how fragile was her courage.

"Let's just do it, okay?" she said, and shoved open her car door. Pride kept her walking with grim determination into the building. It propelled her through the security check-in at the outer control desk, where she and Dean presented their badges and handed in their weapons. As they waited for an escort, she read the Dress Code, posted in the visitor process area:

*The following items are not allowed to be worn by any visitor: Bare feet. Bathing suits or shorts. Any clothing that displays gang affiliation. Any clothing similar to that issued to an inmate or uniformed personnel. Double-layered clothing. Drawstring clothing. Easy-access clothing. Excessively baggy, loose, thick, or heavy clothing . . .*

The list was endless, proscribing everything from hair ribbons to underwire bras.

A corrections officer finally appeared, a heavyset man dressed in MCI summer blues. "Detective Rizzoli and Agent Dean? I'm Officer Curtis. Come this way."

Curtis was friendly, even jovial, as he escorted them through the first locked door and into the pedestrian trap. Rizzoli wondered if he would be so pleasant if they were not law enforcement officers, part of the same brotherhood. He told them to remove their belts, shoes, jackets, watches, and keys and to place them on the table for his examination. Rizzoli took off her

Timex and laid it down next to Dean's gleaming Omega. Then she proceeded to shrug off her blazer, just as Dean was doing. There was something uncomfortably intimate about the process. As she unbuckled her belt and pulled it out of her trouser loops, she felt Curtis staring at her, the way a man watches a woman undress. She took off her low-heeled pumps, set them down beside Dean's shoes, and coolly met Officer Curtis's gaze. Only then did he avert his eyes. Next, she turned her pockets inside out and followed Dean through the metal detector.

"Hey, lucky you," said Curtis as she stepped through. "You just missed being the patdown search of the day."

"What?"

"Every day, our shift commander sets a random number for which visitor gets patted down. You just missed it. Next person who comes through's gonna be it."

Rizzoli said, dryly, "Getting felt up would've been the highlight of my day."

"You can put everything back on now. And you two get to keep your watches on."

"You say that like it's a privilege."

"Only attorneys and officers of the law can wear watches beyond this point. Everyone else has to check in all their jewelry. Now I gotta stamp your left wrists, and you can go into the pods."

"We have an appointment to see Superintendent Oxton at nine," said Dean.

"He's running behind schedule. Asked me to take you to see the prisoner's cell first. Then I'll bring you over to Oxton's office."

Souza-Baranowski Correctional Center was MCI's newest facility, with a state-of-the-art keyless security system operated by forty-two graphic-interfaced computer terminals, Officer Curtis explained. He pointed out numerous surveillance cameras.

"They're recording live twenty-four hours a day. Most visitors never even see a live guard. They just hear the intercom telling them what to do next."

As they walked through a steel door, down a long hallway, and through another series of barred gates, Rizzoli was fully aware that every move she made was being monitored. With just a few taps on a computer keyboard, guards could lock down every passage, every cell, without leaving their control room.

At the entrance to Cell Block C, a voice on the intercom instructed them to hold up their passes against the window for inspection. They restated their names, and Officer Curtis said: "Two visitors here to inspect Prisoner Hoyt's cell."

The steel gate slid open and they entered Cell Block C's day-room, the common area for prisoners. It was painted a depressing shade of hospital green. Rizzoli saw a wall-mounted TV set, couch and chairs, and a Ping-Pong table where two men were clacking a ball back and forth. All the furniture was bolted down. A dozen men dressed in prisoners' blue denim simultaneously turned and stared.

In particular, they stared at Rizzoli, the only woman in the room.

The two men playing Ping-Pong abruptly halted their game. For a moment, the only sound was the TV, tuned to CNN. She gazed straight back at the prisoners, refusing to be intimidated, even though she could guess what each man was surely thinking. Imagining. She did not notice that Dean had moved closer until she felt his arm brush hers and she realized he was standing right beside her.

A voice from the intercom said: "Visitors, you may proceed to Cell C-8."

"It's this way," said Officer Curtis. "Up one level."

They ascended the stairway their shoes setting off clangs against the metal steps. From the upper gallery, which led past individual cells, they could look down into the well of the day-room. Curtis led them along the walkway until he came to #8.

"This is the one. Prisoner Hoyt's cell."

Rizzoli stood at the threshold and stared into the cage. She saw nothing that distinguished this cell from any other — no photographs, no personal possessions that told her Warren Hoyt had once inhabited this space — yet her scalp crawled. Though he was gone, his presence had imprinted the very air. If it was possible for malevolence to linger, then surely this place was now contaminated.

"You can step in if you want," said Curtis.

She entered the cell. She saw three bare walls, a sleeping platform and mattress, a sink, and a toilet. A stark cube. This was how Warren would have liked it. He was a neat man, a precise man, who had once worked in the sterile world of a medical laboratory, a world where the only splashes of color came from the tubes of blood he handled every day. He did not need to surround himself with lurid images; the ones he carried in his mind were horrifying enough.

"This cell hasn't been reassigned?" said Dean.

"Not yet, sir."

"And no other prisoner's been in here since Hoyt left?"

"That's right."

Rizzoli went to the mattress and lifted up one corner. Dean grasped the other corner, and together they hoisted up the mattress and looked beneath it. They found nothing. They rolled the mattress completely over, then searched the ticking for any tears in the fabric, any hiding places where he might have stashed contraband. They found only a small rip on the side barely an inch long. Rizzoli probed it with her finger and found nothing inside.

She straightened and scanned the cell, taking in the same surroundings that Hoyt had once stared at. Imagined him lying on that mattress, eyes focused on the bare ceiling as he spun fantasies that would appall any normal human being. But Hoyt would be excited by them. He would lie sweating, aroused by the shrieks of women echoing in his head.

She turned to Officer Curtis. "Where are his possessions? His personal items? Correspondence?"

"In the superintendent's office. We'll go there next."

"Right after you called this morning, I had the prisoner's belongings brought up here for your inspection," said Superintendent Oxton, gesturing to a large cardboard box on his desk. "We've already gone through it all. We found absolutely no contraband." He emphasized this last point as though it absolved him of all responsibility for what had gone wrong. Oxton struck Rizzoli as a man who did not tolerate infractions, who'd be ruthless at enforcing rules and regulations. He would certainly ferret out all contraband, isolate all troublemakers, demand that lights-out was on the dot every night. Just a glance around his office, with photos showing a fierce-looking young Oxton in an army uniform, told her this was the domain of someone who needed to be in control. Yet for all his efforts, a prisoner had escaped, and Oxton was now on the defensive. He had greeted them with a stiff handshake and barely a smile in his remote blue eyes.

He opened the box and removed a large

Ziploc bag, which he handed to Rizzoli. "The prisoner's toiletries," he said. "The usual personal care items."

Rizzoli saw a toothbrush, comb, washcloth, and soap. Vaseline Intensive Care Lotion. She quickly set the bag down, repulsed by the thought that Hoyt had used these items every day to groom himself. She could see light-brown hairs still clinging to the comb's teeth.

Oxton continued removing items from the box. Underwear. A stack of *National Geographic* magazines and several issues of the *Boston Globe*. Two Snickers bars, a pad of yellow legal paper, white envelopes, and three plastic rollerball pens. "And his correspondence," said Oxton as he removed another Ziploc bag, this one containing a bundle of letters.

"We've gone through every piece of his mail," Oxton said. "The State Police have the names and addresses of all these correspondents." He handed the bundle to Dean. "Of course, this is only the mail he kept. There was probably a certain amount he threw out."

Dean opened the Ziploc bag and removed the contents. There were about a dozen letters, still in their envelopes.

"Does MCI censor prisoner mail?" Dean asked. "Do you screen it before you give it to them?"

"We have the authority to do so. Depending on the type of mail."

"Type?"

"If it's classified privileged, the guards are only allowed to glance inside for contraband. But they're not allowed to read it. The correspondence is private, between sender and prisoner."

"So you'd have no idea what was written to him."

"If it's privileged mail."

"What's the difference between privileged and unprivileged mail?" asked Rizzoli.

Oxton responded to her interruption with a glint of annoyance in his eyes. "Nonprivileged mail is from friends and family or the general public. For instance, a number of our inmates have picked up pen pals from the outside who think they're performing a charitable service."

"By corresponding with murderers? Are they crazy?"

"Many of them are naive and lonely women. Susceptible to being used by a con artist. Those types of letters are nonprivileged and the guards have the authority to read and censor them. But we don't always have time to read them all. We deal with a large volume of mail here. In Prisoner Hoyt's case, there was a lot of mail to inspect."

"From whom? I'm not aware he had much family," said Dean.

"He got a lot of publicity last year. It caught the interest of the public. They all wanted to write to him."

Rizzoli was appalled. "Are you saying he got *fan* mail?"

"Yes."

"Jesus. People are nuts."

"The public gets a thrill from talking to a killer. Something about being in touch with fame. Manson and Dahmer and Gacy, they all got fan mail. Our prisoners get marriage proposals. Women send them cash, or photos of themselves in bikinis. Men write wanting to know what it feels like to commit murder. The world is full of sick fucks, pardon my French, who get a charge out of knowing a real live killer."

But one of them had gone beyond just writing to Hoyt. One had actually joined Hoyt's exclusive club. She stared at the bundle of mail, enraged by this tangible evidence of the Surgeon's fame. Killer as rock star. She thought of the scars he had carved in her hands, and each of the fan letters was like another stab of his scalpel.

"What about privileged mail?" said Dean. "You said it's not read or censored. What classifies a letter as privileged?"

"It's confidential mail that comes from certain state or federal officials. An officer of the court, for instance, or the attorney general. Mail from the president, the governor, or law enforcement agencies."

"Did Hoyt receive such mail?"

"He may have. We don't keep records of every item of mail that comes in."

"How do you know when a letter's really privileged?" said Rizzoli.

Oxton looked at her with impatience. "I just told you. If it's from a federal or state official —"

"No. I mean, how do you know it's not fake or stolen stationery? I could write escape plans to one of your prisoners and mail it in an envelope from, say, Senator Conway's office." The example she'd chosen had not been random. She watched Dean and saw his chin snap up at the mention of Conway's name.

Oxton hesitated. "It's not impossible. But there are penalties —"

"So it's happened before."

Reluctantly, Oxton nodded. "There've been several cases. Criminal information's been sent under the guise of official business. We try to stay alert to it, but occasionally something slips through."

"And what about outgoing mail? The letters Hoyt sent? Did you screen those?"

"No."

"None of it?"

"We had no reason to. He was never considered a problem inmate. He was always cooperative. Very quiet and polite."

"A model prisoner," said Rizzoli. "Right."

Oxton fixed her with an icy glare. "We have men in here who'd rip your arms off and laugh about it, Detective. Men who'd snap a guard's neck just because a meal didn't suit them. A prisoner like Hoyt was not high on our list of concerns."

Dean calmly redirected the conversation back

to the issue at hand. "So we don't know who he may have written to?"

That matter-of-fact question seemed to douse the warden's rising irritation. Oxton turned from Rizzoli and focused instead on Dean, one man to another. "No, we don't," he said. "Prisoner Hoyt could have written to anyone."

In a conference room down the hall from Oxton's office, Rizzoli and Dean pulled on latex gloves and spread the envelopes addressed to Warren Hoyt on the table. She saw a variety of stationery, a few pastels and florals, and one imprinted with *Jesus saves*. Most absurd of all was the stationery decorated with images of frolicking kittens. Yes, just the thing to send to the Surgeon. How amused he must have been to receive that.

She opened the envelope with the kittens and found a photo inside, of a smiling woman with hopeful eyes. Also enclosed was a letter, written in a girlish hand, the *i*'s dotted with cheery little circles:

*To: Mr. Warren Hoyt, Prisoner*
*Massachusetts Correctional Institute*
*Dear Mr. Hoyt,*
*I saw you on TV today, as they were walking you to the courthouse. I believe I am an excellent judge of character, and when I looked at your face, I could see so much sadness and pain. Oh, such a great deal of pain! There is goodness in*

*you; I know there is. If only you had someone to help you find it within yourself . . .*

Rizzoli suddenly realized she was clenching the letter in rage. She wanted to reach out and shake the stupid woman who had written those words. Wanted to force the woman to look at the autopsy photos of Hoyt's victims, to read the M.E.'s account of the agony they had suffered before death mercifully ended their ordeals. She had to make herself read the rest of the letter, a saccharine appeal to Hoyt's humanity and the "goodness that's inside us all."

She reached for the next envelope. No kittens on this stationery, just a plain white envelope containing a letter written on lined paper. Once again, it was from a woman who had enclosed her photo, an overexposed snapshot of a squinting bleached blonde.

*Dear Mr Hoit,*
*Can I have you're autograph? I have collect many signitures from people like you. I even have Jeffry Dahmer's. If you like to keep writing to me, that would be cool. Your friend, Gloria.*

Rizzoli stared at words she could not believe any sane human being would write. *That would be cool. Your friend.* "Jesus Christ," she said. "These people are nuts."

"It's the lure of fame," said Dean. "They have no lives of their own. They feel worthless, nameless. So they try to get close to someone who does have a name. They want the magic to rub off on them, too."

"Magic?" She looked at Dean. "Is that what you call it?"

"You know what I mean."

"No, I don't get any of it. I don't get why women write to monsters. Are they looking for romance? A hot time with a guy who'd turn around and gut them? Is that supposed to bring excitement into their pathetic lives?" She shoved back her chair, stood up, and paced over to the wall of slit-shaped windows. There she stood with arms tightly crossed, staring out at a narrow strip of sunlight, a blue bar of sky. Any view, even this meager one, was preferable to gazing at Warren Hoyt's fan mail. Surely Hoyt had enjoyed the attention. He would have considered each letter fresh proof that he still held power over women, that even here, locked away, he could twist minds, manipulate them. Turn them into his possessions.

"It's a waste of time," she said bitterly as she watched a bird flit past buildings where men were the ones in cages, where bars held monsters, not birdsong. "He isn't stupid. He would have destroyed anything linking him to the Dominator. He'd protect his new partner. He certainly wouldn't leave behind anything useful for us to track."

"Maybe not useful," said Dean, rustling papers behind her. "But definitely illuminating."

"Oh yeah. Like I want to read what these nutty women have written to him? It makes me sick."

"Could that be the point?"

She turned and looked at him. A bar of light through the slit window slashed down his face, illuminating one bright blue eye. She had always thought his features striking, but never more so than at that moment, facing him across the table. "What do you mean?"

"It upsets you, reading his fan mail."

"It ticks me off. Isn't that obvious?"

"To him, as well." Dean nodded to the stack of letters. "He knew it would upset you."

"You think this is all to screw around with my head? These letters?"

"It's a mind game, Jane. He left these behind for you. This nice collection of mail from his most ardent admirers. He knew that eventually you'd be right here, where you are now, reading what they had to say to him. Maybe he wanted to show you that he *does* have admirers. That even though you despise him, there are women who don't, women who are drawn to him. He's like a spurned lover, trying to make you jealous. Trying to throw you off balance."

"Don't mind-fuck me."

"And it's working, isn't it? Look at you. He's got you wound up so tight you can't even sit still. He knows how to manipulate you, how to mess around with your head."

"You're giving him too much credit."

"Am I?"

She waved at the letters. "This is all supposed to be for my benefit? What, I'm the center of his universe?"

"Isn't he the center of yours?" Dean said quietly.

She stared at him, unable to come up with a retort because what he had said struck her, at that instant, as the unassailable truth. Warren Hoyt *was* the center of her universe. He reigned as dark lord over her nightmares and dominated her waking hours as well, always poised to step out of his closet, back into her thoughts. In that cellar, she had been marked as his, the way every victim is marked by an assailant, and she could not obliterate his stamp of ownership. It was carved into her hands, seared into her soul.

She returned to the table and sat down. Steeled herself for the remainder of the task.

The next envelope had a typed return address: *Dr. J. P. O'Donnell, 1634 Brattle Street, Cambridge, MA 02138*. Near Harvard University, Brattle Street was a neighborhood of fine homes and the educated elite, where university professors and retired industrialists jogged the same sidewalks and waved to each other across manicured hedges. It was not the sort of neighborhood where one expected to find a monster's acolyte.

She unfolded the letter inside. It was dated six weeks ago.

*Dear Warren,*

*Thank you for your last letter, and for signing the two release forms. The details you've provided go a long way toward helping me understand the difficulties you've faced. I have so many other questions to ask you, and I'm glad you're still willing to meet with me as planned. If you have no objections, I would like to videotape the interview. You know, of course, that your help is absolutely essential to my project.*

*Sincerely, Dr. O'Donnell*

"Who on earth is J. P. O'Donnell?" Rizzoli said.

Dean glanced up in surprise. "Joyce O'Donnell?"

"The envelope just says Dr. J. P. O'Donnell. Cambridge, Mass. She's been interviewing Hoyt."

He frowned at the envelope. "I didn't know she'd moved to Boston."

"You know her?"

"She's a neuropsychiatrist. Let's just say we met under hostile circumstances, across the aisle of a courtroom. Defense attorneys love her."

"Don't tell me. An expert witness. She goes to bat for the bad guys."

He nodded. "No matter what your client's

done, how many people he's killed, O'Donnell is happy to provide mitigating testimony."

"I wonder why she's writing to Hoyt." She re-read the letter. It had been written with the utmost respect, praising him for his cooperation. Already she disliked Dr. O'Donnell.

The next envelope in the stack was also from O'Donnell, but it did not contain a letter. Instead she pulled out three Polaroids — strictly amateurish snapshots. Two of them had been taken outdoors in daylight; the third was an indoor scene. For a moment she just stared, the hairs on the back of her neck standing straight up, her eyes registering what her brain refused to accept. She jerked back, and the photos dropped from her hands like hot coals.

"Jane? What is it?"

"It's me," she whispered.

"What?"

"She's been following me. Taking photos of me. She sent them to *him*."

Dean rose from his chair and circled to her side of the table to look over her shoulder. "I don't see you here —"

"Look. *Look*." She pointed to the photo of a dark-green Honda parked on the street. "It's mine."

"You can't see the license number."

"I can recognize my own car!"

Dean flipped over the Polaroid. On the back, someone had drawn an absurd smiley face and had written in blue felt-tip ink: *My car.*

Fear beat its drum in her chest. "Look at the next one," she said.

He picked up the second photo. This one, too, had been taken in daylight, and it showed the facade of a building. He didn't need to be told which building it was; last night he had been inside it. He turned over the photo and saw the words: *My home.* Beneath the words was another smiley face.

Dean picked up the third photo, which had been taken inside a restaurant.

At first glance, it appeared to be just a poorly composed image of patrons seated at dining tables, a waitress blurred in action as she crossed the room carrying a coffeepot. It had taken Rizzoli a few seconds to zero in on the figure seated just to the left of center, a woman with dark hair, her face seen only in profile, her features obscured against the glare of the window. She waited for Dean to recognize who the woman was.

He asked softly: "Do you know where this was taken?"

"The Starfish Cafe."

"When?"

"I don't know —"

"Is it a place you visit often?"

"On Sundays. For breakfast. It's the one day of the week when I . . ." Her voice faded. She stared at the photo of her own profile, the shoulders relaxed, face tilted downward, gazing at an open newspaper. It would have been a Sunday paper. Sunday was when she treated herself to breakfast at the Starfish. A morning of French toast and bacon and the comics.

And a stalker. She'd never known someone was watching her. Taking photos of her. Sending them to the very man who pursued her in her nightmares.

Dean flipped over the Polaroid.

On the back was drawn yet another smiley face. And beneath it, enclosed in a heart, was a single word:

*Me.*

# Sixteen

*My car. My home. Me.*

Rizzoli rode back to Boston with her stomach knotted in anger. Although Dean sat right beside her, she didn't look at him; she was too focused on nursing her rage, on feeling its flames consume her.

Her rage only deepened when Dean pulled up in front of O'Donnell's address on Brattle Street. Rizzoli stared at the large Colonial, the clapboards painted a pristine white, accented by slate-gray shutters. A wrought-iron fence enclosed a front yard with a manicured lawn and a pathway of granite pavers. Even by the upscale standards of Brattle Street, this was a handsome house that a public servant could never dream of owning. Yet *it's the public servants like me who face down the Warren Hoyts of the world and who suffer the aftershocks of those battles,* she thought. She was the one who bolted her doors and windows at night, who jerked awake to the echo of phantom footsteps moving toward her bed. She fought the monsters and suffered the consequences, while here, in this grand house, lived a woman who offered those same monsters a sympathetic ear, who walked into courts of law and defended the indefensible. It was a house built on the bones of victims.

The ash-blond woman who answered the door was as meticulously groomed as her residence, her hair a gleaming helmet, her Brooks Brothers shirt and slacks crisply pressed. She was about forty, with a face as creamy as alabaster. Like real alabaster, that face revealed no warmth. The eyes projected only chilly intellect.

"Dr. O'Donnell? I'm Detective Jane Rizzoli. And this is Agent Gabriel Dean."

The woman's eyes locked on Dean's. "Agent Dean and I have met."

And obviously made an impression on each other — not a favorable one, thought Rizzoli.

Clearly not pleased about the visit, O'Donnell was mechanical and unsmiling as she ushered them through the large foyer and into a formal sitting room. The couch was white silk on a rosewood frame, and Oriental carpets in rich shades of red accented the teak floors. Rizzoli knew little about art, but even she recognized that the paintings hanging on the walls were originals, and probably quite valuable. More bones of victims, she thought. She and Dean sat on the couch, facing O'Donnell. No coffee or tea or even water had been offered to them, a not-so-subtle clue that their hostess wanted this to be a brief conversation.

O'Donnell got right to the point and addressed Rizzoli. "You said this was about Warren Hoyt."

"You've corresponded with him."

"Yes. Is there a problem with that?"

"What was the nature of that correspondence?"

"Since you know about it, I assume you've read it."

"What was the nature of that correspondence?" Rizzoli repeated, her tone unyielding.

O'Donnell stared at her a moment, silently gauging the opposition. By now she understood Rizzoli *was* the opposition, and she responded accordingly, her posture stiffening into a suit of armor.

"First I should ask you a question, Detective," countered O'Donnell. "Why is my correspondence with Mr. Hoyt of any concern to the police?"

"You know that he's escaped custody?"

"Yes. I saw it on the news, of course. And then, the State Police contacted me to ask if he had tried to reach me. They contacted everyone who corresponded with Warren."

*Warren.* They were on a first-name basis.

Rizzoli opened the large manila envelope she'd brought with her and removed the three Polaroids, encased in Ziploc bags. These she handed to Dr. O'Donnell. "Did you send these photos to Mr. Hoyt?"

O'Donnell merely glanced at the images. "No. Why?"

"You hardly looked at them."

"I don't need to. I never sent Mr. Hoyt any photos of any kind."

"These were found in his cell. In an envelope with your return address."

"Then he must have used my envelope to store them." She handed the Polaroids back to Rizzoli.

"What, exactly, did you send him?"

"Letters. Release forms for him to sign and return."

"Release forms for what?"

"His school records. Pediatric records. Any information that might help me evaluate his history."

"How many times did you write him?"

"I believe it was four or five times."

"And he responded?"

"Yes. I have his letters on file. You can have copies."

"Has he tried to reach you since his escape?"

"Don't you think I would tell the authorities if he had?"

"I don't know, Dr. O'Donnell. I don't know the nature of your relationship with Mr. Hoyt."

"It was a correspondence. Not a relationship."

"Yet you wrote him. Four or five times."

"I visited him, as well. The interview's on videotape, if you'd like to have it."

"Why did you talk to him?"

"He has a story to tell. Lessons to teach us."

"Like how to butcher women?" The words were out of Rizzoli's mouth before she could think about it, a dart of bitter emotion that failed to pierce the other woman's armor.

Unruffled, O'Donnell replied: "As law enforcement, you see only the end result. The brutality the violence. Terrible crimes that are the natural consequence of what these men have experienced."

"And what do you see?"

"What came before, in their lives."

"Now you're going to tell me it's all due to their unhappy childhoods."

"Do you know anything about Warren's childhood?"

Rizzoli could feel her blood pressure rising. She had no desire to talk about the roots of Hoyt's obsessions. "His victims don't give a damn about his childhood. And neither do I."

"But do you know about it?"

"I'm told it was perfectly normal. I know he had a better childhood than a lot of men who don't cut up women."

"Normal." O'Donnell seemed to find this word amusing. She looked at Dean for the first time since they'd all sat down. "Agent Dean, why don't you give us your definition of normal?"

A look passed between them, hostile echoes of an old battle not fully resolved. But whatever emotions Dean was now feeling did not register in his voice. He said, calmly: "Detective Rizzoli is asking the questions. I suggest you answer them, Doctor."

That he had not already wrestled away control of the interview surprised Rizzoli. Dean struck her as a man accustomed to taking control, yet in this he had ceded to her and had chosen instead the role of observer.

She had allowed her anger to scattershoot the conversation. Now it was time to reclaim command, and for that she would need to keep her anger in check. To proceed calmly and methodically.

She asked, "When did you start writing to each other?"

O'Donnell responded, just as businesslike: "About three months ago."

"And why did you decide to write him?"

"Wait a minute." O'Donnell gave a startled laugh. "You have it wrong. I didn't initiate this correspondence."

"Are you saying Hoyt did?"

"Yes. He wrote me first. He said he'd heard of my work on the neurology of violence. He knew I'd been a defense witness in other trials."

"He wanted to hire you?"

"No. He knew there was no chance his sentence could be altered. Not at this late date. But he thought I'd be interested in his case. I was."

"Why?"

"Are you asking why was I interested?"

"Why would you waste any time writing to someone like Hoyt?"

"He's exactly the sort of person I want to know more about."

"He's been seen by half a dozen shrinks. There's nothing wrong with him. He's perfectly normal, except for the fact he likes to kill women. He likes to tie them down and slice open their abdomens. It turns him on to play surgeon. Except he does it while they're wide awake. While they know exactly what he's doing to them."

"Yet you called him normal."

"He's not insane. He knew what he was doing, and he enjoyed it."

"So you believe he was simply born evil."

"That's exactly the word I'd use for him," said Rizzoli.

O'Donnell regarded her for a moment with a gaze that seemed to bore straight into her. How much did she see? Did her psychiatric training enable her to peer through one's public mask, to see the traumatized flesh below?

Abruptly O'Donnell rose to her feet. "Why don't you come into my office?" she said. "There's something you should see."

Rizzoli and Dean followed her down a hallway, shoes muffled by the wine-red carpet running the length of the corridor. The room she led them into was a stark contrast to the richly decorated sitting room. O'Donnell's office was devoted strictly to business: white walls, bookshelves lined with reference texts, and standard metal filing cabinets. Walking into this room, thought Rizzoli, would snap one instantly into work mode. And it seemed to have precisely that effect on O'Donnell. With grim purpose, she crossed to her desk, snatched up an X-ray envelope, and carried it to a viewing box mounted on the wall. She thrust a film into the clips and flipped a switch.

The viewing box flickered on, backlighting an image of a human skull.

"Frontal view," said O'Donnell. "A twenty-eight-year-old white male construction worker. He was a law-abiding citizen described as considerate, a good husband. A loving father to his six-year-old daughter. Then he was hurt at a work site when a beam swung into his head." She looked at her two visitors. "Agent Dean probably sees it already. How about you, Detective?"

Rizzoli moved closer to the light box. She did not often study X rays, and she could only focus on the broader picture: the dome of the cranium, the twin hollows of the eye sockets, the picket fence of teeth.

"I'll put up the lateral view," said O'Donnell, and she slid a second X ray onto the box. "Do you see it now?"

The second film showed the skull in profile. Rizzoli could now see a fine web of fracture lines radiating backward from the front of the cranium. She pointed to them.

O'Donnell nodded. "He was unconscious when they brought him into the E.R. A CT scan showed hemorrhaging, with a large subdural hematoma — a collection of blood — pressing on the frontal lobes of his brain. The blood was surgically drained, and he went on to recover. Or rather, he appeared to recover. He went home and eventually returned to work. But he was not the same man. Again and again, he lost his temper on the job and was fired. He began to sexually molest his daughter. Then, after an argument with his wife, he beat her so brutally her corpse was unrecognizable. He started pounding and he couldn't stop. Even after he'd shattered most of her teeth. Even when her face was reduced to nothing but pulp and bone fragments."

"You're going to tell me it can all be blamed on *that?*" said Rizzoli, pointing to the fractured skull.

"Yes."

"Give me a break."

"Look at that film, Detective. See where the fracture is located? Consider which part of the brain lies right beneath it." She turned and looked at Dean.

He met her gaze without expression. "The frontal lobes," he said.

A faint smile twitched on O'Donnell's lips. Clearly she enjoyed the chance to challenge an old rival.

Rizzoli said, "What's the point of this X ray?"

"I was called in by the man's defense attorney to perform a neuropsychiatric evaluation. I used what we call the Wisconsin Card Sort Test and a Category Test from the Halstead-Reitan Battery. I also ordered an MRI — magnetic resonance imaging — scan of his brain. All of them pointed to the same conclusion: This man suffered severe damage to both his frontal lobes."

"Yet you said he fully recovered from the injury."

"He *appeared* to recover."

"Was he brain-damaged or wasn't he?"

"Even with extensive damage to the frontal lobes, you can still walk and talk and perform daily functions. You could have a conversation with someone who's had a frontal lobotomy and you might not detect anything wrong. But he is most certainly damaged." She pointed to the X ray. "What this man has is called frontal disinhibition syndrome. The frontal lobes affect our foresight and judgment. Our ability to control inappropriate impulses. If they're damaged, you become socially disinhibited. You display inappropriate behavior, without any feelings of guilt or emotional pain. You lose the ability to control your violent impulses. And we all have them, those moments of rage, when we want to strike back. Ram our car into someone who's cut us off in traffic. I'm sure you know what it feels like, Detective. To be so angry you want to hurt someone."

Rizzoli said nothing, silenced by the truth of O'Donnell's words.

"Society thinks of violent acts as manifestations of evil or immorality. We're told we have ultimate control over our own behavior, that each and every one of us has the free will to choose *not* to hurt another human being. But it's not just morality that guides us. Biology does as well. Our frontal lobes help us integrate thoughts and actions. They help us weigh the consequences of those actions. Without such control, we'd give in to every wild impulse. That's what happened to this man. He lost the ability to control his behavior. He had sexual feelings toward his daughter, so he molested her. His wife made him angry, so he beat her to death. From time to time, we all have disturbing or inappropriate thoughts, however fleeting. We see an attractive stranger, and sex flashes into our heads. That's all it is — just a brief thought. But what if we gave in to the impulse? What if we couldn't stop ourselves? That sexual impulse could lead to rape. Or worse."

"And that was his defense? 'My brain made me do it'?"

Annoyance sparked in O'Donnell's eyes. "Frontal disinhibition syndrome is an accepted diagnosis among neurologists."

"Yeah, but did it work in court?"

A cold pause. "Our legal system is still working with a nineteenth-century definition of insanity. Is it any wonder the courts are ignorant of neurology as well? This man is now on death row in Oklahoma." Grimly O'Donnell jerked the films from the light box and slid them into the envelope.

"What does this have to do with Warren Hoyt?"

O'Donnell crossed to her desk, picked up another X-ray envelope and withdrew a new pair of films, which she clipped onto the light box. It was another set of skull films, a frontal and lateral view, but smaller. A child's skull.

"This boy fell while climbing a fence," said O'Donnell. "He landed facedown, hitting his head on pavement. Look here, on this frontal view. You can see a tiny crack, running upward about the level of his left eyebrow. A fracture."

"I see it," said Rizzoli.

"Look at the patient's name."

Rizzoli focused on the small square at the edge of the film, containing identifying data. What she saw made her go very still.

"He was ten years old at the time of the injury," said O'Donnell. "A normal, active boy growing up in a wealthy Houston suburb. At least, that's what his pediatric records indicate, and what his elementary school reported. A healthy child, above-average intelligence. Played well with others."

"Until he grew up and started killing them."

"Yes, but *why* did Warren start killing?" O'Donnell pointed to the films. "This injury could be a factor."

"Hey, I fell off a jungle gym when I was seven. Whacked my head against one of the bars. I'm not out there slicing people."

"Yet you do hunt humans. Just as he does. You are, in fact, a professional hunter."

Rage blasted Rizzoli's face with heat. "How can you compare me to him?"

"I'm not, Detective. But consider what you're feeling right now. You'd probably like to slap me, wouldn't you? So what's stopping you? What is it that holds you back? Is it morality? Good manners? Or is it just cool logic, informing you that there'll be consequences? The certainty that you'll be arrested? All these considerations together keep you from assaulting me. And it's in your frontal lobes where this mental processing takes place. Thanks to those intact neurons, you're able to control your destructive impulses." O'Donnell paused. And added with a knowing look, "Most of the time."

Those last words, aimed like a spear, found their mark. It was a tender point of vulnerability. Only a year ago, during the Surgeon investigation, Rizzoli had made a terrible mistake that would forever shame her. In the heat of a chase, she had shot and killed an unarmed man. She stared back at O'Donnell and saw the glint of satisfaction in the other woman's eyes.

Dean broke the silence. "You told us Hoyt was the one who contacted you. What was he hoping to gain by all this? Attention? Sympathy?"

"How about plain human understanding?" said O'Donnell.

"Is that all he asked from you?"

"Warren is struggling for answers. He doesn't know what drives him to kill. He does know he's different. And he wants to know why."

"He actually told you this?"

O'Donnell went to her desk and picked up a

file folder. "I have his letters here. And the videotape of our interview."

"You went to Souza-Baranowski?"

"Yes."

"At whose suggestion?"

O'Donnell hesitated. "We both thought it would be helpful."

"But who actually brought up the idea of a meeting?"

It was Rizzoli who answered the question for O'Donnell. "He did. Didn't he? Hoyt asked for the meeting."

"It may have been his suggestion. But we both wanted to do it."

"You don't have the faintest idea why he really asked you there," said Rizzoli. "Do you?"

"We had to meet. I can't evaluate a patient without seeing him face-to-face."

"And while you were sitting there, face-to-face, what do you suppose he was thinking?"

O'Donnell's expression was dismissive. "You would know?"

"Oh yeah. I know exactly what goes on in the Surgeon's head." Rizzoli had found her voice again, and the words came out cold and relentless. "He asked you to come because he wanted to scope you out. He does that with women. Smiles at us, talks nicely to us. It's in his school records, isn't it? 'Polite young man,' the teachers said. I bet he was polite when you met him, wasn't he?"

"Yes, he was —"

"Just an ordinary, cooperative guy."

"Detective, I'm not so naive as to think he's a normal man. But he was cooperative. And he was troubled by his actions. He wants to understand the reasons for his behavior."

"So you told him it was because of that bonk on the head."

"I told him the head injury was a contributing factor."

"He must have been happy to hear that. To have an excuse for what he did."

"I gave him my honest opinion."

"You know what else made him happy?"

"What?"

"Being in the same room with you. You did sit in the same room, didn't you?"

"We met in the interview room. There was continuous video surveillance."

"But there was no barrier between you. No protective window. No Plexiglas."

"He never threatened me."

"He could lean right up to you. Study your hair, smell your skin. He particularly likes to smell a woman's scent. It turns him on. What really arouses him is the smell of fear. Dogs can smell fear, did you know that? When we get scared, we release hormones that animals can detect. Warren Hoyt can smell it, too. He's like any other creature who hunts. He picks up the scent of fear, of vulnerability. It feeds his fantasies. And I can imagine what his fantasies were when he sat in that room with you. I've seen what those fantasies lead to."

O'Donnell tried to laugh but couldn't quite pull it off. "If you're trying to scare me —"

"You have a long neck, Dr. O'Donnell. I guess some would call it a swan neck. He would have noticed that. Didn't you catch him, just once, staring at your throat?"

"Oh, *please*."

"Didn't his eyes sort of glance down, every so often? Maybe you thought he was looking at your breasts, the way other men do. But not Warren. He doesn't seem to care much about breasts. It's throats he's attracted to. He thinks of a woman's throat as dessert. The part he can't wait to slice into. After he finishes with another part of her anatomy."

Flushing, O'Donnell turned to Dean. "Your partner's way out of line here."

"No," said Dean quietly. "I think Detective Rizzoli's right on target."

"This is sheer intimidation."

Rizzoli laughed. "You were in a room with Warren Hoyt. And you didn't feel intimidated then?"

O'Donnell fixed her with a cold stare. "It was a clinical interview."

"You thought it was. But he considered it something else." Rizzoli moved toward her, a move of quiet aggression that was not lost on O'Donnell. Though O'Donnell was taller and more imposing in both stature and status, she could not match Rizzoli's unrelenting fierceness, and she flushed even deeper as Rizzoli's words continued to pummel her.

"He was polite, you said. Cooperative. Well, of course. He had exactly what he wanted: a woman in the room with him. A woman sitting close enough to get him excited. He hides it, though; he's good at that. Good at holding a perfectly normal conversation, even as he's thinking about cutting your throat."

"You are out of control," said O'Donnell.

"You think I'm just trying to scare you?"

"Isn't it obvious?"

"Here's something that should really scare the shit out of you. Warren Hoyt got a good whiff of you. He's been turned on by you. Now he's out, and he's hunting again. And guess what? He never forgets a woman's scent."

O'Donnell stared back, fear at last registering in her eyes. Rizzoli could not help but derive some satisfaction from seeing that fear. She wanted O'Donnell to have a taste of what she herself had suffered this past year.

"Get used to being afraid," said Rizzoli. "Because you need to be."

"I've worked with men like him," said O'Donnell. "I know when to be afraid."

"Hoyt is different from anyone you've ever met."

O'Donnell gave a laugh. Her bravado had returned, braced by pride. "They're all different. All unique. And I never turn my back on any of them."

# Seventeen

*My dear Dr. O'Donnell,*

*You asked about my earliest childhood memories. I have heard that few people retain memories of their lives from before the age of three, because the immature brain has not acquired the ability to process language, and we need language to interpret the sights and sounds we experience during infancy. Whatever the explanation for childhood amnesia may be, it does not apply to me, as I remember certain details of my childhood quite well. I can call to mind distinct images which, I believe, date back to when I was about eleven months old. No doubt you'll dismiss these as fabricated memories, built on stories I must have heard from my parents. I assure you, these memories are quite real, and if my parents were alive, they would tell you that my recollections are accurate and could not have been based on any stories I might have heard. By the very nature of the images, these were not events my family was likely to talk about.*

*I remember my crib, wooden slats painted white, the rail dimpled with gnaw marks from my teething. A blue blanket that had some sort of tiny creatures printed on it. Birds or bees or maybe little bears. And over the crib, a soaring contraption which I now know was a mobile, but at the time struck me as something quite magical. Glittering, always moving. Stars and moons and planets, my father later told me, just the sort of thing he would hang over his son's crib. He was an aerospace engineer, and he believed that you could turn any child into a genius if you just stimulated the growing brain, whether it be with mobiles or flash cards or tapes with his father's voice reciting the multiplication tables.*

*I have always been good at math.*

*But these are memories I doubt you have much interest in. No, you are searching for the darker themes, not my memories of white cribs and pretty mobiles. You want to know why I am the way I am.*

*So I suppose I should tell you about Mairead Donohue.*

*I learned her name years later, when I told an aunt about my early recollections, and she said, "Oh, my God. You actually remember Mairead?" Yes indeed, I remember her. When I call to mind the images from my nursery, it is not my mother's face but the face of Mairead that stares down at me over the railing of my crib. White skin, marred by a single mole which perches like a blackfly on her cheek. Green eyes that are both beautiful and cold. And her smile — even a child as young as I was could see what adults are blind to: there is hatred in that smile. She hates the household where she works. She hates the stink of diapers. She hates my hungry cries which interrupt her sleep. She hates the circumstances which have brought her to this hot Texas city, so different from her native Ireland.*

*Most of all, she hates me.*

*I know this, because she demonstrates it in a dozen quiet and subtle ways. She does not leave any evidence of her abuse; oh no, she is too clever for that. Instead her hatred takes the form of angry whispers, soft as a snake's hiss, as she leans over my crib. I cannot understand the words, but I hear their venom, and I see the rage in her narrowed eyes. She does not neglect my physical needs; my diaper is always fresh and my milk bottle warmed. But always, there are the secret pinches, the twisting of my skin, the sting of alcohol dabbed straight on my urethra. Naturally I scream, but there are never any scars or bruises. I am simply a colicky baby, she tells my parents, born with a nervous disposition. And poor, hardworking Mairead! She is the one who must cope with the screaming brat, while my mother tends to her social obligations. My mother, who smells of perfume and mink.*

*So this is what I remember. The startling bursts of pain. The sound of my own screaming. And above me, the white skin of Mairead's throat as she cranes forward into my crib to deliver a pinch or a jab to my tender skin.*

*I don't know if it's possible for a child as young as I was to hate. I think it's more likely we are merely bewildered by such punishment. Without the capacity to reason, the best we can manage is to link cause and effect. And I must have understood, even then, that the source of my torment was a woman with cold eyes and a milk-white throat.*

Rizzoli sat at her desk and stared at Warren Hoyt's meticulous handwriting, both margins neatly lined up, the small, tight words marching in a straight line across the page. Although he had written the letter in ink, there were no corrections or crossed-out words. Every sentence was already organized before his pen touched paper. She thought of him bent over this page, slender fingers poised around the ballpoint pen, his skin sliding across the paper, and suddenly she felt the almost desperate need to wash her hands.

In the women's rest room she stood scrubbing with soap and water, trying to eradicate any trace of him, but even after she'd washed and dried her hands, she still felt contaminated, as though his words had seeped like poison through her skin. And there were more of these letters to read, more poison still to be absorbed.

A knock at the rest room door made her stiffen.

"Jane? Are you in there?" It was Dean.

"Yes," she called out.

"I've got the VCR ready in the conference room."

"I'll be right there."

She looked at herself in the mirror and was not happy with what she saw. The tired eyes, the look of shaken confidence. Don't let him see you like this, she thought.

She turned on the tap, splashed cold water on her face, and blotted herself dry with a paper towel. Then she stood up straight and took a deep breath. Better, she thought, staring at her reflection. Never let them see you sweat.

She walked into the conference room and gave Dean a curt nod. "Okay. Are we ready?"

He already had the TV on, and the VCR power light was glowing. He picked up the manila envelope that O'Donnell had given them and slid out the videotape. "It's dated August seventh," he said.

Only three weeks ago, she thought, unsettled by how fresh these images, these words, would be.

She sat down at the conference table, pen and legal pad ready to take notes. "Start it."

Dean inserted the tape and pressed PLAY.

The first image they saw was the neatly coifed O'Donnell, standing before a white cinder-block wall and looking incongruously elegant in a blue knit suit. "Today is August seventh. I'm at the Souza-Baranowski facility in Shirley, Massachusetts. This subject is Warren D. Hoyt."

The TV flickered to black; then a new image flared onto the screen, a face so abhorrent to Rizzoli that she rocked back in her chair. To anyone else, Hoyt would seem ordinary, even forgettable. His light-brown hair was neatly trimmed, and his face had the pallor of confinement. The denim shirt, in prison blue, hung a size too large on his slender frame. Those who had known him in his everyday life had described him as pleasant and courteous, and this

319

was the image he projected on the videotape. A nice, harmless young man.

His gaze shifted away from the camera, and he focused on something that was off-screen. They heard a chair scrape and then O'Donnell's voice speaking.

"Are you comfortable, Warren?"

"Yes."

"Shall we start, then?"

"Any time, Dr. O'Donnell." He smiled. "I'm not going anywhere."

"All right." A sound of O'Donnell's chair creaking, the clearing of her throat. "In your letters, you've already told me quite a bit about your family and your childhood."

"I tried to be complete. I think it's important that you understand every aspect of who I am."

"Yes, I appreciate that. It's not often I get the chance to interview someone as verbal as you. Certainly not anyone who's tried to be as analytical as you are about your own behavior."

Hoyt shrugged. "Well, you know the saying about the unexamined life. That it's not worth living."

"Sometimes, though, we can take the self-analysis too far. It's a defense mechanism. Intellectualism as a means of distancing ourselves from our raw emotions."

Hoyt paused. Then said, with a faintly mocking note: "You want me to talk about feelings."

"Yes."

"Any feelings in particular?"

"I want to know what makes men kill. What draws them to violence. I want to know what goes through your head. What you feel, when you kill another human being."

He said nothing for a moment, pondering the question. "It's not easy to describe."

"Try to."

"For the sake of science?" The mockery was back in his voice.

"Yes. For the sake of science. What do you feel?"

A long pause. "Pleasure."

"So it feels good?"

"Yes."

"Describe it for me."

"Do you really want to know?"

"It's the core of my research, Warren. I want to know what you experience when you kill. It's not morbid curiosity. I need to know if you experience any symptoms which may indicate neurologic abnormalities. Headaches, for instance. Strange tastes or smells."

"The smell of blood is quite nice." He paused. "Oh. I think I've shocked you."

"Go on. Tell me about blood."

"I used to work with it, you know."

"Yes, I know. You were a lab technician."

"People think of blood as just a red fluid that circulates in our veins. Like motor oil. But it's quite complex and individual. Everyone's blood is unique. Just as every kill is unique. There is no typical one to describe."

"But they all gave you pleasure?"

"Some more than others."

"Tell me about one that stands out for you. One that you remember in particular. Is there one?"

He nodded. "There's one that I always think about."

"More than the others?"

"Yes. It's been on my mind."

"Why?"

"Because I didn't finish it. Because I never got the chance to enjoy it. It's like having an itch you can't scratch."

"That makes it sound trivial."

"Does it? But over time, even a trivial itch begins to consume your attention. It's always there, prickling your skin. One form of torture, you know, is to tickle the feet. It may seem like nothing, at first. But then it goes on for days and days without relief. It becomes the cruelest form of torture. I think I've mentioned in my letters that I know a thing or two about the history of man's inhumanity to man. The art of inflicting pain."

"Yes. You wrote me about your, uh, interest in that subject."

"Torturers through the ages have always known that the subtlest of discomforts, over time, become quite intolerable."

"And has this itch you mentioned become intolerable?"

"It keeps me up at night. Thoughts of what

might have been. The pleasure I was denied. All my life I've been meticulous about finishing what I start. So this disturbs me. I think about it all the time. The images keep playing back in my head."

"Describe them. What you see, what you feel."

"I see her. She is different, not like the others at all."

"How so?"

"She hates me."

"The others didn't?"

"The others were naked and afraid. Conquered. But this one is still fighting me. I feel it when I touch her. Her skin is electric with rage, even though she knows I've defeated her." He leaned forward, as though about to share his most intimate thoughts. His gaze was no longer on O'Donnell but on the camera, as though he could see through the lens and stare directly at Rizzoli. "I feel her anger," he said. "I absorb her rage, just by touching her skin. It's like white heat. Something liquid and dangerous. Pure energy. I've never felt so powerful. I want to feel that way again."

"Does it arouse you?"

"Yes. I think about her neck. Very slender. She has a nice, white neck."

"What else do you think about?"

"I think about taking off her clothes. About how firm her breasts are. And her belly. A nice, flat belly . . ."

"So your fantasies about Dr. Cordell — they're sexual?"

He paused. Blinked, as though shaken from a trance. "Dr. Cordell?"

"That's who we're talking about, isn't it? The victim you never killed, Catherine Cordell."

"Oh. I think of her, too. But she's not the one I'm talking about."

"Who are you talking about?"

"The other one." He stared at the camera with a look of such intensity that Rizzoli could feel its heat. "The policewoman."

"You mean the one who found you? That's the woman you fantasize about?"

"Yes. Her name is Jane Rizzoli."

# Eighteen

Dean stood up and pressed STOP on the VCR. The screen went blank. Warren Hoyt's last words seemed to hang like a perpetual echo in the silence. In his fantasies, she had been stripped of her clothing and her dignity, reduced to naked body parts. Neck and breasts and belly. She wondered if that was how Dean now saw her, if the erotic visions that Hoyt had conjured were now imprinted in Dean's mind as well.

He turned to look at her. She had never found his face easy to read, but in that instant the anger in his eyes was unmistakable.

"You understand, don't you?" he said. "You were meant to see this tape. He laid a path of bread crumbs for you to follow The envelope with O'Donnell's return address led to O'Donnell herself. To his letters, to this videotape. He knew you'd see it all, eventually."

She stared at the blank TV. "He's talking to me."

"Exactly. He's using O'Donnell as his medium. When Hoyt talks to her, in this interview, he's really talking to you. Telling you his fantasies. Using them to scare you, humiliate you. Listen to what he says." Dean rewound the tape.

Once again, Hoyt's face appeared on the screen. "It keeps me up at night. Thoughts of what might have been. The pleasure I was denied. All my life I've been meticulous about finishing what I start. So this disturbs me. I think about it all the time. . . ."

Dean pressed STOP and looked at her. "How does that make you feel? Knowing you're always on his mind?"

"You know damn well how it makes me feel."

"So does he. That's why he wanted you to hear it." Dean pressed FAST FORWARD and then PLAY.

Hoyt's eyes were eerily focused on the audience he couldn't see. "I think about taking off her clothes. About how firm her breasts are. And her belly. A nice, flat belly . . ."

Again Dean hit STOP. His gaze made her flush.

"Don't tell me," she said. "You want to know how that makes me *feel*."

"Exposed?"

"Yes."

"Vulnerable."

"*Yes.*"

"Violated."

She swallowed and looked away. Said, softly: "Yes."

"All the things he wants you to feel. You told me he's attracted to damaged women. To women who've been violated. And that's precisely the way he's making you feel now. With mere words on a videotape. Just like a victim."

Her gaze shot back to his. "No," she said. "*Not* a victim. Do you want to know what I'm really feeling right now?"

"What?"

"I'm ready to tear that son of a bitch into shreds." It was an answer launched on pure bravado, the words punched into the air. It took him aback, and he just frowned at her for a moment. Did he see how hard she was working to keep up the front? Had he heard the false note in her voice?

She forged ahead, not giving him the chance to see past her bluff. "You're saying he knew, even then, that I'd eventually see this? That the tape was meant for me."

"Didn't it sound that way to you?"

"It sounded like any sicko's fantasy."

"Not just any sicko. And not just any victim. He's talking about you, Jane. Talking about what he'd like to do to *you*."

Alarms crackled through her nerve endings. Dean was turning it personal again, aiming it like an arrow straight at her. Did he enjoy seeing her squirm? Did this serve any purpose except to heighten her fears?

"At the time this was recorded, he already had his escape planned," said Dean. "Remember, he was the one who contacted O'Donnell. He knew she'd talk to him. She couldn't resist the offer. She was an open microphone, recording everything he said, everything he wanted people

327

to hear. You, in particular. Then he set loose a logical sequence of events, leading right to this moment, with you watching that videotape."

"Is anyone that brilliant?"

"Isn't Warren Hoyt?" he asked. It was another arrow launched to pierce her defenses. To drive home the obvious.

"He's spent a year behind bars. He had a year to nurse his fantasies," said Dean. "And they were all about you."

"No, it was Catherine Cordell he wanted. It's always been Cordell —"

"That's not what he told O'Donnell."

"Then he was lying."

"Why?"

"To get at me. To rattle me —"

"Then you do agree. This tape was meant to end up in your hands. It's a message directed at *you*."

She stared at the blank TV. The ghost of Hoyt's face still seemed to be staring at her. Everything he'd done was aimed at rattling her universe, destroying her peace of mind. It's what he'd done to Cordell before he'd moved in for the kill. He wanted his victims terrified, broken down by exhaustion, and he harvested his prey only after they'd been thoroughly ripened by fear. She had no denials left to offer, no defense against the obvious.

Dean sat down and faced her across the table. "I think you should withdraw from this investigation," he said quietly.

Startled, she stared at him. *"Withdraw?"*

"It's become personal."

"Between me and a perp, it's always personal."

"Not to this degree. He wants you on this case, so he can play his little games. Insinuate himself into every aspect of your life. As lead detective, you're visible and accessible. Fully immersed in the hunt. And now he's starting to stage the crime scenes for your benefit. To communicate with *you*."

"All the more reason for me to stay on."

"No. All the more reason for you to walk away. To put some distance between you and Hoyt."

"I never walk away from anything, Agent Dean," she shot back.

After a pause, he said dryly: "No. I can't imagine you ever do."

She was the one leaning forward now, in an attitude of confrontation. "What's your problem with me, anyway? You've had it in for me from the start. You talked to Marquette behind my back. You raised doubts about me —"

"I never questioned your competence."

"Then what is your problem with me?"

He responded to her anger in a voice that was calm and reasoned. "Consider who we're dealing with. A man you once tracked down. A man who blames you for his capture. He's still thinking about what he'd like to do to you. And you've spent the same year trying to forget what *he* did. He's hungry for a second act, Jane. He's laying the foundation, drawing you right in where he wants you. It's not a safe place to be."

"Is it really my safety you're concerned about?"

"Are you implying I have another agenda?" he asked.

"I wouldn't know. I haven't figured you out yet."

He stood and went to the VCR. Ejected the tape and slid it back in the envelope. He was stalling for time, trying to come up with a believable answer.

He sat down again and looked at her. "The truth is," he said, "I haven't figured you out, either."

She laughed. "Me? What you see is what you get."

"All you'll let me see is the cop. What about Jane Rizzoli, the woman?"

"They're one and the same."

"You know that's not true. You just won't let anyone see past the badge."

"What am I supposed to let them see? That I'm missing that precious Y chromosome? My badge is the only thing I *want* them to see."

He leaned forward, his face close enough to invade her personal space. "This is about your vulnerability as a target. It's about a perp who already knows how to twist the screws on you. A man who's managed to get within striking distance. And you never even knew he was there."

"Next time I will know."

"Will you?"

They stared at each other, their faces as close as two lovers. The dart of sexual desire that shot through her was so sudden and unexpected it felt like both pain and pleasure at once. Abruptly she pulled back, her face hot, and even though her gaze met his from a safer distance, she still felt exposed. She was not good at hiding her emotions, and she'd always felt hopelessly inadequate when it came to flirting or engaging in all the other small dishonesties that play out between men and women. She strove to keep her expression unchanged but found she could not keep looking at him without feeling transparent to his gaze.

"You do understand there'll be a next time," he said. "It's not just Hoyt now. There are two of them. If that doesn't scare the hell out of you, it should."

She looked down at the envelope containing the videotape, which Hoyt had meant her to see. The game was just beginning, advantage Hoyt, and yes, she was scared.

In silence she gathered up her papers.

"Jane?"

"I heard everything you said."

"It doesn't make a difference to you. Does it?"

She looked at him. "You know what? A bus could hit me when I cross the street outside. Or I could keel over at my desk from a stroke. But I don't think about those things. I can't let them take over. I almost did, you know. The nightmares — they just about wore me down. But

331

now I've got my second wind. Or maybe I've just gone numb and I can't feel anything anymore. So the best I can do is put one foot in front of the other and keep on marching. That's how to get through this, just *keep on marching*. That's all any of us can do."

She was almost relieved when her beeper went off. It gave her a reason to break eye contact, to look down at the digital readout on her pager. She felt him watching her as she crossed to the conference room phone and dialed.

"Hair and Fiber. Volchko," a voice answered.

"Rizzoli. You paged."

"It's about those green nylon fibers. The ones lifted from Gail Yeager's skin. We found identical fibers on Karenna Ghent's skin as well."

"So he's using the same fabric to wrap all his victims. No surprises there."

"Oh, but I do have one little surprise for you."

"What's that?"

"I know which fabric he used."

Erin pointed to the microscope. "The slides are all ready for you. Take a look."

Rizzoli and Dean sat down facing each other, eyes pressed to the microscope's double teaching head. Through the lenses, they saw the same view: two strands, laid side by side for comparison.

"The fiber on the left was lifted from Gail Yeager. The one on the right from Karenna Ghent," said Erin. "What do you think?"

"They look identical," said Rizzoli.

"They are. They're both Dupont nylon type six, six, drab green. The filaments are thirty-denier, extremely fine." Erin reached into a folder and took out two graphs, which she laid on the countertop. "And here's the ATR spectra again. Number one is from Yeager, number two from Ghent." She glanced at Dean. "You're familiar with Attenuated Total Reflection techniques, Agent Dean?"

"It's an infrared mode, isn't it?"

"Right. We use it to distinguish surface treatments from the fiber itself. To detect any chemicals that have been applied to the fabric after weaving."

"And were there any?"

"Yes, a silicone rub. Last week, Detective Rizzoli and I went over the possible reasons for such a surface treatment. We didn't know what this fabric was designed for. What we did know was that these fibers are heat- and light-resistant. And that the threads are so fine that, if woven together, they'd be watertight."

"We thought it might be a tent or a tarp," said Rizzoli.

"And what would the silicone add?" asked Dean.

"Antistatic properties," said Erin. "Some tear and water resistance. Plus, it turns out, it reduces the porosity of this fabric to almost zero. In other words, even air can't pass through it." Erin looked at Rizzoli. "Any guesses what it is?"

"You said you already know the answer."

"Well, I had a little help. From the Connecticut State Police Lab." Erin placed a third graph on the countertop. "They faxed that to me this afternoon. It's an ATR spectrograph of fibers from a homicide case in rural Connecticut. The fibers were lifted from the suspect's gloves and fleece jacket. Compare it to Karenna Ghent's fibers."

Rizzoli's gaze flew back and forth between the graphs. "The spectra match. The fibers are identical."

"Right. Only the color's different. The fibers from our two cases are drab green. The fibers from the Connecticut homicide came in two different colors. Some were neon orange; others were a bright lime green."

"You're kidding."

"Sounds pretty gaudy, right? But aside from the color, the Connecticut fibers match ours. Dupont nylon type six, six. Thirty-denier filaments, finished with a silicone rub."

"Tell us about the Connecticut case," said Dean.

"A skydiving accident. The victim's chute failed to open properly. Only when these orange and lime-green fibers turned up on the suspect's clothing did it turn into a homicide investigation."

Rizzoli stared at the ATR spectra. "It's a parachute."

"Exactly. The suspect in the Connecticut homicide tampered with the victim's chute the night before. This ATR is characteristic for parachute fabric. It's tear-resistant, water-resistant. Easily packed away and stored between uses. That's what your unsub is using to wrap his victims."

Rizzoli looked up at her. "A parachute," she said. "It makes the perfect shroud."

# Nineteen

Papers were everywhere, file folders lying open on the conference table, crime scene photos layered like glossy shingles. Pens scratched on yellow legal pads. Although this was the age of computers — and there were a few lap-tops powered up, screens glowing — when information is spilling fast and furious, cops still reach for the comfort of paper. Rizzoli had left her own laptop back at her desk, preferring to jot down notes in her dark, assertive scrawl. The page was a tangle of words and looping arrows and little boxes emphasizing significant details. But there was order to the mess, and security in the permanence of ink. She flipped to a fresh page, trying to focus her attention on Dr. Zucker's whispery voice. Trying not to be distracted by the presence of Gabriel Dean, who sat right next to her, taking his own notes, but in far neater script. Her gaze wandered to his hand, thick veins standing out on his skin as he gripped the pen, the cuff of his shirt peeking out white and crisp from the sleeve of his gray jacket. He'd walked into the meeting after she had and had chosen to sit beside her. Did that mean anything? *No, Rizzoli. It only means there was an empty chair next to you.* It was a waste of time, a diversion, to be caught up in such thoughts. She felt scattered, her attention fracturing in different directions, even her notes starting to wander in a skewed line across the page. There were five other men in the room, but it was only Dean who held her attention. She knew his scent now and could pick it out, cool and clean, from the room's olfactory symphony of aftershave scents. Rizzoli, who never wore perfume, was surrounded by men who did.

She looked down at what she'd just written:

*Mutualism: symbiosis with mutual advantage to both or all organisms involved.*

The word that defined Warren Hoyt's pact with his new partner. The Surgeon and the Dominator, working as a team. Hunting and feeding off carrion together.

"Warren Hoyt has always worked best with a partner," said Dr. Zucker. "It's how he likes to hunt. The way he used to hunt with Andrew Capra, until Capra's death. Indeed, Hoyt *requires* the participation of another man as part of his ritual."

"But he was hunting on his own last year," said Barry Frost. "He didn't have a partner then."

"In a way, he did," said Zucker. "Think about the victims he chose, here in Boston. All of them were women who'd been sexually assaulted — not by Hoyt, but by other men. He's attracted to damaged women, women who've been marked by rape. In his eyes, that made them dirty, contaminated. And therefore approachable. Deep down, Hoyt is afraid of normal women, and his fear makes him impotent. He can only feel empowered when he thinks of them as inferior. Symbolically destroyed. When he hunted with Capra, it was Capra who assaulted the women. Only then did Hoyt use his scalpel. Only then could he derive full satisfaction from the ritual that followed." Zucker looked around the room and saw heads nodding. These were details that the cops in this room already knew. Except for Dean, they had all worked on the Surgeon investigation; they were all familiar with Warren Hoyt's handiwork.

Zucker opened a file folder on the table. "Now we come to our second killer. The Dominator. His ritual is almost a mirror image of Warren Hoyt's. He's not afraid of women. Nor is he afraid of men. In fact, he chooses to attack women who live with male partners. It isn't just a matter of the husband or boyfriend being inconveniently present. No, the Dominator seems to *want* the man there, and he goes in prepared to deal with him. A stun gun and duct tape to immobilize the husband. The positioning of the male victim so he's forced to watch what happens next. The Dominator doesn't just kill the

338

man straightaway, which would be the practical move. He gets his thrills by having an audience. By knowing another man is there to watch him claim his prize."

"And Warren Hoyt gets his thrills by watching," said Rizzoli.

Zucker nodded. "Exactly. One killer likes to perform. One likes to watch. It's a perfect example of mutualism. These two men are natural partners. Their cravings complement each other. Together, they're more effective. They can better control their prey. They can combine their skills. Even while Hoyt was still in prison, the Dominator was copying Hoyt's techniques. He was already borrowing elements from the Surgeon's signature."

This was a point Rizzoli had recognized before anyone else, but no one in the room acknowledged that particular detail. Perhaps they'd forgotten, but she hadn't.

"We know Hoyt received a number of letters from the general public. Even from prison, he managed to recruit an admirer. He cultivated him, maybe even instructed him."

"An apprentice," said Rizzoli softly.

Zucker looked at her. "That's an interesting word you use. Apprentice. Someone who acquires a skill or craft under the tutelage of a master. In this case, it's the craft of the hunt."

"But which one is the apprentice?" said Dean. "And which one is the master?"

Dean's question unnerved Rizzoli. For the

past year, Warren Hoyt had represented the worst evil she could imagine. In a world where hunters stalked, none could match him. Now Dean had brought up a possibility she didn't want to consider: that the Surgeon was but an acolyte to someone even more monstrous.

"Whatever their relationship," said Zucker, "they are far more effective as a team than as individuals. And as a team, it's possible the pattern of their attacks will change."

"How so?" asked Sleeper.

"Until now, the Dominator has chosen couples. He props up the man as his audience, someone to watch the assault. He wants another man there, to see him claim the prize."

"But now he has a partner," said Rizzoli. "A man who'll watch. A man who *wants* to watch."

Zucker nodded. "Hoyt just might fill the pivotal role in the Dominator's fantasy. The watcher. The audience."

"Which means he may not choose a couple next time," she said. "He'd choose . . ." She stopped, not wanting to finish the thought.

But Zucker was waiting to hear her answer, an answer he had already arrived at. He sat with head cocked, pale eyes watching her with eerie intensity.

It was Dean who said it. "They'll choose a woman, living alone," he said.

Zucker nodded. "Easy to subdue, easy to control. With no husband to worry about, they can focus all their attention on the woman."

★ ★ ★

*My car. My home. Me.*

Rizzoli pulled into a parking space at Pilgrim Hospital and turned off the ignition. For a moment she did not step out of the car but sat with doors locked, scanning the garage. As a cop, she'd always considered herself a warrior, a hunter. Never had she thought of herself as prey. But now she found herself behaving as prey, wary as a rabbit preparing to leave the safety of its den. She, who had always been fearless, was reduced to casting nervous glances out her car window. She, who had kicked down doors, who'd always joined the first wave of cops barreling into a suspect's home. She caught a glimpse of herself in the rearview mirror and saw the wan face, the haunted eyes, of a woman she scarcely knew. Not a conqueror, but a victim. A woman she despised.

She shoved open the door and stepped out. Stood straight, reassured by the weight of her weapon, holstered snugly at her hip. Let the bastards come; she was ready for them.

She rode alone in the garage elevator, shoulders squared, pride trumping fear. When she stepped off again, she saw other people, and now her weapon felt unnecessary, even excessive. She tugged down her suit jacket to keep the holster concealed as she walked into the hospital, and stepped into the elevator, joining a trio of fresh-faced medical students with stethoscopes poking out of their pockets. They traded

341

medical-speak among themselves, showing off their freshly minted vocabulary, ignoring the tired-looking woman standing beside them. Yes, the one with the concealed weapon on her hip.

In the ICU, she walked straight past the ward clerk's desk and headed to cubicle #5. There she halted, frowning through the glass partition.

A woman was lying in Korsak's bed.

"Excuse me. Ma'am?" a nurse said. "Visitors need to check in."

Rizzoli turned. "Where is he?"

"Who?"

"Vince Korsak. He should be in that bed."

"I'm sorry; I came on duty at three —"

"You were supposed to call me if anything happened!"

By now, her agitation had attracted the attention of another nurse who quickly intervened, speaking in the soothing tones of one who has dealt often with upset relatives.

"Mr. Korsak was extubated this morning, ma'am."

"What do you mean?"

"The tube in his throat — the one to help him breathe — we took it out. He's doing fine now, so we transferred him to the intermediate care unit, down the hall." She added, in defense: "We *did* call Mr. Korsak's wife, you know."

Rizzoli thought of Diane Korsak and her vacant eyes and wondered if the phone call had even registered, or if the information had simply dropped like a penny into a dark well.

By the time she reached Korsak's room, she was calmer and back in control. Quietly she poked her head inside.

He was awake and staring at the ceiling. His belly bulged beneath the sheets. His arms lay perfectly still at his sides, as though he was afraid to move them lest he disturb the tangle of wires and tubes.

"Hey," she said softly.

He looked at her. "Hey," he croaked back.

"You feel like having a visitor?"

In answer, he patted the bed, an invitation for her to settle in. To stay.

She pulled a chair over to his bedside and sat down. His gaze had lifted again, not to the ceiling, as she'd thought at first, but to a cardiac monitor that was mounted in the corner of the room. An EKG blipped across the screen.

"That's my heart," he said. The tube had left him hoarse, and what came out was barely a whisper.

"Looks like it's ticking okay," she said.

"Yeah." There was a silence, his gaze still fixed on the monitor.

She saw the bouquet of flowers that she'd sent that morning resting on his bedside table. It was the only vase in the room. Had no one else thought to send flowers? Not even his wife?

"I met Diane yesterday," she said.

He glanced at her, then quickly looked away, but not before she'd seen dismay in his eyes.

"I guess she didn't tell you."

He shrugged. "She hasn't been in today."

"Oh. She'll probably be in later, then."

"Hell if I know."

His reply caught her by surprise. Perhaps he'd surprised himself as well; his face suddenly flushed.

"I shouldn't've said that," he said.

"You can say whatever you want to me."

He looked up at the monitor again and sighed. "Okay, then. It sucks."

"What does?"

"Everything. Guy like me goes through life, doing what he's supposed to do. Brings in the paycheck. Gives the kid whatever she wants. Never takes a bribe, not once. Then suddenly I'm fifty-four and *wham,* my own ticker turns against me. And I'm lying flat on my back, thinking: *What the hell was it all for?* I follow the rules, and I end up with a loser daughter who still calls Daddy whenever she needs money. And a wife who's zonked out of her head on whatever crap she can get from the pharmacy. I can't compete with Prince Valium. I'm just the guy who puts a roof over her head and pays for all the friggin' prescriptions." He gave a laugh, resigned and bitter.

"Why are you still married?"

"What's the alternative?"

"Being single."

"Being alone, you mean." He said the word *alone* as if that was the worst option of all. Some people make choices hoping for the best; Korsak had made a choice simply to avoid the worst. He gazed up at his cardiac tracing, the twitching green symbol of his mortality. Bad choices or good, it had all led to this moment, in this hospital room, where fear kept company with regret.

And where will I be at his age? she wondered. Flat on my back in a hospital, regretting the choices I made, yearning for the road I never took? She thought of her silent apartment with its blank walls, its lonely bed. How was her life any better than Korsak's?

"I keep worrying it's gonna stop," he said. "You know, just go flat-line. That'd scare the shit out of me."

"Stop watching it."

"If I stop watching, who the hell's gonna keep an eye on it?"

"The nurses are watching out at the desk. They've got monitors out there, too, you know."

"But are they really *watching* it? Or are they just goofing off, talking about shopping and boyfriends and shit? I mean, that's my frigging heart up there."

"They've got alarm systems, too. Anything the least bit irregular, their machine starts squealing."

He looked at her. "No shit?"

"What, you don't trust me?"

"I dunno."

They regarded each other for a moment, and

she was pricked by shame. She had no right to expect his trust, not after what had happened in the cemetery. The vision still haunted her, of a stricken Korsak, lying alone and abandoned in the darkness. And she — so single-minded, so oblivious to everything but the chase. She could not look him in the eye, and her gaze dropped, settling instead on his beefy arm, crisscrossed with tape and I.V. tubing.

"I am so sorry," she said. "God, I'm sorry."

"For what?"

"Not looking out for you."

"What're you talking about?"

"Don't you remember?"

He shook his head.

She paused, suddenly realizing that he truly did not remember. That she could stop talking right now and he would never know how she'd failed him. Silence might be the easy way out, but she knew she couldn't live with the burden.

"What do you remember, about the night in the cemetery?" she asked. "The last thing?"

"The last thing? I was running. I guess we were running, weren't we? Chasing the perp."

"What else?"

"I remember feeling really pissed off."

"Why?"

He snorted. " 'Cause I couldn't keep up with a friggin' girl."

"And then?"

He shrugged. "That's it. That's the last I remember. Till those nurses here started shoving

346

that goddamn tube up my . . ." He stopped. "I woke up all right. You better believe I let 'em know it, too."

A silence passed, Korsak with his jaw squared, his gaze fixed stubbornly on the EKG monitor. Then he said, with quiet disgust: "I guess I screwed up the chase."

This took her by surprise. "Korsak —"

"Look at this." He waved at his bulging belly. "Like I swallowed a goddamn basketball. That's what it looks like. Or I'm fifteen months knocked up. Can't even run a race with a girl. I used to be fast, you know. Used to be built like a racehorse. Not like I am now. You shoulda seen me back then, Rizzoli. Wouldn't recognize me. Bet you don't believe any of it, do you? 'Cause you just see me like I am now. Broken-down piece of shit. Smoke too much, eat too much."

*Drink too much,* she added silently.

". . . just an ugly tub of lard." He gave his belly an angry slap.

"Korsak, listen to me. I'm the one who screwed up, not you."

He looked at her, clearly confused.

"In the cemetery. We were both running. Chasing what we thought was the perp. You were right behind me. I heard you breathing, trying to keep up."

"Like you gotta rub it in."

"Then you weren't there. You just weren't there. But I kept running, and it was all a waste of time. It wasn't the perp. It was Agent Dean, walking the perimeter. The perp was long gone. We were chasing after nothing, Korsak. A few shadows. That's all."

He was silent, waiting for the rest of the story.

She forced herself to continue. "That's when I should've gone looking for you. I should've realized you weren't around. But things got crazy. And I just didn't think. I didn't stop to wonder where you were. . . ." She sighed. "I don't know how long it took me to remember. Maybe it was only a few minutes. But I think — I'm afraid — it was a lot longer. And all that time, you were lying there, behind one of the gravestones. It took me so long to start searching for you. To remember."

A silence passed. She wondered if he'd even registered what she'd said, because he began to fuss with his I.V. line, rearranging the loops of tubing. It was as if he didn't want to look at her and was trying to focus instead on anything else.

"Korsak?"

"Yeah."

"Don't you have anything to say?"

"Yeah. Forget it. That's what I have to say?"

"I feel like such a jerk."

"Why? 'Cause you were doing your job?"

"Because I should've been watching out for my partner."

"Like I'm your partner?"

"That night you were."

He laughed. "That night I was a friggin' liability. A two-ton ball and chain, holding you back. You been getting all worked up about not looking out for me. Me, I've been lying here getting pissed off for falling down on the job. I mean, *literally*. Kerplunk. I been thinking about all the dumb-ass lies I keep telling myself. You see this gut?" Again he slapped his belly. "It was gonna disappear. Yeah, I believed that, too. That one of these days I was gonna go on a diet and get rid of the tire. Instead, I just keep buying bigger and bigger pants. Telling myself those clothing manufacturers are screwing around with the sizes, that's all. Coupla years from now, maybe I'd end up wearing clown pants. Bozo pants. And a ton of Ex-Lax and water pills wouldn't help me pass my physical."

"You actually did that? Took pills to pass the physical?"

"I'm not saying one way or the other. I'm just telling you that this thing with my heart, it was a long time coming. It's not like I didn't know it could happen. But now that it *has* happened, it pisses me off." He let out an angry snort. Looked up at the monitor again, where his heartbeat was blipping faster across the screen. "Now I got the ticker all stirred up."

They sat for a moment, watching the EKG, waiting for his heart to slow down. She had never paid much attention to the heart beating in her own chest. As she watched the pattern traced by Korsak's, she became aware of her own pulse. She had always taken her heartbeat for granted, and she wondered what it would be like, to hang on every beat, fearful that the next might not come. That the throb of life in her chest would suddenly go still.

She looked at Korsak, who lay with gaze still glued to the monitor, and she thought: He's more than angry; he's terrified.

Suddenly he sat up straight, his hand flying to his chest, his eyes wide in panic. "Call the nurse! Call the nurse!"

"What? What is it?"

"Don't you hear that alarm? It's my heart —"

"Korsak, it's just my pager."

"What?"

She unclipped the pager from her belt and turned off the beeping. Held it up for him to see the digital readout of the phone number. "See? It's not your heart."

He sank back on the pillows. "Jesus. Get that thing outta here. Could've given me a coronary."

"Can I use this phone?"

He was lying with his hand still pressed to his chest, his whole body flaccid with relief. "Yeah, yeah. I don't care."

She picked up the receiver and dialed.

A familiar smoky voice answered: "Medical examiner's office, Dr. Isles."

"Rizzoli."

"Detective Frost and I are sitting here looking at a set of dental X rays on my computer. We've been going down that list that NCIC sent us of missing women in the New England area. This file was e-mailed to me from the Maine State Police."

"What was the case?"

"It's a murder-abduction from June second of this year. The murder victim was Kenneth Waite, age thirty-six. The abductee was his wife Marla Jean, age thirty-four. It's Marla Jean's X rays I'm looking at."

"We've found Rickets Lady?"

"It's a match," Isles answered. "Your girl's now got a name: Marla Jean Waite. They're faxing the records to us now."

"Wait. Did you say this murder-abduction was in Maine?"

"A town called Blue Hill. Frost says he's been there. It's about a five-hour drive."

"Our unsub's got a bigger hunting territory than we thought."

"Here, Frost wants to talk to you."

Frost's cheery voice came on the line. "Hey, you ever had a lobster roll?"

"What?"

"We can get lobster rolls on the way. There's this great lunch shack up on Lincolnville Beach. We leave here by eight tomorrow, we can get there in time for lunch. My car or yours?"

"We can take mine." She paused. And couldn't stop herself from adding: "Dean will probably want to ride with us."

There was a pause. "Okay," Frost finally said,

without enthusiasm. "If you think so."

"I'll give him a call."

As she disconnected, she could feel Korsak's gaze on her.

"So Mr. FBI's part of the team now," he said.

She ignored him and punched in Dean's cell phone number.

"When did that happen?"

"He's just another resource."

"That's not what you thought about him before."

"We've had a chance to work together since then."

"Don't tell me. You've seen another *side* to him."

She waved Korsak into silence as the call went through. But Dean did not answer. Instead, a recorded message came on the line: "Subscriber is not available at this time."

She hung up and looked at Korsak. "Is there a problem?"

"You're the one looks like she has a problem. You get a fresh lead, and you can't *wait* to call your new fibbie pal. What's going on?"

"Nothing's going on."

"Doesn't look that way to me."

Heat flooded her face. She was not being honest with him, and they both knew it. Even as she'd dialed Dean's cell phone number, she'd felt her pulse quicken, and she knew exactly what it meant. She felt like a junkie craving her fix, unable to stop herself from calling his hotel.

Turning her back on Korsak's baleful gaze, she faced out the window as the phone rang.

"Colonnade."

"Could you connect me to one of your guests? His name's Gabriel Dean."

"One minute please."

As she waited, she hunted about for the right words to say to him, the right tone of voice. Measured. Businesslike. *A cop. You're a cop.*

The hotel operator came back on the line. "I'm sorry, but Mr. Dean is no longer a guest here."

Rizzoli frowned, her grip tightening on the phone. "Did he leave a forwarding number?"

"There's none listed."

Rizzoli stared out the window, her eyes suddenly dazed by the setting sun. "When did he check out?" she asked.

"An hour ago."

# Twenty

Rizzoli closed the file containing the pages faxed from the Maine State Police and focused out the window at the passing woods, at the occasional glimpse of a white farmhouse through the trees. Reading in the car always made her queasy, and the details of Marla Jean Waite's disappearance only intensified her discomfort. The lunch they'd eaten on the way did not help matters. Frost had been eager to try the lobster rolls from one of the roadside shacks, and although she'd enjoyed the meal at the time, the mayonnaise was now churning in her stomach. She stared at the road ahead, waiting for the nausea to pass. It helped that Frost was a calm and deliberate driver who made no unexpected moves, whose foot was steady on the gas pedal. She'd always appreciated his utter predictability but never more than now, when she herself was feeling so unsettled.

As she felt better, she began to take note of the natural beauty outside her car window. She'd never ventured this far into Maine before. The farthest north she'd ever made it was as a ten-year-old, when her family had driven to Old Orchard Beach in the summertime. She remembered the boardwalk and the carny rides, blue cotton candy and corn on the cob. And she remembered walking into the sea and how the water was so cold, it pierced straight to her bones like icicles. Yet she had kept wading in, precisely because her mother had warned her not to. "It's too cold for you, Janie," Angela had called out. "Stay on the nice warm sand." And then Jane's brothers had chimed in: "Yeah, don't go in, Janie; you'll freeze off your ugly chicken legs!" So of course she had gone in, striding grim-faced across the sand to where the sea lapped and foamed, and stepping into water that made her gasp. But it was not the water's cold sting she remembered all these years later; rather, it was the heat of her brothers' gazes as they watched her from the beach, taunting her, daring her to wade even deeper into that breath-stealing cold. And so she had marched in, the water rising to her thighs, her waist, her shoulders, moving without hesitation, without even a pause to brace herself. She'd pushed on because it was not pain she feared most; it was humiliation.

Now Old Orchard Beach was a hundred miles behind them and the view she saw from the car looked nothing like the Maine she remembered from her childhood. This far up the coast, there were no boardwalks or carny rides. Instead she saw trees and green fields and the occasional village, each anchored around a white church spire.

"Alice and I drive up this way every July," said Frost.

"I've never been up here."

"Never?" He glanced at her with a look of surprise she found annoying. A look that said, *Where have you been?*

"Never saw any reason to," she said.

"Alice's folks have a camp out on Little Deer Isle. We stay there."

"Funny. I never saw Alice as the camping type."

"Oh, they just call it a camp. It's really like a regular house. Real bathrooms and hot water." Frost laughed. "Alice'd freak out if she had to pee in the woods."

"Only animals should have to pee in the woods."

"I like the woods. I'd live up here, if I could."

"And miss all the excitement of the big city?"

Frost shook his head. "I tell you what I wouldn't miss. The bad stuff. Stuff that makes you wonder what the hell's wrong with people."

"You think it's any better up here?"

He fell silent, his gaze on the road, a continuous tapestry of trees scrolling past the windows.

"No," he finally said. "Since that's why we're here."

She looked out at the trees and thought: The unsub came this way, too. The Dominator, in search of prey. He might have driven this very road, perhaps gazed at these same trees or stopped to eat at that lobster shack at the side of the highway. Not all predators are found in cities. Some wander the back roads or cruise through small towns, the land of trusting neighbors and unlocked doors. Had he been here on vacation and merely spotted an opportunity he could not pass up? Predators go on vacations, too. They take drives in the country and enjoy the smell of the sea, just like everyone else. They are perfectly human.

Outside, through the trees, she began to catch glimpses of the sea and granite headlands, a rugged view she would have appreciated more were it not for the knowledge that the unsub had been here as well.

Frost slowed down and his neck craned forward as he scanned the road. "Did we miss the turn?"

"Which turn?"

"We were supposed to go right on Cranberry Ridge Road."

"I didn't see it."

"We've been driving way too long. It should've come up by now."

"We're already late."

"I know; I know."

"We'd better page Gorman. Tell him the dumb city slickers are lost in the woods." She opened her cell phone and frowned at the weak signal. "You think his beeper'll work this far out?"

"Wait," said Frost. "I think we just got lucky."

Up ahead, a vehicle with an official State of Maine license plate was parked at the side of the road. Frost pulled up beside it, and Rizzoli rolled down her window to talk to the driver. Before she could even introduce herself, the man called out to them:

"You the folks from Boston P.D.?"

"How'd you guess?" she said.

"Massachusetts plates. I figured you'd get lost. I'm Detective Gorman."

"Rizzoli and Frost. We were just about to page you for directions."

"Cell phone's no good down here at the bottom of the hill. Dead zone. Whyn't you follow me up the mountain?" He started his car.

Without Gorman to lead the way, they would have missed Cranberry Ridge entirely. It was merely a dirt road carved through the woods, marked only by a sign tacked to a post: FIRE ROAD 24. They bounced along ruts, through a dense tunnel of trees that hid all views as they climbed, the road winding in switchbacks. Then the woods gave way to a burst of sunlight, and they saw terraced gardens and a green field rolling up to a sprawling house at the top of the hill. The view so startled Frost that he abruptly slowed down as they both stared.

"You'd never guess," he said. "You see that crummy dirt road, and you figure it leads to a shack or a trailer. Nothing like this."

"Maybe that's the point of the crummy road."

"Keep out the riffraff?"

"Yeah. Only it didn't work, did it?"

By the time they pulled up behind Gorman's car, he was already standing in the driveway, waiting to shake their hands. Like Frost, he was dressed in a suit, but his was ill-fitting, as though he'd lost a great deal of weight since he'd bought it. His face, too, reflected the shadow of an old illness, the skin sallow and drooping.

He handed Rizzoli a file and videotape. "Crime scene video," he said. "We're getting the rest of the files copied for you. Some of them are in my trunk — you can take them when you leave."

"Dr. Isles will be sending you the final report on the remains," Rizzoli said.

"Cause of death?"

She shook her head. "Skeletonized. Can't be determined."

Gorman sighed and looked toward the house. "Well, at least we know where Marla Jean is now. That's what drove me nuts." He gestured toward the house. "There's not much to see inside. It's been cleaned up. But you asked."

"Who's living here now?" asked Frost.

"No one. Not since the murder."

"Awfully nice house, to go empty."

"It's stuck in probate. Even if they could put it on the market, it'll be a hard sell."

They walked up the steps to a porch where windblown leaves had collected and pots of withered geraniums hung from the eaves. It appeared that no one had swept or watered in weeks, and already an air of neglect had settled like cobwebs over the house.

"Haven't been in here since July," said Gorman as he took out a key ring and searched for the correct key. "I just got back to work last week, and I'm still trying to get back up to speed. Let me tell you, that hepatitis'll kick the wind out of your sails but good. And I only had the mild kind, Type A. Least it won't kill me. . . ." He glanced up at his visitors. "Piece of advice: Don't eat shellfish in Mexico."

At last he found the right key and unlocked the door. Stepping inside, Rizzoli inhaled the odors of fresh paint and floor wax, the smells of a house scrubbed down and sanitized. And then abandoned, she thought, gazing at the ghostly forms of sheet-draped furniture in the living room. White oak floors gleamed like polished glass. Sunlight streamed in through floor-to-ceiling windows. Here, at the top of the mountain, they were perched above the claustrophobic grip of the woods, and the views ran all the way down to Blue Hill Bay. A jet scratched a white line across blue sky, and below, a boat tore a wake in the water's surface. She stood for a moment at the window, staring at the same vista that Marla Jean Waite had surely enjoyed.

"Tell us about these people," she said.

"You read the file I faxed you?"

"Yes. But I didn't get a sense of who they were. What made them tick."

"Do we ever really know?"

She turned to face him and was struck by the faintly yellowish cast of his eyes. The afternoon sunlight seemed to emphasize his sickly color. "Let's start with Kenneth. It's all his money, isn't it?"

Gorman nodded. "He was an asshole."

"That I didn't read in the report."

"Some things you just can't say in reports. But that's the general consensus around town. You know, we have a lot of trust funders like Kenny up here. Blue Hill's now the in place for rich refugees from Boston. Most of them get along okay. But every so often, you run into a Kenny Waite, who plays this do-you-know-who-I-am? game. Yeah, they all knew who he was. He was someone with money."

"Where did it come from?"

"Grandparents. Shipping industry, I think. Kenny sure didn't earn it himself. But he did like to spend it. Had a nice Hinckley down in the harbor. And he used to tear back and forth to Boston in this red Ferrari. Till he lost his license and had his car impounded. Too many OUIs." Gorman grunted. "I think that pretty much sums up Kenneth Waite the Third. A lot of money, not much brains."

"What a waste," said Frost.

"You have kids?"

Frost shook his head. "Not yet."

"You want to raise a bunch of useless kids," said Gorman, "all you gotta do is leave 'em money."

"What about Marla Jean?" said Rizzoli. She remembered the remains of Rickets Lady laid out on the autopsy table. The bowed tibias and misshapen breastbone — skeletal evidence of an impoverished childhood. "She didn't start out with money. Did she?"

Gorman shook his head. "She grew up in a coal-mining town, down in West Virginia. Came up here to take a summer job as a waitress. That's how she met Kenny. I think he married her because she was the only one who'd put up with his crap. But it didn't sound like a happy marriage. Especially after the accident."

"Accident?"

"Few years ago. Kenny was driving, boozed up as usual. Ran his car into a tree. He walked away without a scratch — just his luck, right? But Marla Jean ended up in the hospital for three months."

"That must be when she broke her thigh-bone."

"What?"

"There was a surgical rod in her femur. And two fused vertebrae."

Gorman nodded. "I heard she had a limp. A real shame, too, 'cause she was a nice-looking woman."

And ugly women don't mind limping, Rizzoli thought, but held her tongue. She crossed to a wall of built-in shelves and studied a photograph of a couple in bathing suits. They were standing on a beach, turquoise water lapping at

362

their ankles. The woman was elfin, almost childlike, her dark-brown hair falling to her shoulders. Now corpse hair, Rizzoli couldn't help thinking. The man was fair-haired, his waist already starting to thicken, muscle turning to flab. What might have been an attractive face was ruined by his vague expression of disdain.

"The marriage was unhappy?" said Rizzoli.

"That's what the housekeeper told me. After the accident, Marla Jean didn't want to travel much. Kenny could only drag her as far as Boston. But Kenny, he was used to heading for St. Bart's every January, so he'd just leave her here."

"Alone?"

Gorman nodded. "Nice guy, huh? She had a housekeeper who'd run errands for her. Did the cleaning. Took her shopping, since Marla Jean didn't like to drive. Kind of a lonely place up here, but the housekeeper thought Marla Jean actually seemed happier when Kenny wasn't around." Gorman paused. "I have to admit, after we found Kenny, the possibility kind of crossed my mind that . . ."

"That Marla Jean did it," said Rizzoli.

"It's always the first consideration." He reached into his jacket for a handkerchief and wiped his face. "Does it seem hot in here to you?"

"It's warm."

"I'm not too good with the heat these days.

Body's still out of whack. That's what I get for eating clams in Mexico."

They crossed the living room, past the spectral forms of sheet-draped furniture, past a massive stone fireplace with a neat bundle of split logs stacked beside the hearth. Fuel to feed the flames on a chilly Maine night. Gorman led them to an area of the room where there was only bare floor and the wall was a blank white, undecorated. Rizzoli stared at the fresh coat of paint, and the hairs on the back of her neck stirred and bristled. She looked down at the floor and saw that the oak was paler here, sanded and revarnished. But blood is not so easily obliterated, and were they to darken the room and spray with luminol, the floor would still cry with blood, its chemical traces embedded too deeply into the cracks and grain of the wood to ever be completely erased.

"Kenny was propped up here," said Gorman, pointing to the newly painted wall. "Legs out in front of him, arms behind him. Wrists and ankles bound with duct tape. Single slash to the neck, Rambo-type knife."

"There were no other wounds?" asked Rizzoli.

"Just the neck. Like an execution."

"Stun gun marks?"

Gorman paused. "You know, he was here about two days when the housekeeper found him. Two warm days. By then, the skin wasn't looking too good. Not to mention smelling too good. Could've easily missed a stun gun mark."

"Did you ever examine this floor under an alternate light source?"

"It was pretty much a bloody mess in here. I'm not sure what we would have seen under a Luma-lite. But it's all on the crime scene video." He glanced around the room and spotted the TV and VCR. "Why don't we take a look at it? It should answer most of your questions."

Rizzoli crossed to the TV, pressed the ON buttons, and inserted the tape into the slot. The Home Shopping Network blared from the TV, featuring a zirconium pendant necklace for only $99.95, its facets sparkling on the throat of a swan-necked model.

"These things drive me crazy," Rizzoli said, fiddling with two different remotes. "I never did learn how to program mine." She glanced at Frost.

"Hey, don't ask me."

Gorman sighed and took the remote. The zirconium-bedecked model suddenly vanished, replaced by a view of the Waites' driveway. Wind hissed in the microphone, distorting the cameraman's voice as he stated his name, Detective Pardee, the time, date, and location. It was five P.M. on June 2, a blustery day, the trees swaying. Pardee turned the camera toward the house and began walking up the steps, the camera's image jittering on the TV. Rizzoli saw geraniums blooming in pots, the same geraniums that were now dead from neglect. A voice was heard, calling to Pardee, and the screen went blank for a few seconds.

"The front door was found unlocked," said Gorman. "Housekeeper said that wasn't unusual. People around here often leave their doors unlocked. She assumed someone was home, since Marla Jean never goes anywhere. She knocked first, but there was no answer."

A fresh image suddenly sprang into view on-screen, the camera aimed through the open doorway, straight into the living room. This was what the housekeeper must have registered as she opened the door. As the stench, and the horror, washed over her.

"She took maybe one step into the house," said Gorman. "Saw Kenny up against the far wall. And all that blood. Doesn't remember seeing much of anything else. Just wanted to get the hell out of the house. Jumped in her car and hit the gas pedal so hard her tires dug tracks in the gravel."

The camera moved into the room, panning across furniture, closing in on the main event: Kenneth Waite III, dressed only in boxer shorts, his head lolling to his chest. Early decomposition had bloated his features. The gas-filled abdomen ballooned out, and the face was swollen beyond resemblance to anything human. But it wasn't the face she focused on; it was the object of incongruous delicacy, placed on his thighs.

"We didn't know what to make of *that*," said Gorman. "It looked to me like some sort of symbolic artifact. That's how I classified it. A way of ridiculing the victim. 'Look at me, all tied up, with this stupid teacup on my lap.' It's just what a wife might do to her husband, to show how much she despises him." He sighed. "But that's when I thought it might be Marla Jean who did it."

The camera turned from the corpse and was moving up the hallway now. Retracing the killer's steps, toward the bedroom where Kenny and Marla Jean had slept. The image swayed like the stomach-churning view through the porthole of a rocking ship. The camera paused at each doorway to offer a glimpse inside. First a bathroom, then a guest bedroom. As it continued up the hallway, Rizzoli's pulse quickened. Without realizing it, she had stepped closer to the TV, as though she, and not Pardee, were the one walking up that long corridor.

Suddenly a view of the master bedroom swung onto the screen. Windows with green damask curtains. A dresser and wardrobe, both painted white, and the closet door. A four-poster bed, the covers pulled back, almost stripped off.

"They were surprised while sleeping," said Gorman. "Kenny's stomach was almost empty of food. At the time he was killed, he hadn't eaten for at least eight hours."

Rizzoli moved even closer to the TV, her gaze

rapidly scanning the screen. Now Pardee turned back to the hallway.

"Rewind it," she said to Gorman.

"Why?"

"Just go back. To when we first see the bedroom."

Gorman handed her the remote. "It's yours."

She hit REWIND, and the tape whined backward. Once again Pardee was in the hallway, approaching the master bedroom. Once again, the view swept toward the right, slowly panning across the dresser, the wardrobe, the closet doors, then focusing on the bed. Frost was now standing right beside her, searching for the same thing.

She hit PAUSE. "It's not there."

"What isn't?" said Gorman.

"The folded nightclothes." She turned to him. "You didn't find any?"

"I didn't know I was supposed to."

"It's part of the Dominator's signature. He folds the woman's nightclothes. Displays them in the bedroom as a symbol of his control."

"If it's him, he didn't do it here."

"Everything else about this matches him. The duct tape, the teacup on the lap. The position of the male victim."

"What you see is what we found."

"You're sure nothing was moved before the video was filmed?"

It was not a tactful question, and Gorman stiffened. "Well, I guess it's always *possible* the first officer on the scene walked in here and decided to move stuff around, just to make things interesting for us."

Frost, ever the diplomat, stepped in to smooth the chop that Rizzoli so often trailed in her wake. "It's not like this perp keeps a checklist. Looks like this time, he varied it a little."

"If it's the same guy," Gorman said.

Rizzoli turned from the TV and looked, once again, at the wall where Kenny had died and slowly bloated in the heat. She thought of the Yeagers and the Ghents, of duct tape and sleeping victims, of the many-stranded web of details that bound these cases so tightly to one another.

*But here, in this house, the Dominator left out a step. He did not fold the nightclothes. Because he and Hoyt were not yet a team.*

She remembered the afternoon in the Yeagers' house, her gaze frozen on Gail Yeager's nightgown, and she remembered the bone-chilling sense of familiarity.

*Only with the Yeagers did the Surgeon and the Dominator begin their alliance. That was the day they lured me into the game, with a folded nightgown. Even from prison, Warren Hoyt managed to send me his calling card.*

She looked at Gorman, who had settled onto one of the sheet-draped chairs and was once again wiping the sweat from his face. Already this meeting had drained him, and he was fading before their eyes.

"You never identified any suspects?" she asked.

"No one we could hang a hat on. That's after four, five hundred interviews."

"And the Waites, as far as you know, weren't acquainted with either the Yeagers or the Ghents?"

"Those names never came up. Look, you'll get copies of all our files in a day or two. You can cross-check everything we have." Gorman folded up his handkerchief and slipped it back in his jacket pocket. "You might want to check the FBI as well," he added. "See if they have anything to add."

Rizzoli paused. "The FBI?"

"We sent a VICAP report way back. An agent from their behavioral unit came up. Spent a few weeks monitoring our investigation, then went back to Washington. Haven't heard a word from him since."

Rizzoli and Frost looked at each other. She saw her own astonishment reflected in his eyes.

Gorman slowly rose from the chair and took out the keys, a hint that he would like to end this meeting. Only as he was walking toward the door did Rizzoli finally summon the voice to ask the obvious question. Even though she did not want to hear the answer.

"The FBI agent who came up here," she said. "Do you remember his name?"

Gorman paused in the doorway, clothes drooping on his gaunt frame. "Yes. His name was Gabriel Dean."

# Twenty-one

She drove straight through the afternoon and into the night, her eyes on the dark highway, her mind on Gabriel Dean. Frost had dozed off beside her, and she was alone with her own thoughts, her rage. What else had Dean withheld from her? she wondered. What other information had he hoarded while watching her scramble for answers? From the very beginning, he had been a few steps ahead of her. The first to reach the dead security guard in the cemetery. The first to spot Karenna Ghent's body posed atop the grave. The first to suggest the wet prep during Gail Yeager's autopsy. He had already known, before any of them, that it would reveal live sperm. *Because he's encountered the Dominator before.*

But what Dean had not anticipated was that the Dominator would take a partner. *That's when Dean showed up at my apartment. That's the first time he took an interest in me. Because I had something he wanted, something he needed. I was his guide into the mind of Warren Hoyt.*

Beside her Frost gave a noisy snort in his sleep. She glanced at him and saw that his jaw hung slack, the picture of unguarded innocence.

Not once, in all the time they'd worked together, had she seen a dark side to Barry Frost.
But Dean's deception had so thoroughly shaken
her that now, looking at Frost, she wondered
what he, too, concealed from her. What cruel-
ties even he kept hidden from view.

It was nearly nine when she finally walked
into her apartment. As always, she took the
time to secure the locks on her door, but this
time it was not fear that possessed her as she
fastened the chain and turned the dead bolts,
but anger. She drove the last bolt home with a
hard snap, then walked straight to the bedroom without pausing to perform her usual
rituals of checking the closets and glancing
into every room. Dean's betrayal had temporarily driven out all thoughts of Warren Hoyt.
She unbuckled her holster, slid the weapon
into her nightstand drawer, and slammed the
drawer shut. Then she turned and looked at
herself in the dresser mirror, disgusted by
what she saw. The medusa's cap of unruly
hair. The wounded gaze. The face of a woman
who has let a man's attractions blind her to
the obvious.

The ringing phone startled her. She stared
down at the Caller ID display: WASHINGTON
D.C.

The phone rang twice, three times, as she
marshaled control over her emotions. When at
last she answered it, she greeted the caller with a
cool: "Rizzoli."

"I understand you've been trying to reach me," said Dean.

She closed her eyes. "You're in Washington," she said, and though she tried to keep the hostility out of her voice, the words came out like an accusation.

"I was called back last night. I'm sorry we didn't get the chance to talk before I left."

"And what would you have told me? The truth, for a change?"

"You have to understand, this is a highly sensitive case."

"And that's why you never told me about Marla Jean Waite?"

"It wasn't immediately vital to your part of the investigation."

"Who the hell are you to decide? Oh, wait a minute! I forgot. You're the fucking *FBI*."

"Jane," he said quietly. "I want you to come to Washington."

She paused, startled by the abrupt turn in conversation. "Why?"

"Because we can't talk about this over the phone."

"You expect me to jump on a plane without knowing why?"

"I wouldn't ask you if I didn't think it was necessary. It's already been cleared with Lieutenant Marquette, through OPC. Someone will be calling you with the arrangements."

"Wait. I don't understand —"

"You will. When you get here." The line went dead.

Slowly she set down the receiver. Stood staring at the phone, not believing what she'd just heard. When it rang again, she picked it up at once.

"Detective Jane Rizzoli?" a woman's voice said.

"Speaking."

"I'm calling to make arrangements for your trip to Washington tomorrow. I could book you on US Airways, flight six-five-two-one, leaving Boston twelve noon, arriving in Washington, one-thirty-six P.M. Is that all right?"

"Just a second." Rizzoli grabbed a pen and notepad and began to write the flight information. "That sounds fine."

"And returning to Boston on Thursday, there's a US Airways flight six-four-oh-six, leaving Washington nine-thirty A.M., arriving Boston ten-fifty-three."

"I'm staying there overnight?"

"That was the request from Agent Dean. We have you booked into the Watergate Hotel, unless there's another hotel you'd prefer."

"No. The, uh, Watergate will be fine."

"A limousine will pick you up at your apartment at ten o'clock tomorrow and take you to the airport. There'll be another one to meet you when you arrive in D.C. May I have your fax number, please?"

Moments later, Rizzoli's fax machine began

to print. She sat on the bed, staring at the neatly typed itinerary and bewildered by the speed with which events were unfolding. At that moment, more than anything, she longed to talk to Thomas Moore, to ask for his advice. She reached for the phone, then slowly put it down again. Dean's caution had thoroughly spooked her, and she no longer trusted the security of her own phone line.

It suddenly occurred to her that she had not performed her nightly ritual of checking the apartment. Now she felt driven to confirm that all was secure in her fortress. She reached in the nightstand drawer and took out her weapon. Then, as she had done every night for the past year, she went from room to room, searching for monsters.

*Dear Dr. O'Donnell,*

*In your last letter, you asked me at what point did I know that I was different from everyone else. To be honest, I'm not certain that I am different. I think that I am simply more honest, more aware. More in touch with the same primitive urges that whisper to us all. I'm certain that you also hear these whispers, that forbidden images must sometimes flash through your mind like lightning, illuminating, just for an instant, the bloody landscape of your dark subconscious. Or you'll walk through the woods and spot a bright and unusual bird, and your very first impulse, before the boot heel of higher morality crushes it, is the urge to hunt it down. To kill it.*

*It is an instinct preordained by our DNA. We are all hunters, seasoned through the eons in nature's bloody crucible. In this, I am no different from you or anyone else, and I find it some source of amusement how many psychologists and psychiatrists have paraded through my life these past twelve months, seeking to understand me, probing my childhood, as though somewhere in my past there was a moment, an incident, which turned me into the creature I am today. I'm afraid I have disappointed them all, because there was no such defining moment. Rather, I have turned their questions around. Instead I ask them why they think they are any different? Surely they have entertained images they're ashamed of, images that horrify them, images they cannot suppress?*

*I watch, amused, as they deny it. They lie to me, the way they lie to themselves, but I see the uncertainty in their eyes. I like to push them to the edge, force them to stare over the precipice, into the dark well of their fantasies.*

*The only difference between them and me is that I am neither ashamed nor horrified by mine.*

*But I am classified the sick one. I am the one who needs to be analyzed. So I tell them all the things they secretly want to hear, things I know will fascinate them. During the hour or so in which they visit me, I indulge their curiosity, because that's the real reason they've come to see me. No one else will stoke their fantasies the way I can. No one else will take them to such forbidden territory. Even as they are trying to profile me, I am profiling them, measuring their appetite for blood. As I talk, I watch their faces for the telltales signs of excitement. The dilated pupils. The craning forward of the neck. The flushed cheeks, the bated breath.*

*I tell them about my visit to San Gimignano, a town perched in the rolling hills of Tuscany. Strolling among the souvenir shops and the outdoor cafes, I came across a museum devoted entirely to the subject of torture. Right, as you know, up my alley. It is dim inside, the poor lighting meant to reproduce the atmosphere of a medieval dungeon. The gloom also obscures the expressions of the tourists, sparing them the shame of revealing just how eagerly they stare at the displays.*

*One display in particular draws everyone's attention: a Venetian device, dating back to the 1600s, designed to punish women found guilty of sexual congress with Satan. Made of iron, and fashioned into the shape of a pear, it is inserted into the vagina of the unlucky accused. With each turn of a screw, the pear expands, until the cavity ruptures with fatal results. The vaginal pear is only one device in an array of ancient instruments meant to mutilate breasts and genitals in the name of the holy church, which could not abide the sexual powers of women. I am perfectly matter-of-fact as I describe these devices to my doctors, most of whom have never visited such a museum and who would no doubt be embarrassed to admit any desire to see one. But even as I tell them about the four-clawed breast rippers and the mutilating chastity belts, I am watching their eyes. Searching beneath their surface repulsion and horror, to see the undercurrent of excitement. Arousal.*

*Oh yes, they all want to hear the details.*

As the plane touched down, Rizzoli closed the file on Warren Hoyt's letter and looked out the window. She saw gray skies, heavy with rain, and sweat gleaming on the faces of workers standing on the tarmac. It would be a steam bath outside, but she welcomed the heat, because Hoyt's words so deeply chilled her.

In the limo ride to the hotel, she stared out through tinted windows at a city she had visited only twice before, the last time for an interagency conference at the FBI's Hoover Building. On that visit, she had arrived at night, and she remembered how awed she'd been at the sight of the memorials, aglow in floodlights. She remembered a week of hard partying and how she'd tried to match the men beer for beer, bad joke for bad joke. How booze and hormones and a strange city had all added up to a night of desperate sex with a fellow conference attendee, a cop from Providence — married, of course. This was what Washington meant to her: The city of regrets and stained sheets. The city that had taught her she was not immune to the temptations of a bad cliché. That although she might think she was the equal of any man, when it came to the morning after, she was the one who felt vulnerable.

In line at the Watergate Hotel registration desk, she eyed the stylish blonde ahead of her. Perfect hair, red shoes with sky-high heels. A woman who looked as if she actually belonged at the Watergate. Rizzoli was painfully aware of her own scuffed and cloddish blue pumps. Girl-cop shoes, meant to be walked in, and walked in a lot. No need for excuses, she thought. This is me; this is who I am. The girl from Revere who hunts monsters for a living. High heels are not what hunters wear.

"May I help you, ma'am?" a clerk called to her.

Rizzoli wheeled her bag to the counter. "There should be a reservation. Rizzoli."

"Yes, your name's right here. And there's a message from a Mr. Dean. Your meeting's scheduled at three-thirty."

"Meeting?"

He glanced up from his computer screen. "You didn't know about it?"

"I guess I do now. Is there an address?"

"No, ma'am. But a car will be here to pick you up at three." He handed her a key card and smiled. "Looks like you're all taken care of."

Black clouds smeared the sky, and the tingle of an approaching thunderstorm lifted the hair on her arms. She stood just outside the lobby, sweating in the rain-heavy air, and waited for the limo to arrive. But it was a dark-blue Volvo that swung into the porte cochere and stopped beside her.

She peered through the passenger window and saw it was Gabriel Dean behind the wheel.

The lock clicked open and she slid into the seat beside him. She had not expected to face him so soon, and she felt unprepared. Resentful that he appeared so calm and in control while she was still disoriented by the morning's travel.

"Welcome to Washington, Jane," he said. "How was the trip?"

"Smooth enough. I could get to like riding in limousines."

"And the room?"

"Way better than I'm used to."

A ghost of a smile touched his lips as he turned his attention to driving. "So it's not all torture for you."

"Did I say it was?"

"You don't look particularly happy to be here."

"I'd be a lot happier if I knew why I was here."

"It'll be clear once we get there."

She glanced out at the street names and realized they were headed northwest, in the opposite direction from FBI headquarters. "We're not going to the Hoover Building?"

"No. Georgetown. He wants to meet you at his house."

"Who does?"

"Senator Conway." Dean glanced at her. "You're not carrying, are you?"

"My weapon's still packed in my suitcase."

380

"Good. Senator Conway doesn't allow fire-arms into his house."

"Security concerns?"

"Peace of mind. He served in Vietnam. He doesn't need to see any more guns."

The first raindrops began to patter on the windshield.

She sighed. "I wish I could say the same."

Senator Conway's study was furnished in dark wood and leather — a man's room, with a man's collection of artifacts, thought Rizzoli, noting the array of Japanese swords mounted on the wall. The silver-haired owner of that collection greeted her with a warm handshake and a quiet voice, but his coal-dark eyes were direct as lasers, and she felt him openly taking her measure. She endured his scrutiny, only because she understood that nothing could proceed unless he was satisfied by what he saw. And what he saw was a woman who stared straight back at him. A woman who cared little about the subtleties of politics but cared greatly about the truth.

"Please, have a seat, Detective," he said. "I know you just flew in from Boston. You probably need time to decompress."

A secretary brought in a tray of coffee and china cups. Rizzoli curbed her impatience while the coffee was poured, cream and sugar passed around. At last the secretary withdrew, closing the door behind her.

Conway set down his cup, untouched. He had not really wanted it, and now that the ceremony had been dispensed with, he focused all his attention on her. "It was good of you to come."

"I hardly had much of a choice."

Her bluntness made him smile. Though Conway observed all the social niceties of handshakes and hospitality, she suspected that he, like most native New Englanders, valued straight talk as much as she did. "Shall we get straight to business, then?"

She set down her cup as well. "I'd prefer that."

Dean was the one who stood and crossed to the desk. He brought a bulging accordion folder back to the sitting area and took out a photograph, which he laid on the coffee table in front of her.

"June 25, 1999," he said.

She stared at the image of a bearded man, sitting slumped, a spray of blood on the whitewashed wall behind his head. He was dressed in dark trousers and a torn white shirt. His feet were bare. On his lap was perched a china cup and saucer.

She was still reeling, struggling to process the image, when Dean laid a second photograph next to it. "July 15, 1999," he said.

Again the victim was a man, this one cleanshaven. Again he had died sitting propped up against a blood-splattered wall.

Dean set down a third photograph of yet an-

382

other man. But this one was bloated, his belly taut with the expanding gases of decomposition. "September 12," he said. "The same year."

She sat stunned by this gallery of the dead, laid out so neatly on the cherry-wood table. A record of horror set incongruously among the civilized clutter of coffee cups and teaspoons. As Dean and Conway waited silently, she picked up each photo in turn, forcing herself to take in the details of what made each case unique. But all were variations on the same theme that she had seen played out in the homes of the Yeagers and the Ghents. The silent witness. The conquered, forced to watch the unspeakable.

"What about the women?" she asked. "There must have been women."

Dean nodded. "Only one was positively identified. The wife of case number three. She was found partly buried in the woods about a week after that photo was taken."

"Cause of death?"

"Strangulation."

"Postmortem sexual assault?"

"There was fresh semen collected from her remains."

Rizzoli took a deep breath. Asked, softly: "And the other two women?"

"Due to the advanced state of decomposition, their identities could not be confirmed."

"But you had remains?"

"Yes."

"Why couldn't you I.D. them?"

"Because we were dealing with more than two bodies. Many, many more."

She looked up and found herself staring directly into Dean's eyes. Had he been watching her the whole time, awaiting her startled reaction? In answer to her silent question, he handed her three files.

She opened the first folder and found an autopsy report on one of the male victims. Automatically she flipped to the last page and read the conclusions:

*Cause of death: massive hemorrhage due to single slash wound, with complete transection of left carotid artery and left jugular vein.*

The Dominator, she thought. It's his kill.

She let the pages fall back into place. Suddenly she was staring at the first page of the report. At a detail she had missed in her rush to read the conclusions.

It was in the second paragraph: *Autopsy performed on 16 July 1999, 22:15, in mobile facility located Gjakove, Kosovo.*

She reached for the next two pathology files and focused immediately on the locations of the autopsies.

*Peje, Kosovo.*

*Djakovica, Kosovo.*

"The autopsies were done in the field," said Dean. "Performed, sometimes, under primitive circumstances. Tents and lantern light. No running water. And so many remains to process that we were overwhelmed."

"These were war crimes investigations," she said.

He nodded. "I was with the first FBI team that arrived in June 1999. We went at the request of the International Criminal Tribunal for the former Yugoslavia. ICTY, for short. Sixty-five of us were deployed on that first mission. Our job was to locate and preserve evidence in one of the largest crime scenes in history. We collected ballistic evidence from the massacre sites. We exhumed and autopsied over a hundred Albanian victims, and probably missed hundreds more that we couldn't find. And the whole time we were there, the killing was *still going on.*"

"Vengeance killings," said Conway. "Completely predictable, given the context of that war. Or any war, for that matter. Both Agent Dean and I are ex-marines. I served in Vietnam, and Agent Dean was in Desert Storm. We've seen things we can't bring ourselves to talk about, things that make us question why we human beings consider ourselves any better than animals. During the war, it was Serbs killing Albanians, and after the war, it was the Albanian KLA killing Serb civilians. There's plenty of blood on the hands of both sides."

"That's what we thought these homicides were, at first," said Dean, pointing to the crime scene photos on the coffee table. "Revenge killings in the aftermath of war. It wasn't our mission to deal with ongoing lawlessness. We were there specifically at the Tribunal's request, to process war crimes evidence. Not these."

"Yet you did process them," said Rizzoli, looking at the FBI letterhead on the autopsy report. "Why?"

"Because I recognized them for what they were," said Dean. "These murders weren't based on ethnicity. Two of the men were Albanian; one was a Serb. But they all had something in common. They were married to young wives. Attractive wives, who were abducted from their homes. By the third attack, I knew this killer's signature. I knew what we were dealing with. But these cases fell under the jurisdiction of the local justice system, not the ICTY, which brought us there."

"So what was done?" she asked.

"In a word? Nothing. There were no arrests, because no suspect was ever identified."

"Of course, there was an inquiry," said Conway. "But consider the situation, Detective. Thousands of war dead buried in over one hundred fifty mass graves. Foreign peacekeeping troops struggling to keep order. Armed outlaws roaming bombed-out villages, just looking for reasons to kill. And the civilians themselves, nursing old rages. It was the Wild West over there, with gun battles erupting over drugs or family feuds or personal vendettas. And almost always, the killing was blamed on ethnic tensions. How could you distinguish one murder from another? There were so many."

"For a serial killer," said Dean, "it was paradise on earth."

# Twenty-two

She looked at Dean. She had not been surprised to hear of his military service. She'd already seen it in his bearing, his air of command. He would know about war zones, and he'd be familiar with the scenario that military conquerors had always played out. The humiliation of the enemy. The taking of spoils.

"Our unsub was in Kosovo," she said.

"It's the sort of place he would thrive on," said Conway. "Where violent death's a part of everyday life. A killer could walk into such a place, commit atrocities, and walk out again without anyone noticing the difference. There's no way of knowing how many murders are written off as mere acts of war."

"So we may be dealing with a recent immigrant," said Rizzoli. "A refugee from Kosovo."

"That's one possibility," said Dean.

"A possibility you've known all along."

"Yes." His answer came without hesitation.

"You withheld vital information. You sat back and watched while the dumb cops ran around in circles."

"I allowed you to reach your own conclusions."

"Yes, but without full knowledge of the facts." She pointed to the photos. "This could have made the difference."

Dean and Conway looked at each other. Then Conway said, "I'm afraid there's even more we haven't told you."

"More?"

Dean reached into the accordion folder and took out yet another crime scene photo. Though Rizzoli thought she was prepared to confront this fourth image, the impact of the photograph struck her with visceral force. She saw a young and fair-haired man with a wisp of mustache. He was more sinew than muscle, his chest a bony vault of ribs, his thin shoulders jutting forward like white knobs. She could clearly see the man's dying expression, the muscles of his face frozen into a rictus of horror.

"This victim was found October twenty-ninth of last year," said Dean. "The wife's body was never found."

She swallowed and averted her gaze from the victim's face. "Kosovo again?"

"No. Fayetteville, North Carolina."

Startled, she looked up at him. Held his gaze as the heat of anger flooded her face. "How many more haven't you told me about? How many goddamn cases are there?"

"These are all we know about."

"Meaning there could be others?"

"There may be. But we don't have access to that information."

She gave him a look of disbelief. "The *FBI* doesn't?"

"What Agent Dean means," interjected Conway, "is that there may be cases outside our jurisdiction. Countries that lack accessible crime data. Remember, we're talking about war zones. Areas of political upheaval. Precisely the places our unsub would be attracted to. Places where he'd feel right at home."

*A killer who moves freely across oceans. Whose hunting area knows no national borders.* She thought of everything she'd learned about the Dominator. The speed with which he'd subdued his victims. His craving for contact with the dead. His use of a Rambo-type knife. And the parachute fibers — drab green. She felt both men watching her as she processed what Conway had just said. They were testing her, waiting to see if she would measure up to their expectations.

She looked at the last photograph on the coffee table. "You said this attack was in Fayetteville."

"Yes," said Dean.

"There's a military base in the area. Isn't there?"

"Fort Bragg. It's about ten miles northwest of Fayetteville."

"How many are stationed at that base?"

"Around forty-one thousand active-duty. It's home to the Eighteenth Airborne Corps, Eighty-second Airborne Division, and Army Special

Operations Command." The fact that Dean answered her without hesitation told her this was information he considered relevant. Information he already had at the tip of his tongue.

"That's why you've kept me in the dark, isn't it? We're dealing with someone who has combat skills. Someone who's paid to kill."

"We've been kept in the dark, just as you have." Dean leaned forward, his face so close to hers that all she could focus on was *him*. Conway and everything else in the room receded from view. "When I read the VICAP report filed by the Fayetteville police, I thought I was seeing Kosovo again. The killer might as well have signed his name, the crime scene was so distinctive. The position of the male victim's body. The type of blade used in the coup de grâce. The china or glassware placed on the victim's lap. The abduction of the wife. I immediately flew down to Fayetteville and spent two weeks with the local authorities, assisting their investigation. No suspect was ever identified."

"Why couldn't you tell me this before?" she said.

"Because of who our unsub might be."

"I don't care if he's a four-star general. I had a right to know about the Fayetteville case."

"If this had been critical to your identifying a Boston suspect, I would have told you."

"You said forty-one thousand active-duty soldiers are stationed at Fort Bragg."

"Yes."

"How many of those men served in Kosovo? I assume you asked that question."

Dean nodded. "I requested a list from the Pentagon of all soldiers whose service records coincide with the places and dates of the slayings. The Dominator is not on that list. Only a few of those men now reside in New England, and none of them have panned out as our man."

"I'm supposed to trust you on that?"

"Yes."

She laughed. "That requires a pretty big leap of faith."

"We're both making a leap of faith here, Jane. I'm betting that I can trust you."

"Trust me with what? So far, you haven't told me anything that justifies secrecy."

In the silence that followed, Dean glanced at Conway, who gave an almost imperceptible nod. With that wordless exchange, they agreed to hand her the vital piece of the puzzle.

Conway said, "Have you ever heard of 'sheep-dipping,' Detective?"

"I take it that term has nothing to do with real sheep."

He smiled. "No, it doesn't. It's military slang. It refers to the CIA's practice of occasionally borrowing the military's special operations soldiers for certain missions. It happened in Nicaragua and Afghanistan, when the CIA's own special operations group — their SOG — needed additional manpower. In Nicaragua, navy SEALs were sheep-dipped to mine the harbors. In Afghanistan, the Green Berets were sheep-dipped to train the mujahideen. While working for the CIA, these soldiers become, essentially, CIA case officers. They go off the Pentagon's books. The military has no record of their activities."

She looked at Dean. "Then that list the Pentagon gave you. The names of the Fayetteville soldiers who served in Kosovo —"

"The list was incomplete," he said.

"How incomplete? How many names were left off?"

"I don't know."

"Did you ask the CIA?"

"That's where I hit walls."

"They won't name names?"

"They don't have to," said Conway. "If your unsub was involved in black ops abroad, it will never be acknowledged."

"Even if their boy's now killing on home turf?"

"Especially if he's killing on home turf," said Dean. "It would be a public relations disaster. What if he chose to testify? What sensitive information might he leak to the press? You think the Agency wants us to know *their* boy's breaking into homes and slaughtering law-abiding citizens? Abusing women's corpses? There's no way to keep that off the front pages."

"So what *did* the Agency tell you?"

"That they had no information that was relevant to the Fayetteville homicide."

"It sounds like a standard brush-off."

"It was far more than that," said Conway. "Within a day of Agent Dean's query to the CIA, he was pulled off the Fayetteville investigation and told to return to Washington. That order came straight from the office of the FBI's deputy director."

She stared at him, stunned by how deeply the Dominator's identity was buried in secrecy.

"That's when Agent Dean came to me," said Conway.

"Because you're on the Armed Services Committee?"

"Because we've known each other for years. Marines have a way of finding each other. And trusting each other. He asked me to make inquiries on his behalf. But I'm afraid I couldn't make any headway."

"Even a senator can't?"

Conway gave her an ironic smile. "A Democratic senator from a liberal state, I should add. I may have served my country as a soldier. But certain elements within Defense will never entirely accept me. Or trust me."

Her gaze dropped to the photos on the coffee table. To the gallery of dead men, chosen for slaughter not because of their politics or ethnicity or beliefs but because they had been married to beautiful wives. "You could have told me this weeks ago," she said.

"Police investigations leak like sieves," said Dean.

"Not mine."

"*Any* police investigation. If this information was shared with your team, it would eventually leak to the media. And that would bring your work straight to the attention of the wrong people. People who'll try to prevent you from making an arrest."

"You really think they'd protect him? After what he's done?"

"No, I think they want to put him away just as much as we do. But they want it done quietly, out of the public eye. Clearly they've lost track of him. He's out of their control, killing civilians. He's become a walking time bomb, and they can't afford to ignore the problem."

"And if they catch him before we do?"

"We'll never know about it, will we? The killings will just stop. And we'll always wonder."

"That's not what I call satisfying closure," she said.

"No, you want justice. An arrest, a trial, a conviction. The whole nine yards."

"You make it sound like I'm asking for the moon."

"In this case, you may be."

"Is that why you brought me here? To tell me I'll never catch him?"

He leaned toward her with a look of sudden intensity. "We want exactly what you want, Jane. The whole nine yards. I've been tracking this man since Kosovo. You think I'd settle for anything less?"

Conway said, quietly: "You understand now,

Detective, why we brought you here? The need for secrecy?"

"It seems to me there's already too much of it."

"But for now, it's the only way to achieve eventual and complete disclosure. Which is, I assume, what we all want."

She gazed for a moment at Senator Conway. "You paid for my trip, didn't you? The plane tickets, the limos, the nice hotel. This isn't on the FBI's dime."

Conway gave a nod. A wry smile. "Things that really matter," he said, "are best kept off the record."

# Twenty-three

The sky had opened up and rain pounded like a thousand hammers on the roof of Dean's Volvo. The windshield wipers thrashed across a watery view of stalled traffic and flooded streets.

"A good thing you're not flying back tonight," he said. "The airport's probably a mess."

"In this weather, I'll keep my feet on the ground, thank you."

He shot her an amused look. "And I thought you were fearless."

"What gave you that impression?"

"You did. You work hard at it, too. The armor always stays on."

"You're trying to crawl inside my head again. You're always doing that."

"It's just a matter of habit. It's what I did in the Gulf War. Psychological ops."

"Well, I'm not the enemy, okay?"

"I never thought you were, Jane."

She looked at him and could not help admiring, as she always did, the clean, sharp lines of his profile. "But you didn't trust me."

"I didn't know you then."

"So have you changed your mind?"

"Why do you think I asked you to come to Washington?"

"Oh, I don't know," she said, and gave a reckless laugh. "Because you missed me and couldn't wait to see me again?"

His silence made her flush. Suddenly she felt stupid and desperate, precisely the traits she despised in other women. She stared out the window, avoiding his gaze, the sound of her own voice, her own foolish words, still ringing in her ears.

In the road ahead, cars were finally starting to move again, tires churning through deep puddles.

"Actually," he said, "I did want to see you."

"Oh?" The word tossed off carelessly. She had already embarrassed herself; she wouldn't repeat the mistake.

"I wanted to apologize. For telling Marquette you weren't up to the job. I was wrong."

"When did you decide that?"

"There wasn't a specific moment. It was just . . . watching you work, day after day. Seeing how focused you are. How driven you are to get everything right." He added, quietly: "And then I found out what you've been dealing with since last summer. Issues I hadn't been aware of."

"Wow. 'And she manages to do her job anyway.' "

"You think I feel sorry for you," he said.

"It's not particularly flattering to hear: 'Look how much she's accomplished, *considering* what she has to deal with.' So give me a medal in the Special Olympics. The one for emotionally screwed-up cops."

He gave a sigh of exasperation. "Do you always look for the hidden motive behind every compliment, every word of praise? Sometimes, people mean exactly what they say, Jane."

"You can understand why I'd be more than a little skeptical about anything you tell me."

"You think I still have a secret agenda."

"I don't know anymore."

"But I must have one, right? Because you *certainly* don't deserve a genuine compliment from me."

"I get your point."

"You may get it. But you don't really believe it." He braked at a red light and looked at her. "Where does all the skepticism come from? Has it been that tough for you, being Jane Rizzoli?"

She gave a weary laugh. "Let's not go there, Dean."

"Is it the part about being a woman cop?"

"You can probably fill in the blanks."

"Your colleagues seem to respect you."

"There are some notable exceptions."

"There always are."

The light turned green, and his gaze went back to the road.

"It's the nature of police work," she said. "All that testosterone."

"Then why did you choose it?"

"Because I flunked home ec."

At that, they both laughed. The first honest laugh they'd shared.

"The truth is," she said, "I've wanted to be a cop since I was twelve years old."

"Why?"

"Everyone respects cops. At least, that's how it seems to a kid. I wanted the badge, the gun. The things that'd make people stand up and take notice of me. I didn't want to end up in some office where I'd just disappear. Where I'd turn into the invisible woman. That'd be like getting buried alive, to be someone no one listens to. No one notices." She leaned an elbow against the door and rested her head in her hand. "Now, anonymity's starting to look pretty good." *At least the Surgeon wouldn't know my name.*

"You sound sorry you chose police work."

She thought of the long nights on her feet, fueled by caffeine and adrenaline. The horrors of confronting the worst that human beings can do to each other. And she thought of Airplane Man, whose file remained on her desk, the perpetual symbol of futility. His own, as well as hers. We dream our dreams, she thought, and sometimes they take us places we never anticipate. A farmhouse basement with the stench of blood in the air. Or a free fall through blue sky, limbs flailing against the pull of gravity. But they are our dreams, and we go where they lead.

She said, at last: "No, I'm not sorry. It's what I do. It's what I care about. It's what I get angry about. I have to admit, a lot of the job's about anger. I can't just stand back and look at a victim's body without being pissed off. That's when I become their advocate — when I let their deaths get to me. Maybe when I *don't* get angry is when I'll know it's time to quit."

"Not everyone has your fire in the belly." He looked at her. "I think you're the most intense person I've ever met."

"That's not such a good thing."

"No, intensity is a good thing."

"If it means you're always on the verge of flaming out?"

"Are you?"

"Sometimes it feels that way." She stared at the rain lashing the windshield. "I should try to be more like you."

He didn't respond, and she wondered if she'd offended him by her last statement. By her implication that he was cold and passionless. Yet that's how he had always struck her: the man in the gray suit. For weeks, he had baffled her, and now, in her frustration, she wanted to provoke him, to make him display any emotion, however unpleasant, if only to prove she could do it. The challenge of the impregnable.

But it was just such challenges that led women to make fools of themselves.

When at last he pulled up in front of the Watergate Hotel, she was ready with a crisp farewell.

"Thanks for the ride," she said. "And for the

revelations." She turned and opened her door, letting in a *whoosh* of warm, wet air. "See you back in Boston."

"Jane?"

"Yes?"

"No more hidden agendas between us, okay? What I say is what I mean."

"If you insist."

"You don't believe me, do you?"

"Does it really matter?"

"Yes," he said quietly. "It matters a great deal to me."

She paused, her pulse suddenly quickening. Her gaze swung back to his. They had kept secrets from each other for so long that neither one of them knew how to read the truth in the other's eyes. It was a moment in which anything could have been said next, anything could have happened. Neither dared to make the first move. The first mistake.

A shadow moved across her open car door. "Welcome to the Watergate, ma'am! Do you need help with any luggage?"

Rizzoli glanced up, startled, to see the hotel doorman smiling at her. He had seen her open the door and assumed she was stepping out of the car.

"I'm already checked in, thank you," she said, and glanced back at Dean. But the moment had passed. The doorman was still standing there, waiting for her to get out. So she did.

A glance through the window, a wave; that

was their good-bye. She turned and walked into the lobby, pausing only long enough to watch his car drive out of the porte cochere and vanish into the rain.

In the elevator, she leaned back, her eyes closed, and silently berated herself for every naked emotion she might have revealed, everything foolish she might have said in the car. By the time she got up to her room, she wanted more than anything to simply check out and return to Boston. Surely there was a flight she could catch this evening. Or the train. She'd always loved riding trains.

Now in a rush to escape, to put Washington and its embarrassments behind her, she opened her suitcase and began to pack. She'd brought very little with her, and it did not take long to pull the spare blouse and slacks from the closet where she'd hung them, to throw them on top of her weapon and holster, to toss her toothbrush and comb into her toilet case. She zipped it all into the suitcase and was wheeling it to the door when she heard a knock.

Dean stood in the hall, his gray suit spattered with rain, his hair wet and glistening. "I don't think we finished our conversation," he said.

"Did you have something else to tell me?"

"Yes, as a matter of fact." He stepped into her room and closed the door. Frowned at her suitcase already packed and ready for her departure.

Jesus, she thought. Someone has to be brave

here. Someone has to grab this bull by the horns.

Before another word could be said, she pulled him toward her. Simultaneously felt his arms go around her waist. By the time their lips met, there was no doubt in either of their minds that this embrace was mutual, that if this was a mistake, they were equally at fault. She knew almost nothing about him, only that she wanted him, and would deal with the consequences later.

His face was damp from the rain, and as his clothes came off they left the scent of wet wool on his skin, a scent she eagerly inhaled as her mouth explored his body, as he made competing claims on hers. She had no patience for gentle lovemaking; she wanted it frenzied and reckless. She could feel him holding back, trying to slow down, to maintain control. She fought him, used her body to taunt him. And in this, their first encounter, she was the conqueror. He was the one who surrendered.

They dozed as the afternoon light slowly faded from the window. When she awakened, only the thin glow of twilight illuminated the man lying beside her. A man who, even now, remained a cipher to her. She had used his body, just as he had used hers, and although she knew she should feel some level of guilt for the pleasure they'd taken, all she really felt was tired satisfaction. And a sense of wonder.

"You had your suitcase packed," he said.

"I was going to check out tonight and go home."

"Why?"

"I didn't see the point of staying here." She reached out to touch his face, to stroke the roughness of his beard. "Until you showed up."

"I almost didn't. I drove around the block a few times. Getting up the nerve."

She laughed. "You make it sound as if you're afraid of me."

"The truth? You're a very formidable woman."

"Is that really how I come across?"

"Fierce. Passionate. It amazes me, all that heat you generate." He stroked her thigh, and the touch of his fingers sent a fresh tremor through her body. "In the car, you said you wished you could be more like me. The truth is, Jane, I wish I could be more like you. I wish I had your intensity."

She placed her hand on his chest. "You talk as if there's no heart beating in there."

"Isn't that what you thought?"

She was silent. *The man in the gray suit.*

"It is, isn't it?" he said.

"I didn't know what to make of you," she admitted. "You always seem so detached. Not quite human."

"Numb."

He had said the word so softly, she wondered if he'd meant it to be heard. A thought whispered only to himself.

"We react in different ways," he said. "The

405

things we're expected to deal with. You said it makes you angry."

"A lot of the time, it does."

"So you throw yourself into the fight. You go charging in, all cylinders firing. The way you charge at life." He added, with a soft laugh, "Bad temper and all."

"How can you *not* get angry?"

"I won't let myself. That's how I deal with it. Step back, take a breath. Play each case like a jigsaw puzzle." He looked at her. "That's why you intrigue me. All that turmoil, all the emotion you invest in everything you do. It feels somehow . . . dangerous."

"Why?"

"It's at odds with what I am. What I try to be."

"You're afraid I'll rub off on you."

"It's like getting too close to fire. We're drawn to it, even though we know damn well it'll burn us."

She pressed her lips to his. "A little danger," she whispered, "can be very exciting."

The evening drifted into night. They showered off each other's sweat and grinned at themselves standing before the mirror, wearing matching hotel robes. They ate a room service dinner and drank wine in bed with the TV tuned to the Comedy Channel. Tonight, there would be no CNN, no bad news to sour the mood. Tonight, she wanted to be a million miles away from Warren Hoyt.

But even distance, and the comfort of a man's arms, could not shut Hoyt from her dreams. She lurched awake in darkness, drenched in the sweat of fear, not passion. Through the pounding of her heart, she heard her cell phone ringing. It took her a few seconds to disentangle herself from Dean's arms, to reach across him toward the nightstand on his side of the bed and flip open her cell phone.

"Rizzoli."

Frost's voice greeted her. "I guess I woke you up."

She squinted at the clock radio. "Five A.M.? Yeah, that's a safe assumption."

"You okay?"

"I'm fine. Why?"

"Look, I know you're flying back today. But I thought you should know before you got here."

"What?"

He didn't immediately answer her. Over the phone, she heard someone ask him a question about bagging evidence, and she realized that at that moment he was working a scene.

Beside her, Dean stirred, alerted by her sudden tension. He sat up and turned on the light. "What's going on?"

Frost came back on the line. "Rizzoli?"

"Where are you?" she asked.

"I got called to a ten sixty-four. That's where I am right now —"

"Why are you answering burglary calls?"

"Because it's your apartment."

407

She went completely still, the phone pressed to her ear, and heard the throb of her own pulse.

"Since you were out of town, we temporarily halted surveillance on your building," said Frost. "Your neighbor down the hall in two-oh-three called it in. Ms., uh —"

"Spiegel," she said softly. "Ginger."

"Yeah. Seems like a real sharp girl. Says she's a bartender down at McGinty's. She was walking home from work and noticed glass under the fire escape. Looked up and saw your window was broken. Called nine-one-one right away. First officer on the scene realized it was your place. He called me."

Dean touched her arm in silent inquiry. She ignored him. Clearing her throat, she managed to ask, with deceptive calmness, "Did he take anything?" Already she was using the word *he*. Without saying his name, they both knew who had done this.

"That's what you'll need to tell us when you get here," said Frost.

"You're there now?"

"Standing in your living room."

She closed her eyes, feeling almost nauseated with rage as she pictured strangers invading her home. Opening her closets, touching her clothes. Lingering over her most intimate possessions.

"It looks to me like things are undisturbed," said Frost. "Your TV and CD player are here. There's a big jar of spare change still sitting on the kitchen counter. Is there anything else they might want to steal?"

*My peace of mind. My sanity.*

"Rizzoli?"

"I can't think of anything."

A pause. He said, gently: "I'll go through it all with you, inch by inch. When you get home, we'll do it together. Landlord's already boarded up the window so the rain won't get in. If you want to stay at my house for a while, I know it'll be fine with Alice. We got a spare room never gets used —"

"I'm okay," she said.

"It's no problem —"

*"I'm okay."*

There was anger in her voice, and pride. Most of all, pride.

Frost knew enough to ease off and not feel offended. He said, unruffled, "Give me a call as soon as you get in."

Dean was watching as she hung up. Suddenly she could not stand to be looked at while naked and afraid. To have her vulnerability on full display. She climbed out of bed, went into the bathroom, and locked the door.

A moment later, he knocked. "Jane?"

"I'm going to take another shower."

"Don't shut me out." He knocked again. "Come out and talk to me."

"When I'm finished." She turned on the shower. Stepped in, not because she needed to wash but because running water barred conversation. It was a noisy curtain of privacy behind which to hide. As the water beat down on her, she stood with head bowed, hands braced on the tiled wall, wrestling with her fear. She imagined it sliding off her skin like dirt and gurgling down the drain. Layer by layer, shedding off. When at last she shut off the water, she felt calm. Cleansed. She dried herself, and in the steamed mirror she caught a glimpse of her face, no longer pale but flushed from the heat. Ready once again to play the public role of Jane Rizzoli.

She stepped out of the bathroom. Dean was sitting in the armchair by the window. He said nothing, just watched as she began to dress, picking up her clothes from the floor as she circled the bed, its rumpled sheets the mute evidence of their passion. One phone call had ended it, and now she moved about the room with brittle resolve, buttoning her blouse, zipping up her slacks. Outside, it was still dark, but for her, the night was over.

"Are you going to tell me?" he said.

"Hoyt was in my apartment."

"They know it was him?"

She turned to face him. "Who *else* would it be?"

The words came out shriller than she'd intended. Flushing, she retrieved her shoes from under the bed. "I have to get home."

"It's five in the morning. Your plane leaves at nine-thirty."

"Do you really expect me to go back to sleep? After this?"

"You'll get into Boston exhausted."

"I'm not tired."

"Because you're wired on adrenaline."

She shoved her feet into her shoes. "Stop it, Dean."

"Stop what?"

"Trying to take care of me."

A silence passed. Then he said, with a note of sarcasm, "I'm sorry. I keep forgetting you're perfectly capable of taking care of yourself."

She paused with her back to him, already regretting her words. Wishing for the first time that he *would* take care of her. That he would put his arms around her and coax her back to bed. That they would sleep holding each other until it was time for her to leave.

But when she turned to face him, she saw that he was out of the chair and already getting dressed.

# Twenty-four

She fell asleep on the plane. As they started the descent into Boston, she woke up feeling drugged and desperately thirsty. The bad weather had followed her from D.C., and turbulence rattled seat-back trays and passengers' nerves as they dropped through the clouds. Outside her window, the wing tips vanished behind a curtain of gray, but she was too tired to register even a twinge of anxiety about the flight. And Dean was still on her mind, distracting her from what she should be focused on. She stared out at the mist and remembered the touch of his hands, the warmth of his breath on her skin.

And she remembered their last words at the airport curb, a cool and rushed good-bye under pattering rain. Not the parting of lovers but of business associates, anxious to get on with their separate concerns. She blamed herself for the new distance between them and blamed him, as well, for letting her walk away. Once again, Washington had turned into the city of regrets and stained sheets.

The plane touched down in a driving rain. She saw ramp personnel splash across the tarmac in their hooded slickers and she was already dreading the prospect of what came next. The ride home to an apartment that would never again feel secure, because *he* had been there.

Wheeling her suitcase from baggage claim, she stepped outside and was hit with a blast of wind-driven rain that angled under the overhang. A long line of dispirited people stood waiting for taxis. Scanning the row of limousines parked across the street, she was relieved to find the name RIZZOLI displayed in one of the limo windows.

She tapped on the driver's side, and the window rolled down. It was a different driver, not the elderly black man who'd brought her to the airport the day before.

"Yes, ma'am?"

"I'm Jane Rizzoli."

"Going to Claremont Street, right?"

"That's me."

The driver stepped out and opened the backseat door for her. "Welcome aboard. I'll put your suitcase in the trunk."

"Thank you."

She slid into the car and gave a tired sigh as she leaned back against rich leather. Outside, horns blared and tires skidded in the pouring rain, but the world inside this limousine was blessedly silent. She closed her eyes as they glided away from Logan Airport and headed for the Boston Expressway.

Her cell phone rang. Shaking off her exhaustion, she sat up and dazedly dug around in her purse, dropping pens and loose change on the car floor as she hunted for the phone. She finally managed to answer it on the fourth ring.

"Rizzoli."

"This is Margaret in Senator Conway's office. I made the arrangements for your travel. I just wanted to double-check that you do have a ride home from the airport."

"Yes. I'm in the limo now."

"Oh." A pause. "Well, I'm glad that was cleared up."

"What was?"

"The limo service called to confirm that you'd canceled your airport pickup."

"No, he was waiting for me. Thank you."

She disconnected and bent down to retrieve everything that had fallen from her purse. The ballpoint pen had rolled beneath the driver's seat. As she reached for it, fingers skimming the floor, she suddenly registered the color of the carpet. Navy blue.

Slowly she sat up.

They had just entered the Callahan Tunnel, which burrowed beneath the Charles River. Traffic had slowed, and they were creeping along an endless concrete tube, its interior lit a sickly amber.

*Navy-blue nylon six, six Dupont Antron. Standard carpet in Cadillacs and Lincolns.*

She remained perfectly still, her gaze turned

toward the tunnel wall. She thought about Gail Yeager and funeral processions, the line of limousines slowly winding toward cemetery gates.

She thought of Alexander and Karenna Ghent, who had arrived at Logan Airport just a week before their deaths.

And she thought of Kenneth Waite and his OUIs. A man who was not allowed to drive, yet took his wife to Boston.

*Is this how he finds them?*

A couple step into his car. The woman's pretty face is reflected in his rearview mirror. She settles back in smooth leather seats for the ride home, never realizing that she's being watched. That a man whose face she has scarcely registered is, at that very moment, deciding that she is the one.

The tunnel's amber lights glided by as Rizzoli built the theory, brick by brick. Such a comfortable car, a quiet ride, the leather seats soft as human skin. A nameless man behind the wheel. All designed to make the passenger feel safe and protected. The passenger knows nothing about the man behind the wheel. But the driver would know the passenger's name. The flight number. The street where she lives.

Traffic was stalled now. Far ahead, she could see the tunnel's opening, a small portal of gray light. She kept her face turned to the window, not daring to look at the driver. Not wanting him to see her apprehension. Her hands were sweating as she reached into her purse and

**415**

grasped the cell phone. She did not take it out but just sat with her hand around it, thinking about what, if anything, she should do next. So far the driver had done nothing to alarm her, nothing to make her think he was anything but what he claimed to be.

Slowly she took the phone from her purse. Flipped it open. In the dim tunnel, she strained to see the numbers so she could dial. Keep it casual, she thought. As though you're just checking in with Frost, not shrieking out an S.O.S. But what would she say? "I think I'm in trouble, but I can't be sure?" She hit the speed-dial for Frost. Heard ringing, then a faint "hello" followed by static.

*The tunnel. I'm in the goddamn tunnel.*

She disconnected. Looked ahead to see how close they were to emerging. At that instant her gaze flicked involuntarily to the driver's rear-view mirror. She made the mistake of meeting his eyes, of registering the fact that he was watching her. That's when they both knew, they both understood.

*Get out. Get out of the car!*

She lunged for the door handle, but he had already triggered the locks. Scrambling to override it, she clawed in panic at the release button.

It was all the time he needed to reach back over the seat, aim the Taser, and fire.

The probe hit her in the shoulder. Fifty thousand volts pulsed into her torso, an electrical jolt that shot like lightning through her nervous system. Her vision went black. She dropped to the seat, her hands useless, all her muscles contracting in a storm of convulsions, her body out of control, quivering in submission.

A drumming noise, pattering above, drew her from the darkness. A fog of gray light slowly brightened on her retinas. She tasted blood, warm and metallic, and her tongue throbbed where she had bitten it. The fog slowly melted, and she saw daylight. They were out of the tunnel, heading . . . where? Her vision was still blurred, but through the window she could make out the shapes of tall buildings against a background of gray sky. She tried to move her arm, but it was heavy and sluggish, the muscles spent from the convulsion. And the view of buildings and trees sliding past the window was so dizzying she had to close her eyes. She focused all her effort on making her limbs obey her commands. She felt muscles twitch, and her fingers closed into a fist. Tighter. Stronger.

*Open the door. Unlock the door.*

She opened her eyes, fighting vertigo, her stomach roiling as the world spun past the window. She forced her arm to straighten, every inch a small victory. Hand now reaching toward the door, toward the lock release button. She pressed it and heard the loud click as it snapped open.

Suddenly there was pressure on her thigh. She saw his face glancing back over the seat as he

417

shoved the Taser against her leg. Another burst of energy pulsed into her body.

Her limbs spasmed. Darkness fell like a hood.

A drop of cold water falling on her cheek. The screech of duct tape being peeled off a roll. She came awake as he bound her wrists behind her back, wrapping the tape several times around before he slit it off the roll. Next he pulled off her shoes, let them thud onto the floor. Peeled off both her trouser socks so the tape would adhere to bare skin. Her vision slowly cleared as he worked, and she saw the top of his head as he leaned into the car, his attention focused on binding her ankles. Behind him, through the open car door, was an expanse of green. Marsh and trees. No buildings. The fens? Had he pulled off in the Back Bay Fens?

Another screech of duct tape, and then the smell of adhesive as it pressed to her mouth.

He stared down at her, and she saw details that she had not bothered to register when the car window had first rolled down. Details that had then been irrelevant. Dark eyes, a face of sharp angles, an expression of feral alertness. And excitement about what came next. A face that no one would register from the backseat of a car. They are the faceless army dressed in uniforms, she thought. The people who clean our hotel rooms and haul our luggage and drive the limousines in which we ride. They move in a parallel world, seldom noticed until they are needed.

Until they intrude into ours.

He picked up her cell phone from the floor where it had fallen. Dropped it onto the road and slammed his heel down, smashing the phone into a bundle of crumpled plastic and wires, which he kicked into the bushes. No enhanced 911 would lead the police to her.

He was all efficiency now. The seasoned professional, doing what he does best. He leaned into the car, dragged her toward the door, then lifted her into his arms without even a grunt of effort. A special ops soldier who can march for miles with a hundred-pound pack strapped to his back would find little challenge in the transfer of a 115-pound woman. Rain splattered her face as she was carried to the rear of the car. She caught a glimpse of trees, silvery in the mist, and a dense tangle of undergrowth. But no other cars, even though she could hear them beyond the trees, the *whish-whish* of traffic, like the sound of the ocean when you hold a seashell to your ear. Close enough to raise a muffled howl of despair in her throat.

The trunk was already open, the drab-green parachute laid out and waiting to receive her body. He dropped her inside, went back to the car for her shoes, and threw those in with her as well. Then he closed the trunk, and she heard him turn the key in the lock. Even if she got her hands free, she would not be able to escape this black coffin.

She heard his door slam shut; then the car was

moving again. Heading toward a meeting with a man she knew would be waiting for her.

She thought of Warren Hoyt. Thought of his bland smile, his long fingers encased in latex gloves. She thought of what he would be holding in those gloved hands, and terror engulfed her. Her breaths quickened and she felt she was suffocating and could not suck in air deeply enough, quickly enough, to keep from smothering. She twisted in panic, thrashing like a crazed animal, desperate to live. Her face slammed against her suitcase, and the blow momentarily stunned her. She lay exhausted, cheek throbbing.

The car slowed down and stopped.

She went rigid, heart punching at her chest, as she waited for what came next. She heard a man say, "Have a nice day." The car was rolling again, picking up speed.

A tollbooth. They were on the Turnpike.

She thought of all the small towns that lay to the west of Boston, all the empty fields and tracts of forest, the places where no one else would think to stop. Places where a body might never be found. She remembered Gail Yeager's corpse, bloated and veined with black, and Marla Jean Waite's scattered bones, lying in the stillness of woods. So goes the way of all flesh.

She closed her eyes, focusing on the rumble of the road beneath the tires. Going very fast. By now, well beyond the Boston city limits. And what would Frost be thinking as he waited for her call? How long before he realized something had gone wrong?

*It makes no difference. He won't know where to look. No one will.*

Her left arm was growing numb from her weight, the tingling now unbearable. She rolled onto her belly, and her face pressed against the silky parachute fabric. The same fabric that had shrouded the corpses of Gail Yeager and Karenna Ghent. She imagined she could smell death in its folds. The odor of putrescence. Repulsed, she tried to rise to a kneeling position and hit her head against the roof of the trunk. Pain bit her scalp. The suitcase, small as it was, left little room in which to maneuver, and claustrophobia was making her panic again.

*Control. Goddamn it, Rizzoli. Take control.*

But she could not shut out images of the Surgeon. She remembered his face looming above her as she'd lain immobilized on the cellar floor. Remembered waiting for the slash of his scalpel, and knowing that she could not escape it. That the best she could hope for was a swift death.

And that the alternative was infinitely worse.

She forced herself to breathe slowly, deeply. A drop of warmth slid down her cheek, and the back of her head stung. She had cut her scalp and now it was bleeding in a steady trickle, dripping onto the parachute. Evidence, she thought. My passage marked by blood.

*I'm bleeding. What did I hit my head against?*

She raised her arms behind her, fingers skimming the trunk roof, seeking whatever it was that had pierced her scalp. She felt molded plastic, a smooth expanse of metal. Then, suddenly, a sharp edge of a protruding screw pricked her skin.

She paused to ease her aching arm muscles, to blink blood from her eyes. She listened to the steady thrum of the tires over the road.

Still moving fast, Boston far behind them.

*It is lovely, here in the woods. I stand surrounded by a ring of trees, whose tops pierce the sky like the spires of a cathedral. All morning it has rained, but now a shaft of sunlight breaks through the clouds and spills onto the ground where I have hammered four iron stakes, to which I have looped four lengths of rope. Except for the steady drip from the leaves, it is silent.*

*Then I hear the rustle of wings and I look up to see three crows perched on the branches overhead. They watch with strange eagerness, as though anticipating what comes next. Already they know what this place is, and now they wait, flicking their black wings, drawn here by the promise of carrion.*

*Sunshine warms the ground and steam curls from the wet leaves. I have hung my knapsack on a branch to keep it dry, and it droops there like heavy fruit, weighed down by the instruments inside. I do not need to inventory the contents; I have assembled them with care, fondling their cold steel as I placed them into the knapsack. Even a year of confinement has not dulled my familiarity, and when my fingers* close around a scalpel, it feels as comfortable as a handshake with an old friend.

Now I am about to greet another old friend.

I walk out to the road to wait.

The clouds have thinned to wisps, and the afternoon has grown close and warm. The road is little more than two dirt ruts, and a few tall weeds poke up, their fragile seed heads undisturbed by the recent passage of any car. I hear cawing, and look up to see that the three crows have followed me, and are waiting for the show.

Everyone likes to watch.

A thin curl of dust rises beyond the trees. A car is coming. I wait, my heart beating faster, my hands sweating with anticipation. At last it swings into view, a gleaming black behemoth moving slowly up the dirt road, taking its dignified time. Bringing my friend to see me.

It will be a long visit, I think. Glancing up, I see that the sun is still high, leaving us hours of daylight. Hours of summer fun.

I move to the center of the road and the limousine rolls to a stop in front of me. The driver steps out. We don't need to exchange a word; we merely look at each other and smile. The smile of two brothers, united not by family bonds, but by shared desires, shared cravings. Words on a page brought us together. In long letters did we spin our fantasies and forge our alliance, the words flowing from our pens like the silky strands of a spiderweb binding us together. Bringing us to these woods where crows watch with eager eyes.

*Together we walk to the rear of the car. He is excited about fucking her. I can see the bulge in his pants, and I hear the sharp rattle of the car keys in his hands. His pupils are dilated, and his upper lip gleams with sweat. We stand beside the trunk, both of us hungry for the first look at our guest. For the first delicious whiff of her terror.*

*He thrusts the key in the lock and turns it. The trunk hood rises.*

*She lies curled on her side, blinking up at us, her eyes dazed by the sudden light. I am so focused on her, I do not immediately register the significance of the white bra, trailing from one corner of the small suitcase. Only as my partner leans forward to haul her from the trunk do I understand what it means.*

*I shout, "No!"*

*But already she has brought both her hands forward. Already she is pulling the trigger.*

*His head explodes in a mist of blood.*

*It is a strangely graceful ballet, the way his body arches as it falls backward. The way her arms swing toward me with unerring precision. I have time only to twist sideways, and then the second bullet bursts from her gun.*

*I do not feel it pierce the back of my neck.*

*The strange ballet continues, only now it is my own body that performs the dance, arms flinging a circle as I hurtle through the air in a swan's dive. I land on my side, but there is no pain on impact, only the sound of my torso slamming against dirt. I lie waiting for the ache, the throb, but there is nothing. Only a sense of surprise.*

*I hear her struggle out of the car. She has been lying cramped in there for over an hour, and it takes her several minutes to make her legs obey.*

*She approaches me. Shoves her foot against my shoulder, rolling me onto my back. I am fully conscious, and I look up at her with full comprehension of what is about to happen. She points the weapon at my face, her hands shaking, her breath coming in short, sharp gasps. Smeared blood has dried on her left cheek like war paint. Every muscle in her body is primed to kill. Every instinct screams at her to squeeze the trigger. I stare back, unafraid, watching the battle play out in her eyes. Wondering which form of defeat she will choose. In her hands she holds the weapon of her own destruction; I am merely the catalyst.*

*Kill me, and the consequences will destroy you.*

*Let me live, and I will forever inhabit your nightmares.*

*She releases a soft sob. Slowly she lowers the weapon. "No," she whispers. And again, louder. Defiantly: "No." Then she straightens, takes a deep breath.*

*And walks back to the car.*

# Twenty-five

Rizzoli stood in the clearing, looking down at the four iron stakes that had been pounded into the earth. Two for the arms, two for the legs. Knotted cord, already looped and waiting to be tightened around wrists and ankles, had been found nearby. She avoided lingering over the obvious purpose of those stakes. Instead she moved around the site with the businesslike demeanor of any cop looking over a crime scene. That it would have been her limbs restrained to the stakes, her flesh rent by the instruments contained in Hoyt's knapsack, was a detail she kept at a distance. She could feel her colleagues watching her, could hear the way their voices grew hushed when she came near. The bandage over her sutured scalp conspicuously labeled her as the walking wounded, and they were all dealing with her as though she were glass, easily shattered. She could not abide that, not now, when she needed, more than ever, to believe she was not a victim. That she was in full control of her emotions.

And so she walked the site, as she would have any other crime scene. The site had already been photographed and picked over by the

State Police the evening before and the scene was officially released, but this morning Rizzoli and her team felt compelled to examine it as well. She tramped with Frost into the woods, tape measure whicking in and out of the canister as they measured the distance from the road to the small clearing where the State Police had discovered Warren Hoyt's knapsack. Despite the personal significance of this circle of trees, she viewed the clearing with detachment. Recorded in her notebook was a catalog of what had been found inside the knapsack: scalpels and clamps, retractor and gloves. She'd studied the photos of Hoyt's footwear impressions, now cast in plaster, and had stared at evidence bags holding knotted cords, without stopping to think about whose wrists those cords were intended for. She glanced up to check the changing weather, without acknowledging to herself that this same view of treetops and sky would have been her last. Jane Rizzoli the victim was not here today. Although her colleagues might watch her, waiting for a glimpse, they would not see her. No one would.

She closed her notebook and glanced up to see Gabriel Dean walking toward her through the trees. Although her heart lifted at the sight of him, she greeted him with merely a nod, a look that said, Let's keep it business.

He understood, and they faced each other as two professionals, careful not to betray any hint of the intimacies they had shared only two days before.

"The driver was hired six months ago by VIP Limousines," she said. "The Yeagers, the Ghents, the Waites — he drove them all. And he had access to VIP's pickup schedule. He must have seen my name on it. Canceled my scheduled pickup so that he could take the place of the driver who should have been there."

"And VIP checked out his job references?"

"His references were a few years old, but they were excellent." She paused. "There was no mention of any military service on his résumé."

"That's because John Stark wasn't his real name."

She frowned at him. "Identity theft?"

Dean gestured toward the trees. They moved out of the clearing and started walking through the woods, where they could speak in private.

"The real John Stark died September 1999 in Kosovo," said Dean. "U.N. relief worker, killed when his Jeep hit a land mine. He's buried in Corpus Christi, Texas."

"Then we don't even know our man's real name."

Dean shook his head. "Fingerprints, dental X rays, and tissue samples will be sent to both the Pentagon and Central Intelligence."

"We won't get any answers from them. Will we?"

"Not if the Dominator was one of theirs. As far as they're concerned, you've taken care of their problem. Nothing more needs to be said or done."

"I may have resolved their problem," she said bitterly. "But mine is still alive."

"Hoyt? He'll never be a concern to you."

"God, I should have squeezed off one more shot —"

"He's probably quadriplegic, Jane. I can't imagine any worse punishment."

They emerged from the woods, onto the dirt road. The limousine had been towed away last night, but the evidence of what had transpired here still remained. She looked down at the dried blood where the man known as John Stark had died. A few yards away was the smaller stain where Hoyt had fallen, his limbs senseless, his spinal cord turned to pulp.

*I could have finished it, but I let him live. And I still don't know if it was the right thing to do.*

"How are you, Jane?"

She heard the note of intimacy in his question, an unspoken acknowledgment that they were more than merely colleagues. She looked at him and was suddenly self-conscious about her battered face and the lump of bandage on her scalp. This was not the way she'd wanted him to see her, but now that she stood facing him there was no point hiding her bruises, nothing to do but stand straight and meet his gaze.

"I'm fine," she said. "A few stitches on my scalp, a few sore muscles. And a really bad case of the uglies." She waved vaguely at her bruised face and laughed. "But you should see the other guy."

"I don't think it's good for you to be here," he said.

"What do you mean?"

"It's too soon."

"I'm the one person who should be here."

"You never cut yourself any slack, do you?"

"Why should I need to?"

"Because you're not a machine. It will catch up with you. You can't walk this site and pretend it's just another crime scene."

"That's exactly how I'm treating it."

"Even after what almost happened?"

*What almost happened.*

She looked down at the bloodstains in the dirt, and for an instant the road seemed to sway, as though a tremor had shaken the earth, rattling the carefully constructed walls she had put up as shields, threatening the very foundation upon which she stood.

He reached for her hand, a steady touch that brought tears to her eyes. A touch that said: Just this once, you have permission to be human. To be weak.

She said softly, "I'm sorry about Washington."

She saw hurt in his eyes and realized that he had misunderstood her words.

"So you wish it never happened between us," he said.

"No. No, that's not it at all —"

"Then what are you sorry about?"

430

She sighed. "I'm sorry I left without telling you what that night meant to me. I'm sorry I never really said good-bye to you. And I'm sorry that . . ." She paused. "That I didn't let you take care of me, just that once. Because the truth is, I really needed you to. I'm not as strong as I like to think I am."

He smiled. Squeezed her hand. "None of us is, Jane."

"Hey, Rizzoli?" It was Barry Frost, calling to her from the edge of the woods.

She blinked away tears and turned to him. "Yeah?"

"We just got a double ten fifty-four. Quik-Stop Grocery Store, Jamaica Plain. Dead store clerk and a customer. The scene's already been secured."

"Jesus. So early in the morning."

"We're next up for this one. You good to go?"

She drew in a deep breath and turned back to Dean. He had released her hand, and although she missed his touch, she felt stronger, the tremor silenced, the ground once again solid beneath her feet. But she was not ready to end this moment. Their last good-bye in Washington had been rushed; she wouldn't let it happen again. She wouldn't let her life turn into Korsak's, a sad chronicle of regrets.

"Frost?" she said, her gaze still on Dean.

"Yeah?"

"I'm not coming."

"What?"

"Let another team take it. I'm just not up to it right now."

There was no response. She glanced at Frost and saw his stunned face.

"You mean . . . you're taking the day off?" Frost said.

"Yeah. It's my first sick leave. You got a problem with that?"

Frost shook his head and laughed. "About goddamn time, is all I can say."

She watched Frost walk away. Heard him still laughing as he headed into the woods. She waited until Frost had vanished among the trees before she turned to look at Dean.

He held open his arms; she stepped into them.

# Twenty-six

*Every two hours, they come to check my skin for bedsores. It is a rotating trio of faces: Armina on day shift, Bella on evenings, and on the night shift the quiet and timid Corazon. My ABC girls, I call them. To the unobservant, they are indistinguishable from each other, all of them with smooth brown faces and musical voices. A chirpy chorus line of Filipinas in white uniforms. But I see the differences between them. I see it in the way they approach my bed, in the various ways they grasp me as they roll my torso onto one side or the other to reposition me on the sheepskin cover. Day and night, this must be done, because I cannot turn myself and the weight of my own body pressing down upon the mattress wears away at the skin. It compresses capillaries and interrupts the nourishing flow of blood, starving the tissues, turning them pale and fragile and easily abraded. One small sore can soon fester and grow, like a rat gnawing at the flesh.*

*Thanks to my ABC girls, I do not have any sores — or so they tell me. I cannot verify it because I can't see my own back or buttocks, nor can I feel any sensation below my shoulders. I am completely dependent on Armina, Bella, and Corazon to keep me healthy, and like any infant, I pay rapt attention to those who tend me. I study their faces, inhale their scents, commit their voices to memory. I know that the bridge of Armina's nose is not quite straight, that Bella's breath often smells of garlic, and that Corazon has just the hint of a stutter.*

*I also know they are afraid of me.*

*They know, of course, why I am here. Everyone who works on the spinal cord unit is aware of who I am, and although they treat me with the same courtesy they offer all the other patients, I notice they do not really look me in the eye, that they hesitate before touching my flesh, as though they are about to test a hot iron. I catch glimpses of the aides in the hallway, glancing at me as they whisper to each other. They chatter with the other patients, asking them about their friends and families, but no such questions are ever put to me. Oh, they ask me how I am feeling and whether I slept well, but that is the extent of our conversation.*

*Yet I know they are curious. Everyone is curious, everyone wants a peek at the Surgeon, but they are afraid to come too close, as though I might suddenly spring up and attack them. So they cast quick glances at me through the doorway, but do not come in unless duty calls them. The ABC girls tend to my skin, my bladder, and my bowels, and then they flee, leaving the monster alone in his den, chained to the bed by his own ruined body.*

*It's no wonder I look forward so eagerly to Dr. O'Donnell's visits.*

*She has been coming once a week. She brings her*

cassette recorder and her legal notepad and a purse full of blue rollerball pens with which to take notes. And she brings her curiosity, wearing it fearlessly and unashamedly, like a red cloak. Her curiosity is purely professional, or so she believes. She moves her chair close to my bed and sets up the microphone on the tray table so it will catch every word. Then she leans forward, her neck arching toward me as though offering me her throat. It is a lovely throat. She is a natural blonde, and quite pale, and her veins course in delicate blue lines beneath the white-wash of skin. She looks at me, unafraid, and asks her questions.

"Do you miss John Stark?"

"You know I do. I've lost a brother."

"A brother? But you don't even know his real name."

"And the police, they keep asking me about it. I can't help them, because he never told me."

"Yet you corresponded with him all that time from prison."

"Names were unimportant to us."

"You knew each other well enough to kill to-gether."

"Only the one time, on Beacon Hill. It's like making love, I think. The first time, you're still learning to trust each other."

"So killing together was a way of getting to know him?"

"Is there a better way?"

She raises an eyebrow, as though she's not quite sure if I'm serious. I am.

435

"You refer to him as a brother," she says. "What do you mean by that?"

"We had a bond, the two of us. A sacred bond. It's so hard to find people who completely understand me."

"I can imagine."

I'm alert to the merest hint of sarcasm, but I don't hear it in her voice, or see it in her eyes.

"I know there must be others like us out there," I say. "The challenge is to find them. To connect. We all want to be with our own kind."

"You talk as though you're a separate species."

"Homo sapiens reptilis," I quip.

"Excuse me?"

"I've read that there's a part of our brain that dates back to our reptilian origins. It controls our most primitive functions. Fight and flight. Mating. Aggression."

"Oh. You mean the Archipallium."

"Yes. The brain we had before we became human and civilized. It holds no emotions, no conscience. No morals. What you see when you look in the eyes of a cobra. The same part of our brain that responds directly to olfactory stimulation. It's why reptiles have such a keen sense of smell."

"That's true. Neurologically speaking, our olfactory system is closely related to the Archipallium."

"Did you know I've always had an extraordinary sense of smell?"

For a moment she simply gazes at me. Again, she does not know if I am serious or I am spinning this theory for her because she is a neuropsychiatrist *and I know she will appreciate it.*

*Her next question reveals she has decided to take me seriously: "Did John Stark also have an extraordinary sense of smell?"*

*"I don't know." My stare is intent. "Now that he's dead, we'll never know."*

*She studies me like a cat about to pounce. "You look angry, Warren."*

*"Don't I have reason to be?" My gaze drops to my useless body, lying inert on the sheepksin pad. I don't even think of it as my body any longer. Why should I? I can't feel it. It is just a lump of alien flesh.*

*"You're angry at the policewoman," she says.*

*Such an obvious statement does not even deserve a response, so I give none.*

*But Dr. O'Donnell is trained to zero in on feelings, to peel away scar tissue and expose the raw and bloody wound beneath. She has sniffed the aroma of festering emotions and now she moves in to tweeze and scrape and dig.*

*"Do you still think about Detective Rizzoli?" she asks.*

*"Every day."*

*"What sort of thoughts?"*

*"Do you really want to know?"*

*"I'm trying to understand you, Warren. What you think, what you feel. What makes you kill."*

*"So I'm still your little lab rat. I'm not your friend."*

*A pause. "Yes, I can be your friend —"*

*"It's not why you come here, though."*

"To be honest, I come here because of what you can teach me. What you can teach all of us about why men kill." She leans even closer. Says, quietly: "So tell me. All your thoughts, however disturbing they may be."

There is a long silence. Then I say, softly, "I have fantasies. . . ."

"What fantasies?"

"About Jane Rizzoli. About what I would like to do to her."

"Tell me."

"They're not nice fantasies. I'm sure you'll find them disgusting."

"Nevertheless, I would like to hear them."

Her eyes have a strange glow to them, as though they are lit from within. The muscles of her face have tensed with anticipation. She is holding her breath.

I stare at her and I think: Oh yes, she would like to hear them. Like everyone else, she wants to hear every dark detail. She claims her interest is merely academic, that what I tell her is only for her research. But I see the spark of eagerness in her eyes. I sniff her pheromonal scent of excitement.

I see the reptile, stirring in its cage.

She wants to know what I know. She wants to walk in my world. She is finally ready for the journey.

It's time to invite her in.

We hope you have enjoyed this Large Print book. Other Thorndike, Wheeler or Chivers Press Large Print books are available at your library or directly from the publishers.

For more information about current and upcoming titles, please call or write, without obligation, to:

Publisher
Thorndike Press
295 Kennedy Memorial Drive
Waterville, ME    04901
Tel. (800) 223-1244

Or visit our Web site at:
www.gale.com/thorndike
www.gale.com/wheeler

OR

Chivers Press Limited
Windsor Bridge Road
Bath BA2 3AX
England
Tel. (01225) 335336

Or visit the Chivers Web site at:
www.chivers.co.uk

All our Large Print titles are designed for easy reading, and all our books are made to last.